Table of Con

Forgotten Sins
A Hunters Series Thriller
 # 9
Glenn Trust

Copyright © 2023

Forgotten Sins

By Glenn S. Trust

All rights reserved

Dedication

For the readers

FREE Book Here!

**They thought they found paradise ... It was hell,
and Chance Wills was an unlikely Savior**

Join us at Glenn Trust Books and receive a free download of his modern-day western crime thriller *Mojave Sun.*

You can download your Free copy today at **this link** >>>
https://bf.glenntrustbooks.com/h31utr5ms2

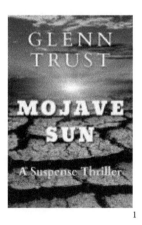

1

No Spam – We never share your address... Ever.

Part One – A Cold Trail

1. Something Else

He was hunting, moving carefully—step, one foot, listen, wait a few seconds, then the other—winding his way along a deer trail that zig-zagged through the pines and oaks around a steep hillside. He heard scuffling ahead in the brush and stopped in his tracks, controlling his breathing, waiting.

The scuffling noise stopped, and he waited some more. After a minute, he saw movement and lifted the rifle to peer through the scope. It took a few seconds for him to discern the deer's outline blending in with the surrounding undergrowth. A buck. A good-sized one, ten-point rack, and well-muscled from feeding on the abundant browse covering the Appalachian slopes—hackberry, oak, elm, hickory, acorns, meadow grasses, and the ever-present Georgia pines.

The buck sensed he was being watched and froze, trying to blend into the landscape background. After a minute, he turned his head slowly and peered through the trees at the man with the rifle fifty yards away. His antlers caught a beam of sunlight through the trees, spotlighting each point so that they stood out, clear and defined. The man gave an appreciative smile. The buck was a handsome animal and seemed to know it, showing himself proudly, as if challenging the man to make the first move.

It was a standoff, watching each other, waiting for the other to declare his intentions. The man lowered the rifle. He wasn't hunting deer that day.

At the movement, the buck snorted and bounded away, and the man resumed his hike through the woods. He was an experienced hunter and made no sound audible more than a few feet away. Eyes scanning ahead, he planned the placement of each step before his boot touched the ground and his leg raised to move forward again. It was a slow process, but he had time. When his prey came into sight, he would be waiting.

By late morning, he came to a cluster of dense brush surrounding a small clearing. He parted the undergrowth with a gloved hand just enough to peer into the clearing. A small shack stood in the center, not much more than a lean-to.

He watched for several minutes, listening, searching for some sign they had returned early. When he was sure the shack was empty, he crossed the clearing, went inside, made himself comfortable on an empty milk crate, and leaned against the back wall to wait.

The shack and deer camp had been there for fifty years. Occasionally, the owner—the man he was waiting for—would haul in some new planks to patch things, but he wasn't much of a carpenter, and the shack leaned at a precarious angle.

The man with the rifle relaxed, munching sunflower seeds from his pocket, spitting shells on the plank floor. Sometime after noon, he heard a noise, distant but clear. He checked his rifle and thumbed off the safety.

They came crashing through the underbrush into the clearing. Two men, one older than the other, father and son with the same red faces and stocky frame, but the father's bulk turning to fat now with age.

"Gotta take a shit!" the son called out and headed to the closet-sized outhouse at the back edge of the clearing.

"I need a beer," his father said, walking inside the shack, squinting into the gloom as his eyes adjusted. "Son of a bitch. What the fuck are you ..."

"Don't make a sound." The man with the rifle rose from the egg crate, the muzzle centered on the newcomer's forehead. "Lean your rifle against the wall."

"Alright, alright." The older man dropped the rifle's butt on the floor and let it fall against the wall. "Just be careful with that thing."

They stood facing each other, one hard-eyed, holding his rifle steady. The other was wide-eyed, his red face turning pale and terrified, staring into the rifle's muzzle. A minute passed, and then another, and the man in the outhouse came out and shouted, "Daddy, you don't want to go in there anytime soon. Had a blowout! Nearly shit my ..."

He came into the shack and stopped in his tracks, his head swiveling back and forth as he looked from the man with the rifle to his father, standing frozen in the center of the small room. "What the fuck ..." He started to raise the rifle hanging from one hand at his side.

"Don't do it!" his father shouted. "Look at his eyes. He wants you to try, so he can kill you."

"He's gonna kill us anyway," the son said, but let the rifle dangle from his sweaty palm until it thumped on the floor.

The man holding the rifle on them nodded at the wall. "Lean it over there."

The son leaned the gun beside his father's, and the rifle-man said, "Good."

He reached into a pocket of the daypack slung over his shoulder and pulled out two sets of handcuffs. "Turn around, hands behind your backs."

"Wh-what you doing?" the son stammered.

"Shut up," his father said. "You can damned well see what he's doing. Won't be any reasoning with him. He never was the reasoning sort." He turned his head and spoke over his shoulder to rifle-man. "You won't get away with this."

The cuffs ratcheted shut on his wrists and then on his son, who began whimpering, "Please ... no ... you know I never did nothing intentional. Never meant to do no harm. You gotta know that. It was just ..." He looked to the side at his father. "It was him ... all him!"

"Head out." The rifle-man motioned them forward with the rifle's barrel.

Father and son stumbled outside, squinting in the sunlight. "Move out," rifle-man ordered.

"Which way?" the old man asked.

"Across the clearing, through those bushes. There's a deer trail. Follow it."

They found the deer trail and started walking, rifle-man behind with the Winchester .30-06 pointed at their backs. After a mile, rifle-man said, "Go to the right here."

"Where?" the father said, eyeing the surrounding brush and hillside that rose precipitously from the deer trail.

"Push through and start up the hill."

"Like this?" the older man said and motioned awkwardly behind his back with his cuffed hands. "Liable to fall and break my ass."

"Better than what happens if you don't start moving," rifle-man said.

The two men started up the slope, their feet slipping in the dirt and pine straw. Progress was slow and tedious. Five steps up, slide back two or three, and then five more scrambling steps. With their hands cuffed behind their backs, they were forced to wedge their legs and feet into any crevice they could find for a hold and then push upward.

Rifle-man kept his distance, following the trail they blazed up the slope. He waited now and then as they scrambled and helped each other up, pushing with their shoulders and knees, looking back to see the rifle still pointed in their direction. He was in no hurry, and if it took all day and night to climb up, he was fine with it.

It didn't take all day, but it was late afternoon when they made it up to a high ledge with a cliff rising above. They stopped on the ledge, panting hard, and looked out over the wooded valley two thousand feet below. Rifle-man took a water bottle from his daypack and sipped.

"I could use a swallow of that," the father said, his voice a dry croak, his mouth and tongue parched.

Rifle-man ignored him and put the bottle back in the pack.

"You son of a bitch," the son whined. "Give us a goddammed drink!"

"Move." Rifle-man pointed with the rifle along the ridge.

Father and son stared at him for a second, and it seemed they might be considering the possibility of rushing him, overpowering him, getting the rifle and handcuff keys away, and then blowing his brains out. Rifle-man waited, the look on his face sending the message that he almost wished they would try. But they didn't, and the truth was, he was glad because he had something better planned for them.

The father saw the hardness in his eyes and turned. "Let's go."

They started along the narrow ledge, the two cuffed men staying away from the edge and the steep slope to the valley below. They had gone another half mile when rifle-man said, "Stop here."

"Why? What's here? What are you going to do?" The son was close to panicking.

His father looked at him with disgust and said, "Shut up."

Rifle-man reached to the side and pulled a fallen tree limb to reveal a cut in the rock face. "In there."

"I ain't goin' in there," the son said, shaking his head. "No way. Not unless I know what you're going to do."

"You really want to know that?" rifle-man said, smiled for the first time, and shrugged. "I could just do it here."

"C'mon," the father said. "We keep him talking, we still got a chance." He looked at rifle-man and sneered, "He'll fuck up. He always does."

"Yeah, right," his son muttered, hoping it was true. "He'll fuck up."

The father, older and heavier, started squeezing his thick body through the crevice in the rock wall, popping through suddenly like a champagne cork. He staggered into an almost pitch-black cave. His son followed a few seconds later, stumbling into his father.

Rifle-man pointed the rifle barrel through the opening and called inside, "Move away."

The two men backed deeper into the cave, away from the crevice entrance. Rifle-man, leaner and in better shape, came through and stepped aside, allowing a narrow beam of sunlight to point like an arrow across the rocks.

"Over there." He motioned with the rifle.

"Where?" the old man said. "It's dark as shit. We're likely to fall a thousand feet down some hole."

"Move," rifle-man said.

The two men shuffled backward across the cave's rock-strewn floor until they came up against another rock wall. Without a word, rifle-man stepped to the side, leaned the rifle against the wall, and took a nine-millimeter pistol from his belt.

"Y-you c-can't do this," the son blubbered, in tears now.

With the pistol pointed at them, rifle-man reached down with a hand and retrieved something from the cave floor. "Face the wall."

"What the hell, you doin', boy?" The older man's frightened protest echoed shrilly around them.

The two men turned, the younger one sobbing, his father trembling but trying to put on a tough front. Rifle-man turned on a small battery-powered lantern and then lifted a heavy chain from the floor. It required only a few seconds to weave the chain between their arms and around the handcuff links behind their backs. Secured at one end by a bolt sunk through the links into the rock, he looped the other end back around to the starting point, ran a padlock through the links, and snapped it shut. It was an industrial-grade lock, as big as a man's hand, and guaranteed by the manufacturer to withstand several tons of prying force. He put the pistol back in his belt, stepped back, and surveyed his work.

Months earlier, he'd begun planning, packing in the heavy chain, securing it to the rock wall with a twelve-inch rock bolt sunk into the cave wall. That had taken some time and a good deal of sweat and backbreaking labor, but he got it done, carrying the tools in his daypack—hammers, chisels, a diamond-tipped manual auger, heavy wrenches. Once he had the bolt and chain secure, he waited for the right time. Yesterday he'd learned the two men were at the deer camp. It was the right time.

Now, handcuffed and chained together, the men stood silently, waiting for their captor to say something. When he did not, they looked at each other, then managed an awkward shuffling turn, twisting the chain taught as they did. The older man understood their situation. Looped together, hands cuffed behind, they had about eight feet of space to shuffle about. He jerked his hands and arms behind him, pulling at the chain, testing its strength. "You think you're pretty fucking smart, don't you, boy!"

Rifle-man said nothing, turned off the lantern, then walked to the cave's crevice entrance, and disappeared.

"No!" the younger man screamed like a frightened child. "You can't leave us here like this! Nooo..."

"You son of a bitch!" his father shouted. "I get out of here, I'll fucking kill you, you little pissant bastard."

He was back on the ridge, now making his way around the slope and down to the deer trail. A hundred yards from the cave entrance, their screams and shouts were barely audible. When he had gone another hundred, the only sounds were the birds and animals scurrying through the brush and the breeze rustling the trees.

The cave was one of hundreds in Georgia, formed by seismic activity along the fault lines that ran through north Georgia and the Appalachians. For a million years, the upward heaving and thrusting of the earth's crust had formed pockets in the underground rock, creating caves like this one. Some were well known, but not all. Before today, only one person knew of this cave.

As a boy wandering the hills and mountains, rifle-man had discovered it. He made it his sanctuary. Only one other person knew about it, his brother, and he would never reveal its location. It had been their special place. A place that no one else knew about. A place where they were safe. Now it would be something else.

2. The George Mackey Rule

"Coming up behind you," Marco Santoro said, just loud enough for the microphone in his earbud to pick it up. He stopped at a red light alongside a glistening metallic red, tricked-out Mercedes GLS class SUV.

"10-4," George Mackey responded as he waited in a small economy-sized car parked along the curb a block ahead.

The bass from some unidentifiable music thumped inside the Mercedes' tinted and sealed windows. Marco ignored it and the people inside the SUV. There was no way to see through the darkened windows, even if he had wanted to, but he didn't. He already knew who was inside.

A driver and another armed gangbanger up front. Behind and sitting alone, Hermilo 'Hermie' Mendoza, gang organizer and one of the largest drug traffickers in the state. Three additional armed gangbangers sat behind Hermie.

Marco watched the traffic signal, waiting for the light to turn green, the steering wheel, seat, and windows vibrating around him as the bass from the Mercedes pounded. When the light changed, he made a left turn, proceeded a block to the next signal, and turned right, now heading in the same direction as the SUV on a parallel street.

Ahead, George waited for the Mercedes to roll past and pulled away from the curb when it was a block ahead. "Get ready, Ponce."

"Standing by," Gary 'Ponce' Poncinelli replied from his position, parked in an alley two blocks ahead.

It was a multi-unit vehicle surveillance and tail. Rotating the tail vehicles every couple of blocks, they were taking no chances of being detected. Savannah's squares and parks simplified the process, affording them plenty of side streets and alleys to turn out so the next car could take over as the tail vehicle.

Hermie Mendoza was a big fish in the Savannah underworld. The hope was that he would lead them to an even bigger fish. No one knew who that was exactly, but every law enforcement agency in Georgia had been trying to discover who he worked with ... or for.

The operating assumption was that he was working with one of the Mexican cartels. Coming to that conclusion did not require any particularly shrewd investigative efforts. The cartels were pretty much tied into all drug trafficking in the country to some degree, but discovering which cartel Hermie worked with had become a puzzle gnawing at investigators for months.

***

The Savannah P.D. had been trying to build a case against Hermie Mendoza for several months and were getting nowhere. The narcotics unit decided they could use an assist and asked the mayor to put in a call to the governor and request assistance from the OSI—Office of Special Investigations.

The reasons for calling in the OSI were mainly tactical. Unfortunately, the potential public relations boost for the mayor and city council also injected a hefty dose of self-serving politics into the operation.

Tactically, the more expertise involved, the better. A year earlier, the OSI had broken up a human trafficking ring with international and cartel connections. Interpol had taken an interest in the case, and the OSI's experience in dealing with them would be helpful to the local detectives working the Mendoza case if they discovered he was working with a cartel outside the country.

Politically, no one wanted to fumble this one and take the blame for letting an unidentified cartel operate freely in the state. If somehow the surveillance was blown and the investigation went to hell, the city administration could blame the elite OSI team. On the other hand, if they were successful, they could take the spotlight and the credit for cracking a major drug operation.

The Savannah mayor's office assigned a police liaison to head up the task force. Captain Leonard Stoneman was one of those police officers who had built a career on political connections and favors. The badge he carried was a tool for advancing his personal interests more than to enforce the law. The standard police motto—To Protect and Serve—were words he used when addressing community groups, assuring them of his and the mayor's personal devotion to the safety of every voting citizen of Savannah. Stoneman was good at speeches, but he was not a street cop.

Politics aside, at the urging of the lieutenant commanding the narcotics unit, a call went out to the OSI, or as the media called them, the Hunters. George and the team were happy to lend a hand and get back into some real action. Since breaking up the human trafficking ring in south Georgia, things around the office had been quiet. Usually, in the law enforcement world, quiet was a good thing, but in the big game of Good Guys versus Bad Guys, they began to feel like they were losing their competitive edge.

The OSI deputy director, Andy Barnes, a former Atlanta homicide detective, jumped at the opportunity to get his team back on the field in a major case. He sent a crew of investigators led by George Mackey to Savannah to work with the local narcotics detectives. Their mission was to set up surveillance, prepare to net Mendoza, and pressure him to identify his cartel contacts.

The first part of their plan was to develop a major case against Mendoza. They needed to bring charges that would allow them to present him with serious prison time if he didn't cooperate. Mendoza had been remarkably smart or lucky for a career criminal. A few minor busts on his rap sheet were the only ammunition investigators had to urge him to cooperate, and they were all closed cases. Whether it was brains or luck, Mendoza was always careful to set up his criminal enterprises so that others took the fall if things went the wrong way for them.

The OSI team and local narcotics investigators devised a plan to hit him with a serious felony charge that would land him in federal prison if convicted. They worked with an informant who cooperated to avoid facing federal charges of interstate drug trafficking for running a load of meth and fentanyl. The informant was not about to turn on Mendoza directly and send him to prison with his testimony. Others had tried to make that deadly mistake.

Instead, they pressured the informant to feed Mendoza information that a major cartel representative contacted him while he was making the run. They even gave the fictitious cartel leader a name—Raoul Santiago. The imaginary cartel leader, Santiago, was not happy that Mendoza was infringing on his turf, but he wanted to meet with Mendoza to see if they could work together and expand both their businesses. The informant bandied about the huge numbers in shared profits that Santiago supposedly offered to share to preserve the peace and grow their businesses.

If they could lure Mendoza into making a major interstate drug deal and record him in the process, they'd have what they wanted. Dangling a serious prison sentence in front of him would give them the leverage they needed to pressure him to reveal his cartel contacts and take them farther up the ladder of traffickers one rung at a time.

Mendoza might be a killer at heart, but not with his own hands, and the prospect of serious conflict with a Mexican cartel, even one he didn't know, was alarming. He agreed to meet the cartel leader but, as always, was cagey and demanded that it be at a place of his choosing to be revealed on the very day of the meeting.

That was the plan. It was complicated, had a lot of moving parts, and would take time to work. That was why the OSI was in Savannah, working with the local narcotics unit. The only wrinkle in the operation was the arrangement with the mayor's office that required them to work under the titular command of Captain Leonard Stoneman.

***

"He's all yours," George said, turning off Bull Street at Monterrey Square.

"On him," Ponce said. "Get ready, John."

"Standing by." John Rodham was the fourth member of the OSI team assigned to the case.

A minute later, Ponce said, "Taking a left on Harris. We're now westbound toward MLK Boulevard."

"10-4," Rodham said, accelerating down a side street to get into position and adjust for the change in direction. "It'll take me a minute to get there."

"We'll pick him up." Lieutenant Dwayne Hicks headed the Savannah narcotics unit and had a team of detectives working the surveillance with the OSI. "They may be heading for I-16."

"All units, do not allow that vehicle to leave the city limits." Captain Stoneman was cruising nearby, making a show of being in command.

"Negative," George said immediately. "The plan is to follow to the meet location he selected and then send in our undercover man and backup units. Continue to follow."

"You have no authority here. The OSI is here to support our operation," Stoneman snapped back over the communications net. "Lieutenant Hicks, did you copy my order?"

There was a pause before Hicks answered. "Captain, the correct move is to follow until we get to the meeting location, then record him taking our deal. Without that, we get nothing."

"Goddammit!" Stoneman shouted over the comms. "That vehicle is not to leave the city limits! Are you clear?"

It was clear. Stoneman wanted to ensure the full credit for the arrest went to the Savannah P.D. An arrest outside the city where Savannah P.D. had no jurisdiction would put the OSI in the spotlight.

George ignored Stoneman and tried one more time. "Your department can take the credit, but all units stay on plan. Continue to follow the subject vehicle without making contact."

"Lieutenant, are you clear on my orders!" Stoneman roared.

"I'm clear," Hicks responded, and the detectives listening in could hear him take a deep breath before he added, "All due respect, that is the wrong thing to do, Captain. We don't have what we need to bring serious charges against him."

"I'm on the Mercedes," Rodham said as he took over the tail from Ponce. "On MLK, taking the ramp toward I-16. Advise."

"Stay on it," George said immediately. "Continue the tail. We'll get ahead and pick it up down the road."

"Stop that vehicle!" Stoneman was almost screaming now.

"Stay with the Mercedes," George repeated calmly. "Stay with the plan."

"Hicks! Ignore any further communication from the OSI and get your ass up there and stop that vehicle!"

"I'm not in position to do that just yet, Captain. The OSI units are closest. Recommend allowing them to continue the tail until he gets to the meet location."

"Lieutenant, get your ass up there and make the stop inside the city, or you can kiss your pension goodbye."

The pause was longer this time, but when Hicks spoke, he said, "All units, make the stop."

A uniform patrol car sped by Rodham's undercover vehicle and pulled behind the Mercedes. Two narcotics undercover cars were behind, and together, they wedged the Mercedes to the shoulder.

"OSI units, back off," George said over the comms. "Support the Savannah units."

Within a few minutes, all the OSI units and two more local narcotics undercover cars were on the scene. Weapons drawn, they ordered the gangbangers out and put them face down on the ground while they took their guns and searched the vehicle. George and the OSI team watched. With the arrest in progress, they had nothing else to do except watch their plan evaporate.

An unmarked but clearly official Savannah P.D. car pulled up behind the others. Captain Stoneman got out and hurried up to where the action was. The Savannah city limit sign on I-16 was less than a quarter mile ahead. Stoneman gave a satisfied nod, already considering the briefing he would provide the media about the exemplary work of the task force the mayor had appointed him to lead.

One by one, Hermie Mendoza and his gangbangers were cuffed and loaded into separate police vehicles. Mendoza complied and never resisted. He shook his head and gave a wry smile at the officers who cuffed him. "What you think you got me on?"

"Weapons charges," Lieutenant Hicks said. "Lot of guns in your car."

"Not mine." Mendoza shook his head and grinned. "Didn't know those boys was even carrying."

"Bullshit," Hicks muttered but knew that in the end, they had nothing substantial on Mendoza and definitely not enough to persuade him to rat out a cartel.

Stoneman strutted around the scene, pointing and giving unnecessary orders to the narcotics detectives, making sure they all understood who was in charge. Then he noticed George and the OSI team watching and stomped over, full of righteous anger. "I'll be reporting you to your superiors," he seethed without preliminaries.

"Is that a fact?" George said with a dry smile.

"Yes, it's a goddammed fact." Stoneman leaned. "I've heard about you, Mackey ... the things you've done and got away with, but you won't get away this time."

"Really?" The smile spread across George's face.

"Insubordination, attempting to countermand an order from a senior officer during a crucial operation, trying to circumvent the chain of command," Stoneman said, his face reddening as he spoke.

"That all?" George said, and his air of indifference disconcerted Stoneman even more.

"That's plenty ... enough ammunition to shoot holes in the governor's precious little OSI."

Still smiling, George said, "What about calling you a stupid son of a bitch?"

"Calling me a ..." Stoneman's eyes bulged as if they might pop from their sockets. "You can't ..."

George turned and walked to his car.

"Where the hell do you think you're going?" Stoneman said. "Get your ass back here. I'm not finished with you!"

Marco, Ponce, and Rodham stood to the side, fighting back the laughter that threatened to erupt.

"What the hell are you grinning at?" Stoneman shouted.

"Nothing," Marco said. "Just that George has this rule he lives by."

"What rule is that?" Stoneman said, the red flush on his face spreading down his neck

Marco grinned, looked at the others, and they repeated the George Mackey rule in unison. "Never argue with a stupid son of a bitch."

Laughing outright now, Marco and the others followed George to their cars. Stoneman stood sputtering on the side of the road. The Savannah narcotics detectives turned away, their shoulders heaving with suppressed hilarity.

3. A Familiar Face

"Buxton oughta do something about this damn road." Sheriff Doyle Sutter clutched the steering wheel with both hands as the pickup nosed down into a three-foot depression with a bone-jarring thud. A second later, it popped back up, the front tires spinning off the ground before slamming back onto the packed gravel and clay. "Son of a bitch gonna pay for the repairs if I lose the suspension on this truck," Sutter muttered and gritted his teeth as the pickup bounced into another rut.

A mile after pulling off the paved county road, he drove into the cleared yard of an old frame house that dated back over a hundred years. Originally, it was the home of Ezekiel and Magdalora Buxton. Along with their nine children, they were one of the original families to settle this part of the Appalachian foothills on land left vacant after the U.S. government forced the original Cherokee owners out and sent them west on the Trail of Tears.

By the time Ezekiel arrived in 1848, remnants of the Cherokees were long gone or plowed under. His grandson, Elmore, built the house in the clearing and then passed it to his oldest son, who did the same, and on through the generations until it ended up in the hands of Oxford 'Ox' Buxton. It was Ox's wife Mimsy, who had called Sheriff Sutter out that day.

Sutter braked the pickup to a stop in the bare dirt yard, got out, hitched his baggy pants up over absurdly narrow hips, and ambled toward the porch. His uniform hung and fluttered off his skeletal frame like a gunny sack off a scarecrow. Mostly, it was an assortment of odd and mismatched pieces passed from sheriff to sheriff over the years and added to according to their tastes—navy blue pants, brown shoes, and an army green shirt with a patch on the left shoulder that read *Bayne County, Georgia, Est. 1840.*

Mimsy came out on the porch as Sheriff Sutter crossed the yard. "Thank God you came out, Doyle. I'm about to die of worry."

"And a good morning to you, too," Sutter said, smiling. "What's the problem, Mimsy?"

"It's Ox and my boy Harley. I haven't heard from them in a week."

"Thought they went up to that deer camp Ox keeps back in the hills," Sutter said, pulling out a pack of cigarettes and lighting up. He rested a boot on the bottom porch step and leaned against the rail as he puffed. "No phone service up there, but I don't expect there's anything to worry about. He knows what he's doing ... been hunting these hills since he was a boy. Been out there with him some myself."

"Ox said they'd be back in three or four days, and it's been eight." Mimsy shook her head. "Not like him to not be back when he said. I'm worried, Doyle. Woke up with a sick feeling in my stomach about it."

"A sick feeling, huh." Sutter shook his head with a laugh, and the cigarette hanging from his lips dropped ashes to the porch planks. "No offense, but strictly speaking, from a law enforcement point of view, a sick feeling isn't much to go on."

"Something's wrong. I know it," Mimsy insisted. "I need you to go check on them, Doyle."

"Alright," Sutter sighed. "I got a shift at the Kwik Pak tonight, but I'll go check on them tomorrow."

"If something's wrong, things might be worse for them by tomorrow," Mimsy said, her brow wrinkled with concern.

"Probably nothing wrong except Ox got to drinking and lost track of the days. You know how he is, Mimsy." Sutter tossed the cigarette into the yard and stood straight, tugging his belt higher around his waist. "Look, I can't miss my shift. County barely pays me enough to meet the rent payment. I got to have that shift tonight, but I promise I'll go check on them tomorrow." He smiled. "And when I get up there, I'll drink a few of Ox's beers as payment for the trouble."

"Alright," Mimsy said, tugging nervously at her lip and calling after Sutter as he turned toward the eight-year-old pickup the county provided. "You find him, Doyle, and tell him to come on back down. Tell him he's got me worried sick."

"Not sure that's going to motivate him to come home, but I'll pass the message." Sutter lifted a hand in acknowledgment and chuckled as he walked away. Ox Buxton was not one to give a shit about worrying someone else, including Mimsy ... especially Mimsy.

Besides, to Sheriff Sutter's mind, Ox being away to parts unknown was a good thing. Time passed more peacefully when Ox Buxton was away.

Fifteen minutes later, he bounced his way back down the Buxtons' dirt road and out onto the paved county road. The remainder of the afternoon passed quietly, and at four o'clock, he headed to the Kwik Pak convenience store out on the state highway. Pulling into the lot, he threw a hand up and waved to a deputy parked across the highway. Toby Jones was one of three deputies who patrolled Bayne County along with the sheriff.

With a population of just under two thousand and no industry to speak of, funding the sheriff's department was an ongoing challenge. The county's scanty pay forced Sutter and his deputies to work extra jobs to make ends meet. The truth was that for the deputies like Jones, law enforcement was their second job, not a primary source of income. Jones was a carpenter when he wasn't in a patrol car. Brian Mecham was a plumber, and the third deputy, Dave Pascal, sold used cars for his father. Sutter's duties as sheriff prevented him from doing much more than working as the Kwik Pak's night clerk.

The county's lack of tax revenue might have caused them to close up the sheriff's office, but fortunately, a five-mile stretch of state highway cut across the southern tip of the county. This provided a source of revenue from traffic citations, usually paid on the spot by travelers eager to be on their way and not held up in some hillbilly backwater waiting for the local magistrate, Judge Meeks, to pull himself away from a fishing hole to find them guilty. Best to just pay the fine and move on.

Deputy Jones, partially concealed behind a billboard, returned Sutter's wave, and pointed a radar gun at a semi-rig coming down a long grade into the county. The speed limit changed abruptly from sixty to forty-five at the county limits, and the driver used the air brakes to slow the eighty-thousand-pound rig. It was too little, too late.

Jones flipped on the blue lights as the truck passed at over fifty miles an hour. Sutter could see the wide grin on his deputy's face as he pulled out, the kind of grin that came from the thrill of hooking a big fish, and Jones had a big one on the line. It took almost half a mile for the truck to pull over onto the narrow shoulder with Jones behind.

"Go get 'em, boy," Sutter said, smiling, and went inside the store.

"Wonderin' if you was comin'," Maddie Carter, the day shift clerk, said. Gray-haired and tipping the scale at three hundred pounds, Maddie sat in her customary position, a high, padded stool behind the cash register.

"Sorry," Sutter said, glancing at the clock on the wall behind Maddie. He was three minutes late. "Got held up on sheriff work."

"Humph," Maddie grunted. "More like taking a nap behind the Pentecostal church."

Sutter ignored her and went into the back room, where he removed his uniform shirt and put on a thin polyester smock with *Kwik Pak* embroidered over the left breast. When he returned to the front, Maddie was already waddling out the door, the satchel bag she used to carry her lunch draped over her shoulder. Sutter figured if he stopped her and looked inside the bag, he'd find it loaded with pilfered bags of chips and candy bars.

He didn't stop her. What would be the point? The store owner, Maddie's brother Earl, would never dare prosecute her for shoplifting.

Things were quiet in the store. The evening rush of customers wouldn't start until five, so he went to the back, used a dolly to bring out several boxes of canned goods, and began stocking shelves.

He was just lining up a row of canned pears when the door chimed. A dark-haired young man came in, walked to the cooler in the back, and pulled out a six-pack of beer. Ambling down an aisle, he looked over the assortment of snacks, grabbed a bag of chips, and headed to the cash register.

Sutter left the canned pears to ring up the beer and chips, eyeing the young man, who looked vaguely familiar. "Gonna need to see some I.D.," he said. "Gotta be eighteen to buy beer."

"I'm twenty-one," the young man said.

"Even so, need to see that I.D."

"Sure." The young man reached into his back pocket, retrieved a worn brown leather wallet, and pulled out his driver's license.

"William H. Payne," Sutter said, reading the license and looking back at the young man's face. "You have a familiar face. From around here?"

"Nope. Just passing through," the young man said, smiling, and nodded at the license in Sutter's hand. "Everything check out?"

Sutter's brow wrinkled as he studied the young man, trying to see under the two-inch beard he wore. Damn kids all had beards these days, so they all looked the same. Like trying to tell one pine cone from another.

He glanced back at the license and nodded. "Like you said. Twenty-one years old. Need a bag?'

"Nope. I'm good. Thanks." The young man took the chips and beer from the counter and started toward the door.

"Hold on a second," Sutter called out.

The young man, William Payne, stopped and turned with a smile. "Sure. What's up?"

"You remind me of someone."

"Who's that?" Payne stood by the door, holding the bag of chips and the beer tucked under an arm.

"Old Ned Hodgett."

"Who?" Payne's brow wrinkled

"Ned Hodgett. Grew up with him."

"Don't know him," Payne said, shaking his head.

"Played on the high school football team together. Good ole boy, Ned was ... until the accident."

"Accident," Payne said patiently, waiting for Sutter to get to the point.

"Yep." Sutter nodded. "Stopped in this very store and grabbed him a six-pack, just like you. He was about your age, too, at the time. Went tearing down this highway in his daddy's pickup, driving too fast and drinking those beers. Next thing you know, he drifts off the road and ends up plowing into a tree."

Sutter's brow wrinkled, and his head shook slowly side to side as if remembering the tragedy. "He survived, but he went through the windshield. Had the world ahead of him and a good life planned. UGA was scouting him as a linebacker. It all changed the instant he hit that tree. He lived, but his brain was never right after that. Now, old Ned doesn't know whether he's coming or going ... lives with his old mama on a little bit of disability the government gives him. Just sits there on the porch waiting for her mama to feed him and get him to the toilet. They say she even wipes his ass for him after, though I've never seen that for myself."

"That's a sad story." Payne smiled and lifted the six-pack. "If you're worried about this, I never drink and drive."

"Good. That's good," Sutter said, nodding. "You see, I'm sort of the sheriff around here."

"Sort of?" Payne said.

"Well." Sutter grinned. "That doesn't sound right, I suppose. Yes, I am the sheriff, and even though I'm here, I have deputies out working tonight, so I just wanted you to know to be careful."

"Thanks, Sheriff, I will be," Payne said. "Anything else?"

"No." Sutter shook his head. "That's about it. Just be careful and have a good evening, son."

"You too, Sheriff."

Payne walked from the store to an old pickup parked by one of the gas pumps. Sutter watched him go and smiled. People passing through the county stopped for gas, to buy a Coke or beer, or to use the restroom and never suspected that the skinny man behind the cash register was the county sheriff. Doyle Sutter liked it that way.

Something about William Payne had caused him to say more than usual. Maybe it was the eyes and nose above the beard, a certain sadness about them. Or, it could have been the confident way he moved and talked, but underneath, there was something else.

Sutter watched Payne pull onto the highway, hoping Toby Jones would leave him alone. Toby was just returning from stopping the semi-rig and pulled in beside the billboard. He eyed the young man leaving in the pickup but ignored him and aimed his radar gun down the highway.

Good. Let him be on his way. Sutter watched the young man disappear down the highway and muttered uneasily, "I swear I've seen that face before."

4. Probably Shouldn't Have Said That

George Mackey was expecting the call, waiting in his car. He answered on the first chime. "What's up, Andy?"

"I think that's my question, George." Andy Barnes sat back in his chair with the phone screwed to his ear. This was a private conversation, and George tended to speak loudly enough to be heard by everyone within thirty feet, even when the speaker was turned off. "Tell me what happened with the Mendoza arrest and why we just wasted a chance to get to his cartel connection."

"You want the sanitized version or the truth?" George asked more harshly than he would typically have with Andy, but it had been a long, draining day, and he was feeling short-tempered.

Andy was at the end of an equally long day and was not in the mood for attitude, not even from his lead investigator. "Cut the shit and spit out," he snapped back. "I just got off the phone with the governor and Savannah's mayor. They're pissed off. Tell me why?"

"They're pissed off?" George let out a laugh. "That's funny."

"They weren't laughing," Andy said. "Mayor Crest called the governor, blaming you for blowing the arrest."

"Blowing the arrest!" Not only was George worn out by the day's events, he was now royally pissed and not in the mood to deal with more bullshit. "You know better than that, Andy. We didn't blow anything!"

"Explain," Andy said tersely.

"Alright. We had the surveillance team in place, alternating the tail vehicles ... standard stuff until we got near the city limits when the mayor's flunky ordered his people to move in and arrest Mendoza."

"You mean Leonard Stoneman, a Captain in the Savannah P.D. and aide to the mayor."

"If you say so," George said with a smirk. "Definitely connected to a politician ... acted like one. He was so hellbent on having the arrest go down in his jurisdiction that we never got a chance to follow Mendoza to his contact. Stoneman had his guys pick up Mendoza to make sure they could take credit on the six o'clock news."

"That's not quite the story they're giving," Andy said.

"For the record," George sighed. "I don't give a shit what story they're giving, and frankly, Stoneman's not a real cop."

"For the record, I know and believe your version, if that matters to you," Andy said less sharply, trying to ease the tension on the call.

"It does," George said and took a deep breath to calm down. Andy Barnes was a good boss, fair, evenhanded, and not one to jump to conclusions regardless of who was yapping in his ear.

"Good," Andy said. "Because I need all the details. The mayor and Stoneman told the governor we blew the surveillance,"

"That's bullshit," George said, his jaw tightening.

"According to Stoneman, Mendoza made you ... spotted you and our tail cars ... and he had no choice but to order his men to make the arrest prematurely."

"Like I said, that's bullshit," George snapped.

"And like I said, I believe you," Andy shot back. "Now tell me what happened so I can make our case to the governor."

George reviewed the events of the day. He wrapped it up with, "And that's when the stupid son of a bitch told his people to stop Mendoza and make the arrest ... right at the city limits."

"Thanks, George. That'll help next time I speak with Governor Fullman. One more thing, though.""

"What's that?" George asked, although he knew what was coming.

"Did you call Stoneman a stupid son of a bitch?"

"I did," George replied without hesitation, adding, "His face took on an interesting shade of red ... kind of purple around the edges."

"Alright then," Andy said, fighting back the urge to laugh. "Will you do something for me?"

"Sure. If I can."

"Good. Go see Mayor Crest in the morning. She wants a meeting at eight o'clock sharp."

"I'll be there," George said.

"Smooth things over with her. This was supposed to be a big case ... a chance to get close to a major cartel player in Georgia. We need to stay in the mix."

"You mean you want me to apologize," George said quietly.

"I mean smooth things over. Explain how things went down from our perspective, make it a matter of disagreement between professionals, but eliminate the animosity ... take the personalities out of it."

"You mean I can't call him a stupid son of a bitch anymore," George said dryly.

"That would be a start," Andy laughed out loud this time. "Look, George. It would be nice if Stoneman had kept his cool ... let everyone do their job, but he didn't, and you know why."

"Politics," George interrupted.

"Yes." Andy paused before agreeing. "Politics ... public relations... whatever you want to call it, but the mayor will not take the blame for Stoneman's knee-jerking and shutting things down prematurely. He's her appointee, and frankly, she wanted the credit for the arrest in her city."

"Stoneman's an asshole ... a dumb one," George threw back. "If he's the mayor's appointee, that means she's ..."

"Stop," Andy said. "It doesn't matter. They are what they are. We've dealt with assholes before."

"We have, but these assholes blew a major investigation ... a chance to move on the cartels, and they did for politics."

"So, what else is new?" Andy said. "For now, I need you to fix things. We still have a chance to hit back hard at the cartels. Savannah P.D. has their hands on Mendoza. We need to find a way to use him."

"You mean turn him into an informant," George said.

"I mean, this case is bigger than Savannah. The cartels are here in Georgia, killing people. We are not going to sit back and let that happen. That means we cooperate with Savannah ... do things their way, play their game until we get the intel to work our way back up to the major cartel players." Andy paused and added. "So, yes. We need to turn Mendoza and see where it takes us."

"Mendoza isn't the kind to turn. He knows what his cartel contacts will do if they ever found out." George said but knew Andy was right. They couldn't just throw their hands in the air and call it a day. He sighed and said, "Alright, I'll play nice and try to smooth things over."

"That's all I'm asking," Andy said. "Unfortunately, we have to deal with a guy like Stoneman, but those are the cards we've been dealt, so help me out on this one, and let's focus on the job."

"Will do, and I'm sorry for the problem," George said softly.

"Don't be sorry, George. Just asking for your help."

"Okay," George almost whispered this time. He slumped back in the car seat, fatigued, the irritation in his voice suddenly dissipated, his voice sounding far away and almost disinterested. He stared out the windshield. "Whatever you say, Andy."

"Thank you," Andy said quietly. Something wasn't right, not the usual ball-busting George Mackey on the phone. The voice speaking to him had become distant, indifferent even. Andy felt the need to clarify. "This is not an ass-chewing, George. Just an explanation. You understand that, right?"

"I understand," George said. "Don't worry. I'll take care of it."

"Alright," Andy said, still concerned. "Check in with me after you meet with the mayor tomorrow."

"Sure. Will do," George said. "Anything else?"

"No, that about covers it."

"Alright. Talk to you tomorrow, then."

Andy still had the phone at his ear when George disconnected. He laid it on the table and replayed the conversation in his mind. George Mackey had been part of the Office of Special Investigations since its inception. Focused, engaged, dedicated, persistent—those were words Andy would have used to describe the Mackey approach to his work. That was not the man he had just spoken with.

George drove back to the tiny motel on the city's outskirts where he and his team were staying. Marco, Ponce, and John leaned on their cars in the parking lot, waiting for him.

"What's up?" Marco asked and exchanged a glance with the others as George plodded toward them, brow furrowed, eyes down, focused on the ground as if pondering some problem.

"Not much," George said, looking up at them, forcing a smile. "Orders from above. They want us to stay engaged with Savannah P.D., so I gotta make up with Stoneman."

"You're shitting me," Ponce said. "Make up with that prick? The P.D. here is fine ... all pros, but Stoneman is ..." He shook his head, grinned, and the others joined him in repeating the phrase of the day, "A stupid son of a bitch."

They laughed. George frowned and said, "Yeah, well, I probably shouldn't have said that."

"Far as I can see, it's true," John Rodham said.

"Maybe so." George shrugged. "But the governor called Andy, and I've got to go make nice with Stoneman and the mayor in the morning." He looked at Marco. "I want you to come with me, maybe help me keep things on an even keel."

"Not sure how much help I'll be, but I'll tag along if you want," Marco said, his usual cocky undercover persona replaced by concern. He'd never seen George down like this before, not over some asshole politician pretending to be a cop.

"Alright, that's settled," Ponce said, hoping to spin George out of his mood. "Let's go grab some food and a couple of beers."

"You all go. I'll grab a burger later." George turned and walked across the parking lot.

Marco watched and shook his head, the look of concern deepening. "I've never known George to be down ... not like that."

"Tired, maybe," John said. "Been putting in some long hours on Mendoza."

"Maybe." Marco shook his head. "Not like him, though. The look on his face."

"Yeah," Ponce said. "Almost like he'd checked out ... was somewhere else."

In his room, George kicked off his shoes and leaned back on the bed, staring at the ceiling for several minutes before he pulled out his cell phone and thumbed the number.

Sharon Price answered immediately. "Been waiting for you to call."

"Sorry, got tied up." George took a deep breath and closed his eyes.

"I heard," Sharon said. "Andy told me the mayor and some asshole captain called the governor complaining because they blew the case on Mendoza but wanted to pass the buck to you."

"That's about the size of it."

"Are you okay, babe?"

"I guess." George let out a deep breath. "Honestly, I don't know."

"Want to talk about it?" Sharon asked.

"Nope. Right now, I want to talk about something ... anything else besides this case. How was your day?"

5. I Do Know You

"You out there, Doyle?" Carol Digby, the Bayne County Clerk, keyed the microphone on her desk and waited for a response.

Her office resided in an old storefront off the town square in Dykes, Georgia, the county seat, and served as the center of operations for all county staff, including the tiny sheriff's department. With a budget that barely put fuel in the vehicles and paid the sheriff and his deputies their small salaries, a full-time dispatcher was out of the question. Carol was happy to add the task to her meager list of duties. Fielding incoming calls for the sheriff and advising him over the old radio on a table beside her desk gave her something to gossip about with her friends.

She waited a minute and then repeated her call more emphatically, "Doyle Sutter. Are you out and about? Time to get up!"

A few seconds passed before Sheriff Sutter croaked, "I'm up," yawning as he spoke.

"You sound terrible," Carol said, stifling a laugh. "Late night?"

"Pulled some overtime at the Kwik Pak stocking shelves last night."

"Sure it wasn't a bender with the boys?" It was a joke. Everyone in the county knew that Doyle Sutter was a hard-core, born-again Baptist who never drank ... almost never, at least.

Truth was that he only backslid for special occasions—births, deaths, Fourth of July, weddings, and the like. When he did, it was never more than a jar or two of home-distilled white lightning with Bob Thompson and his sons behind the Thompson barn and out of view of his constituents and Brother Simmons, the local Baptist preacher.

"What you got?" Sutter said into the portable radio he kept charging by the bedside. He slid his legs over the side of the bed and sat up straight, stretching and scratching.

"Mimsy Buxton called and wanted to know if you've been out to check on her husband and son at the deer camp."

"Told her I'd get to it today," Sutter growled, annoyed.

"Well, she called," Carol replied. "No need to snap at me."

"Sorry. Just tired." Sutter stood, stretched again, and with the radio in hand, went to the bathroom to relieve himself. "Let her know I'm going to have a look for them, and I'll let her know later this afternoon when I get back."

"Okay," Carol said and reached for the phone to call Mimsy Buxton.

Sutter finished peeing and wandered through the small two-bedroom house he lived in with his wife, Chloe. Coffee was waiting for him on the kitchen table.

Chloe stood at the stove, scrambling eggs. "Heard you stirring. Thought I'd get your breakfast going."

He nodded, plopped in a vinyl-covered chair, and lifted the coffee cup. "Thanks."

Chloe put the eggs on a plate in front of him, then poured a cup for herself and dropped into a chair across the table. They sat quietly while Sutter ate. There wasn't really anything to speak about. The day would pass as each day had for almost twenty years.

He would go off for the day, being the sheriff in a county where not much happened, and then to a second job, the latest at the Kwik Pak on the state highway. She would tidy up the house, then go into Dykes for any food or sundries they needed. After that, she would head off to her job as a waitress at a diner on the interstate twenty miles away in another county.

Childless, despite trying for a baby the first ten years of their marriage, they filled their lives with meaning where they could. To say they were a particularly happy couple might be an overstatement, but they weren't unhappy either. Life was what it was, simple with a few highlights. After returning from a stint in the army, Doyle had been elected sheriff, mainly because nobody else wanted the job. He was into his fifth term now, and it seemed he might remain the sheriff until he retired.

Chloe was a quiet person who found fulfillment in small ways. On Sunday, she taught bible lessons to the adult class. Wednesdays, she led the women's prayer and study group. Saturday afternoons were spent volunteering at the senior center in Dykes.

Sutter slowly chewed the last bite of eggs, swallowed the last drop of coffee, and sighed. "Guess I better get moving, or Mimsy Buxton won't be giving us a minute of peace."

"What's she on about?" Chloe asked.

"Says she hasn't heard from Ox or Harley since they went up to that shack Ox calls his deer camp."

"Oh." Chloe sipped coffee. It was not unusual for her to be in the dark about what her husband called his sheriffing. Mornings at the table were about the only times they had to talk, and they rarely did much of that.

Sutter left his plate and cup on the table. Chloe cleaned up the dishes and ran the vacuum while he went to shower and shave. When he returned to the living room, dressed in the same hodgepodge of a uniform he'd worn every day that week, he gave her a peck on the cheek and said, "See you tonight."

"Have a good day," Chloe said, returning the kiss, and then sat in a chair in front of the television as the door closed. She pulled out her bible and flipped the channel to a local cable station that broadcast faith-based programs, primarily Baptist and Pentecostal, for sixteen hours a day. The remaining eight hours were filled with infomercials that all promised two of whatever they were selling for the small sum of $19.99, plus a small fee for shipping and handling.

Sutter pulled the county pickup out of the driveway and keyed the mic. "Carol, this is Doyle."

"I hear you, Sheriff," Carol Digby replied immediately. Things were quiet around the county offices that day, and she had nothing to do except listen for radio calls and file some property tax exemptions.

"On duty and heading up to check things out at Buxton's deer camp," Sutter said. "Be out of radio and phone contact for a while up there."

"10-4," Carol replied, sighing. Now she had one less duty for the day and was trying to figure out how to fill her time. She pulled out her phone and brought up a solitaire game. "Call in when you're back in service, and I'll let Mimsy know."

"10-4."

Sutter pulled off the main county road a few minutes later and began winding up into the Appalachian foothills. Within a couple of miles, he was out of radio contact, and his cell phone bars showed no service.

He muttered a few words that Brother Simmons would not have condoned. "Damned Buxton gotta have a deer camp up in the hills. He's got plenty of land and could just put up a deer stand like everybody else. Plenty of damned deer around, but no, Buxton has to do things different, do things his own damn way."

Sutter carried on the conversation with himself for ten miles until he came to a gravel road that switchbacked up a steep hill. He turned and followed it up for another two miles until he came to Buxton's big dually pickup with its blackened diesel exhaust stacks extending above the cab.

He got out, found the trail to the shack across the road, and started up the slope. It was a two-hundred-yard climb from the road to the clearing, and he was breathing heavily when he came out from under the trees. He paused at the tree line and looked around the clearing.

Things were quiet. There was plenty of sound from the breeze rustling the trees, animals foraging in the woods, and birds chirping, but he'd expected to hear some human sounds coming from the shack—drunken laughter, noise, loud talking, maybe even a gunshot fired off as a joke. There ought to be some sign that Ox and his boy Harley forgot about going back home because they had hunkered down on a beer-drinking binge.

Sutter wouldn't have called the silence in the clearing eerie, but it was surely odd. He took a few steps into the open and figured maybe they were inside, sleeping off the beer. That made sense. He called out, "Ox! Harley! You in there?"

Sutter took a few more steps and added, "Don't be shooting off your guns in my direction! It's just me, Doyle Sutter!"

He stood for a second, waiting for a response, then shrugged his shoulders and walked toward the shack, a little less worried that they might fire off a round at him if he surprised them. They must have really tied one on to be sleeping it off this late in the day.

He found the shack's door ajar and pushed it with the toe of his boot, peering inside. He could just make out a cot against the back wall. The blankets were piled up on it, but he couldn't tell if anyone was under them.

"Ox ... Harley," he said softly as he stepped inside to let his eyes adjust to the gloom. Scanning the interior from left to right, he caught his breath and froze.

"I thought you might come ... was hoping you'd be the one to come looking for them."

"You ..." Sutter squinted, eyes narrowing to study the young man's face. "You're the fella from last night at the Kwik Pak ... showed me your I.D. for the beer."

"That's right," the young man said, his eyes cold and hard over the smile below. He sat on a milk crate leaning against the wall, a rifle resting on his knee.

"William ... something," Sutter said, trying to remember.

"Payne ... William Payne." The young man nodded and moved, so the rifle pointed at Sutter's face. "Take off your gun belt and lay it on the floor ... do it slow."

"Where's Ox and Harley?" Sutter asked, surprise and fear making him unable to do anything but stare alternately at the rifle barrel and the smile on Payne's face.

"You'll see soon enough." Payne stood and motioned with the rifle. "The gun belt ... on the floor ... now."

Hands shaking, Sutter unfastened the belt's buckle so that it and his sidearm slid off his narrow hips and dropped to the floor with a thump.

Payne nodded. "Good. Now, take out your handcuffs and put one over your left wrist, then put your hands behind your back."

Sutter complied, ratcheted a cuff over his wrist, and turned to face the wall to have his arms jerked roughly behind his back, and the other handcuff snapped around his right wrist. Payne spun him around again so that he could see his face clearly.

Sutter's brow furrowed, and then, as if a light had switched on, he nodded in recognition. Voice trembling, he said, "I do know you."

"Yes," William Payne said, and the broadening smile on his face sent a chill down Doyle Sutter's spine.

6. Step Up

Marco met George in the motel parking lot and handed him coffee in a paper cup. "From the pot in the lobby. Shitty coffee, but it's hot."

"Thanks," George said, taking the coffee. "You drive."

"Me?" Marco saw the same distracted look on George's face from the day before. He shrugged. "Right, I'll drive."

The drive to city hall through the morning traffic took twenty minutes. George sat quietly, looking out the window, lost in his thoughts. Marco assumed he was steeling himself for what would probably be an ass-chewing from the mayor.

***

A news broadcast the night before had featured Captain Stoneman in full uniform standing before the cameras. As press conferences went, it was pretty mundane. Stoneman and the mayor were proud of the excellent work done by the Savannah Police Department in arresting Hermilio Mendoza, a known drug dealer.

When he finished his prepared remarks, a reporter raised her hand.

Stoneman smiled and called on her, "Carla, always first with a question. Go ahead."

"Thank you," Carla returned the smile, then got down to business. "Captain Stoneman, sources tell me that there is a cartel chief that your investigators hoped to get close to through this investigation. Can you tell us how if that effort is proceeding now that Mendoza is behind bars? Have you confirmed any links to the cartels, or has the Mendoza arrest put that on the back burner, so to speak?"

"Ah, yes, well, that's an interesting question and, uh ..." Stoneman cleared his throat and said, "I assure you we have every intention of following up with our investigation into cartel expansion into Georgia, and if it hadn't been for the failures of ... well, some of our partners from other agencies ... we would be pursuing those cartel connections at this moment." He smiled.

"But for now, we have Mendoza in custody, and we're going to make the best of the situation."

"Can you be more specific?" Carla, the reporter, asked. "What agency failures in the arrest?"

"Let's just say some of our partners acted prematurely, and we were forced to make an arrest instead of continuing our surveillance of Mendoza," Stoneman said, a sober look on his face expressing his disappointment at the outcome of the investigation.

"By other agencies," Carla persisted, "Do you mean the Governor's Office of Special Investigations?"

Stoneman gave a final smile. "Unfortunately, I can't discuss any details of our ongoing active investigation. I'm sure you understand." Before another question was asked, Stoneman strode briskly from the podium.

***

"Did you see the news report last night?" Marco asked as he drove.

"What?" George turned from his reverie, staring out the window.

"The news last night. That son of a bitch threw the blame on us for blowing the Mendoza surveillance," Marco said.

"Oh." George nodded. "I saw. He didn't actually name us."

"No, but it won't take long for the media to figure out which agency was working the case with Savannah. That son of a bitch has some fucking nerve." Marco was becoming more agitated as he spoke. "Calls off the tail and blows our surveillance so his people can arrest Mendoza inside the city, then blaming us ... the other agency. It's bullshit, pure and simple bullshit ..." Marco stopped his tirade, a smile of understanding spread across his face. He turned to George. "You're the *source*, aren't you? You told that reporter about the blown investigation."

"Seemed like the thing to do." George shrugged. "We can't say anything officially to the press, but I figured someone should throw a bone, off the record, for that reporter and her colleagues to go after."

Marco laughed. "Now that's the George Mackey I know."

George resumed his stare out the window.

They arrived at city hall fifteen minutes before the scheduled meeting, went through the security checkpoint, and were ushered into the mayor's reception area. Their eight o'clock appointment did not begin until eight-thirty-five.

Mayor Sondra Crest came directly to the point as they sat in hard chairs, positioned in front of her desk like school children called to the principal's office. "I have registered a complaint with the governor."

George and Marco sat silently without replying. There was nothing to say, and they weren't about to beg for forgiveness.

A few seconds passed, and the mayor broke the silence. "I told him that his vaunted Office of Special Investigations interfered and ruined our investigation into cartel activities … activities that impact the entire state, not just Savannah."

Crest paused again, waiting for a response. George said nothing, so she continued, "Specifically, you, Investigator Mackey. Your interference at the arrest of Hermilio Mendoza made it impossible to pursue our investigation into his cartel connections."

George said nothing, but Marco had enough. "The investigation was blown because you …" Marco turned, glaring at Stoneman. "You gave the order to arrest Mendoza within the city limits of Savannah rather than continue the surveillance. If not for that, he might have led us to his cartel connection yesterday. At the least, we'd still have an active investigation."

"I don't have to tolerate this kind of talk from you," Stoneman sputtered, surprised that a mere investigator would dare such an outburst to a ranking officer and aide to the mayor.

"It's alright," George said to Marco. "The mayor called this meeting. Let her speak."

Arguing was pointless. It was clear the mayor and Stoneman had no intention of accepting any blame. With the word out about the blown investigation, they were in full deflect-the-blame mode. It was politics as usual, and George had been around long enough to know that facts rarely mattered when politicians were involved.

Mayor Crest continued her rant for several minutes, throwing out words like incompetent, bungling, and inept. When she finished, she said, "Is there anything you'd like to say, Investigator Mackey?"

For ten years, George Mackey had worked cases for the OSI, had been at the center of every major investigation, and before that, twelve years as a deputy sheriff in Pickham County. He was no stranger to job-related stress. He could feel sympathy for the pain and suffering of victims, then push it aside so he could deal with the criminals who victimized them. As for politicians, he'd dealt with his share of their bullshit—sheriffs, governors, district attorneys, lawyers ... mayors.

So why was this so different? He didn't know, but he did know that he was no good for this investigation like this. He made a spontaneous decision. "Whatever blame you attribute to the OSI team should be placed on me."

Crest's eyes raised in surprise, and she cast a sideways glance at Stoneman. "Anything to say about that, Captain?"

Stoneman sat up straight, took a second to clear his throat, and gathered his thoughts. This was a surprise. George Mackey was willing to bury the hatchet to move things forward. Even more than that, he was falling on his sword.

The truth was that Stoneman had received his own ass-chewing from the mayor for the botched press conference. The question from the reporter prompted by her unnamed source had cast doubt on the importance of the Mendoza arrest. It also pressured them to continue the cartel investigation, and the mayor knew Stoneman had no idea where to begin that investigation without OSI assistance.

He began, "Your acceptance of responsibility does not change the fact that ..."

"You know what, you're right," George interrupted, looked at Mayor Crest, and nodded. "You're both right. I think things might run more smoothly with someone else as your OSI contact."

"What are you saying?" Crest said, the surprise on her face cracking through the tough-mayor veneer as she sat up straight. "You're quitting? You do that, and I'll be on the phone with the governor before you leave the building."

"I'm saying that this investigation is too important to the state for personality clashes to get in the way." He looked at Marco, whose expression was even more stunned than the mayor's. "Investigator Santoro will be your liaison with the OSI. He is an expert in undercover operations and can assist your investigators in working Mendoza and finding a way to get to his cartel contacts."

"This was not the purpose of the meeting," Mayor Crest said. "I called you here to ..."

George lifted a hand and interrupted. "You called me here to smooth the ruffled feathers of the captain here. I don't know why that's so important to you. Maybe he helps get the vote out for you. Maybe he contributed to your campaign, or he's married to one of your relatives."

Crest nearly came out of her chair. "You don't have the right to speak to me that way or to question my motives!"

"Not questioning anything," George said. "Merely pointing out that I don't care about your motives for calling the governor and demanding a face-to-face with me. I care about getting our hands on Mendoza's cartel contact setting up shop in our state."

"I will not tolerate this sort of insolence from *you*!" Crest raged, and the unspoken words hung in the air for everybody to understand—from you, a *mere detective from south Georgia ... a redneck ... a nobody.*

"If you wanted an apology for what I said to your Captain ..." George looked at Stoneman, whose face was nearly as red as it was the day before after hearing the George Mackey rule. "Captain, you have my apology. What I said to you was out of line."

George stood. "I think that should wrap things up, Mayor. I will withdraw from the case, and Investigator Santoro will take over for the OSI."

"You don't have the right to quit!" Crest said.

George looked down at her and understood. He nodded and said, "You're right. I will tell my superiors that you removed me from the case, that it was your decision to send me back to Atlanta in the best interests of the investigation."

"That's not what I mean," Crest said, but she was no longer shouting.

It *was* what she meant, but George didn't argue. He looked at Marco. "If you'll give me a ride back to the motel, I'll get my things and head back to Atlanta. Then you can come back and coordinate with Captain Stoneman." He looked at Mayor Crest and threw her a bone to smooth things over for Marco. "Would that be acceptable, Mayor?"

"Fine," Crest said sharply. "Get out of my office."

"Yes, Ma'am," George said and turned for the door with a stunned Marco Santoro trailing.

In the car on the way back, Marco said, "This isn't right. It's Stoneman. He's a ..."

"I make a mistake ..." George raised a hand to stop him in mid-sentence. "I let Stoneman piss me off and pissed him off in return. I'm sorry for that because he's the one you have to work with now."

"I'm not going to be able to handle this any better than you," Marco said. "They'll be sending me back to Atlanta right behind you."

"No, you can do it. Think of it as an undercover operation, working an informant, except now you're undercover, working the good captain and Mendoza." George smiled. "I've seen you work a suspect. You can do this, Marco."

When they reached the motel, George put out a hand and shook Marco's. "You'll do fine. Don't get distracted like I did, and remember that the main thing is finding a way to get to Mendoza's cartel contact."

"You planned this all along, didn't you?" Marco said, brow furrowed and a wry smile on his face.

"Planned?" George shook his head and shrugged. "Not a plan ... just wanted things to refocus on the investigation and take the personality conflicts out of the equation. Besides, it's time for you to take the lead."

"I'm an undercover cop, George." Marco shook his head. "A pretty good one, but not a leader."

"You're a leader now," George said. "So, step up and do the job."

7. No Choice

William Payne motioned up the slope with the rifle. "Up there."

"Where are you taking me?" Sheriff Sutter asked, frozen in place. He had no desire to move off the deer trail. There might not be much chance of it, but at least here, some hunter might come along and maybe prevent Payne from doing whatever he had planned.

"Up the hill," Payne said and pointed the rifle at Sutter's face. "Start climbing."

Sutter began the scramble up to the ridge, with Payne trailing at a safe distance behind in case he came tumbling down on top of him. He didn't and made it to the ridge, panting and wheezing, leaning back against the rock face and away from the drop-off.

Payne came up and motioned him along the ridge path. Sutter shuffled along, trying to come up with an escape plan. He peered over the edge down the hillside. The slope was steep, and a fall would likely result in broken legs or neck. He considered throwing himself over and trying to roll and bounce down anyway, but Payne had the rifle pointed at him and could easily put a bullet through his back if he tried.

Out of choices, Sutter was working himself up to chance the fall when Payne said, "Stop." He pulled at some brush and tree limbs piled against the rock face, revealing the crevice. He pointed the rifle at Sutter and said, "Through there."

"In there?" Sutter turned, standing with his shoulders across the opening, shaking his head. "I'm not going in there."

Payne smiled and slammed the butt of the rifle into his groin. Hands cuffed behind him, Sutter slumped, groaning, unable to clutch his throbbing testicles.

"You're going in one way or the other," Payne said. "Get moving."

Sutter turned and pushed himself sideways through the crevice opening. His gaunt stature made it a much easier process than it had been for Ox Buxton a week earlier.

"What in the hell ..." Sutter said, choking. He stood in the dark, trying not to breathe the foul odor inside. "Smells like shit in here."

Payne followed him through, prodded him forward with the rifle's barrel, and turned on the lantern he'd left by the entrance. The dim light cast a yellow glow around the cave, and Doyle Sutter's eyes opened wide in shocked disgust.

"My God, boy! What have you done here?"

Hands cuffed behind them and secured to the rock wall by the chain, Ox and Harley Buxton knelt slumped over on the floor, their arms twisted unnaturally, backward and up as they hung from the chain. For the first day and a half, they had managed to stand, leaning and supporting each other. Toward the end of the second day, Ox's legs gave out. Exhausted, he passed out and collapsed to the cave floor, the handcuffs and chain behind his back dislocating his shoulders as he fell. Harley managed to hang on until the next day before collapsing by his father's side. Younger and more limber, his shoulder had not come out of the socket, but the pain was maddening.

Two more days followed without food or water. Dehydrated, older, and in poor physical condition, Ox died the next night. Harley listened to his father's last rattling gasps, and when they ceased, he sobbed, "No, daddy ... you can't leave me here alone ... no, please, not alone."

Now, nearing the end of the fifth day in the cave, Harley clung to life, but just barely. Both men had defecated on themselves within the first twenty-four hours, filling the small cave with an unspeakable stench. They continued to produce urine for another day, adding acrid ammonia fumes to the disgusting odor. After that, their kidneys began to shut down. Toxins built up in their remaining organs until they followed suit, turning themselves off one by one. As their body functions ceased, their lives ebbed away. Ox had succumbed first, but his son would not be far behind.

Wide-eyed, Sutter gasped on seeing what remained of the two men. Some animal had begun eating at Ox's flesh, crawling up to his face to get at the mouth's soft, tender parts and the nasal cavities. Insects crawled over his body, in and out of the wounds left by the animals.

Harley's eyes fluttered open for a moment, but Sutter could see no sign of recognition there, no indication that he hoped the newcomer was bringing his deliverance. Even if he had, there was no strength left to ask for it or even to plead for mercy.

While Sutter stared in horror at the spectacle, Payne took the pistol from his belt and pointed it at the sheriff. Then he unfastened the padlock, ran the end of the chain between Sutter's arms and over the handcuffs, and refastened the chain to the wall with the padlock.

Sutter turned to face him., shaking his head. "You can't do this."

Payne smiled. "I already have."

"Look, I get it," Sutter said, speaking rapidly, knowing there wasn't much time left to make his case. "I understand what you're doing."

"Do you?" Payne's eyebrows lifted curiously, but there was something there besides curiosity ... something dark and driven.

"I do ... I do," Sutter said, the words pouring out in a flood as if they might wash away the darkness he saw behind Payne's eyes. "I absolutely understand what you are doing, and believe it or not, I don't blame you."

"You don't blame me?" Payne smirked, and sarcasm dripped from his words. "That's really nice to know."

"You have to hear me out. What you're doing here ..." Sutter shook his head. "This is the wrong way to go about things. It won't get you what you want. You're a smart kid. You must know that. So be smart, and let me get out of here, and we can talk about what to do next."

Payne knelt and turned off the lantern.

"No, listen," Sutter cried out. "I had no choice! Don't you understand? I had no choice."

"There's always a choice," Payne said, then disappeared through the crevice in the rock wall and covered it again with the fallen tree branches.

"No!" Sutter shouted after him. "You don't understand!"

Harley Buxton died that night. Sutter sobbed in the darkness, kicking at the bodies on the cave floor. "You sonsabitches! You gave me no choice! I had no choice!"

They would be Sutter's last words, but no one heard them, and no one would ever repeat them.

8. Worry

Maddie Carter shuffled to the Kwik Pak's door and pushed it open. Leaning against the door frame to steady her bulk, she waved across the highway to the county patrol vehicle parked behind the billboard. The deputy looked up for a moment and then focused on his radar gun, aimed at an oncoming SUV. It passed by with a whoosh, and the deputy pulled his vehicle onto the highway, blue lights flashing. A few seconds later, he gave a quick yelp on the siren, and the speeding SUV pulled to the shoulder.

Maddie turned from the door, huffing and puffing her way back to the counter, and with a grunt, hefted her bulk onto the stool behind the cash register. "That Toby Jones, pretending he didn't see me," she muttered and shifted, trying to get comfortable. "Too busy writing tickets to pay attention to a taxpayer. I know he damn well saw me!"

She was right. Ten minutes later, Jones wheeled his sheriff's department cruiser into the parking lot and came through the door, smiling. "What can I do for you, Maddie?" he said, walking to the cooler to grab a Coke.

"Find that damned Sheriff of yours and tell him to get here to work." Maddie crossed her fat arms over her chest, her lips pursed in a way that gave her round face the look of a pouting child.

"Don't have to find him," Jones said, twisting off the Coke's cap. "I know where he is. Went up in the mountains to check on the Buxton men at that deer camp Ox keeps up there. Mimsy sent him."

"Well, give him a call on that damned radio and tell him to get his damned ass back down here to work. I been here all day, and I need to get off my feet."

Jones almost laughed. He'd never seen Maddie Carter go farther on her feet than to the bathroom or back and forth from her car. She spent all day, every day, on that stool or in the dilapidated recliner in her living room at home.

He didn't laugh but shook his head and explained, "Can't do it, Maddie. No radio or cell service up there."

"So, what the hell am I supposed to do?" she snapped at the deputy. "He should have been back by now."

"Might have had to track them down in the hills if they're out hunting," Jones said. "No telling how long that took."

"More likely, sitting there with them drinking beer until he can't see straight and staying out of sight of that preacher, Simmons," Maddie grumbled.

Maddie came from a Presbyterian family who found Baptist ways a little too holier than thou. Presbyterians were solid drinkers and not ashamed of it. She said, "Anyway, I need you to get him here."

"I wish I could help you, Maddie, but like I said, no radio or cell service, and I've got patrolling to do." Jones turned for the door. "I'm sure the sheriff will show up soon as he gets done checking on the Buxton men."

"You can pay for that Coke," Maddie said, frowning.

"Sure." Deputy Jones grinned, reached in his pocket, put the money on the counter, and walked to the door. "Keep the change, Maddie."

"I damned well will!" Maddie said.

Toby Jones worked traffic a while longer, looking for speeders, then headed around the county, patrolling slowly just to make time pass. Coming back in from the country roads, he drove around the town square in Dykes and stopped by the county offices to make his hourly check for messages on the phone recording machine. Carol Digby left at five and the machine was the only method of contacting the sheriff's department after hours.

There was one message. Jones hit the play button and listened.

"*This is Mimsy Buxton. I'm just calling to see if Doyle ... I mean ... if Sheriff Sutter was able to check up on my men up at the deer camp. He said he'd let me know, but I haven't heard anything today, so I ... well, I just wanted to see if there was any news, so if anyone gets this message, let me know if he found Ox and Harley.*" There was a pause for a few seconds, Mimsy thinking what else to say, and then she said simply, "*Alright, so, this is Mimsy Buxton ...goodbye.*"

Deputy Jones considered calling her on the office phone, but decided against it. There didn't seem to be any sense in worrying Mimsy with word that Sutter hadn't checked in yet. Sutter would be back in the morning and could tell her himself.

He scrawled out a note and left it on Carol Digby's desk, telling her that the sheriff hadn't shown up at the Kwik Pak, but he wasn't too concerned. Maddie Carter was probably right about Doyle sitting in the shack drinking beer with Ox and Harley until it got too dark to make his way back out to the road on foot. The sheriff would turn up in the morning and could make his own explanation to Mimsy and to Maddie. Jones broke into a grin as he wrote the note, thinking he'd like to be a fly on the wall at the Kwik Pak when Sutter tried to explain his absence. Then he went out and began cruising toward the state highway to look for another speeder.

At eleven PM, part-time deputy Brian Mecham relieved Jones. He made a quick tour around the county, then returned to the county offices to sleep the night away in Carol Digby's chair, as he did most nights. He set the alarm on his phone to make sure he was out on patrol before she arrived in the morning, then leaned back and dozed off.

When Carol unlocked the offices at the exact stroke of eight o'clock, Mecham drove around the corner and parked as if he'd been out riding all night. He checked in, told her about Mimsy Buxton's message on the machine, and reported all had been quiet overnight.

Carol no sooner sat at her desk when the phone rang. She recognized the number as Doyle Sutter's home phone.

"Running late again today, Sheriff?" she said, grinning.

"Is Doyle there?" Chloe Sutter said without preliminaries, speaking fast.

"Hi, Chloe. No, he's not here. Thought maybe he was feeling under the weather ... late night again."

"I haven't seen him," Chloe said. "And I'm worried."

"Haven't seen him? You mean he left home early?"

"No, I mean, I came home from work after my shift last night and went to bed like usual. Doyle gets off at the Kwik Pak later and comes to bed when he gets home, but I woke up, and he's not here! His side of the bed never was slept on."

"You didn't notice that he wasn't there during the night?" Carol asked.

"I take a sleeping pill and wear earplugs at night. Doyle snores something terrible. So, I never hear him come in, but he's always here in the morning." Chloe paused to catch her breath. "Except this morning ... he isn't here."

Carol saw the note Toby Jones left for her, read it, and decided not to read it to Chloe. The woman was already working herself into a state of panic, and there was no reason to worry her more.

"Well, I know he went up to check on the Buxton men at their shack in the hills. He got a late start, and it gets dark early up there in the hill shadows. Probably took a while to find Ox and Harley tramping around, and then figured he'd sit tight until daylight instead of chance breaking a leg trying to walk down to the road. You know how Doyle's a careful man that way, and with no phone or radio up there, he couldn't let you know."

"He told me about checking on the Buxton," Chloe said. "Didn't say anything about it taking him into the night."

"Just the same, it probably did," Carol said with the official-sounding confidence of the County Clerk and unofficial sheriff department dispatcher. "Tell you what. I'll give it a while longer, and if we haven't heard from Doyle, I'll have Toby Jones go check on him. Means we'll be without any law down here in the county for a while, but we'll find Doyle for you."

Chloe said nothing for several seconds, breathing deeply to calm the worry that threatened to flare up into panic again. "Alright, you're probably right. He was playing it safe and decided to wait until daylight."

"That's right," Carol said, chuckling. "And when he gets back, he owes you a nice dinner for the worry, maybe at that new Italian place over in Cumming and a night in a motel. You tell him I said so."

"I will." Chloe forced a smile. "Thanks, Carol."

The call ended at eight-ten in the morning. Carol looked out the window into the still shaded dawn. Deep in the Appalachian hills, the sun would not rise above the ridge tops for another couple of hours. The gloom in the valleys and ravines would last until noon. She frowned, muttering, "Damned inconsiderate, Doyle Sutter, to get us all worrying like this first thing in the morning."

9. Doubts

The phone chimed. George was expecting the call and answered, "Mackey."

"Get your ass back to Atlanta!"

"Already on the way," George said.

Governor Ben Fullman disconnected the call without another word. Less than a minute passed before George's phone chimed again. "What can I do for you, Andy?"

"You're going to get a call from the governor," Andy said quickly.

"Thanks for the heads up, but he already called," George said. "He didn't sound happy."

"He's not." Andy sighed. "I was hoping I could head things off this morning before he got wind of your meeting with the mayor."

"Doesn't matter," George said matter-of-factly. "Warning me wouldn't have changed anything. Marco can handle the investigation. Staying would have only made it more difficult for the team. I left Savannah of my own accord."

"I know," Andy said and chuckled. "I think that pissed Fullman off the most ... took his steam away so he couldn't do any political grandstanding ... give you an ass-chewing in front of the mayor to earn some payback points with her. No doubt, he'll be looking for her support when the next election rolls around."

"Anyway, sorry for the trouble it caused you, Andy." George meant it. Andy Barnes was the kind of boss who always had your back.

"No trouble, George," Andy said. "You did the right thing. We'll get through this. Fullman will get over it."

"Oh, I imagine an ass-chewing is gonna happen," George said.

"You're probably right," Andy agreed with a laugh. "But for now, get your ass in gear and get back here. Bob Shaklee wants to share a big announcement this afternoon."

"What's the big announcement?" George asked.

"Not at liberty to say," Andy said. "It's Bob's deal, but he'll be glad you're back to hear it in person."

"Okay, then. My ass is in gear," George said.

The drive from Savannah to the Twin Towers, Georgia State Office buildings should have taken a little over four hours, but George stayed off the interstate and took back highways and county roads, so he could think things through. There hadn't been much time for that recently.

He wondered if he was losing it ... burning out. That happened sometimes ... a lot of times ... to police officers.

Burnout.? He didn't feel burned out. Then what?

So why get pissed off with the mayor and her flunky? You've dealt with politicians before, put up with their interference and maneuvering, and always found a way to do your job.

Now that he had cooled off from his conversation with Mayor Crest, he began to feel guilty about leaving Marco and the team in the lurch back in Savannah. Maybe he should have played nice with the mayor and that dipshit, Stoneman.

He let out a sigh. Thinking things through was not reassuring him that he'd done the right thing. He focused on driving and tried to put the Mendoza case out of his mind for a while.

Somewhere around Covington, he picked up I-20 and made his way into Atlanta. Forty minutes later, he parked and walked around the capitol grounds toward the State Office Building.

The sky was cloudless and deep blue, the sun glittering off the capitol's gold dome as he'd seen it do hundreds of times. It was a landmark known to all Georgians. The gold to gild it came from Dahlonega, Georgia, home of the nation's first gold rush. Like George Mackey, the building had history, good and bad.

When constructed, the new capitol symbolized the new post-civil war south, a place of hope for the future. At the same time, segregationists, including notable governors like Lester Maddox, used it and the legislature it housed as a bulwark to try to fend off cries for racial equality. Yet, today, one of the most visited and revered places on the capitol grounds was the Martin Luther King Jr. statue.

Watching a group of tourists take pictures before it, George considered his past, good and bad. Faces flooded his memory, people he'd hurt and helped. Lives saved and lives taken. Investigations worked, cases solved, some too late. Like all history, his was all jumbled together. The good and bad, the dark and light, black and white, mixed until everything appeared gray in his mind. That was his state of mind as he crossed the capitol lawn.

He found Andy and the entire OSI team in the conference room they used as a command center. The original team of four had grown to more than a dozen investigators. Bob Shaklee, the Office of Special Investigations director, and founder, smiled as George walked in, the last to arrive. He sat beside Sharon Price and Johnny Rincefield at the end of the table closest to Bob and Andy. The entire OSI team was now present except for Marco and the group working with Savannah P.D.

Andy grinned and called out, "George! Took you long enough to get here! We were getting worried about the steely-eyed deputy from Pickham County."

"Sorry." George shrugged. "Took the back roads. After screwing up the case in Savannah, I wanted to take the time to think things through."

"Bullshit," Andy said. "You didn't screw up anything. You handled that captain just fine ... typical Mackey fashion."

There was laughter around the table. Andy continued, "Anyway, Bob asked me to get you all together because he wanted to share something with you."

Andy looked at Bob, seated at the head of the table, smiling, and listening to the banter between the team members, the team he'd brought together from nothing. He leaned forward and said simply, "I wanted you all to know that I turned in my papers to the governor today."

Surprised eyes stared at Bob for a few seconds, absorbing what their leader had just said. Putting in his papers could only mean one thing, but George said, "You turned in your papers? You mean ..."

"Yep," Bob said, nodding emphatically. "Pulling the pin ... retiring."

"I'll be damned," George said, openly surprised. "I'll just be damned." He looked at the others. The surprise on their faces turned to smiles.

A flurry of "Congratulations!" came at him from all sides.

"We're happy for you, Bob, and for Celia," Sharon said. "You've both earned it."

"Well, I know she has," Bob said.

He and Celia had put in their time and held their marriage together against the odds. Statistically, only about one in four law enforcement officers are married to their original spouses at the end of their careers. Bob and Celia held it together for thirty-three years. They deserved to spend the remainder of their days together celebrating life and a successful journey through it and not worrying about whether he would come home at the end of the day.

"I can't believe it," George grinned, shaking his head in mock disbelief. "Bob Shaklee retiring. An era has ended."

The OSI team knew they would genuinely miss Bob Shaklee. To George, he was one of the truly good people he had run across in life, always there for the team, mentoring, building them up, and guiding them when necessary. That thought sent a pang of guilt through his conscience for the way he left the team in Savannah in the lurch.

"Bob, I'm truly happy for you," George said, genuinely pleased for his boss and friend. "Don't know how we're going to manage without you."

"You'll manage," Bob said and nodded at Andy. "I'm leaving you in good hands. Andy will be moving up to director, reporting to the governor."

"That's great!" George beamed at Andy. "You deserve it."

"Thanks, George," Andy said and nodded at Sharon. "There's more. Sharon will move up to Deputy Director."

"That's fantastic!" George leaned over and gave her a peck on the cheek. "Guess this means there's no excuse if I don't follow orders."

"Never has been any excuse," Sharon quipped back.

They laughed, and Bob added, "One more thing, George. It's a good thing you made it back today. You're not getting out of here without a scar. The governor is appointing you OSI Chief of Field Operations."

"Chief of ..." George shook his head. "No, that's Andy's job ... Sharon's now that she's the Deputy Director."

"Not anymore," Bob said. "Case volume is up, and Sharon will continue to head up technology. We need an experienced person to head the team in the field. Can't think of anyone better suited for that than you."

George was silent for several seconds, then said, "The governor appointed me? You sure about that?"

"Well, granted, the appointment was made before your conversation with that ..." Bob looked up as if trying to recall a word, grinned, and said, "That stupid son of a bitch in Savannah."

Laughter broke out around the table.

"But I will make sure it happens as my parting concession from the governor. He'll gripe and bluster, but you are officially the Chief of Field Ops ... effective today."

"Are you alright, George?" Sharon asked, leaning to the side to take his hand.

George frowned for a moment, thinking that his first act running field operations had been to abandon his people in Savannah. Then he shook his head to clear his thoughts and forced a smile. "Sorry. No, I'm fine, and this is great news ... about your retirement and all. I'm not so sure about the field ops thing." The smile widened. "Are we going to celebrate?"

"As a matter of fact, there's a retirement dinner tonight. Are you up for that after your drive back?"

"Always up for dinner if you're buying."

"Perfect." Bob stood. "Let's get moving."

They adjourned and regrouped at an upscale watering hole in Buckhead. It was fancier than George's usual hangouts, but Celia and Andy's wife, Deirdre, had planned everything. They sat around an oak table in cushioned chairs in a private room, sipping expensive cocktails and chatting about Bob and Celia's plans for the future.

The meal was a five-star selection of fish, beef, lamb, and assorted poultry. The restaurant's wine cellar was renowned throughout the south, and the sommelier visited the table to review the wine list. In the case of less sophisticated palates like George's, he made suggestions and helped them choose.

The room was filled with warmth and nostalgia. They had been through much together.

George met Sharon and Bob when the Georgia Bureau of Investigation assigned them to work with him to find a serial killer on a rampage in south Georgia. The following year, a series of murders across the state brought them together again. Andy Barnes from the Atlanta P.D homicide division and Johnny Rincefield, a State Patrol pilot, joined the team.

Others had come on board over the years as the investigative load increased. They were more than comrades serving in a common cause. They were friends.

The evening ended amid a flurry of hugs, handshakes, and congratulatory wishes. "I've still got some time before I'm gone," Bob assured them. "Governor made me give him thirty days' notice." His eyes narrowed. "So, make sure your asses are at work on time in the morning."

Everyone laughed and went their separate ways. When they arrived home, George and Sharon helped each other undress, a preliminary to the love-making that would follow.

Afterward, George lay on his back staring at the ceiling while Sharon snuggled close, breathing softly, her hair spread across his chest. He thought about the day and his doubts about the decision to leave Marco and the others in Savannah. Is that what Bob would have done ... Andy ... Sharon? He wasn't so sure. He was happy for Bob and Celia, for Andy and Sharon, but he wasn't so sure about himself after the way he'd handled things in Savannah.

Chief of Field Operations. The position meant nothing if he wasn't qualified, and after a day of guilt at abandoning the Savannah team, he had serious doubts about his qualifications.

10. We Have a Problem

The phone rang as Carol Digby unlocked the door to the county offices. She dropped her handbag and lunch sack on the desk and answered. "Bayne County Clerk. How may I help you?"

"Thank God you're there," Chloe Sutter said breathlessly. "I've been waiting all night to call. Didn't want to bother you at home."

"Morning, Chloe. What's the problem? Doyle not coming in again today?" She gave a disapproving shake of her head and dropped into her chair. "Those Buxton boys must have convinced him to stay and tie one on."

"He never came home," Chloe said, and her voice sounded like she might burst into tears. "No word ... nothing. I checked with Maddie Carter at the Kwik Pak, and he never showed up for work again last night."

"Never showed up for ..." Carol paused. Letting his sheriff duties go for a day was one thing, but Doyle Sutter was not one to lose a source of income ... not deliberately, at least.

"No," Chloe said. "I got back from my job and waited up ... didn't take the sleeping pill like usual ... stayed up all night, waiting for him because he never came in the night before." She sobbed, the words choked off in her throat before she asked, "Did Toby Jones ever get up to the deer camp to check like you said?"

"No," Carol said. "I'm sorry, Chloe. It was hectic around here yesterday, and by the time I remembered it was getting close to dark time ... too late to go traipsing around up there. I guess I figured Doyle had already come back down."

"He didn't," Chloe said, sobbing now. "Not a word from him."

"Alright, I'm going to send Toby Jones up to look for him right now and tell him to get his butt back home."

"Thanks, Carol. Please call me as soon as you hear. I'm worried sick."

"Promise I'll call as soon as I hear something."

Carol hung up and was just dialing Toby Jones's number when the phone rang again. It was Mimsy Buxton.

"Morning, Mimsy," Carol said and added before Mimsy could speak. "Still haven't heard anything, but I'm sending Toby Jones up to check on your men and the sheriff."

"And the sheriff?" Mimsy said. "You mean Doyle went up and is still gone?"

"Chloe said he never came home."

"Oh, my God," Mimsy said breathlessly. "What could be going on up there?"

"Nothing!" Carol said brusquely to cut her off before she followed suit with Chloe and started blubbering on the phone. "Just a bunch of grown men out in the woods, drinking beer and acting like boys. Figured they'd take a little vacation from their responsibilities, but I'll tell you one thing." Carol paused to take a breath. "There will be hell to pay when they get back. Doyle Sutter may think he's got a lock on being the sheriff after all these years, but when I get through with him, he's going to wish he'd stayed up in those hills."

"You really think they're just drinking beer up at the shack?" Mimsy asked.

Carol didn't know what to think at this point, but she said, "I'd bet on it. Now, I have to get Toby Jones to go up and drag them back down here."

"Alright, but let me know when he finds them."

"I will." Carol disconnected the call. Irritated at having her day disrupted first thing in the morning and her annoyance rising like a pot heating up to boiling, Carol stabbed the numbers on the phone with a stiff forefinger.

Toby Jones answered, "What's up, Carol?"

"I need you to head up the mountain and find Doyle and the Buxton men."

"They're not back yet?" Toby said.

"Well, why would I say I need you to go get them if they were back?" Carol snapped.

"Sorry, Carol," Toby said and pulled the phone a little farther from his ear. "Thing is, I'm in the middle of a job right now ... doing a bathroom remodel at the Seymour house."

Webley Seymour was the county commission chairman. Carol nodded, undeterred. "You tell Web, I said to get moving and go find the sheriff. His bathroom can wait."

"But, Carol, this job is gonna pay me ..."

"Toby Jones, I don't care what the job pays or what Web Seymour is going to say," Carol interrupted. "You tell him two of his voting constituents, along with the sheriff, are missing, and I'm sending you up there to find them. You're a deputy sheriff in Bayne County, and if you want to stay one, you'll do what I say. Get up there, find them, and if you have to, you drag them back down. You can tell Web I said so, so get to it."

"Yessum," Toby replied like a scolded child. "I'll head up right away."

Unsurprisingly, the chairman of the county commission did not argue when Toby told him that Carol Digby wanted him to leave and check on the sheriff. Politicians like Web Seymour came and went, filling seats on the county commission for a couple of terms to bolster their egos and standing in the county ... and so their families would have something interesting to add to their obituaries one day. For all intents and purposes, since being appointed twenty-two years earlier, Carol Digby had been the unofficial Bayne County chief executive.

Toby left his tools at Web Seymour's house, promised to be back in a couple of hours, and climbed in his pickup. He was on official county business, but the old police cruiser the county provided him would be useless for this assignment. Purchased at auction from one of the metro Atlanta police departments, the Ford Crown Victoria was fine for chasing down speeders on the state highway but was too low to the ground and lacked four-wheel-drive. It could never handle the mountain back roads.

Toby headed out of Dykes, turned off onto the dirt road that wound its way up into the hill country, and found Doyle Sutter's pickup parked behind the Buxton's truck. He set the parking brake in his own vehicle and climbed out. As he turned and scanned the hills for movement, he listened for sounds. There were none. No voices or drunken laughter to validate Carol's suspicion that they were binge drinking. None of the usual noises men make when away from civilization. Nothing.

Toby called out, "Doyle Sutter! Ox Buxton! Harley! You boys up here? Shout out and let me know."

There was no response, not even an echo from the hills heavily blanketed in trees and undergrowth. "Shit," he muttered and headed up the hillside path toward the Buxton's shack. He pushed through the last bit of brush at the edge of the clearing and called out, "Hello, the shack! It's Toby Jones."

There was no answering shout.

"Dammit," he muttered, then shouted, "I'm coming in! If you boys are there, don't be shooting in this direction."

He made his way across the clearing and peered inside the open door. Something rustled in a corner, and he jumped aside as a raccoon scurried out, chittering at him for disturbing its exploration of the shack.

Toby stepped inside to find ... nothing. There was no sign that anyone had been in the shack recently. No food leftovers and no beer cans. No rumpled sleeping bags from the night before. None of the usual clutter you'd expect from a couple of men away from their wife and mother.

He walked around the interior, turned back to the door, and froze in his tracks, his eyes fixed on the two rifles leaning against the wall and a gun belt with a holstered pistol on the floor. Toby recognized it as belonging to Doyle Sutter. Up to now, he had been annoyed by Carol's orders to go find the sheriff, but not overly concerned. Now, an eerie sense of dread crept up his spine.

His eyes darted around the shack's interior, and he backed hurriedly outside. Eyes scanning the trees and hills, he explored the clearing without finding any sign that the men had been there. A barely discernible trail headed into the brush on the far side. Probably made by deer or other game passing through when the hunters weren't around. He walked towards it and considered following it to see what he could find, then decided against it. If Sutter and the Buxtons had gone up the deer trail and not come back, he was not about to follow suit without some backup.

He turned back to the path that led up from the road, checking over his shoulder every few seconds. When he descended to the dirt road, he examined Sutter's and the Buxton's vehicles and found them locked and undisturbed. He knew they had made it to the shack because their firearms were still there. After that, he had no clue, but if Doyle Sutter had gone missing looking for the Buxton, he had no desire to be next.

He climbed back into his pickup and drove away as rapidly as he dared on the dirt roads. Every minute or so, he checked his cell phone for service, but it wasn't until he came out into the narrow valley leading into Dykes that he could make a call. One eye on the road, he thumbed in the county clerk's number.

Carol Digby answered immediately. "What'd you find, Toby?"

"Nothing," Toby said, breathless, as if he'd been running.

"What do you mean, nothing?"

"I mean nothing ... they're gone ... no one around ... no sign of anybody, except their guns left behind."

"You say their guns ..." Carol started, but Toby cut her off.

"Get hold of Brian Mecham and Dave Pascal. Have them meet me at your office, and let Web Seymour know we have a problem."

11. Talk About It

"Are we going to talk about it?" Sharon looked at him over the top of her first cup of coffee.

"About what?" George said, avoiding her gaze. He knew what she wanted to talk about, but he wasn't sure he could. How could he explain something that he didn't even understand himself completely?

The lovemaking the night before had been warm and comfortable, if not filled with their usual passion. When it was finished, he lay quietly staring at the ceiling, lost in his thoughts, as if their passion had only been a brief distraction from a problem churning around in his mind, but he couldn't put his finger on the problem.

Sharon was concerned. He could see it in her eyes, feel it in her uncertain touches as they made love, knowing something troubled him but giving him the space to sort it out before talking about it. Now, in the morning light, there was no way she was going to put off discussing it any longer.

"Cut the bullshit, Mackey," Sharon said with her usual blunt but smiling charm. "You've been lost in a haze somewhere since you got back from Savannah. Start explaining."

"I guess I have been ..." George paused. "Preoccupied. That's what I've been, I suppose."

"You suppose?" Sharon frowned. "After all this time together ... the things we've been through, things we've seen, what we've been to each other ... for each other ... I know when something is eating away at you." She thumped the coffee cup down on the table so that he looked up. "Start talking, Mackey."

"Not sure I can explain. Why don't you start?"

"Me?" Sharon shook her head. "You're the one in a funk. I just want to understand ... and help if I can."

"It's that obvious?"

"Obvious? Hell, yes, it's obvious, and not just to me ... to all of us ... me, Andy, Bob, the rest of the team ... the way you pretended to be there last night at Bob's retirement dinner, but your mind was somewhere else." She shook her head. "You want me to start, okay. Here goes. What's on your mind right now?"

"On my mind?" George frowned.

"Right now. Don't think about it. Just say the first word that comes into your mind, and we'll start there."

He stared into the space above her head for a few seconds, then took a deep breath and said, "Tired. I guess that's on my mind."

"Good." Sharon nodded. "Now, tell me what you mean. You need more sleep ... tired of the job ... me?"

"Not you." George smiled. "Never you." He shrugged. "And I get enough sleep. I guess if you want me to boil it down to a word ... the job."

"So, what does that mean?" Sharon asked, her voice quiet. "You want to resign? Do something else?"

"No." George shook his head. "The job ... it's what I do ... who I am. I don't know what else I would do."

"Then what?"

He sat back, thought for a moment, thinking, while she waited, letting him sort out his thoughts. Finally. He looked up and said, "Do you ever wonder if any of it makes a difference?"

"The job?" Sharon shook her head. "No. Never. It makes a difference. I've never doubted it."

"What if *I* do?" George asked. "What does that say about me ... my ability to do the job?"

"That you're human." Sharon reached out and took his hand between hers. "We all have our moments of weakness, George."

"Except you. You just said it. You've never doubted what we do ... that it makes a difference."

"I have never doubted the job," she said softly. "But I have doubted *myself* plenty of times. We all have times like that." She smiled. "Even the great George Mackey is allowed to have his doubtful moments."

"Guess I never felt this way before," he said, shrugging. "Like I've lost it ... the fire. I'm just going through the motions these days, not really engaged, and you know this is not the kind of job where you can just put in your time. Do that, and eventually, someone will get hurt ... and it will be because of me." He shook his head. "I can't let that happen."

"You would never let that happen, George," she said, her tone softer, then more bluntly in her Sharon-way, she added, "So, knock it off. You're overthinking this."

"I'm not so sure. I told Marco I was leaving for the good of the investigation, but it wasn't true. I sat there with that mayor and her flunky, listening to their bullshit, and it just hit me. It all seemed pointless ... tedious ... like nothing will ever change or make a difference in the big scheme of things." He shrugged. "So, I just gave up, turned it over to Marco ... put him in their crosshairs ... abandoned him and the others."

"No," Sharon interrupted. "You didn't abandon them. You made your point to the mayor, put her on notice, and showed her by example that there are bigger issues here than egos and who gets to take credit for the investigation."

Sharon shrugged and added, "Maybe she'll get it, but you set the example, did what was right for the case, and Marco and the others saw it. The way I see it, that was a training moment ... one they will remember."

"A training moment? Not so sure about that." George raised his eyebrows and gave her a doubtful look. "But you were right. I needed to talk things through. Thank you for that."

"No thanks necessary, but can I make one more suggestion?"

"Would it stop you if I said no?" George asked.

"Nope," Sharon said. "We can talk more later, but for now, sit on our conversation for a while. Don't bring it up with Bob or Andy. Let's let Bob retire without worrying about your crisis of doubt. He's been there for us through the years. Let's not send him off with a last worry about what he is leaving behind. And Andy has enough on his plate with his transition to director and dealing with the governor."

"You're right," George said, feeling guilty that she had to remind him. He'd been too caught up in his doubts. It was time to shake it off. "This is just between us."

"Good." Sharon let go of his hand, stood, and pulled her robe around her. "Now, let's get our asses to work. Haven't you heard? There's crime and mayhem in the streets."

12. We Need More People

It wasn't much of a search party, but it was the best Deputy Toby Jones could put together on short notice. Brian Mecham, the third shift deputy, was waiting at Carol Digby's office when he came down from the hills. Dave Pascal worked the swing shift, filling in when Sheriff Sutter and the others were off. He arrived fifteen minutes after Jones' return, wearing loafers, slacks, and a sweater.

Jones eyed him doubtfully. "We're not going to church, Sam."

"You said come quick, so I came quick from the car lot. Figured you wouldn't want me to take the time to run by the house and change."

Jones nodded at his feet. "Those shoes aren't going to cut it where we're going."

"Don't worry about me. Got my hunting boots in the truck. What's going on? Carol said the sheriff wandered off ... missing or something."

"Not wandered," Jones said and nodded. "But missing, yeah. He went to check on the Buxton men at their shack up on the mountain. Hasn't been seen now in two days. I couldn't find any sign of them at the shack, so we need to go back and do some searching."

"No sign?" Pascal gave a scornful sake of his head. "Damn big area up in there. You expect the three of us to cover it?"

"Figure three was better than just me alone," Jones snapped back. "And as the senior deputy, I expect you to lend a hand to do what we can to find the sheriff."

"Fine. You're the boss, being the *senior deputy* and all," Pascal said, his mocking tone not lost on the others. "What's the plan?"

"We head back up to the shack, and if they still aren't around, we try to find them," Jones said.

"And if they are there?" Pascal asked and shook his head. "Wasted time and effort."

"I doubt they will be. I found the Buxtons' rifles leaning against the wall inside and the sheriff's gun belt on the floor next to them."

"His gun belt." Dave began and smirked. "You coulda said that up front and saved all the discussion."

"Saying it now," Toby snapped back.

"Let's get moving." Brian Mecham listened to the exchange between the other deputies with his arms folded across his chest as he sat on the edge of Carol Digby's desk. Now he shook his head and headed for the door. "We're wasting daylight."

Jones made his way up to the deer camp for the second time that day. Mecham and Pascal followed in their personal pickups. It was afternoon by the time they left the trucks on the road behind Sutter's and made their way up the path to the shack.

Jones called out from the edge of the clearing, "In the shack! Doyle, Ox, Harley! Anyone there?"

Jones expected no answer, and there was none. He led the way across the clearing and stepped aside for Mecham and Pascal to enter. "See for yourselves and then tell me what you think."

They weren't inside long. When they emerged, squinting into the afternoon sun, Mecham nodded. "Doesn't look good, Toby."

"Yeah. No way Doyle would leave his gun belt on the floor," Pascal said. He looked around the clearing. "What next?"

"This way," Jones headed off toward the brush on the far side of the clearing. "There's a game trail there."

"You didn't check it?" Pascal said with disdain.

"No, I didn't." Jones turned to stare at him, his eyes narrowed and hard, his face signaling that he had had enough of Pascal's attitude. "We don't know why, what, or who is behind these men disappearing. What good would it have been for another to go missing with no sign?"

"Seems like a good *senior deputy* might have done a little investigating on his own?" Pascal quipped with his usual smirk.

"Shut up, Sam," Mecham snapped and looked at Jones. "You did good, Toby. Right thing is to get some backup. We don't need any more missing people up here, and the more eyes, the better." He motioned to the game trail. "Let's check it out ... together, where we can watch each other's backs."

Jones nodded and led the way through the brush. Mecham followed, and Pascal brought up the rear, silent now that Mecham had taken sides with Jones.

The three men followed the trail, zigzagging around the mountain and up the slope. In places, it was barely discernible, and they had to scout around to pick it up again. Everywhere, they came across signs of wildlife using the trail. In places, it was covered with deer droppings. In others, they stepped over bobcat and coyote scat, signs that the predators in the area hunted the young deer. What they did not find was any sign of the three missing men.

The sun sank behind the highest ridge tops, and Jones held up a hand. Even with the flashlights they carried, there was a severe risk of turning an ankle or breaking a leg trying to navigate the uneven trail in the dark. "Best turn back now. Night will be coming on soon."

For once, Pascal gave him no argument. They backtracked along the trail, through the clearing by the shack, and then down the path to their vehicles. By the time they were turned around and headed back to Dykes, they needed their headlights, the cones of light bouncing off the pine trees and boulders lining the dirt road.

They found County Chairman Web Seymour waiting with Carol Digby in the county office. He sprawled back in Carol's chair while she sat in one of the thinly padded metal chairs reserved for visitors. When Jones and the others came through the door, he leaned forward, grinned, and shouted out in his best good ole boy drawl, "You find them boys' drinkin' hole up there on that mountain?"

"We need more people," Jones said without preliminaries, and then explained everything they'd seen and done to find the missing men.

"You need more people? Well, by God, I'll get you more people," Seymour said. Pulling out his cell phone, he punched in a number, watching the others to make sure they were paying attention. A few seconds later, Seymour said, "This is Web Seymour, Bayne County Commission Chairman. I want to speak with the governor."

13. That Went Well

The phone on the desk chirped annoyingly. He looked at the display. It was the call he'd been expecting all morning.

Bob Shaklee answered, and before he could speak, Governor Fullman barked, "You and Barnes drag his ass over here."

There was no need to ask whose ass the governor wanted dragged. "Be right there."

The line was already dead. To be expected, he thought.

A minute later, he stood in the doorway to Andy Barnes' office, leaning casually against the metal jamb like a man talking about the weather and killing time. "We've been summoned."

"Later than I thought it would be." Andy looked up from Marco's latest report on the Mendoza investigation and interaction with the Savannah mayor.

"Yep." Bob nodded. "That's probably not a good thing. It's better to let him blow off his steam early than let it build up all morning." He shrugged. "Anyway, you're taking over, so you might as well get off to a good start dealing with the latest tempest in a teapot."

"This shouldn't be a damned tempest." Andy stood. "We work for him. He should try to have our backs now and then."

"When it's convenient, yes, but not when politics are involved." Bob shrugged. "Get used to it. Few more weeks, and it'll just be you while I sun myself on some beach."

"Uh-hmm, any idea which beach?" Andy grabbed his suit coat from the hook on the back of his office door. "I might want to join you."

"Still to be decided." Bob grinned. "Celia's working on it."

They stopped by the conference room on the way out. George sat at one of the laptops arranged on the desk for use by the investigators when not in the field.

"It's time," Bob said from the doorway.

George looked up and then at the time on his phone beside the laptop. "He's late. Thought we'd have this over by now."

"Nope." Bob grinned. "He probably had staff working all night, preparing bullet points for the ass chewing he's planning."

They laughed and headed for the elevator, down to ground level, and across the capitol lawns. The banter ended as other workers, busily going about their day, passed and greeted them.

The gold dome above glittered in the morning sun, a cheerful setting for what would not be a pleasant meeting. They showed their badges and IDs, passed through the security checkpoint, and made their way to the suite of executive offices.

The governor's assistant, Toni Garber, greeted them as they entered the reception area. "Thanks for coming, Bob." She nodded at his deputy, soon-to-be-director. "You too, Andy."

She turned to George. "Agent Mackey, I assume you know why the governor wants to see you."

"You assume correctly." George gave an indifferent shrug.

"Probably not the demeanor to have when you go in," she warned. "He is not in a good mood, and it might be best not to antagonize him."

"I figure he's already antagonized. My demeanor isn't going to change that." George spoke in a weary tone, as if he might yawn in her face and couldn't care less about the governor's mood. "Let's just get it done."

"Fine." Garber turned and ushered them into the governor's office.

Fullman sat behind his desk, rifling through a file. He looked up, tossed it on the desk, and scowled. "Good. You're here."

Bob, Andy, and George lined up in front of the desk. As the group's leader, Bob spoke. "What can we do for you, Governor?"

"Don't fucking play games with me!" Fullman glared at them, his eyes moving from face to face until they rested on George. "You know goddam well why you're here!"

"I do." George nodded.

"Gross insubordination to the mayor of one of the state's largest cities and voter demographics. I have it from several sources that you fucking called her aide a stupid son of a bitch!" Fullman paused to take a breath. "Do you deny it?"

"No." George shook his head. "That's what I did."

"I should fire you on the spot." Fullman lifted a paper, waving it like a flag over the desk. "Unfortunately, I can't. Do you know what this is?"

Fullman didn't wait for a response. "It's a fucking press release! That's what!" He tossed it on the desk. "Staff released it to the media yesterday. It'll hit the news today. Know what it says?"

George and the others remained silent. There was no reason to play guessing games with Fullman. Let him keep talking without interruption, like taking the cover off a boiling pot until it simmers down. Except Fullman was not simmering down.

"Tell them," Fullman barked at Garber, standing to his right.

"Yes, sir. "Garber picked up the press release and scanned it as she spoke. "The governor announces the organizational change to the OSI after Bob's retirement. Barnes' promotion to Director, Sharon Price to Deputy Director, and you ..." She looked at George. "To Chief of Field Operations, along with glowing accounts of your investigative successes."

"That's right," Fullman interrupted. "It paints you as a goddammed hero, and the press had it before you pulled your bullshit with Mayor Crest. I can't rescind it."

"You could." George shrugged. "Won't hear any complaints from me."

Andy and Bob exchanged a glance at that remark, but said nothing.

"No! I can't!" Fullman roared. "I as much as said you walk on investigative water in that press release." He shook his head. "It's already in the news cycle, so now I can't take it back ... without looking like a fool for appointing you in the first place. And if I pulled it, you know damned well the media would have a field day at my expense."

Politics as usual. The law-and-order governor could not reverse himself on the promotion without raising questions about his judgment in the first place.

Andy listened, biting his tongue, thinking he should say something to the sanctimonious prick, berating a man who had put his life on the line more than once. Doing so would only make it worse for all of them in the future, so he remained silent.

Bob, on the other hand, stood quietly, waiting. When it seemed Fullman's rage had subsided a bit, he said, "Agent Mackey will still be an excellent Chief of Field Operations. The issues with Mayor Crest will blow over in time and ..."

"Damn it!" Fullman slammed his hand down on his desk, his rage rising again to a crescendo. "I don't want the issues gone in time. I want them gone now!" He stared at George. "But since I can't fire your ass now, I want you out of my sight ... far away."

George waited, prepared to take whatever was coming without complaint. He had no intention of making things difficult for Bob and Andy by arguing with the governor.

"Something came up this morning, far away from here, up in Bayne County."

"A case?" Bob asked.

"No, a fucking cookie sale!" Fullman sneered. "Yes, a case, and I want him to take the lead." He jerked his head in George's direction. "There's a missing sheriff up there, and I want Mackey up there, looking for him and out of my sight."

"A missing ..." Bob's brow furrowed.

"Sheriff," Fullman finished for him. "Disappeared."

"Not sure I follow," Bob said. "You mean a missing person, and it's the sheriff?"

"I mean, Doyle Sutter, sheriff up in Bayne County, went up on a mountain to check on a couple of good ole boys, and he never came down."

"Signs of foul play?" Bob asked.

"Now, how the hell should I know?" Fullman snapped. "That's your department." He looked at George. "His department."

"Of course, we understand that." Bob took the governor's attitude without flinching. "I mean, has there been a search for him?"

"Local deputies looked for him and the two boys who didn't come back from their hunt camp. No sign of any of them, but the consensus is they probably went off on a drunk somewhere."

"Alright," Bob nodded, taking the lead to avoid throwing gas on the fire by having George interact directly with Fullman. "What is it you want from the OSI?"

"What do you think I want?" Fullman frowned, annoyed. "Find the fucking sheriff. Bring him home to his loving wife."

"I see," Bob nodded as if he was considering the governor's instructions before he said, "With all due respect, this isn't really an OSI case."

"Any case I assign you is an OSI case!" Fullman rumbled.

"Of course, but what you're asking here is a matter for the GBI. They have more resources and can coordinate the search for the sheriff and the missing persons," Bob said. "And as you previously instructed, we are knee-deep in the Savannah investigation. George is here, but we still have a team there, and the Chief of Field Operations should supervise their activities from here."

"I know damn well what I *previously instructed*!" Fullman's rumble increased in volume again. He turned his eyes to Andy. "I'm changing my instructions. Barnes can oversee the Savannah investigation."

"Not sure I understand why a missing person, sheriff or not, is a case for the OSI," Bob said, although he understood very well and was not about to let Fullman get away without saying it out loud. Andy needed to see what he would deal with once Bob retired.

"It's a case for you because I say it is!" Fullman snapped. "But fine. I'll play your game. The Bayne County commission chairman called me and asked to have the OSI look into things. Name's Web Seymour, old family, original settlers in the area. He has a lot of clout with people, the press, local media outlets ... not just in Bayne County, but across north Georgia."

"You mean this is about politics," Bob said.

"Yes, dammit! Politics!" Fullman's face reddened. "You want me to say it? Fine, I'll say it. I owe Web Seymour just like I owe Mayor Crest in Savannah. That's how the game is played, and you've been around long enough to know it, Shaklee. So, I'm sending the OSI's *Chief of Field Operations* to handle things personally."

"There couldn't be that many voters up in Bayne County." After the verbal lashing Fullman gave George, Bob would not let it go so easily. He smiled before adding, "Seems like a misallocation of resources to send our best investigator to ..."

"Enough!" Fullman slammed his hand down on the desk. "I don't give a shit about resources or how many voters there are in Bayne County. I owe Seymour ... maybe not as much as Mayor Crest, but your job is to make him think we're doing everything possible to find his missing sheriff."

"Just wanted to hear you say it, Governor," Bob said quietly, his tone controlled and non-accusing.

"Don't take that holier-than-thou attitude with me, Shaklee." Fullman's eyebrows lowered, angry. "You might keep in mind that politics is why I'm here ... the reason you and the OSI exist. Because of politics, my predecessor brought you in to form the Office of Special Investigations. I'm sending Mackey, end of story."

Fullman turned his scowl in George's direction. "Word of warning. Take your time about things up there. Stay gone ... out of my sight. I can't fire you ... yet ... but I can send you where I don't have to see your face."

George nodded and spoke before Bob could drag things on longer. "Understood, Governor."

"Fine," Bob interjected calmly, nodding pleasantly as if they were discussing the weather. "Now that you've clarified things, we'll get on it. Who's our contact in Bayne County?"

"I have the information here," Toni Garber said, handing over a file folder and hiding the grin that threatened to spread across her face. Bob Shaklee was unique—a government employee who refused to be intimidated by her boss, in theory, the most powerful person in Georgia—and Garber loved it.

"Thanks." Bob took the folder without opening it and handed it to George.

"You'll find the report from the deputy who made the initial investigation," Garber said, "Along with telephone numbers for him, the county clerk, and Commission Chairman Seymour."

"Thanks, Toni." Bob looked at Fullman. "Anything else, Governor?"

"No." Fullman scowled. "You can leave, but I want a daily report from you, not Mackey."

"I'll make sure you get a daily report." Bob turned and walked from the office before Fullman could say anything else.

Andy and George followed without speaking. They were outside, crossing Martin Luther King, Jr. Drive, headed back to the state office building, when he broke into a grin. "That went well, don't you think?"

They were still laughing as they walked through the lobby of the State Office Building.

14. I Won't Hurt You

It was a nondescript truck, just a service vehicle like a thousand others roaming the streets on any given day. An old-style shell covered the truck's bed and tool and equipment compartments lined both sides. No company name or phone number was on the door panels to drum up business, but the words—*Fast and Friendly Service / We keep you plugged in and powered up*—were stenciled on the sides. Anyone who noticed would assume the man in the truck was an electrician, but no one noticed.

William Payne steered it through the streets of Cumming, Ga, winding his way out to one of the housing developments bordering Lake Lanier. They had been springing up along the lake's shores since 1956 when the Army Corps of Engineers built a dam and reservoir along the Chattahoochee River basin north of Atlanta.

Some of the higher-end neighborhoods he passed were gated, with security officers, keypads, and cameras watching who came and went. The one he drove into was one of the ungated developments. The houses there were older, dating from the seventies, but still very nice, with tree-lined streets and backyards that were farther from the shore but still overlooked the lake.

Payne stopped along the curb at the end of a cul-de-sac and stepped out, pulling a ball cap down low over his head and the shaggy wig he wore over his close-cropped hair. The smell of freshly cut grass drifted through the air, and Payne gave a brief wave to an old man on a riding mower two houses away. It was getting late in the season, and the lawn didn't need mowing, but the old man rode around, swallowed up in an oversized sweater and floppy trail hat, hunched over the mower's steering wheel with a determined look. He barely glanced at the man in khaki-tan work clothes who got out of the truck at the end of the cul-de-sac and never noticed him give a friendly wave.

Payne turned and rummaged around in one of the truck-bed compartments for a minute, took out a tool belt, and hung it around his waist. He turned as the old man on the mower disappeared around the side of his house, the engine's humming fading to a distant buzz. Good, he thought, his eyes scanning the nearby homes for anyone else outside.

He knelt by the sealed transformer between the two nearest yards, took a screwdriver from his tool belt, and made movements that might make anyone who saw him believe he was working on the box. No one came out to question what he was doing. No one peeked out a window or came outside to investigate. Why should they? There were always service trucks in the neighborhood.

Satisfied that no one had noted his presence, he returned to the truck, took a football-sized box and a clipboard from a compartment, and then walked to the nearest house's front door. A short path of stone pavers wound through a small flower garden to the front porch. He was careful to stay on the path and rang the doorbell.

A small dog inside let out a sharp bark, its nails clicking as it scurried across a tiled floor loud enough that Payne could hear it outside. The dog continued barking while heavier footsteps shuffled toward the door.

Inside, Doris Mills came to the door. She was a widow, alone since the death of her husband Morris five years earlier. The house on the lake—near the lake, actually, as they were not wealthy—had been their dream home.

"Lucy, hush." Doris Mills used a slippered foot to push the dog, a pug-chihuahua mix, to the side as she peeked through the sidelight.

A young man in neat work clothes nodded and smiled, and Doris cracked the door open and said, "Can I help you?"

"Yes, ma'am." Payne looked at the clipboard for a moment, then said. "Mrs. Mills, is that right?"

"Yes, I'm Doris Mills." She opened the door a hair wider. After all, the young man knew her name.

"Mrs. Mills, I'm Rick Sager, an electrician, doing some contract work for the power company. They sent me out to replace your power meter." Payne motioned with his head toward the street. "All of them actually with these new meters."

"New meters? Why would they do that?" Doris asked, then looked down at Lucy, sniffing and growling at Payne's shoes. "Lucy, leave the man alone and get inside."

Lucy ignored her and let out a sharp bark to let her and the man know she was running things at the moment. Doris smiled and shrugged, "Sorry ..."

She leaned forward to see the name patch on Payne's shirt. "Sorry, Rick. She doesn't mind so well."

"No problem, Mrs. Mills. I've got a couple at home ... just mutts, but they let me know who's boss."

Doris laughed. "They will do that, but what would we do without them?"

"Be a lot lonelier," Payne said with a smile and nod.

"That's for sure," Doris said. "Now, you were saying something about my power meter?"

"Yes, ma'am. They've got me out here replacing them with these new smart meters."

"Smart meter." Doris shook her head. "Never heard of anything like that."

"They've been around for a few years, but we're just getting out here to your neighborhood." Payne pulled the top open on the box in his arms. "Want to see it?"

Doris peeked over the cardboard edge and shook her head. "Looks like a regular old meter to me. What makes it smart?"

"The power company can read it remotely from their office. They won't have to send a meter reader around anymore." He shrugged. "Reduces costs, they say."

"Reduces cost ...humph." Doris gave a smirk. "Sounds to me like nobody wants to work anymore."

"Well, it keeps me employed." Payne grinned. "I just need to get to your power meter to change it out."

"On the side of the house, behind the fence. Gate's unlocked."

"Thank you, ma'am."

"Am I going to lose power now?" Doris asked. "I'm in the middle of my show ... *Days of Our Lives*. Haven't missed an episode in years."

"No, ma'am. I can get it done without cutting power." He smiled. "Go back to your show. I'll come back and let you know when I'm finished so you can sign off that everything's working when I leave."

"That's fine, then." Doris turned to close the door. "Come on, Lucy." The dog gave a final yap as the door closed.

"Nice young man," Doris muttered, shuffling back to the sofa and her television. "At least he's out working, not like a lot of young people, sitting around letting their parents take care of them." She eased herself down onto the sofa and picked up the remote. "He should get a haircut, though."

Payne walked around to the side of the house, opened the gate, and when he was out of sight, made a quick examination of the backyard. Like the front, it was nicely, if simply, landscaped with the typical signs of care by a gardener with time on her hands. Planter boxes bordered the walkways, and small, well-tended garden beds surrounded the base of every tree. There was not a weed or blade of stray grass anywhere.

At the bottom of the backyard, a long slope led down to a wooded ravine. He could just make out Lake Lanier lapping at the shoreline a little way along the ravine. The Mills home was modest compared to many of the more lavish ones with full lake frontage. He stood for a moment looking down the slope, looking for movement, some sign of anyone aware of his presence. There was none. He'd picked the right day.

He made his way through the yard, careful not to step into the soft ground around the garden beds, mostly staying on the paver walks. After stopping by the side of the house to retrieve his props—the new meter and clipboard—he walked out to the truck.

Kneeling by the curbside transformer box, he scanned the street as if he were finishing up the job. It was quiet. It had been quiet on every test run he'd made for the last month, using different vehicles, alert to activity in the street and surrounding yards. This was an older neighborhood with tree-filled yards that nearly hid most houses from the street. The residents, like Doris Mills, were predominantly elderly. If they happened to wander outside, it would be to enjoy their landscaped and wooded lake views, not a service truck on the road. Still, he was careful and meticulous in his planning and precautions.

Cranking up the truck, he backed into the driveway all the way to the house until the bumper almost touched the garage door. Then he took a toolbox from the truck, settled the hat farther down on his head, and returned to the front door.

When he rang the bell, Lucy barked again and ran across the tiles. A few seconds later, Doris peeked out the sidelight again and then opened the door, wide this time.

"Done so soon?" Doris said. "You certainly work fast."

She started to smile at the young man with the name patch that read Rick Sager, but he stepped in quickly, forcing her back from the door, pushing it shut as he did. It happened so quickly, Doris nearly fell over and stumbled back against the wall.

"What are you doing?" she said, too shaken to scream for help, not that anyone would have heard it if she had.

"No sound," Payne said, opening the toolbox and taking out the roll of duct tape like the ones he'd seen used in almost every abduction he had ever witnessed in a movie.

"No, please, no …" She shook her head, pleading.

He ignored her pleas and, in a few seconds, wrapped three layers of tape around her mouth and head, careful not to obstruct her nose and breathing. Three more wraps of tape went around her wrists and then three around her ankles as Doris sobbed and shook her head. Then he lifted her over his shoulder like a flour sack and made his way through the house, Lucy yapping at his heels the entire time.

There had been no way to explore the house's interior during his surveillance, but it didn't take long to find the laundry room and interior entrance to the garage. He went into the garage and shut the door quickly, leaving Lucy snarling, scratching, and barking, trying to follow.

Placing Doris on the concrete floor, he pressed the garage door opener button and went to the truck backed up outside. He opened the hatch to the shell covering the bed and then went back for Doris. Lifting her once more over his shoulder, he carried her to the truck's bed and laid her inside. She had no time to struggle before he slammed the hatch cover shut.

Pressing the exterior keypad button, he closed the garage door, walked calmly to the front of the truck, and climbed into the driver's seat. He drove away slowly, minding the speed limit through the nearly empty streets, and made his way back to U.S. Highway 19, where he turned north. Fifteen minutes from Dahlonega, he turned onto a county road, heading northeast, always winding deeper into the southern end of the Appalachian Mountains.

The last leg of the trip took him three miles over a barely discernible dirt trail that ended abruptly beside a shack in a clump of pines. It was a forgotten place, far from the city's sprawl and development. Someone lived there once, but tax assessor records showed that the county had taken the property for non-payment of taxes nearly fifty years earlier.

Payne never bothered to buy it. There was no need, and there would be no record of his name on any bill of sale or title transfer. The shack was so distant from any development that the chance of someone stumbling upon it was minuscule. They would have to be as determined as he had been to find a place as remote as this one.

Payne went to the rear, opened the hatch, and pulled Doris out by the feet. Slinging her over his shoulder again, he walked to the shack, pushed the plank door open with a foot, and set her gently on the floor against the back wall.

He looked around the single room. Everything was as he left it. Everything was ready.

After finding the old shack and verifying that no one owned it, he had spent a month preparing it for today. Driving up whenever he had free time, he brought lumber to reinforce the walls. Then he brought sacks of concrete and five-gallon water cans to set posts through the rotted planks, anchoring them with concrete three feet deep into the ground below. That was the most challenging part of the job.

The last task, setting the heavy chains and eyebolts in the posts, was comparatively easy. When he finished with that, he'd spent two days and nights in the shack just to make sure no one came around. No one did, and he was satisfied.

He took out the handcuffs he'd left in the shack and cuffed Doris' wrists behind her back, looping the cuff links over the heavy chain between the posts. Taking out his knife, he thumbed open the blade, and Doris' eyes widened in terror.

He ignored her and cut the duct tape from her ankles and around her mouth. As the tape came off, she gasped and sobbed. He waited, standing over her as he closed the knife and dropped it back in his pocket.

When she caught her breath between sobs, Doris managed to ask, "W-why ... w-who are you?"

Payne reached up and pulled off the ball cap and wig. Their eyes met, and Doris began shaking her head frantically. A long, low, gasping wail echoed off the shack walls.

"No ... no, you don't understand ... I didn't do ... it was never ..." She rocked her head violently, as if by shaking it hard enough, she might transport herself back to Lucy and her house by the lake. Her aging body and bones quivered with fear. "Please ... please don't hurt me."

He looked at her with eyes that seemed more sad than angry and said, "I won't hurt you."

15. A Ride in the Mountains

"If you want to talk about it, we can." Bob Shaklee lounged in the passenger seat looking at cows on a hillside, an OSI cap pulled low on his forehead. It was the day after the governor assigned George the missing sheriff case.

"I knew it." George sighed and smiled. "You've been talking to Sharon. That's why you said you wanted to tag along on my exile to the mountains."

"I wanted to tag along to get some time in the field before I pull the pin." Bob shrugged. "And yes, Sharon and I spoke because I could see something was worrying her and asked her. We talked. She explained, and then asked me not to trouble you, that you needed to work things out for yourself." Bob turned toward George. "So here I am, letting you work things out for yourself and ready to do some real investigating for a change." He grinned. "Even if it's only a missing person case. Oh, and before you get annoyed with Sharon for speaking with me, I already knew something was eating away at you."

"You did?"

"George, it's written all over you. I may not have done any real investigating in a while, but I can still read people."

"And what is it you think you're reading here?"

"In you? Only that something's weighing on your mind." Bob shrugged. "But I'm not troubling you about it, just throwing it out there because you asked." He shrugged" And if you want to talk about it, I'm happy to listen."

George was silent for ten miles. Bob looked at the cows on the hillsides.

There was no reason to be annoyed with Bob for asking about the problem. It was what he did. He took care of the team, a combination father figure and friend. If somebody had a problem, Bob was the one they went to and talked it through.

He might disagree, but he had the unique ability to point out issues without making the other party defensive or berating them for a stupid idea, and he had heard a lot of stupid ideas over the years. George knew he had gone to Bob with his share of stupid ideas or problems over the years.

Another ten miles passed, and he spoke. "Seems like everybody wants me to talk, so I might as well.

81

"If you want," Bob said, still looking out the window, a listening ear and nothing more like a father confessor.

"Okay, here goes. Ever wonder what it all means?"

Bob listened without speaking or looking in his direction.

"The cases, the people—good and bad—the ones who get hurt and the ones who hurt them. It's a never-ending cycle, and in the end, nothing changes. Lock one asshole up, and another comes along to take his place. There's no final victory ... no good over evil, no happy ending. Life isn't a comic book with superheroes."

George looked at Bob, who remained silent. "Not going to say anything?"

"You want me to?" Bob turned his head away from the window.

"I'm talking. I guess you should throw in your two cents' worth."

"Okay, you're right, George. It's a never-ending cycle. There will always be assholes to lock up because they hurt others. What's it mean?" Bob shrugged. "Only this. The assholes you put away aren't there to hurt anyone else, at least not for a while ... for as long as they stay put away."

"So, it's about locking up a never-ending stream of assholes?" George shook his head and gave a wry smile. "Reminds me of that scene from the old Lucy show where she and Ethel are trying to wrap up little chocolate balls that are coming too fast on the conveyor belt and can't keep up, so they shove them down their clothes or in their mouths, but that's not what the candy factory was paying them to do."

Bob laughed. "Never heard it put like that, but I suppose the analogy has some validity. There will always be people coming down the conveyor belt who want to hurt others, take advantage of them, take everything they have. You do what you do to stop them and take them away so they can't hurt anyone. That doesn't mean there won't be more coming down the belt."

He paused and waited for George to glance in his direction. "But there are others ... the ones who won't be hurt because you did your job." Bob shrugged. "That's what it means, I suppose ... what it's all about. Now, ask yourself a question."

"What's that?" George said.

"Is stopping those others from being hurt enough for you to keep doing your job? If it is, then you keep plugging away. If not, I guess you have to make a career decision."

"That's your advice? Keep plugging away or give it up and do something else?"

"Not advice." Bob shook his head. "Just laying it out. That's the situation ... the job. Not everyone can do it, but someone has to, or the assholes, the hurters, win and take over the world."

They drove in silence for a while. Bob resumed looking out the window, letting George sort through things on his own.

"Thanks, Bob," George said after a while. "For laying it all out like that, but there's something else."

"What's that?"

"This promotion." He shook his head. "I don't want it."

"Bullshit," Bob said. "You're the right person for the job."

"I left the team in Savannah. Got pissed and just walked away."

"You laid out the truth. That captain is a stupid son of a bitch. They should have let the investigation proceed as planned, and you told them as much." Bob grinned. "In your own distinct way."

"Is that how you would have handled things?"

"Probably not." Bob smiled. "I wouldn't have had the balls to say it, but it's not a bad thing that you did. Just a different style."

"Different style?" George shook his head. "I'm not a leader, Bob, not like ..."

"Stop. You are a leader, George." Bob shrugged. "Let's face it. We are not the same. I've never been the investigator you are, but that doesn't mean I'm not a damned good investigator, and you aren't me. That doesn't mean you're not a leader, just different. Don't try to be me or anyone else. You lead the field teams the way you handle everything else, and you'll do fine. The team will respect you." Bob nodded. "Trust me. You are the right person for the job."

He leaned back in the seat. "Now, if you'll excuse me, all this talk has worn me out. I'm gonna just sit here and enjoy the scenery for a while." Outside, the foothills grew and merged into a continuous chain of rounded summits that flowed north, merging with the Appalachian Mountains.

George said nothing more. Bob did what he always did, said his piece, and left you to decide whether the words had merit. George knew they did.

16. What Could We Do?

Henry Rush eased himself down the ramp leading from the front porch of Lara Jean's Personal Care Home. He and the five other residents, all in their eighties, simply called it *the home*.

Steadying himself with a cane, he focused on putting one foot in front of the other. The ramp, built to accommodate wheelchairs, had a shallow pitch, but a fall at his age would be life-changing, and life had changed enough over the years for Henry Rush.

So, he took his time and made it safely to the old concrete sidewalk that led to the street. He proceeded carefully. The sidewalk was serviceable but cracked and heaved up in a few places from the roots of a live oak planted too close a hundred years earlier. The State Healthcare Facility Regulation inspector had given Lara Jean Wainwright and her husband, Bobby, a written warning on the last inspection visit. They said the sidewalk posed a trip hazard to the six seniors—three men and three women—housed there, and it must be repaired before their next inspection. That was three months ago, but money was tight, and the Wainwrights were still trying to find a contractor to do the work in exchange for small monthly payments.

"See ya later, Doc," his roommates, two old men, called from their wicker rockers on the front porch.

Rush raised a hand for a second without looking back, hunched over and the other hand maintaining a white-knuckle grip on the cane. They watched him descend to take his walk every day, but never joined him. Both were wheelchair-bound, able to pull themselves up and onto the rockers, or the bed, or the toilet, but that was the extent of their physical activity.

Henry Rush was their hero. At eighty-seven years old, he maintained his morning walk routine, bathed himself, and made his bed daily. When necessary, he would go into the kitchen to ask Lara Jean for their afternoon snacks when she forgot to hand them out.

Rush shuffled along the shoulder of the street in an older, working-class neighborhood. There were no sidewalks or curbs in this part of Valdosta, Georgia.

Small frame homes, mostly painted white, lined both sides of the street. Many of the houses had long since seen their best days and were in decay, their railings rusted, paint chipped and scaling off the siding. Some had plywood nailed over broken windows because the owners could not afford to replace them. A few, like the one the Wainwrights owned and operated as a personal care facility for seniors, were in reasonably good shape. Still, all were small affairs, with two or three bedrooms at most. Lara Jean and Bobby had added an extra bathroom to their home to satisfy the state inspectors, and this added to their financial woes.

For a man who had once been a practicing physician, it was an inauspicious place to spend his final years. Doctor Henry Rush had no choice.

Doctoring, as he called it, in a tiny rural community was not always a lucrative undertaking. Between the cost of maintaining an office, satisfying regulators, licenses, and required ongoing training, expenses were high. The simple fact was that there weren't enough sick and injured patients to cover the costs. Doc Rush had taken up other jobs to make ends meet.

He served as the county coroner for many years, an easy enough task that brought him a steady paycheck. Then there was his investment in a hardware and feed store and a small horse farm. The store brought in some cash. The horse farm drained it away.

Still, with an eye on a cottage down on the St. Mary's River across from Cumberland Island and a distant view of the Atlantic beyond, he and his wife, Evelyn, had planned a neat little retirement. That was before they diagnosed Evelyn with breast cancer. Treatments lasted five years, and in the end, the cancer took her anyway.

The cost of her medical care drained away their financial resources. Rush sold everything he could to pay the bills, including his share of the hardware and feed store. Nobody wanted any part of the horse farm. When all the bills were paid, he had a small county pension for his service as the coroner and the interest he earned on the money from the sale of his house.

It was his daughter Rose who found the personal care home. It was affordable ... just barely ... and her father wanted to live out his years some place warm. Valdosta, Georgia might not have been a condo on the Gulf coast, but it was a stone's throw from the Florida line, and it was warm ... very warm.

Rose got her father settled at Lara Jean's, then returned to Atlanta, where her husband underwrote insurance policies for a national company known for its annoyingly repetitive television commercials. She promised to visit with the grandchildren as often as possible. He hadn't seen her for eight months, and the grandchildren had never been to visit. He told himself that was understandable. Atlanta was a three-and-a-half-hour drive away. The children had school, and his daughter and son-in-law had work.

That was alright, he told himself. Life was good enough for now. Anyway, it wouldn't be long before he joined Evelyn.

He made it to the end of the block and turned down a dirt lane that ran behind a row of shotgun houses. A service pickup truck was stopped halfway along the path. Its rear hatch door was up, and the tailgate dropped. To the side, a young man knelt over a transformer box that provided electrical services to the nearby houses. As Doc Rush passed, the young man stood and smiled. Rush nodded, returned the smile, and shuffled by, hunched over, hand gripping the cane.

He had just passed the truck's rear bumper when the young man's arms were around his frail frame, lifting him off his feet and depositing him in the truck's bed. "What ... what are you doing?" Rush managed to sputter.

William Payne moved swiftly and with precision, his reflexes and reaction times honed in another place and another time. He leaned over the frail, trembling man and secured him with handcuffs to a heavy rail welded to the side of the bed. His grip was firm but gentle enough not to hurt or break the old man's brittle bones. As with the Buxton men, Sheriff Sutter, and Doris Mills, he had no intention of hurting the old man.

"You?" Rush's eyes widened with recognition as Payne leaned over him. "I always wondered if I'd see you again."

Payne said nothing, but looked into his eyes for a moment. He wore no disguise this time. There was no need. As with the others, he'd taken his time selecting the right place for their encounter, watching the old man's movements every day for months. It was a painstaking chore. What he really wanted was to get this over with quickly, but that wouldn't do. It had to be this way, if it was to mean anything.

Finally, he decided on this neighborhood, in this alley behind a row of dilapidated houses. There were no cameras here to recording backyards, and there were no witnesses.

Payne lifted the tailgate and slammed the rear hatch down, sealing Rush into the back of the same truck Doris Mills had occupied a few days earlier. The drive to the shack in the north Georgia woods took much longer this time. Payne was in no hurry, drinking Cokes and munching peanuts he'd bought at a convenience store when he topped off the truck's gas tank that morning. There was no reason to rush and risk attracting the attention of some bored cop patrolling I-75.

Five hours later, they arrived at the shack in the woods. When Payne dropped the tailgate and reached in to uncuff Rush, he stopped. The old man was still and quiet. Payne leaned close and felt a faint breath of air on his cheek. Still alive. Good.

He released the handcuff from the rail and pulled Rush from the truck's bed as carefully as possible. Then, as he had Doris Mills, he lifted old Doc Rush's frail body over his shoulder and carried him inside.

The smell was overpowering, and Rush began to move about, agitated as he regained consciousness. Payne placed him on the floor beside Doris Mills's body. She hadn't lasted long. He'd only been gone a few days, but it was evident that she was dead. Rigor mortis had set in, her bowels and bladder emptied, and insects and mice had helped with decomposition by taking bites from her flesh.

Rush shook his head slowly to clear it and looked around, trying to understand. "Where is this place?"

Payne said nothing as he fastened the handcuffs to the same chain that still held Doris' wrists secure.

Rush's face and nose wrinkled at the stench. He turned his head to the side. "Who is ..." His eyes opened wide as he stared into Doris' dead face. "No ... she's ..." Rush shook his head. "No, you can't do this, son. Don't ..."

"I'm not your son," Payne said, speaking for the first time, ratcheting the handcuffs closed.

"Please, I know I should have done something," Rush said, twisting his head to watch Payne leave and close the door behind him. "No!" he shouted.

A moment later, the pickup's engine cranked up, and he heard it move away over the rocky ground, leaving him alone in the shack with Doris Mills. He looked into her dead eyes, tears trickling down his pale cheeks, and asked her, "What could we do?"

Doris Mills made no reply.

17. Short-timer and a Peacock

They arrived in Dykes, the county seat of Bayne County, without fanfare. George parked on the square and led the way into the county offices. Web Seymour, Carol Digby, and Toby Jones, dressed in his mismatched uniform, met them.

Seymour, seated in Carol's chair, spoke first. "You must be the boys Fullman sent up."

"Governor Fullman assigned us to assist your deputy in locating Sheriff Sutter," George said dryly.

"Expected you yesterday." Seymour shook his head. "Don't like to be kept waiting."

"We had some other issues to clear off our plates." George began to wonder if he should have told Fullman to shove it when he ordered him as far away from Atlanta as possible. Dealing with this strutting peacock was not in his job description.

"More important than doing what the governor ordered. Is that a fact?" Seymour's mouth twitched into a smirk.

"More important than a missing sheriff, who we were told is probably off drinking with his buddies." George was not about to get into the details of the Savannah investigation that had preoccupied him yesterday afternoon. He was also tired of the inquisition. "Who exactly are you?"

Seymour's mouth twitched a little, and he straightened up in the chair, leaning forward across the desk on his elbows. "Webley Seymour, Bayne County Commission Chairman, and I ask the questions here, so who the hell are you?"

"Agent Mackey." George eyed the pretentious asshole doing the 'Boss Hogg' impression. "And for the record, when it comes to this investigation, we'll ask the questions."

"That a fact? We'll see." Seymour leaned back again in the chair and put his hands behind his head, the lord of the realm examining his underlings. "Who's your partner here?"

"Ask him yourself," George said.

Bob stepped forward and gave a nod. "Agent Shaklee." He stared down at the man, who was apparently the biggest fish in a very small pond, and didn't realize how small his pond was.

"What exactly do you two ... *agents* ... do for Fullman?"

"I'm the Director of the Office of Special Investigations. Agent Mackey is the OSI Chief of Field Operations," Bob said quickly, not sure whether George was likely to laugh in the man's face or ream him a new asshole. In George's present state of mind, both were possibilities.

"Glad to see Fullman is taking this seriously," Seymour said. "Lot of support came his way from up here in these hills during the last election."

"He appreciates the support of all the voters," Bob replied and decided it was time to ignore Seymour. He turned to Toby Jones. "You must be the deputy who conducted the initial search and made the report."

"Yes, sir." Toby nodded, completely awed at standing in the presence of the OSI ... the Georgia equivalent of investigative royalty.

"From your report, we understand that the sheriff's wife and ..." Bob pulled a notepad from his pocket where he had jotted down a few details from the report. "Mrs. Buxton made the initial reports that the men were missing."

"Yes, sir." Jones nodded solemnly. "I took down everything they said."

"Good." Bob nodded. "You can come with us. We'd like to speak with the complainants and familiarize ourselves with the case."

"Yes, sir." Jones came from his position in the rear behind Carol Digby, the look of relief on his face unmistakable.

George wondered if he was relieved to have them there to lead the investigation or to have a reason to get away from Seymour. Both, he decided.

Seymour pushed himself up from the desk. "I'll join you."

"Not necessary," Bob said, turning toward the door. "We'll take your statement in due course."

"Statement?" Seymour's eyes narrowed. "You don't seem to understand. I'm the chairman of the county commission, and I ..."

"Actually, you don't understand," Bob said, cutting him off. "The governor sent us to find your missing sheriff. This is now an OSI investigation, and from this point forward, we will control it. As Agent Mackey said, we will ask the questions, meaning no one interferes or speaks with witnesses but us. No one becomes involved in the case without our permission. No one gives directions regarding the case except us." Bob smiled. "Standard procedure, of course."

"Who the ... what do you think ... You have no ..." Web Seymour suddenly could not put a complete sentence together.

Bob turned away from the sputtering Bayne County commission chairman. Like Toby Jones, Carol Digby had remained silent through the introductions but was now working hard to stifle a laugh. A wide-eyed Jones followed George and Bob to the sidewalk around the courthouse square.

"Well, that was interesting." George allowed himself a chuckle. "Wonder how long before the governor is on the phone. He's gonna be pissed you didn't give that pompous asshole the kid-glove treatment."

"Let him be pissed." Bob shrugged. "One of the advantages of being a short-timer. They can't really fuck with you."

George grinned. "I think I might just like this assignment."

Bob took out his notepad and scanned it for a few seconds, then looked at Toby Jones. "You ride with us. We're going to go see Mimsy Buxton first, then the sheriff's wife."

"Yes, sir." Jones nodded, cast a sideways glance at the window at the county clerk's office to find Webley Seymour glaring at him through the glass. "Can we just go, now ... please?"

18. Fate

Mimsy Buxton cracked the front door open and peered out at the two strangers standing on the porch. "Ox and Harley aren't here," she said so softly that George had to lean forward.

"I'm sorry, ma'am. What did you say?" he asked.

"Ox and Harley aren't around," Mimsy said, managing to lift her voice above a whisper. "Who are you?"

"It's me, Mimsy," Toby Jones said from the side, out of view. George moved so she could see the deputy through the partially open door. "These men are from the state. They're going to help us find Ox and Harley."

Mimsy cracked the door a little wider now, still not inviting them inside but reassured by the deputy's presence. "They're gone up to the deer camp," she said. "Almost three weeks now. Should have been back two weeks ago. You going up to search for them?"

"Deputy Jones is going to take us to the deer camp to look around, but I have to ask a question." George gave a friendly smile. "Why'd you wait until last week to call the sheriff?"

"Ox doesn't like me in his business much." Mimsy's eyes darted to the floor, and she shrugged. "He might have a reason for staying up at the camp, but I don't know what it is, and I ... sort of got worried something mighta happened."

"Maybe if we could come in for a minute," George suggested, "It might help us find your husband and son. Just to ask a few questions, that's all." He waited as she hesitated, then added, "It really would be a big help."

"I don't know," she mumbled, still looking at the floor. "I only wanted Doyle Sutter to go up and have a look around for them."

"We know." Toby Jones nodded. "Doyle's missing too. That's why we want to talk ... just a few questions, Mimsy."

"Alright." She nodded and looked up for a second, then back down at the floor as she backed away from the door so they could enter, then pointed to a sofa and chair. "You can sit ... if you want."

Jones went in first, followed by George, then Bob. The three arranged themselves on the sofa. George pushed his notepad into his shirt pocket and leaned forward, elbows on knees, smiling. Mimsy was already nervous, and scribbling down everything she said would only make her more so and less likely to communicate. He figured that between the three of them, they could remember the important details.

George waited for her to sit. She straightened the old print flowered dress that looked like something from the 1960s, lowered herself, and folded her hands in her lap. Then he waited for her to look up and meet his gaze. She finally did and immediately looked down at her hands.

"You say your husband might have a reason for staying up at the deer camp longer than you expected," George said. "Any idea what the reason might be?"

"No." Mimsy shook her head. "But Ox does things his way, is all."

"And he doesn't like you prying into his business. That it?"

"Doesn't like anybody in his business," Mimsy said.

"And what business is that?" George asked.

"Fixes things for people. Cars, tractors, mechanical things ..." Mimsy looked at George and smiled for the first time as if she found something good to say about her husband. "Ox is good like that ... can fix just about anything."

"Where does he fix things for people? A shop in Dykes?"

"No, he stays close to home and makes them bring their broke things out here." She nodded toward the door. "Out in the barn behind the house. That's where he works."

"Well, that sure keeps things simple," George nodded and smiled. "He must bring in pretty good money to support this place, with no rent to pay on the shop and all."

"He does alright, I guess." Mimsy gave another of her submissively deferential shrugs. "Ox says we got all we need, and the place is paid for ... inherited from his parents."

"That makes for a pretty nice life out here in the hills, I guess. I know a lot of people would like to trade places with you."

Mimsy looked up at that, surprised, but said nothing.

"So, he and your boy Harley ... how old is Harley?"

"Twenty-nine ... going on thirty in two months."

"Right ... almost thirty... a grown man, then." George nodded.

"That's right. He's grown," Mimsy said. "Works with his father, learning how to fix things." She shook her head and allowed herself a brief smile. "But he's not good at it ... not like his father."

"So, Ox and Harley work together, spend a lot of time together."

"Right." Mimsy nodded.

"And they went up to the deer camp on the mountain together." George's brow furrowed, as if trying to puzzle out a thought. "There wasn't any trouble between them, was there?"

"Trouble?" Mimsy looked surprised. "You mean Harley giving Ox trouble?" She shook her head. "No, Harley would never do that."

"Okay," George continued. "So, they went up to deer camp just like they normally would this time of year."

"Yes, that's right ... just like normal," Mimsy said. "Except they always came back before."

"Right." George nodded thoughtfully and said, "I have to ask you. Are there people who don't like your husband, people who might be angry at him?"

"You mean angry enough to hurt him and Harley?" Mimsy shrugged. "There's lots of folks that don't care much for Ox, or Harley either, for that matter. They can be hard to take at times, but I don't know of anyone so mad they might want to hurt them."

"I'm sure that's true," George said mildly. "You understand. I had to ask to be sure so we can eliminate anything else."

"I understand." Mimsy was looking at her hands, fingers opening and closing, twisting nervously in her lap again.

George and Bob noticed and exchanged a look. Something wasn't right. There was more, but pressing her now would only drive her farther into her shell. It was time to change the subject and put her at ease, if that was possible. George swiveled his head around to look at the furnishings and pictures on the wall. "That picture there, the old one, is that your family or Ox's?"

"That one," Mimsy looked up and smiled. "That's mine. Mama's holding my little brother Joey, and I'm holding Daddy's hand." The smile faded from Mimsy's face. "They're all gone now ... mom and dad dead of cancer five years apart. Joey got killed in Afghanistan doing something with the army."

"I'm really sorry to hear that," George said, waited a few seconds, eyes focused on the picture, and then asked, "Mind if I take a closer look?"

"Sure, you can look," Mimsy said and watched him stand and walk to the wall to examine the picture up close.

"Yep, I definitely see the family resemblance," George said. "You and your mother have the same face and smile."

"You think so?" Mimsy said, smiling again.

"I do." George nodded. "She was a very pretty lady."

"Yes, she was. Everyone said so." Mimsy looked down at her lap again, but the smile widened across her face.

The interview lasted another thirty minutes without Mimsy knowing she was being interviewed. George chatted with her like a neighbor who just happened to drop by for coffee. They talked about life in the hills. Growing up in Bayne County, and how they celebrated birthdays and Christmases, and the Fourth of July. In her soft voice, she told him she missed her mother and father terribly, but most of all, her brother.

As they talked, bits of information about her relationship with her husband and son came out. They helped color in the picture that was the life of Mimsy Buxton. Details she would have denied if questioned directly emerged as snippets of conversation that others would miss or ignore, but the investigators missed nothing.

There were no signs of physical abuse, but it was undeniable that she was emotionally controlled and abused. Ox made all the decisions, controlled all the money, and disregarded any idea that was important to her.

When she wanted a puppy to keep her company, he said no. The next time she mentioned it, he told her if she ever brought a dog home, he would kill it. Mimsy believed him completely and never brought the subject up again.

Harley learned from his father and treated his mother in much the same way. If she scolded him for misbehaving, he locked her in a closet while his father laughed. He demanded that his mother wait on him hand and foot. If she didn't move quickly enough, there was always the threat of being locked in the closet again while Ox laughed.

Bob Shaklee and Deputy Jones listened without speaking, mentally recording the information George extracted in his pleasant, non-threatening way. They could not help but wonder why she had stayed, but both knew it was not uncommon for a woman to stay in an abusive relationship.

Fear kept them there. Fear of the unknown, of having to survive in a frightening and intimidating world. Threats of what would happen if they ever tried to leave. Even in an abusive relationship, there was the security of knowing what to expect out of life. For many, the devil they knew was less terrifying than the one they did not.

When they finished, George said, "One more thing, Mrs. Buxton."

"Yes?"

"Mind if we take a look around in the barn ... you know, Ox's workshop where he fixes things?"

The fleeting look of worry on her face was noticeable, but she recovered quickly and said, "Sure, I suppose so."

Mimsy led the way out to the barn, opened the door, and stepped aside. They entered and wandered about as if merely curious about Ox's tools and equipment, making mental notes of everything they saw.

George stopped before a metal door, out of place in the weathered wood barn. "What's in here?"

"Storeroom," Mimsy said and looked away. "Just Ox's supplies."

"Can I see?" George asked.

"Locked," Mimsy said. "Ox has the key."

"Oh." George smiled. "Makes sense. Working man has to protect his tools."

"I suppose so." Mimsy turned to the barn's entrance. "We should go now. Ox might not like me bringing you in here."

They said their goodbyes in the yard and promised to do everything possible to find her husband and son. Driving out the dirt road to the highway, Toby Jones muttered, "She'd be better off if we never found them."

George nodded, and Bob said, "I can't disagree."

"Mimsy's been like that ever since I've known her," Jones said. "And Ox has been the way he is. She's just the kind of woman he would pick out for a wife ... the kind of woman who would say yes, too afraid to say no, and afraid no one else might ever ask her if she did."

***

Tucked back in the trees on an overlooking hill, William Payne watched through binoculars. He saw the three men arrive and waited while they spoke to Mimsy Buxton, then went into the house. He watched closely when they entered the barn, came out, and then left a few minutes later.

Mimsy stood in the yard for several minutes after they drove away. The sun had finally made its way up over the hills, and she held a hand to her forehead to shade her eyes as she scanned the slopes. Once, she looked directly in his direction. Through the binoculars, he sensed that she knew she was being watched and that her fate was being decided.

When she went into the house, Payne lowered the binoculars. He sat for a long while, hidden in the trees, listening to the birds, feeling the breeze on his face, smelling the pines, trying to make up his mind about something, doing what Mimsy suspected—deciding her fate.

19. Free Meal

After interviewing Mimsy Buxton, the OSI team spent the rest of the day organizing an expanded search party. At the same time, the Bayne County deputies—Toby Jones joined by Brian Mecham, and Dave Pascal—huddled in a corner of the county clerk's office, muttering among themselves. They were more than a little overwhelmed.

They stared at Bob Shaklee and George Mackey like star-struck teens gawking at the latest music video obsessions. To them, these were real big-city cops, pros who had solved murders, dealt with terrorists, and been involved in life-and-death struggles. By contrast, after attending the state's Basic Mandate Law Enforcement eleven-week training course at the regional Academy in Athens, the deputies returned to rural Bayne County where not much happened ... ever. Since then, their law enforcement experience mostly entailed bringing in revenue through traffic citations and locking up an occasional town drunk on a Saturday, mainly without the need to do more than open the cell door and say, "Get on in there, son."

The first help to arrive was a lieutenant and three troopers from the Georgia State Patrol barracks thirty miles away. The State Patrol came through Bayne County, making courtesy rounds during the day, but spent most of their time cruising the interstates and U.S. highways. Having them arrive within a couple of hours after one call by Bob Shaklee to the patrol commander, a colonel in Atlanta, added to the deputies' awe.

Bob Shaklee and George Mackey worked the phones, calling in more resources. Bob was on the phone at one point with a loud, blustering, and easily recognizable voice. The Bayne County deputies exchanged awestruck looks as Governor Fullman's voice boomed over the speaker.

"Whatever you need," the governor said and added with his usual bombast. "You tell Mackey to get the job done. Find me that sheriff!"

It was late afternoon when the contingent of state troopers arrived in Dykes—too late to head up on the mountain and search with night coming on. Pulled away from their usual patrol duties, they had no idea why they had been summoned to the smallest county in the state. So, they milled around in Carol Digby's office, waiting for instructions.

Commission Chair Web Seymour blew into the office with his usual gust of pomposity, took one look at the gathering, and bellowed, "What the hell is this?"

"Organizing the search party," Bob said, looking up from a map spread out on a desk, where he and George marked out search quadrants and briefed the Lieutenant in charge of the troopers.

"Search party?" Seymour's arms flew up like a bantam rooster puffing its wings. "You should be out there searching now!"

"Lot of territory to cover up in those mountains" Bob shook his head. "Sheriff Sutter could be anywhere. These state troopers are a start, but they won't be near enough manpower. Besides, it'll be dark in a couple of hours, and there's no way to search that terrain in the dark."

"I want my sheriff found!" Seymour was shouting now.

"If he's up there, we'll find him," Bob replied calmly, unflustered by the red-faced man doing his best to intimidate everyone in the room. "Your deputies have already searched the area of the deer camp and came up with nothing. The next step is to expand the search area, and we can't do that without more people. Better to go out organized with enough people than wander without a plan and hope we find them. A company of National Guard will be here tomorrow."

"They better be," Seymour grumbled, lowering his voice. "Hate to make another call to the governor."

"Call whoever you want," Bob said, dismissing Seymour with a shrug and returning to the map. "The Guard will be here tomorrow. Now, go away and let us do our jobs."

"You forget who you're talking to," Seymour sputtered. "I am the goddammed chairman of this county, and I'll ..."

"We know exactly who you are, "Bob interrupted. "And we know why we're here. You puffed your chest and had the governor send us up to handle this, so get out of the way, and we'll do our jobs ... without your interference."

The three deputies watched, more awed than ever. No one, at least no one in Bayne County, back talked Web Seymour, but these state boys didn't seem to give a rip about who he was. When the commission chairman's eyes darted their way, they stared at the floor, clenching their jaws to suppress the grins on their faces.

Standing alone in the room, ignored by the OSI and state troopers, Seymour did what most politicians would do. He started speaking authoritatively and giving orders to the only people who could not safely ignore him.

"When these state people get their asses organized," he told the deputies. "You make sure you are there, in the lead. That's our sheriff you're going up there to find. You make sure you're the ones who bring him back down. Don't let those fancy state badges get in your way." He leaned toward the deputies. "And by God, don't you forget who's paying you."

With that, the county commission chairman stormed from the building. George watched the exchange from the side, and as Seymour left, he gave an understanding nod to the deputies. He was more than a little familiar with small-time politicians carrying their self-importance around on their shoulders, always ready to throw it in the face of those who could only stand there and take it. "Don't worry," he said. "We'll let you take the lead when we find the sheriff."

Relieved, Toby Jones nodded. "Thanks. I know we're not experts at this, but ..." He shrugged. "Well, you heard Seymour. He expects us to be there."

"You will be," George said. He looked at Bob. "It's a little late in the day to do a full search, but how about we have these deputies lead us up to the scene? Be good to get the lay of the land before the Guard gets here, and the circus begins."

"Good idea," Bob said. He turned to the trooper in charge, a lieutenant whose nameplate read R. Giles. "Want to join us, Lieutenant?"

"Let's do it." Giles looked at the troopers who had accompanied him. "Need you back first thing in the morning."

One trooper looked up from a chair, leaning back on two legs, reclining against a wall. "Came a long way, LT, just to be sent home."

"You know why we're here. Governor's orders. Be here." Giles looked at Bob. "What time?"

"National Guard should be here by eight. Have your people here at seven, and we'll review the search grids. Your troopers and the Bayne County deputies will lead the search teams and make sure the guardsmen don't accidentally contaminate any crime scene if we find one."

Giles turned to the troopers. "Report here at seven AM."

The troopers shuffled out, mumbling.

"Typical cluster fuck."

"Yeah. Hurry up and wait."

"Politicians involved. What did you expect?"

"Corporal Rusk!" Giles called out to the trooper, grumbling the loudest.

A grizzled, gray-haired trooper wearing two stripes on his sleeves turned in the door while the others scurried out to the street. "Lieutenant?"

"Stop the bullshit."

"Sir?" Rusk said mildly, unintimidated by the bars on the Lieutenant's epaulets. He was a twenty-five-year State Patrol veteran. Once, he had worked the interstates around Atlanta. Now, he spent his days cruising the rural state highways of north Georgia and biding his time until retirement. His civil service status would protect his position from any but the most flagrant violations of Patrol Policy. No wet-behind-the-ears lieutenant with shiny new bars was going to intimidate him.

"You are supposed to be a senior trooper, and I expect you to show an example for the others."

Rusk's lips twitched into a defiant smile. "Anything else, LT?"

"Be here at seven," Giles barked.

Rusk's smile widened. He turned without acknowledging and walked to the street where the other troopers waited. Giles watched them huddle for a moment. Rusk nodded at the office's plate-glass window and laughed. The others smiled, nodded, then moved to their patrol cruisers and departed.

Giles turned back to the OSI team, red-faced and uneasy that they had watched the trooper's public display of insubordination. Bob smiled to put him at ease. "Don't worry, Lieutenant. It's an unusual assignment ... not exactly usual patrol duties. They'll get in line once we give them something to do tomorrow."

"Right." Giles nodded, putting on a stern face to hide his embarrassment.

"What say we head up the mountain and scope things out before dark?" George said, changing the subject.

"Let's do it." Bob agreed.

Jones, Mecham, and Pascal led the way up the mountain in Jones' pickup. George and Bob followed, with Giles trailing in his State Patrol SUV.

Rolling to a dusty stop along the dirt road behind Sheriff Sutter's pickup, they climbed out and looked around.

"Lot of ground up here," Bob said.

"Let's see what we can see." George nodded at the deputies. "Lead on."

The sun had already lowered behind the western hilltops. Twilight would turn to night in an hour.

"This way," Toby Jones said, leading the way up the trail to the shack at the deer camp.

They crossed the clearing and entered, stopping inside the door to let their eyes adjust to the gloom. Nothing had changed. The rifles still leaned against the wall, and Sheriff Sutter's gun belt lay on the floor nearby.

"You didn't think to secure their weapons?" Lieutenant Giles said with a disapproving shake of his head.

"Well, I ...," Jones sputtered, red-faced. "I mean, we didn't know ..."

"Makes sense," George said quickly, deflecting Giles' star away from the deputy.

After the interaction with Trooper Rusk, Giles felt the need to prove his status as a command officer. Taking it out on a country deputy with minimal training was not the way.

"If this is a crime scene," George continued, "it gives us a chance to see things exactly as the deputy found them. If not, and the missing parties returned, we wouldn't want to leave them without weapons and defenseless. Besides, it's not likely someone was going to stumble on the shack up here."

Jones shifted uneasily and stared at the bare floor. Giles grunted and nodded. "I suppose."

"Deputy," George said. "Good job preserving the scene, and now that we've seen it, I think you can take the weapons with you and secure them as potential evidence."

"Right," Jones said, gathering up the rifles and gun belt.

George led the way and exited the shack into the deepening dusk. The group spent a few minutes walking around the clearing and checking the surrounding brush. Jones parted some branches and showed them the deer trail he had followed. He said doubtfully, "I'll take you up a ways ... if you want."

"Tomorrow's soon enough," George said. "No need to break a leg up here wandering in the dark when we aren't familiar with the terrain."

They picked their way carefully in the deepening gloom, down the path to the vehicles. By the time they were off the mountain and on the county road leading to Dykes, full dark had come on.

***

Not a mile away, scavengers were feasting in a cave formed four hundred and eighty million years earlier when tectonic forces created a landscape that once rivaled the Rockies and the Alps. Doyle Sutter might have survived a little longer if not for his frantic struggles to free himself, expending vast amounts of energy, sweating, and sobbing. For two days, he pulled, twisted, and turned. The handcuffs cut gouges into his wrists, but he could not free himself.

By the third day, he was too weak to do more than call for help. He knew it was futile, that the probability that anyone would come along the deer trail from the clearing, then climb the slope and find the cave. Still, he shouted and screamed for hours until his parched vocal cords produced only a whisper.

Small animals had been visiting the corpses of Ox and Harley, biting off bits for their suppers, snarling at each other in the dark as they fought for the best morsels. A few of them decided to find out what Sutter tasted like. His wail was barely a whimper as tiny teeth ripped and tore at him. He tried feebly to kick them away, but they were faster, had vision adapted to the dark, and were hungry. The more he struggled against them, the more determined their assaults became.

Had he been in better physical condition, he might have lasted a little longer, but he wasn't. A congenital heart arrhythmia that would have prevented him from passing the physical exam into any police academy had not prevented him from being elected as the county sheriff. The more he struggled to escape, the weaker he became until the arrhythmia brought on a stroke. More helpless than before, he hung from the chain, one side of his body paralyzed, his mouth drooping, saliva dripping down his chin to the rock floor.

Exhausted and delirious, dehydrated and starving, his hold on this world was as tenuous as one of the spider webs that had drifted over him and clung maddeningly to his face in the cave's pitch black. He died that night, whimpering and sobbing until his breaths faded away.

The cloying stench of Ox and Harley Buxton's rotting bodies, and now Sutter's, attracted more hungry creatures. Such bounty was uncommon in nature, and they were not about to waste it.

The scavengers continued their feast, now completely unhampered by his struggles. The gods had been generous to them lately, and they would not be denied their free meal.

20. The Word

"Where are you?" Sharon reclined on the sofa and turned down the television.

George looked out into the dark from the motel room. An old-style neon sign, hanging precariously from a pole, swung in the breeze blowing off the mountains. Half of the letters were burned out. "The Continental Inn," he said as he closed the curtains and flopped down on the bed, stretching out and yawning.

"Sounds plush ... five stars even."

"Not even close. Maybe two stars only because I haven't seen a rat ... yet."

"Sorry," Sharon said. "I'd say I wish I was with you, but ..."

"It's not really that bad. Just very ... rustic." George chuckled. "Right up my redneck alley."

"Why, Mr. Mackey, I thought our association might have upped your standards."

"When it's the only place in town, standards go out the window."

"You could have driven home for the night," Sharon held the phone close as if whispering in his ear. "I miss your warm butt."

"Sorry. I miss yours too, but I'm beat, and a two-and-a-half-hour drive back to the city was too far. We want to get started early in the morning. Lot of territory to cover up in the hills." George said. "Bob decided to stay too."

"Ohh? Sounds cozy."

"Not so much. He's in the next room, probably doing what I'm doing ... checking in with the boss."

"Celia?" Sharon laughed. "That's what you think? That we ladies are the boss? Who'd a thunk it."

They both laughed, feeling good, playful, and enjoying the banter with no other pressures.

"Please, baby, I don't do a thing without your approval," George said, closing his eyes and grinning.

"Right," Sharon laughed. "Except call a mayor a stupid son of a bitch."

"It wasn't the mayor. It was her aide."

"I stand corrected," Sharon said.

They were silent, smiling, enjoying being close, even if it was over the phone.

After a minute, Sharon said, "So, tell me about the case."

He stretched out on the twin bed in a small room in a motel that probably didn't see three guests in a month. Visitors were so rare that the county clerk, Carol Digby, had to find the owner, Jack Winton, at a local bar and arrange a room for the two OSI investigators.

After grabbing a quick dinner at a café on the town square, George and Bob headed to their rooms. Jake went back to the bar.

"Not much to report. The sheriff and two locals disappeared from a deer camp up on a mountain. No trace of them, just their guns left behind, including Sutter's sidearm."

"Their firearms left behind? That's not good. Foul play, you think?"

"Could be," George said. "Smells like it, but it could be just a bunch of dumbasses lost on the mountain. Until we find them, there's no telling. Law enforcement up here is a little shaky in the training department."

"I can imagine," Sharon said. "Small town ... small budget ... part-time cops. Good thing you and Bob are there to take the lead."

"Not much lead to take right now. Just a search. The terrain is pretty rough, and the locals know the area. We'll get more feet on the ground for them, but the ball's in their court until we find something or someone. For all we know, the sheriff and his buddies got drunk and fell off a cliff or down a ravine."

"Well, hurry up and get it done." Sharon paused and smiled, imagining his face, eyes closed, leaning back on a pillow, phone to his ear. She whispered. "I miss you, Mackey."

"I miss you too, babe. Won't be long. I expect we'll know something in another day or so, and I'll be headed back."

"Good." They rarely used the word *love*, but she knew she loved George Mackey and was confident he felt the same for her.

Their relationship began as colleagues working on a case. It soon became friendship—a real one, not colored by sexual or romantic undertones. When the romance happened, it came naturally, like sliding into a comfortable garment. It was enough to stretch out and talk into each other's ear over the phone tonight.

"I think I'm going to turn in now. Gotta get an early start tomorrow," George said and yawned after a few minutes. "Love you."

Sharon smiled, a little surprised he'd used *the word* but happy he had. "Love you too," she said.

They disconnected, and George stared at the ceiling for a few minutes, wondering how the Mendoza investigation in Savannah was going and feeling a little guilty once again that he'd gotten booted off the case, leaving Marco and the team to fend for themselves. Sleep forgotten, he picked up the phone again and punched the speed dial.

"What's up, boss?" Marco answered immediately.

"Just checking in," George said. "How's it going?"

"About as expected. A little icy around here for the last couple of days, but I was able to sit with the narcotics team here and work on a plan to follow up on Mendoza."

"Tell me."

The briefing was short and simple. As they expected, Mendoza's lawyer had no trouble getting the weapons charges dismissed, claiming he had no knowledge that the men with him were armed when the police stopped his car. Predictably, his men were not about to turn rat and inform on him to save themselves from some jail time. A little time in jail was a badge of honor in their world, but turning on Mendoza would be a death sentence.

That all worked in favor of continuing the investigation. The plan was simply to continue surveillance on him until they could pin something bigger on the drug dealer or until he led them to his cartel contacts.

"Sounds like a plan," George said as Marco wrapped things up.

"Good as we can come with, anyway." Marco paused and let out a chuckle. "By the way."

"What?"

"Stoneman is still a stupid son of a bitch."

George laughed. "I should have never let him get to me. I should be there with you now."

"George, we've got it under control. Right now, there's nothing to do but keep an eye on Mendoza until he fucks up again, and one thing is certain."

"He will fuck up again," they repeated in unison. It was their philosophical way of dealing with the fact that sometimes a bad guy slipped through their fingers. The bad guy was always bound to be back in their sights, sooner or later. In Mendoza's case, they expected it to be sooner.

They ended the call, but George couldn't shake the feeling that he had let the team down. He shook his head. Don't think about that. Find the missing sheriff, make the governor happy, and then get back into action.

He closed his eyes and kicked his shoes off. They thumped on the floor, but he lay awake, staring at the ceiling.

21. Helluva Show

"Coffee," George said without preliminaries. "I need coffee."

"Right in the breakroom." Carol Digby nodded at a door leading into a small room that was little more than a closet with a sink, water tap, and a coffeemaker set up on a table.

George nodded and said, "Thanks," then shuffled to the coffee maker like a zombie just out of the grave.

"Cups in the cabinet over the sink," Carol called after him. She looked at Bob. "Is he going to be alright?"

"He'll make it." Bob smiled. "He has another investigation in progress and has a lot on his mind. He's just tired. You know how it is."

"Oh." Carol nodded, but had no idea how it was. "Must be something very important to wake him up in the middle of the night."

She felt compelled to fish for more information. After all, having real investigators from Governor's OSI right here in a sleepy backwater like Bayne County would raise questions around the county. Once they departed, she would be expected to fill the locals in on all the juicy details. She smiled inwardly, imagining the procession in and out of her office, hashing it all over again for weeks. People would look for excuses, make them up if they had to—this tax bill's not right or is the commission meeting on the fourth or fifth. They'd take turns to avoid looking too nosey, but they'd be there, eager to hear the latest gossip about their missing sheriff and those damned no-good Buxton men. And Carol would have it all for them, every detail.

"Just the job," Bob said cryptically, and changed the subject. "Is this when you normally open the county office?"

"No." Carol smiled. "I opened early, knowing what time you had everyone coming. This is sort of a special occasion ... the OSI ... the Hunters ... in town, and a big search party coming in and all. A lot of excitement for a place like Bayne County, and people around here are going to want me to document it all for later consumption. Probably sounds funny ... coming from Atlanta to a place like this."

"Not funny," Bob said. "We work all over the state ... lots of small communities. Locals usually have a special interest in what we do, so I get the excitement, but you didn't mention finding your missing sheriff. Seems like that would be the topic of most concern."

"Doyle Sutter?" Carol gave a short laugh. "Sure, we're all concerned. Lots of theories floating around town, but the one that seems to have the most followers is just what we've been saying. Doyle and those Buxton men got to drinking and lost track of time. Fell asleep under a tree, maybe, or went out scouting deer and got lost. Your search party will likely stumble over them and wake them up."

She threw her head back and laughed harder. "That'll be something when you drag them back down here. They'll have some explaining to do. That's for sure."

"I see." Bob nodded. There was no reason to raise her concerns about what they had found at the shack—weapons neatly stacked against the wall and a gun belt lying on the floor. Despite the possible signs of foul play, the locals might be right, and by-the-book law enforcement procedures did not seem to be a prerequisite for wearing a badge in Bayne County.

George yawned and listened from the tiny breakroom as he sipped black coffee from a foam cup. He wasn't quite ready to face the world, and he had to be ready in the next few minutes.

After the call with Marco, he'd spent most of the night twisting and turning from side to side, finally drifting back to sleep at 4:00AM. When his alarm went off at 5:00, he moaned, crawled from the bed, and stood under an icy shower to shock his mind awake. Fifteen minutes later, he and Bob were in the car headed to the county office.

Bob commented on his fatigued appearance. George reviewed his call with Marco and rested his head against the passenger window, dozing as Bob drove.

**

The three Bayne County deputies had talked it over the night before, sitting on the tailgate of Jones' pickup, drinking beers and reviewing the day's excitement.

"What do you think it means?" Toby Jones said, turning up a brown, longneck bottle. "Doyle's gun belt left there in the shack."

"Don't know that it means anything at all." Dave Pascal shrugged and sipped his own beer.

"There's an explanation," Brian Mecham said confidently, leaning back on the tailgate. "I mean, what are the odds that they all just disappeared without any reason."

"Hell, Brian," Jones said. "I know there's an explanation. I'm just wondering what it is."

"You think some boogie man came along and snatched them?" Pascal laughed. "Or maybe aliens swooped in and carried them off."

Mecham laughed with him. Jones scowled in return, not appreciating the laughter.

"Don't think anything," he said. "Just asking the question, and no, I don't think some boogie man came along or aliens." He sipped the beer and continued. "Doyle and the Buxtons can take care of themselves. They know the backcountry."

He raised a hand and began ticking off the timeline of events on his fingers. "First, Ox and Harley go up, and Mimsy never hears from them. That has to be ... what? Over three weeks now. Next, Doyle goes up to check on them and doesn't come back. All of them leave their guns in the shack, so it seems like they never felt concerned about anything."

"All true." Mecham nodded. "So?"

"So, it seems like too much time in between the disappearances for them to be tied together somehow." Jones's brow furrowed as he tried to reason it out.

"And then you went up alone and came back in one piece, and after that, we all went up," Pascal said and shrugged. "Nothing happened to any of us, so what does that tell you?"

"I don't know," Jones said. "That's what I'm wondering."

"Well, I'll tell you what it means to me," Pascal stood up straight. "Pretty simple, really. It means there is no boogie man or aliens or bear or bigfoot wandering around up there snatching up people." He turned his beer up, drained it, and reached for another in the cooler in the pickup's bed.

"Then what?" Mecham asked, annoyed as usual at Pascal's know-it-all swagger.

"Simple," Pascal said, twisting the cap off the beer. "They went somewhere on their own, of their own free will. My guess is they're off rutting with one of those back hills trailer whores over toward Dalton. Having such a good time, they lost track of time."

"Bullshit," Mecham spat out. "Ox and Harley for sure would pull something like that, but Doyle's not the type."

"Oh hell, he's just the type, and tell me you wouldn't go off and do the same in his position ... at his age." Pascal looked them both in the eye and smiled. "Look, he's married all these years. No kids. Wife is always at work, or he's working the Kwik Pak if not at the county. How much time do you think they spend together in that house or in their bed? Might not have been his idea, but I'll bet Ox and Harley talked him into it, and now he's bundled up with some plump ass rubbing up and stroking him right on the ..."

"You're an asshole," Jones said in disgust. "I'm with Brian. Doyle's not the type."

"Suit yourself." Pascal shrugged. "But unless you've got a better idea, that's what I say is going on." He grinned. "Gonna be fun, though. State Patrol, National Guard, those OSI boys from the governor." He nodded. "It'll be a helluva show tomorrow. I'll bet they even bring in some news crews from Atlanta, cameras and all."

Jones and Mecham nodded and reached into the cooler for beers. Pascal was an asshole, but he was right about one thing. It was going to be one hell of a show.

The next morning, the deputies bustled into the county clerk's office dressed in their finest Rambo outfits ready for their adventure. Dressed in camo as if they were about to rope down from a chopper on a special forces mission. Each wore their sidearms in military flap-style holsters and carried a rifle slung over their shoulders. It would have been an understatement to say they were a little excited to be involved with the OSI in the day's activities.

Like most of the county's population, they expected their missing sheriff to turn up with the Buxton men at some point. But this was the biggest damn deal to hit the Bayne County sheriff's office since ... well, there hadn't ever been anything like this in their memories, and they were going to make the most of the excitement.

George watched from the breakroom closet, shook his head, blinked his bleary eyes, and sucked down more black coffee.

22. Crime Scene

The state patrol troopers arrived precisely on time at 7AM. The trucks carrying the National Guard rolled into Dykes an hour later, circling the courthouse square and giving it the appearance of an occupied town in a war zone. Local traffic slowed, and townsfolk gawked as the vehicles lined up around the square.

The locals gathered at their hangouts to watch the show—several women at the café drinking coffee, men on the sidewalk outside the hardware store. All whispered and murmured among themselves about the missing sheriff and *them damn Buxton boys.*

"Sutter shoulda knowed better than to head up there alone. They all get to drinkin' and no tellin' what might happen."

"Doyle never was the sharpest tack in the box. That's why he took to government work."

Laughter.

"Still, I hope nothing bad happened to him. He might not have been too smart, but he was good company. Treated people fair."

"True enough. Not a mean bone in his body."

"For all we know them, Buxton coulda killed him and threw him down Taney's Ravine."

"Buxton is mean, but he ain't no killer."

"More likely they got drunk and fell down the ravine, and ole Doyle got too close and fell in after 'em."

"If he did, it's gonna be a hard day trying to find him. They say Ole General Sherman marched a whole Union company of scouts down there, and they never seen them again."

"Yep, lots of places for a person to fall off a cliff or down a hole and never be seen again."

"That'd be a damn shame, for sure. Whatever else he might be, Doyle Sutter's too good a man to have his life wasted on someone like Ox Buxton or his dumbass son, Harley."

"That's the damn truth."

Heads nodded in agreement

National Guard troops had been dispatched from a support unit, a motor vehicle maintenance company with minimal field experience. They jumped down from the trucks, wandering the square and mingling with each other and the locals, with no idea what was expected of them.

George eyed them doubtfully. "We're as likely to end up losing one of them off a cliff as we are to find the sheriff."

"Let's make sure that doesn't happen," Bob said. "They might be National Guard, but they're civilians when it comes to this kind of work. Keep them where it's safe as much as possible."

They waited while the Guard captain in charge of the troops gathered them on the courthouse square. As military formations go, it was a very informal formation. The troops talked with one another, laughing at jokes and breaking ranks to make runs to the café across the street for coffee. Most seemed to think this was a holiday from their day jobs.

A few griped at the inconvenience of being pulled away from their lives to fulfill the agreement they'd made when they enlisted in the Guard. After all, it was supposed to be a part-time deal, a way to make a little extra cash, wear a uniform one weekend a month, and head off for a two-week adventure once a year, all of it scheduled so that their commitment to Uncle Sam and the State of Georgia would not interfere with their lives.

Still, most were happy to be there, strutting around the square in their BDUs for the locals to see. At the same time, they gawked at the state troopers, deputies, and OSI men, carrying sidearms. This was a real adventure, something to tell their friends about over a beer.

The captain called them together. "Gather up, everyone!"

The Guard troops shuffled around, forming an irregular arc in front of the courthouse steps. Bob nodded, and George stepped up a step and began the briefing. He kept it short and simple. They would divide into three groups, each guided by one of the Bayne County deputies.

The National Guard contingent would form two of the two groups and fan out into lines along the dirt road to the deer camp, proceeding in formation up and down the slope from there, searching for some sign of the missing persons. If they found a body, or anything that might be a clue as to what happened, they were to touch nothing and immediately contact the OSI team on the radios the deputies carried. If they found a survivor, they were to render first aid and call in for medical support from the EMTs who would accompany them as far as they could, in an ambulance a neighboring county had provided.

"Questions?" George asked, wrapping things up. There were none. "Good. Let's go."

The Guard loaded into their trucks, George and Bob rode with Toby Jones, and the state troopers followed in Lieutenant Giles' patrol cruiser. By the time they arrived at the road near the deer camp, the morning sun was up over the ridges and peaks, but deep shadows still obscured the valleys and ravines.

The teams moved out to cover their assigned search areas. Brian Mecham led a team to the west around the mountain, and Dave Pascal led the team to the east. They would search methodically up and down the slopes from there, making their way around the mountain. The morning gloom, uneven terrain, and heavy underbrush in places made progress slow.

Toby Jones led George, Bob, and Lieutenant Giles with his state troopers back up the path to the clearing by the shack. From there, they spread out to search up the slope.

They didn't go far. In minutes, they had climbed as far as they could. Rocky bluffs hung out above, rising another two feet. They searched around the bottom of the cliffs for bodies or signs of injuries, then returned to the clearing. George sent the state patrol contingent down the slope to continue the search. He, Bob, and Toby Jones returned to the shack to see if they had missed any clues regarding the men's disappearance.

They hadn't. Nothing had changed since the day before or since Jones' first visit, searching for Sheriff Sutter.

"What about the deer trail you found at the edge of the clearing?" George asked when they went outside.

"Over there," Jones nodded.

"Let's check it out," George said, and Jones led the way.

They wound around the mountain on the trail for more than a mile until it disappeared into the undergrowth, then turned and backtracked to search up the slope from the deer trail. They hadn't gone far when George stopped and held up a hand.

"What?" Bob said.

"There." George pointed. "Looks like another game trail heading off up the slope."

Bob and Toby Jones looked at the point in the brush George indicated. Bob's brow furrowed. "Not much of a trail. Not sure even a deer could make that climb."

"They could," Jones said, nodding. "Seen them do it up here a hundred times, getting themselves up places I'd never try."

"They came up looking for deer. Could be they were on a trail and followed a deer that way." George shrugged. "I'm going up." He pushed his way past some brush and started climbing. Jones was behind him, with Bob bringing up the rear.

They moved even more slowly than before. Rocks and loose dirt slipped under their feet, and they grabbed whatever they could to keep from sliding back down the slope. They were panting heavily when they reached a ledge at the base of a towering rock wall that extended upward to the mountain's summit.

"Which way now?" Bob said.

George looked both ways along the ledge and nodded. "That way looks like easier traveling."

"Interesting, don't you think?" George said over his shoulder, leading the way again past a point where the slope below steepened to a nearly vertical drop.

"What's that?" Bob panted, trying not to look down. The ledge they followed was part of the rock bluff they had found rising above the shack.

"We're headed back in the direction of the clearing again," George said. "A couple of hundred feet above it, but if we keep going, we should be able to see down into the clearing. Might be something we can see from up here we didn't pick up below."

"Maybe," Bob said, eyes on his feet and stepping carefully along the ledge.

As it turned out, they did not make it back around to the deer camp. After another hundred feet, George held up his hand. "Stop."

"What is it?" Bob asked.

"Smell that?"

Bob inhaled, wrinkled his nose, and nodded. "Something dead."

"Right."

Toby Jones peered over the ledge. "Could be coming from down there. Maybe they were tracking a deer, and they slipped."

"Could be," George said, "but why track a deer without your rifles, and how would Sheriff Sutter know to look for them up here?"

"We found it," Bob said.

George looked at Jones. "Deputy? What do you think?"

He shook his head. "I don't think Sheriff Sutter would have come up here, probably wouldn't have found it, and if he did, he would have come back to town for help. Too dangerous a place to be moving around on your own."

George nodded and looked up at the rock wall and along the ledge. Something had died ... nearby. It might be at the bottom of the rock bluff, but he didn't think so. The stench of death was coming from some place closer.

He took a few more steps, stepping around a bulge in the cliff wall, sliding his hand along the rock face to steady himself as the ledge narrowed. "Here," he said suddenly and reached for his cell phone. "This is where it's coming from."

A narrow opening, not over two feet wide, extended along one edge of the bulging rock upward from the ledge, forming a vertical crevice. Sliding sideways through the opening, an animal, or a person, could get to whatever was inside.

"I'll check it out. Probably nothing, or just a dead animal."

"Or a bear with a deer carcass waiting for someone to invade his turf," Bob warned.

"Thanks a hell of a lot for that," George said, and grinned. "But I don't think a bear could get in there."

"Just the same, there could be other ways in from above. Be careful."

"Always," George said, turning on the cell phone's flashlight as he squeezed through the gap. A moment later, they heard him say, "Son of a bitch."

"What is it?" Bob called in from the entry.

"They're here."

Bob came through the opening, blinked as his eyes adjusted, and put a hand over his mouth and nose to block the thick, putrid stench. It was useless. The cloying scent of death and decay quickly permeated everything—clothes, hair, skin, filling their nasal passages so they could taste it in the backs of their throats. Three decaying bodies, ravaged by scavengers and leaking their body fluids, lay on the floor of a small cave.

They had expected to find the missing men dead, but finding and smelling them in this condition forced Bob Shaklee, hardened investigator that he was, to mumble, "Holy shit."

Toby Jones came through the opening and immediately gagged. "Damn!" he said and turned to leave.

"Wait," George ordered and pointed. "Is that them?"

Jones stopped, turned, and stared at one of the bodies in the beam from George's flashlight. "He nodded. "That one there looks like Doyle ... Sheriff Sutter." He swallowed hard. "My God, it looks like something's been eating on his face."

"And the others?" George said, without giving him time to think about the sheriff's condition.

Jones' eyes followed the flashlight beam. "Could be," he said. "Probably is. Look to be about the right size as Ox and Harley, but I can't say for sure. I mean, the way they're falling apart and leaking out like that." He gagged again, and his cheeks puffed in and out as if trying to hold back a burst of vomit.

"Not in here," George said sharply. "Crime scene."

Hand over his mouth, Jones nodded and hurried back through the opening to the ledge, where he leaned against the rock wall, gagged again, and sent a stream of projectile vomit splashing on the rocks two hundred feet below.

23. A Heavy Chore

Inside the cave, George used his phone camera to record what they found. "We need a forensics team."

"Working on it," Bob said, returning to the ledge where the elevation allowed him to pick up a cell signal. He contacted Sharon Price in the OSI office, briefly explained what they discovered, and had her dispatch a GBI forensics team. To expedite things, he added, "Have Johnny Rincefield fly them to the Bayne County Airport in Dykes. Tell him we may want him to hang around until we sort things out."

"Rince will be happy about that. He's been flying drug enforcement patrol along the interstates for the GBI. He's ready to sink his teeth into some real detective work."

"Good," Bob said. "We are also going to need the GBI's Body Recovery Team. They'll need full rescue equipment, and tell them to make sure they send rock climbers with rescue experience."

"Not sure they have anyone like that," Sharon said.

"Tell them to find someone."

"Right. What else?" Sharon asked.

Bob thought for a moment. Someone had to brief the governor, but he didn't have the time or desire to deal with his bluster now. "Do me a favor, and you and Andy call Fullman and update him on what we found."

"He's going to want to hear that directly from you, Bob," Sharon said.

"You can tell him I'm too damned busy to call right now!"

Sharon pulled the phone away from her ear as his voice rose. "Alright, we'll call the governor, but you owe us ... big time."

"I know, Sharon." Bob's voice returned to its usual calm tone. "Sorry. Just a lot going on here."

Bob ended the call and turned to Toby Jones. "You ready to help?"

"Yes, sir," Jones nodded.

"Get on the radio and call in the other teams. Tell them we found the missing persons, but don't go into detail. Have one of your deputies go back to Dykes and meet our chopper and the GBI forensics team and bring them back to the clearing. Then you lead them up here." He looked over the ledge and shook his head. "Not sure how we're going to get their gear up here. We'll need to haul it up on ropes."

"Might be an easier way." Jones looked up at the rock wall. "The mountain summit is up there, another couple of hundred feet. Maybe the helicopter could lower the gear down by rope. Be faster and easier if the chopper pilot can handle it."

"He can handle it," Bob said.

"Yes, sir. Then I can get ropes from our volunteer fire department and have them meet him when he lands."

"Good idea, deputy," Bob said. "When you get back to the clearing, see if a couple of those National Guard mechanics can help operate the winch in the chopper. You'll need to stay at the clearing and lead the forensics team up on foot." Bob nodded. "I guess we have a plan. Let's get it done."

"Yes, sir," Jones said, happy to be contributing something more than nausea and to have a task to take his mind off of what he'd witnessed in the cave.

Bob was on the phone again, to Johnny Rincefield this time, explaining the need to lower the gear from the chopper to the ledge and confirming that the plan it workable. "What do you think, Rince? Can you handle that?"

"You give me someone capable enough to handle the winch and not fall out the door, and I'll get it done."

"Good. They'll meet you at the airport."

Jones turned to head back along the ledge, talking to the other search teams on the radio. By the time he was back at the clearing, Rince was airborne from Atlanta with the forensics team and their gear. Brian Mecham and Dave Pascal waited in the clearing with the National Guard and state troopers.

Jones explained the plan without going into detail about what they'd found. Then he sent Mecham and two of the National Guard mechanics in one of their trucks to the Bayne County airfield.

He turned to the state troopers and Lieutenant Giles. "GBI is sending a forensics team. Mr. Shaklee said this whole area is officially a crime scene now."

"Right." Giles turned to his men and gave orders to secure the scene and all the approaches to the clearing. Dave Pascal was assigned to assist, and the National Guard troops were dispatched around the perimeter to prevent curious locals from wandering in and disturbing any evidence they might not have found yet.

By the time Mecham and the mechanics arrived at the airport, Rince had the helicopter on final approach. Once on the ground, he hopped out and bustled about, overseeing the gear loading into the helicopter. The Bayne County Volunteer Fire Department was standing by with ropes, harnesses, straps, and buckles to secure it all.

Mecham piled the three forensics techs into the pickup, headed back up to the clearing, and turned them over to Jones. They were making their way along the deer trail to the path up to the ledge when Jones radioed back to get the helicopter enroute.

Rince piloted the chopper while the mechanics practiced operating the door winch he'd demonstrated before taking off. They may not have been much good at fieldwork, but were capable and experienced at working with their hands. In short order, they could operate the winch like experts or near enough for what they had to do.

Jones led the very nervous forensics technicians along the ledge to the cave. Documenting and collecting evidence from the most gruesome crime scenes was one thing, but their job description did not cover risking a two-hundred-foot fall.

They found George and Bob on the ledge outside the cave. George breathed in the clean, fresh air as deeply as he could, trying to clear the smell of decay from his nose and lungs.

Then he took one final deep breath and led the forensics team inside. The techs pulled out the Tyvek hazmat coveralls, masks, and latex gloves they'd stuffed in their pockets and followed.

It took a minute inside for them to don the gear between gasps for fresh air. Then George showed them the scene and detailed what he wanted. The forensics team began by photographing everything with the cameras they'd carried on straps around their necks.

Not long after they began, the helicopter arrived over the summit with their gear. Bob and Toby Jones signaled to Rince that he was in position, and the Guard mechanics on board began lowering the cases holding the forensics team equipment—fingerprint kits, evidence, body fluid sample materials, UV lights, magnifying equipment to find the smallest particles of evidence, and a wide assortment of collection bags and containers. Before the day was done, they would use all of it.

The sun was lowering by the time the forensics team completed their work. Bob and George decided to hold off until morning before trying to recover the bodies. The GBI's Body Recovery Team would have to rope down from above, enlarge the opening with an electric jackhammer, load the corpses into body bags and litters, and haul them by rope to the summit to be loaded onto another helicopter. Doing all of that in the dark was too risky, and after all, the bodies weren't going anywhere.

A second GBI forensics team arrived by car later in the day to process the clearing and shack for evidence. The results were minimal. Other than the fact that the plan was intricate, well-planned in advance, and seemed personally directed at the victims, nothing in the cave or the shack provided clues to the killer's identity.

When the forensics teams completed their work, a rotation for site security was set up with the National Guard troops. They would watch over the scene until the bodies were recovered the next day.

With all the details covered, George and Bob climbed into Toby Jones' pickup and headed back down the mountain. When he got a strong cell signal, Bob was on the phone with Andy and Sharon in the OSI office. George leaned his head against the window and closed his eyes. It was the end of a long and gruesome day, and he was exhausted.

"How long, do you think?" Jones asked as he drove. He'd recovered somewhat from the shock of finding his sheriff's body in a state of decomposition. Now, he wanted justice for Doyle Sutter.

"How long?" George said without opening his eyes.

"You know ... until we find the killer?" Jones said.

"I don't know," George said. "The trail is as cold as they get, and my brain is fried right now." He looked over at Jones and nodded reassuringly. "But we'll get on it first thing tomorrow. It's best to rest on it tonight and look at it again in the clear light of day."

"Okay." Jones was quiet for a moment, his forehead wrinkled as if trying to solve a problem.

George noticed. "What's the matter, deputy?"

Jones shrugged. "It's just that I need to tell them something."

"Sorry." George understood immediately. Someone had to let Mimsy Buxton and Chloe Sutter know their husbands were not coming home. "Sometimes I get caught up in the investigation and forget there are some things you need to handle locally."

"They're gonna ask questions, is all?" The concern on Jones' face deepened. "I don't know what to say."

"Fair enough." George nodded and sat up straight. "Keep it simple. Don't go into the details of what we found. No reason to upset them with what we saw. They'll be upset enough. Just let them know we found them dead in a cave ... cause of death unknown."

"Unknown?" Jones asked. "But ..."

"Unknown for now," George repeated. "It's true enough until the medical examiner makes the official determination of the cause of death. Tell them we'll give them a full briefing once we have more information."

"Right, simple." Jones nodded.

"And you don't have to mention what I said about this being a cold trail." George had made more than a few death notifications and knew it was never easy. Families always wanted more information than could be revealed during an ongoing investigation. "Tell them our task force is working on it, and you and the other deputies are part of it. As soon as we know anything, we'll give them an update."

Jones nodded, but the look of concern remained.

"You've never done this before, have you?" George asked.

"No." Jones shook his head. "Never had any reason to."

"You want some company when you make the notifications?"

Jones thought for a moment and shook his head. "No. They know me. I've been around them all my life. I think it's better coming from someone they know ... more personal, if you know what I mean. Strangers there will just make things harder." He looked at George. "If that's alright with you, I mean."

"Fine by me," George said. "And you're right. It's best coming from someone they know and trust."

"Alright," Jones said and stiffened his shoulders as if preparing himself for a heavy chore.

Part Two – A Bad Beginning

24. It Happened Like This

Clarence Buxton was a certified bully and a drunk. When the locals spoke of him, which they rarely did in his hearing, they simply described him as a *one mean bastard*. Named for his father, he hated the name, so his father took to calling him Junior. He hated that too, and at a young age, insisted on being called Ace. His father had no idea where the name came from and laughed at the idea.

His son didn't give up, and every time someone called him Junior his face reddened and he went home to argue with his father. Eventually, worn down by his arguing, his mother, Letty Buxton, went to her husband. She didn't like the name any more than his father but knew there was no use arguing with the boy any longer

"It's enough. I'm tired of the arguing. Let the boy be called whatever he wants. What difference does it make, anyway?"

"Never been done that way, that's what," Clarence Senior said.

"But what difference does it make?"

"How people going to know whose boy he is or what family he comes from?"

"They'll figure it out," Letty said. "But I'm telling you now, I'm tired of the fighting. Make it stop."

Her husband was quiet for a few seconds then nodded. "Alright. He can call himself whatever the hell he wants, but you tell him. I don't want nothing more to do with the little pissant on the subject of his name."

Clarence Junior Buxton became Ace, but it didn't happen all at once. At first, several classmates laughed and scoffed at the idea. After Ace pounded a few of their heads, the laughter ceased, and they took to calling him Ace. Eventually, everyone in Bayne County who knew him did the same. It was just easier to get along with a Buxton that way.

As Ace grew to adulthood, his reputation as a man who liked a fight spread, but these were no longer schoolyard brawls. On a couple of occasions, he beat men unconscious. No charges were ever pressed by the victims and the sheriff, Harvey Pursall, never prosecuted him, with the explanation that the fights may have been brutal but they were fair fights and the participants willing.

Along with being known as a fighter, Ace became known for his mean streak. Some said it was a mile wide. Others said he was just mean through and through. No one in Bayne County crossed Ace Buxton knowingly.

One autumn day, Clarence Senior died suspiciously in a hunting accident—shot in the back by a .30-06 rifle round. He'd gone off alone after deer and never returned. No suspects were identified, and although the sheriff called it an accident, rumors persisted that one person knew where Clarence always hunted and that person also owned a .30-06 caliber hunting rifle. Ace Buxton typically hunted with his father, but they had been arguing about a twenty-acre parcel of the family farm that demanded be signed over to him as a sort of birthright. Ace had gone around Dykes, bragging about how he was getting the family farm. When it never happened, people began to scoff at the idea—behind Al's back, of course, but he knew anyway.

What the locals didn't know was that Clarence Senior laughed at his son when he came to his father with the demand for the land. "Hah, boy. Get the hell out of here. There'll be time enough for that, but you got to earn it first, and right now, you haven't earned shit."

"You old son of a bitch!"

"I just might be what you say, but for saying it, you don't get shit until I'm dead and gone."

"That might be sooner than you think!" Ace stormed out of the house and stayed away until his father went out hunting that weekend.

"Clarence, you shouldn't be so hard on the boy." Letty Buxton was a Bible-reading, soft-spoken woman whose quiet nature made it difficult for her to intervene when her husband and sons argued, which they often did.

"Hard, my ass," Clarence shot back. "That boy wants something from me, he needs to earn it, and he ain't never earned anything but trouble."

"Yes, I know." Letty nodded. "Still, there are ways to explain it and keep the peace between you two. You know Ace is high-strung and prone to get angry quick. If you took the time to explain things ... give him a goal ... he might come along, and ..." Letty paused.

"And what, woman?" Clarence scowled.

"It's just that ... well, maybe things could be more peaceful here at home. Wouldn't that be nice? To have things more peaceful at home?"

"What did I do to break the peace?" Clarence shook his head. "He comes in here demanding I give what he hasn't earned, and I'm the one breaking the peace?"

"All I'm saying," Letty said, "is, maybe if you would help him see things instead of shouting and laughing him out of the house ... maybe he wouldn't want to fight with you all the time."

"Far as I'm concerned, that boy can go straight to hell. I'm not gonna coddle him. He needs to be a man, and if he wants a fight, I'm the man for it."

"Alright," Letty said meekly, having pushed the limits of questioning her husband as far as she dared. She went to the kitchen, sat in a chair, and opened the Bible she kept handy on the kitchen table's Formica top. Reading the words in it always calmed her after one of the family fights.

A minute later, the front door slammed. Clarence was going off to drink beer with his friends and tell them the laughable story that Ace wanted the land. A week later, Clarence Buxton was dead.

When he never returned from his hunt, Letty called Sheriff Pursall. The search party found Clarence's body up on the mountain near the family's deer camp. The location raised questions because of its proximity to the camp. It seemed unlikely that Clarence was tracking a deer so close to the shack in the clearing. Another hunter would have had to see the clearing before sighting in and pulling the trigger on what he thought was a deer.

In the end, Pursall had a lot of questions, most directed at Ace.

"Don't you own a .30-06 rifle?" he asked.

"Did," Ace said shortly. "Traded it over in Cartersville for a .30-.30 a fella had."

"Uh-huh." Pursall nodded. "And who was the fella you traded it to?"

"Don't remember. It was a swap meet. I didn't get any names. He looked at my rifle, and I looked at his, then we traded."

"I see."

Sheriff Pursall had a lot of other questions, but he didn't push too hard. Pushing Ace was never a good strategy, and Pursall only had a few more years before he could draw his county pension. He had no desire to spend the rest of his career looking over his shoulder dealing with Ace Buxton's vindictive nature. Just so he could say he'd been thorough in his investigation, he went to Letty and asked her if she had any idea who might be angry enough with Clarence to put a bullet through his back.

"Why, no one I know!" she said, her eyes widening at the prospect that her husband had been murdered.

"And everything's been peaceful around here?" Pursall asked.

"Here?" Letty frowned. "What are you getting at, Sheriff?"

"Nothing, really." Pursall shrugged. "Just covering all the bases, so to speak. You know, asking all the questions so we can put things to rest."

"Everything's been peaceful ... here and everywhere else as far as I know."

It was the answer Pursall expected, and if Letty suspected that her son might have murdered his father, she never let on. Pursall figured he'd done what he could and filed a report stating Clarence Buxton died in a hunting accident from a bullet fired by an unknown person.

By default, Ace became the head of the household and owner of the Buxton property. He took over the master bedroom in the house and allowed his mother to live in a small room off the back porch.

Oxford Buxton, ten years younger than Ace, was ten when his father died and idolized his brother. Ace, being who he was, loved being idolized, which meant he and Oxford shared the only close bond either had with anyone. When Oxford came to Ace one day and said he hated the name their father had given him and wanted another name like his brother, Ace thought for a moment and looked his brother up and down.

After a minute, he grinned and said, "Ox."

"What?"

"Ox. That'll be your name from now on. It suits you."

"Ox?" his brother said, smiled and nodded. "Like a bull ... big and strong."

Ace's grin widened. "And mean."

"Ox." His brother nodded emphatically. "I like it!"

From that moment, Oxford became known as Ox. When the word spread about his new nickname, no one argued. Ox had his brother backing him up in the matter, and everyone remembered the lessons learned and thumps received when Ace changed his name.

As Ox grew into manhood, he learned from Ace's harsh, bullying ways, mimicked them, and did everything he could to be even more intimidating than Ace. Eventually, Ox Buxton was an equally despised and feared bully.

They became a team, intimidating and threatening anyone in the county who dared defy them. Both found submissive women with no other prospects of marriage and terrified of living the rest of their lives as the old maids of the county.

That might have been the end of the story, two bullies living out their shabby lives in a small rural community, except they created a killer. It happened like this.

25. No One Hides

"Hold still, boy! You move again, and I'll beat you within an inch of your life!" Ace Buxton, a father now, lifted the wide leather belt high over his son's head, and when the boy flinched, he added, "I swear to God. You move your ass again, and I'll give you ten more and then another ten and another until there ain't nothing left of your back but bare bone."

Hob Buxton couldn't help himself. He let out a piercing yowl as the belt struck his bare back and, despite his father's warning, attempted to pull away and the next blow. True to his word, Ace went to work on his son with renewed vigor, his fury growing with every blow he rained on the boy's back.

"Ace, please, it's enough." Emma Buxton, the boy's mother, spoke softly. Speaking softly was always advisable around her husband. She had no idea what her son had done to merit this latest beating, but it didn't really matter. One real or imagined offense was enough for his father to lay into him.

When she spoke, Ace lowered his arm, the belt dangling from his hand, and she knew she had made a grave mistake. Without speaking, he turned and swung a backhanded fist that knocked Emma to the floor and split her lip.

She crawled to the kitchen to soak up the blood with a dishrag as best she could. Then she did what she always did. She took a pull from the bottle of cheap bourbon she kept stashed under the kitchen sink for just such times. The alcohol stung her battered lips but soothed the other hurts in her life. She winced and took another swallow and another until the bourbon began to ease the sting in her conscience.

Emma had no illusions. She was a weak woman and considered herself a terrible mother. She'd brought two sons into the world, and the days of their birth were the last bit of mothering they would receive, at least within Ace's seeing. She hated herself, blamed herself, and told herself she should stand up to her husband and protect her sons, but she didn't. She was terrified of the man who had fathered her children, an act accomplished more by forcible rape than lovemaking. Standing up to Ace was more frightening than walking outside in a category-five tornado.

Most of the Bayne County population agreed with her assessment of her mothering skills. They said she was a terrible mother from the safety of their front porches and Sunday socials, where there was no danger of being locked up behind closed doors with Al. Some of the harsher critics called her a coward. When the local church ladies gossiped in their Bible study circles and Emma's name came up, they shook their heads and wondered how God could have created a woman like her, lacking the normal mothering instincts. Emma was a coward, pure and simple, they said.

They said other things and used other words, but with all their words, they never came to her to offer a word of comfort or support. None of the local men, who were just as critical of Emma as their wives, ever confronted Ace about his treatment of his wife and sons.

In the front room, the beating continued until, bleeding and sobbing, his cries fading away into the night, Hob fell unconscious. Emma turned the bottle of bourbon up and drank again, hoping the burn would float her away into oblivion so she wouldn't have to hear what came next.

But she was too late. Before the alcohol completely deafened her ears, her younger son, Cal, cried out. "No! Daddy, no!"

The sound of the leather striking flesh, made her wince and cringe. With both hands, she lifted the bottle again and again, draining it until she slumped into a kitchen chair, her chin on her chest, the bottle dangling from a limp hand.

Cal's beating did not last as long as Hob's. It might be that his pleas struck a sympathetic chord with his father and persuaded him to go easier on the boy. It was more likely that Cal was simply weaker than Hob and always succumbed more quickly to his father's violence than his brother. Where Cal pleaded with his father, tried to reason, and apologize for whatever real or imagined offense they may have committed, Hob stood his ground and stared back defiantly. He might howl out in pain, but he never begged for mercy.

When both boys were prostrate on the floor, their father stood over them glaring, panting to catch his breath. A minute passed before he looked around and saw that his wife was not in the front room.

Where the hell was she, he wondered and knew immediately. "Bullshit," he growled. "You're as much to blame for this as them boys," he roared, although he could not have stated precisely what she had done other than to be present when he arrived home.

Ace stormed into the kitchen, reached out with a beefy hand, grabbed a handful of Emma's hair, and threw her to the floor. She never roused from her alcoholic stupor.

He eyed her for a moment and sneered, "You think it's that easy? Think you can hide from me in that bottle?" He spit on the floor beside her. "No one hides from me!"

He leaned over, ripped the faded cotton shift from her body, tore her underwear to tatters, forced her limp legs apart, and raped her on the kitchen floor. When he finished, sweating and grunting, he pushed himself up, glaring down at Emma.

She was awake now, eyes wide, confused, and terrified at the same time. Her hazy mind could think of nothing to do but shake her head and mumble, "No."

"Told you!" Ace roared, swinging a fist into the side of her head so that her eyes fluttered closed, and she sank back into unconsciousness. "Told you. No one hides from me!"

26. Bad Men

Ace and Ox Buxton grew up in Bayne County, had never lived anywhere else, and bragged they'd never been more than fifty miles from the county seat in Dykes, Georgia. Locals joked that they would gladly pay the cost of sending them far away if the brothers left and never returned. It was a joke they never repeated in front of the Buxton brothers.

The truth was that everyone cut them a wide berth, not because they were the toughest men in the county but because they never quit. More than one person they deemed guilty of some offense, real or imagined, learned that crossing the Buxton brothers would result in a never-ending stream of confrontations and harassment. Most people decided it just wasn't worth it. The few who stood up to them spent their time looking over their shoulders, waiting for some act of spiteful retaliation. Mysteriously flattened tires, broken windows, and poisoned pets were common methods of retribution if a Buxton took a disliking to you. For more serious offenses, barns or chicken coops might be discovered burned to the ground.

On at least one occasion, a house fire broke out in the middle of the night. The victim, Bob Toles, was the father of a boy that had been held down by Ox Buxton while his son, Harley, beat the shit out of him for laughing at him one day in school. Toles stopped Ox on the sidewalk in front of the courthouse square, grabbed him by the shirt, and pushed him up against a street lamp.

"You ever lay a hand on my boy again, and I'll give you a beating you won't forget." As big as Ox and all muscle, Toles leaned close into Ox's startled face. "You piece of shit, I swear to God, I'll make you pay."

Astonished passersby stopped in their tracks. Cars and trucks stopped on the street, their drivers craning their necks to see what was happening. No one had ever confronted one of the Buxtons in that manner.

Toles gave Ox a push that sent him stumbling backward and glared at Ox, waiting for a response. When there was none, he spat on the ground at Ox's feet and said, "You've been warned!"

The truth was that Bob Toles was as big and tough as either of the Buxton brothers, and no one doubted that he could do what he promised—beat the shit out of Ox or Ace, or both. But he was also gentle of nature and longsuffering. Had the offense against his son not been so grievous, the confrontation would likely never have occurred. Two boys settling a score with their fists was fine. Schoolyard fights were part of growing up in the rural south, but grown men holding down his fourteen-year-old son so Harley Buxton could flail away at his face was more than a father could bear.

Only the pleading of Cora, his wife, prevented him from doing what he promised that day in front of the courthouse. "They'll come for us," she said. "You know them Buxtons are bad men. We'll all pay the price if you do what you say." She shook her head. "There's got to be another way, Bob."

Toles thought it over for a second, then nodded. "Alright. I'll just give them a warning. They can't be putting their hands on our boy … not ever. I won't hurt no one, although God knows someone should."

Bob Toles was a reasonable man, and delivering a stern warning to Ox instead of beating his ass seemed like a reasonable compromise. So, Bob Toles went to town to deliver his warning and waited until Ox came along, as he did every day, glaring at anyone who dared to look him in the eye or even in his direction.

With a final thump in the chest from his beefy forefinger, he said, "You keep your hands off my boy, Ox. Don't try me on this point." Then he walked away.

When he arrived home, he told Cora to relax. He'd given notice to Ox to stay away from their son, but no violence was done. There was no reason to worry about retribution from the Buxton. "Fact is," Bob said, smiling. "Ox seemed kind of taken aback that anyone would stand up to him. If more people did likewise, those Buxtons wouldn't be near as tough as they seem."

"Lord, I hope you're right," Cora whispered, offering a silent prayer that God would soften the hearts of Ox and Ace, at least regarding the Toles family.

Two nights later, the Toles' house burned to the ground. The volunteer fire department responded, but it was far too late. Miraculously, the family survived. This was primarily because it was summer, and without central air conditioning in the old frame house, they slept with their windows open and an attic fan running to give them some relief from the heat.

When the family dog began barking, they woke and saw what was happening. Toles hollered at his children and grabbed the dog. Then they all kicked the screens from the windows and tumbled to the ground. Bob handed the dog through the window to Cora and was the last one out, escaping just moments before the roof trusses began to give way.

He gathered the family beneath an oak that had stood there since before the old house was built. As a boy, He climbed through its branches, and his children did the same. Now, the oak was all that remained of the homestead. Sobbing, the Toles family stood in the dark, watching the flames consume their home, converting it to glowing embers blowing away in the night sky.

Sheriff Pursall—now in his last term before retirement—conducted an investigation of sorts. As near as it could be determined, the fire started at a broken fitting from the propane tank that provided heating and cooking fuel. How the fitting broke, no one could say. It had never malfunctioned or given the Toles family a problem before, and the propane delivery company swore there was nothing wrong with it when their driver pumped a hundred gallons into the tank three days earlier.

The fire was hot enough to melt the propane tubing and steel tank, creating enough heat to ignite the house's old timbers. It destroyed any evidence of how it started, but everyone knew who was responsible. A week later, Bob Toles closed the garage he'd operated for twenty years, packed up his family in the pickup, and left Bayne County for good.

He would have gladly settled the score man to man. If it had been a matter of facing off with one or both of the Buxtons and if there was no one else to worry about, they could never have run him out of Bayne County. But he had a wife and children. They had survived the fire because their dog barked. If not for that … he didn't want to think about what might have happened. Bob Toles might not have personally feared the Buxton brothers, but he feared for his family. He would not risk their lives.

So, they left Bayne County and never returned. Grins on their faces, Ox and Ace leaned against the courthouse steps, watching the Toles family roll through Dykes in their pickup.

"Good riddance," Cora Toles muttered, glaring through the pickup's windows at the Buxton brothers.

"Sons of bitches," Bob grunted but drove on, swallowing his anger and the bile that welled up in his gut as Ace and Ox grinned and sneered as he went past.

From then on, the locals cut an even wider path to steer clear of Ace and Ox Buxton. For their part, the brothers continued to feed off each other's meanness. Bullying their wives and children and anyone else who got in their way.

The locals nodded to each other, careful not to catch the attention of Ox or Ace, and whispered among themselves.

"Those Buxton brothers are bad men," an outraged citizen would say. "Someone should stand up and do something."

"Who? You? And what would they do?" another would say, "Bob Toles tried to stand up to them, and you saw what happened."

"True enough," the outraged citizen would reply, nodding and then shut up.
Everyone saw what happened to Bob Toles and his family.

27. As Fate Would Have It

"Here, take a pull." Harvey Pursall, now the former sheriff of Bayne County, handed the flask across the desk to Doyle Sutter. "I'd say congratulations are in order."

"Thanks, Sheriff," Sutter said, leaning forward to take the flask. "I believe I will."

"Call me Harvey," Pursall said. "There's a new sheriff in town, thanks to you."

"Nothing I did," Sutter said, took a swallow from the flask, and handed it back. "You set things up. If you didn't stump for me, there's no way I'd have won the election. Web Seymour and his cronies were about to handpick your replacement."

"Wasn't going to let that happen." Pursall shook his head. "Being sheriff here may not be much, but it's important. Seymour thinks Bayne County is so backward we don't need a sheriff. You don't know how many times I've gone around and round with Seymour and the county commission to keep the funding coming."

He sighed and sat back in the chair. "That's why they wanted to appoint one of their own ... someone they could control ... and when the time was right, they could pull the plug on the funding and use the money for one of their pet projects."

"Well, you didn't let that happen." Sutter nodded and held out his hand for the flask.

"No sir, I didn't." Pursall handed the flask back to him, folded his hands over his belly, and smiled. "We may not have big-city crime, but that doesn't mean we don't need someone to keep the peace, and keeping the peace means the person wearing the badge needs to have a certain temperament." "He smiled and nodded. "I believe you have that temperament, Doyle. That's why I got behind you.

"And pushed," Sutter said, laughing. "Pushed pretty hard a few times."

"Well, I knew you wouldn't come along willingly."

***

It was true. Doyle Sutter had never aspired to be the sheriff of Bayne County. He'd helped out as a sort of unofficial part-time deputy, helping direct traffic at Grant's Funeral Parlor when someone died or running kids out from under the bleachers at high school football games. The extra cash the county paid him was nice to have, but he'd never done any real police work. Harvey Pursall was the sheriff and had been for as long as Sutter could remember.

It had taken some convincing. Pursall told him how the county needed a good man to replace him after he retired. Sutter wasn't convinced. He wasn't much more than a security officer and a poor substitute for an old-school lawman like Pursall.

Pursall persisted and spent much of his time the last two years of his term mentoring Sutter and convincing him to run for sheriff. As he built him up in the eyes of the local residents, he also managed to increase Sutter's confidence in his ability to do the job.

"I don't have any qualifications," Sutter had said.

"You got the right temperament," Pursall responded. "That's the most important thing. Sheriffing up here isn't like working for the FBI. You don't have to be an expert criminologist. You get elected, and they send you off to a special training course for new sheriffs like you. Hell, half of them never even saw the inside of a patrol car. Then every so often, you go off to some in-service training the state puts on for sheriffs."

"I don't know, Harvey." Sutter shook his head. "I don't know the first thing about solving crimes. Maybe one of your regular deputies would do better."

"They don't have the right temperament, and that's what you got ... the right temperament. Solid, stable, mature, and not one to be cowed by Web Seymour and his cronies."

Sutter was not convinced. "Like I said, it's just something I never thought about doing."

"Look, you're overthinking this. Crimes around here aren't like in the city. Mostly it's the kind of thing you grew up with in high school ... kids shoplifting, occasional burglary, redneck fistfights."

"Never was much of a fighter in school, and I'll be damned if I know the first thing about investigations, even simple ones," Sutter said, shaking his head.

"Trust me, you'll learn," Pursall said confidently. "Besides, if something serious comes along ... something you don't think you can handle, you call the Georgia State Patrol, and they'll send a trooper to back you. It might take a while, so you stay away from the danger until they get here. And then there's the GBI for any kind of serious investigation. That's what we pay them for."

Eventually, Sutter began to believe Pursall was right. He could handle the job, so after a few months of urging and Pursall explaining the salary and pension benefits he could expect, he said, "Alright, I'll do it."

"Good!" Pursall slammed a fist down on his desk and stood up to shake his hand. "Now let's go win an election so I can retire."

And they did. With Pursall's coaching, he made the rounds and visited key locations and people, asking for their support. Pursall knew the ropes and set it all up. Church congregations, women's clubs, the men's lodges, and local businesses, with Pursall at his side, Sutter visited them all.

Despite Web Seymour's notoriety and power in the county, Doyle Sutter was a shoo-in. Seymour had pushed his son-in-law, Kirby Towson, to run with the promise of a big bonus when they closed down the sheriff's office.

The Bayne County voters weren't fooled. They might be rural and, by big-city standards, politically unsophisticated, but they knew exactly what Web Seymour was up to. Having their own sheriff was a point of pride and distinguished them from the few rural Georgia counties with only a local constable for law enforcement. Besides, Harvey Pursall convinced them that Doyel Sutter was a pretty good man, and they were willing to give him a try.

When the vote came in, it wasn't even close. Doyle Sutter was elected sheriff by a landslide. Seymour was re-elected to the county commission, mostly because he had a pipeline to the governor's office and because he was adept at bringing in state funds for various pet projects, but the voters soundly rejected his meddling in the sheriff's department.

Kirby Towson soon left town, tail between his legs, more intimidated by his father-in-law's disappointment than by the rejection from the voters. Seymour blamed him for losing the election to a nobody like Doyle Sutter. He moved his wife and children to Atlanta, where he took a job selling cars at a dealership whose owner was the son of a college drinking buddy.

***

"Any advice for a rookie?" Sutter asked, sitting across from Pursall.

"Just be yourself," Pursall said. "Get to know the people, and they'll like you well enough." He leaned forward a bit and added, "And be nice to the Buxton boys. They are trouble and will make your life miserable if they get half a chance. Take care of the voters and stay clear of the Buxton boys as much as possible, and one day you'll be sitting here about to collect your pension and passing the badge to the next sheriff."

Then Pursall put his hands down on the desk's polished surface, pushed himself out of his chair, and stepped around. He grinned at Sutter and said, "Take a seat, Sheriff. Give her a spin."

Sutter stepped around the desk and sat in the chair. "Gonna have to make myself a new ass impression in this old chair," he said, wiggling his backside back and forth.

Both men laughed and took another celebratory pull from Pursall's flask. Neither had any idea that things would change one day, despite Pursall's assurance that nothing serious ever happened in Bayne County. As fate would have it, as sheriff, Doyle Sutter would be caught in the middle of it all.

28. The Greater Good

"How you boys doin'?" Sheriff Doyle Sutter stepped off the sidewalk in front of the courthouse to speak to the two boys huddled together in the back of the pickup. He leaned over the side of the bed to look them over. "Looks like you've had a rough day."

Both sat with their backs against the cab wall, knees up, heads down. The smaller of the two trembled and buried his face deep between his knees to keep from looking at the sheriff.

The older looked up and said, "We're fine," but the bruises on his arms and face and the bandage with a dark blood stain over his eye said otherwise.

The younger boy said nothing, but his shoulders shook with a sudden sob.

"You're Ace Buxton's boys, aren't you?"

The older boy nodded and looked away over the side of the pickup's bed as if alert for someone's approach.

"That means you'd be the one they call Hob, right?"

The older boy nodded again.

"Then this younger fella is Calvin," Sutter said, leaning closer, trying to get the boy to look up.

"He goes by Cal," Hob said and looked at the sheriff, then added, "You shouldn't be here."

"Why not?" Sutter smiled. "Just passing the time of day."

"Daddy won't like it," Hob said more firmly. "Now, go and leave us be."

"Don't worry. I'll explain to him. Can't blame an elected official for stopping to say hello and introduce himself to a couple of future voters."

Sutter let out a chuckle. Hob and Cal said nothing and kept their heads down.

"By the way? Shouldn't you boys be in school?"

Hob shrugged.

"Your daddy take you out for the day? Maybe do a little fishing with his sons?"

Hob shrugged again.

"What the hell do you want?" Ace Buxton came out of the hardware store and stormed across the street to the pickup.

Startled, Sutter whirled around, composed himself, and smiled. "Hello, Ace. Just passing the time with your boys."

"The boys are fine, and we're leaving." Ace walked up to within a few inches of Sutter's face. "Now, if you've got business with me, state it, or get your ass out of here."

Most people treated the sheriff with at least a bit of respect, if not for the man, then for the badge. Ace and Ox Buxton were not most people. They tended to push the limits of rude behavior with everybody, and the badge on Sutter's shirt had no tempering effect. If anything it was like waving a red flag in front of a bull.

"No offense intended. Just that it's a school day and here they are in the back of your pickup. Thought maybe you caught them playing hooky." Sutter jerked his head toward Hob, adding, "Looks like your older boy got himself in a helluva fight. I imagine that'll teach him a lesson about cutting class."

"What they been doing is none of your affair. Now, move out of the way before I back over you." Ace pushed past Sutter and jerked the pickup's door open.

Sutter heeded his advice and stepped up on the curb. Harvey Pursall had advised him to stay on the peaceful side of Ace and Ox Buxton, and he had heeded the advice. In a small community like Bayne County, there were too many places and too many ways to run into people who might hold a grudge, and the Buxton boys were famous grudge holders.

Still, as he watched the pickup roar out of town with the boys bumping along in the bed, he decided to pay the school a visit.

***

The Bayne County Consolidated School served the entire county. Funding was always scarce, and providing the usual separate schools to separate younger and older children was impossible. Every child from first grade through twelfth attended the same facility.

Doris Mills, history teacher, and school principal, had known Hob and Cal Buxton since they walked through the school doors. Each had been escorted by their mother, Emma, on their first day. After that, neither she nor her husband Ace ever attended a school function, parent-teacher conference, school play, or the advancement ceremony at the end of every school year.

Hob and Cal were on their own. The teachers found them intelligent but unmotivated and largely isolated from the other students who had been warned by their parents not to get too close. Becoming overly friendly with a Buxton might result in contact with their father, and neither the children nor their parents wanted that. So, Hob and Cal were outsiders. Except for interaction with some of their teachers over the years, they were completely isolated.

Sheriff Sutter parked in the gravel lot beside the small brick building that housed the school and went inside. He found Mills in the small principal's office adjacent to the front door.

"Morning, Doris," he said, standing at the door.

"Sheriff Sutter." Mills smiled. "Don't see you around here much. One of our students get themselves in trouble with the law?"

"No, ma'am. Just had some questions about a couple of the boys I ran across this morning."

"Well, in that case, have a seat and ask away."

"Thanks." Sutter sat in a plastic chair usually reserved for children sent to the principal's office for various disciplinary reasons.

"So, who did you run across today?" Mills asked.

"The Buxton boys, Hob and Cal."

"Oh." Mills brow furrowed. "Were they out and about?"

"So to speak," Sutter said. "Found them huddled down in the back of their father's pickup. They looked pretty concerned that I walked up and spoke to them. The older boy, Hob, was bruised up pretty bad."

"Hmm." Mills sat back in her chair and nodded. "Sounds about right."

"How so?"

"Ace Buxton is a hard man, but he seems to be hardest on his sons."

"You saying he put those bruises on Hob?"

"I'm saying it's not out of the question," Mills said.

"Has Hob been in any fights around school? Sometimes boys get into things without telling the grownups."

"Sometimes." Doris nodded and shrugged. "But I don't know."

"You said them being bruised up sounded about right," Sutter persisted. "What did you mean by that?"

Mills leaned forward and lowered her voice before responding. "I mean, I can't count the number of times those boys have come to school battered and bruised ... broken bones on a couple of occasions ... lots of cuts and split lips."

"You report any of it?" Sutter asked.

"To who? You?" Mills shook her head. "Or Harvey Pursall before he retired. No, I didn't report it ... not officially, at least."

"What does that mean?"

"It means I talked with Harvey a couple of times. He said he would check and ask around, but it didn't come to anything. In the end, he let it drop."

"You never talked to the boys about their treatment at home?" Sutter frowned.

"Don't take that disapproving tone with me, Doyle Sutter." Mills' voice rose a few decibels. "Yes, I asked them a few times ... discreetly and off the record."

"And?"

"And nothing. They either wouldn't speak or said they got in a fight. When I asked with who, they clammed up and wouldn't say another word. I let the matter drop. If they didn't want to report it, I wasn't going to force them. So, don't get judgmental with me."

"Sorry," Sutter said. "That's not what I meant."

"Of course it is," Mills snapped back, then took a breath and forced herself to lean back in the chair again. "Truth is, I've passed judgment on myself plenty of times worried about those boys. I know it's their father who beats them like that, but the last thing I want here is for Ace Buxton to show up at this school making threats ... or worse."

"Worse?"

"You know what happened to Bob Toles and his family when he threatened Ox for putting hands on his boy. I have to think about the school, the other children, and their families. What's happening to those boys is a sin, and I hope Ace Buxton burns in hell, but I had to put the other children ahead of those two boys. I thought it was the greater good." Her eyes narrowed. "So did Harvey Pursall."

"Someone could have gone to Child Protective Services," Sutter offered, knowing the response he would get.

"Who? You?" Mills shook her head. "And what do you think Buxton would do then. He'd know it was you, or me. Harvey and I talked about that too, and we knew that there was no telling what type of murderous act of revenge Buxton would take on the school and everyone associated with it." Mills shook her head. "No, we did what we could. We protected the others. That Hob and Cal had to pay the price for it is terrible but not our fault."

"Alright." Sutter nodded. "I appreciate you talking openly about this with me, Doris." Sutter stood and turned to the door.

"You won't say anything about our conversation, will you, Doyle?"

"No, Doris. I won't say a thing."

His next stop was a small office two blocks off the courthouse square. A bronze plaque on the wall beside the door read, *Henry Rush, MD*. Sutter walked through the door, looked around the empty waiting area, and called out, "Anybody here?"

A graying man in a white lab coat came from the backroom. "Doyle, what brings you here?" Dr. Rush bustled about the waiting area straightening chairs and magazines. "Sorry. My receptionist is off visiting family in Atlanta today, so I thought I'd tidy up some."

"No problem," Sutter said. "I just wanted to ask you some questions about Ace Buxton's boys."

Rush frowned, stopped what he was doing, and turned. "We better go back to my office."

He led the way and, when they were settled into chairs, asked, "What questions, Sheriff?"

Sutter reviewed his encounter with the Buxton boys and their father. The doctor listened attentively, nodding now and then and adjusted his glasses.

"And all of this means what to you?" Rush asked when Sutter finished.

"Don't know that it means anything much," Sutter said. "Maybe more curiosity than anything ... for the moment. I'm in my second year as sheriff and still trying to get a feel for everyone in town. Harvey Pursall told me to tread lightly around the Buxton family, so I haven't really had much to do with them yet."

"If you're smart, you won't ... ever," Rush said bluntly, then leaned forward. "What you really want to know is if I think Ace Buxton is physically abusing his sons."

"I suppose so." Sutter nodded.

"Of course, he is," Rush said sharply. "He beats the shit out of them." He shrugged. "Maybe for a good reason, maybe not, but I've been stitching and patching up those boys almost since they were born."

"Talked to Doris Mills over at the school," Sutter said. "She went through it all with me ... do the best we can for the other children ... protect them and all. I get that. Just wondering if you had any other opinion on that."

"No," Rush said flatly. "There is no other opinion to have. Doris is right. Bayne County is a good place to live and raise a family. Children grow up here, go off to school or into business, start families, and live happy lives."

Rush folded his hand on top of his desk as if reviewing an unpleasant diagnosis with a patient. "In my experience, it's best not to come between a father and his boys. So, I take care of their physical needs, treat their injuries, and yes ..." He nodded solemnly. "I send them home with their father, knowing it will happen again."

"Have you ever thought of reporting it?" Sutter asked and, seeing the look on Rush's face, added quickly, "Not that I am saying you should have. Not accusing you of anything, Doc, just asking."

"Of course, I have thought about reporting the abuse," Rush said, his voice softening. "We all have, but we also all have families and lives here. Unless you tell me, you'll spend the rest of your life camped outside my house with your rifle loaded and ready, I'm doing what I can."

Rush shook his head. "Besides, if you did tell me you'd spend your time watching over me and my family, I wouldn't believe you. What about your family? Your wife? You'd have to take care of them." He gave a wry smile. "You see the dilemma. This is a peaceful community. People get along ... except for the Buxtons. They are the infection among us, and with any infection, unless you are willing to cut off the infected part, you isolate and prevent it from spreading. People around here have decided to isolate the infection and stay as far away from Ace and Ox Buxton as possible."

"And Don't judge us too harshly, Doyle." Rush shrugged. "I'm not a violent man ... not a fighter. Most people around here are like me, hardworking, good people, but not fighters. Unless you're willing to risk everything to take on Buxton, there's no way to stand up to them."

Sutter sat quietly for a few moments before nodding and standing. "Thanks, Doc."

He turned to leave, and Rush felt he had to say something else. Doyle Sutter was struggling with his conscience in the same way that Rush, Sheriff Pursall, Doris Mills, and others had. Most everyone in the county who'd interacted with Hob and Cal felt some pang of guilt for doing nothing to help them. The difference was that Sutter was just coming to grips with it and hadn't had time to reach his own conclusions.

"Doyle," he called out before the door closed. "There's nothing else to do about it. What can we do? We all took a whipping when we were young, sometimes for good reason."

Sutter stopped and turned. "Like that? Like what I saw?" There was no anger or outrage in his voice. The look on his face was one of a man trying to solve a puzzle.

"Maybe not like that," Rush answered. "But sometimes, maybe they were as bad. I don't remember every time because my daddy laid into me plenty when I was a boy. I'm sure I deserved most of the whippings I took from him."

Doyle Sutter spent the rest of the day cruising the county's backroads, pondering his conversations with Doris Mills and Henry Rush. Whatever he decided to do, if it involved going up against the Buxtons, he would do it alone. There would be no help from anyone else.

Rush called it a dilemma. Harvey Pursall had made peace with that dilemma by learning to be friendly with the Buxtons, as much as that was possible. Pursall was not a weak man, but he recognized that he could not stand up alone to a threat that would come from out of nowhere when it came, and one thing was certain. If you stood up to the Buxton brothers, they would become a threat.

Doyle Sutter faced the same dilemma as the rest of Bayne County. He had a wife, family, and home to protect. He remembered something Doris Mills said earlier. Protecting them was the greater good. As he drove and thought things through, he began to think that she might be right.

29. Bless My Boys

Life at home for Hob and Cal Buxton was mainly a matter of staying away from their father and avoiding the next beating. Hob tried to protect Cal as much as possible, taking the blame for his brother's occasional alleged offenses against their father, but these were few. Most of Ace's fury was directed at Hob, anyway.

The reason wasn't clear, except maybe to Ace. Emma begged her husband to ease up on the boy, but as the years passed and Hob approached manhood, Ace's fits of rage directed at his oldest son grew worse. The beatings that accompanied them also became more severe. Hob's tortured life at home came to a head not long after his eighteenth birthday, an occasion that merited no remembrance in the Buxton household other than a whispered, "Happy birthday," from his mother.

He returned home from his after-school job at the hardware store in Dykes to find his father waiting on the front porch, a half-empty fifth of bourbon on the planks beside the step. Ace sat glaring out at the world. Head down, Hob stepped around him and started up the steps without speaking.

"Know what's wrong with you, boy?" Ace stood up, blocking the way, and standing nose to nose with Hob.

Hob waited, silent. The best course of action when Ace was fixed on picking a fight was silence. Just listen to the bullshit, then go inside and check on Cal. Besides, there was no way of guessing what Ace thought was wrong with him today.

"You got no manners. That's what's wrong!" Ace shouted, wavering unsteadily a little on the narrow steps. "I'm your damned father, and you treat me with no respect! What do you got to say to that!"

They stood close, Ace's alcohol tainted and spittle breath in Hob's face, but Hob said nothing. He waited for the tempest to pass or for Ace to do whatever he had in mind, which always involved bruises.

"You little son of a bitch!" Ace lifted a fist and caught Hob on the cheekbone under his left eye, sending him off the steps to the dirt.

It wasn't the first time it had happened, but something changed in Hob. Usually, he would have waited in the yard for his father, prepared to defend himself as best he could, but for some undefinable reason, this time, he didn't wait.

Hob went on the offensive. Who knows why this time and not one of the thousands of others during his life. Hob couldn't have answered the question himself. Whatever triggered it, his breaking point had been reached. Now, years of his own rage boiled out.

Charging headlong into Ace, he knocked him back on the steps. Before his father could regain his balance, Hob grabbed him by the shirt and pulled, sending his father face forward into the ground.

Ace was far more powerful than his son, but Hob was quicker, more agile, and although not as heavily built as Ace, he was well-muscled from physical labor. He leaped on top of Ace and pummeled him with his fists, raining blow after blow down.

Ace slowly recovered from the shock of the attack, managed to force Hob off, and rolled over on his stomach to push himself up to his feet. Hob scrambled away, jumped up, and while Ace struggled to stand, wobbling under the effects of the alcohol and the attack, he reached for the shovel leaning against the porch.

It had come to this. Now, he would finish it.

Raising the shovel to his shoulder like a batter at the plate, he swung, catching Ace in the side of the head. The blow knocked him back to his knees, stunned and swaying.

"It's time, you old bastard!" All the years of beatings and torture at his father's hands crashed through his memory at once like a tidal wave. He swung again, catching Ace in the back.

Ace fell forward on his stomach, moaning. Stunned and in shock, he tried to get his arms under him to push himself up from the ground but fell forward again.

Hob raised the shovel high over his head. It was time to end this now.

"No!" Emma cried out as he was about to crush his father's skull. "No! You can't, Hob!"

She ran to her son and put her arms around him for the first time in years. Her tears streaming down and falling wet his arm caused him to turn his head in surprise. He turned his head to look at her.

"Hob, you can't do it. He might deserve it ..." She shook her head, and more tears fell. "God knows he does deserve it, I know it, but you can't."

Hob turned his head toward her, a look of disbelief on his face. "Why? You said it. He deserves it ... for everything ... for what he's done to you and Cal, to all of us."

"Because they'll put you away in prison, or worse, send you off to death row. They do that around here. I can't lose you ... not like that."

"I'm already lost. I do this for you and Cal. What happens to me after doesn't matter."

"It does matter, son. To me, it matters." Emma cried and sank sobbing to her knees. "I can't lose you like that. I'm not the mother you should have had, not even close. I've cursed myself for it every day since you were born, but I always hoped that when the day came that you left, it would be to a better life far away, not to spend the rest of your years in some Georgia prison. I couldn't bear that, son. Please, I beg you, don't do this."

Slowly, Hob lowered the shovel. He breathed heavily for several seconds, letting his fury dissipate into the afternoon air. Then, he nodded. "Alright, mama."

"Thank you, son. Thank you." Emma wrapped her arms around his knees and hugged him for a minute awkwardly, then she stood, wiping the tears from her face. "Now, you have to go."

"Go?" Hob's forehead wrinkled, eyebrows raised. "Go where?"

"Away," Emma said. "You go to the city, someplace where he can't find you, because when he gets up, he'll come looking. You know how Ace is. After what you did today, he'll kill you."

Hob shook his head. "I can't leave you and Cal. He'll take it out on you."

"No, he won't," Emma said. "Not too much anyway, and we can handle it. We've been handling it for years, but if he finds you, he won't stop until you're dead, and you won't take him by surprise next time."

She took him by the arm, pleading. "Go and make a home somewhere, and when you get settled, Cal can come live with you where it's safe."

He knew she was right. Take his father's life, and he'd go to prison or worse. His mother and brother would be alone to fend for themselves with no family but his uncle, Ox Buxton, just another version of his father. Trading one devil for another was not the answer.

"Alright," he said. "I'll go, but I'll send money back to the bank in Dykes for you and Cal."

"Don't worry about money. Just go before he wakes up and comes to his senses."

Cal had come out on the porch to watch the drama and hear the conversation. He wept, shaking his head. "What am I going to do when you're gone."

"You stay here until I get settled, and I'll send for you. Then you and Mama can live with me, and ..." He nodded at Ace, moaning again, and moving about slightly. "It'll be someplace where that old bastard can't hurt you ever again."

He turned and trotted two miles down the gravel drive to the county road. It was well after dark before he made it to the state highway. Too late to thumb a ride, he slept in the woods at the roadside and, in the morning, began making his way south, hitching rides when anyone stopped for him.

Two days later, Hob Buxton stood in an Army recruiting office in Atlanta. Skills testing, physical exams, and an interview with a neatly uniformed man with bars on his collar took some time. Hob managed to secure a bed at one of the homeless missions downtown, living off the money in his wallet.

The two hundred dollars he'd been paid by the hardware store in Dykes wouldn't last long. With no job prospects or contacts in Atlanta, the Army seemed a good solution to doing what his mother had asked—putting together a life and making a home for Cal and her.

Hob had always been mentally quick and passed the exams easily. Physically, he was a young man in good shape, although the doctor noted on his record the evidence of several previously broken bones, more than one would have expected from even an active boy. Still, since they seemed to have no effect on his physical abilities or strength, the doctor signed off and passed him.

After that, Hob was sworn in and bussed off to basic training. When his pay started coming in, he had the money sent to his bank account in Dykes with instructions to let his mother know it was there and to give her access.

Ace recovered, from his injuries, although he carried a scar on the side of his face from the shovel blade. Fueled by his fury for Hob, his fits of rage worsened. Emma and Cal stayed out of his way as much as possible, but they couldn't avoid him altogether and something—sometimes their mere presence—would trigger a new bout of beatings and abuse.

If anyone asked Ace about Hob's whereabouts, his standard response was, "The little pissant run off, like the sniveling, coward piece of shit he is."

When Ace was not around, Emma and Cal offered up prayers for Hob. Emma's was always the same. "God, please bless my boys and protect them."

30. Emma's Pain Ended

Emma was wrong. Despite the reassurance she gave Hob when he left, she and Cal could not handle the increased abuse Ace rained down on them day after day. She thought of taking Cal and running away, but there was nowhere to run, and even if there was, she had no money or means to travel. They were prisoners.

The house in the woods miles from the nearest neighbor was a dungeon to them, a place from which there was no escape. Ace came and went as he pleased, and Cal was allowed to attend school to keep up appearances. Emma spent all her days sitting at a window, the bottle of bourbon always at hand. Her world became an alcohol-blurred wasteland where she used the bottle to dull the pain of her failure to protect her children and find a means of escape from the monster she'd married.

As for Ace, he liked her drinking. Drinking made his wife even more pliable. He could leave for hours or days and always find her sitting by the window with her bottle, submissive, shrinking away from him if he threw a glance in her direction. Ace Buxton loved the feeling of power he derived from the nervous twitch of her fingers and the tremble in her voice when he spoke to her.

One day, he came in after dark, thumping up the porch steps. The color drained from Cal's face at the sound of his father's heavy steps. Seated on the floor near his mother, he was about to rush to his room at the back of the house when the door burst open. Ace stomped in, eyes blazing angrily, his face red with rage.

They never found out what he was angry about. It didn't matter. Cal moved to a corner and huddled down, trying to make himself as small a target as possible.

"You little fucking shit!" Ace shouted. "I won't have you skulking around in the corners. Get your ass over here!"

Cal huddled down farther, head between his knees.

"Goddamnit! I said get your fucking ass out of that corner!"

Cal huddled down more and began sobbing. "No, Daddy. Please. I didn't do anything."

"Then why the fuck you cowering over there?" Ace hollered and stomped across the room toward him. "You did something ... today or some other day ... it doesn't matter. Either way, you got a beating coming."

"Why?" Cal pleaded. "I've been here all day, like you said."

"Because I said. That's reason enough!"

The first blow struck Cal in the back of the head so that it snapped forward and bashed his nose against his raised knees. He lifted his face, blood pouring from his nose, shaking his head. "Please, Daddy. No more."

"I'm just fucking starting on you, boy."

Ace's heavy fists rained down on Cal's head so that it banged into the wall with every blow. Cal began to fade into unconsciousness, and Ace struck harder. "Stay up and take it, boy, like a man!"

"Ace, stop," Emma whispered from her chair. She focused her bleary eyes on her husband and spoke more loudly. "You're hurting the boy. Stop it."

Ace didn't stop and didn't bother looking her way. He focused on his target, making every blow count.

Emma said nothing more. Why it happened that day is a mystery, or maybe it was an act of God, a whisper into her tortured soul that she had to do something this time.

She pushed herself from the chair, moving robotically as if some switch inside her had been thrown, and electric impulses from an unseen source controlled her body.

Staggering to the shelf by the door where Ace kept his guns, she reached for one of the rifles hanging on a rack but noticed the revolver on the shelf between two boxes of .44 shells. She lifted it, and the weight dragged her frail arm down. Using both hands and all the strength in her arms, she lifted it and turn toward her husband. "Ace, stop. Look at me."

He didn't. When the shot thundered and the pistol bucked in her hands, she nearly dropped it. Emma was almost as surprised as Ace as he spun and howled, clutching the gaping exit wound in his gut where the .44 magnum round exited before plowing into the wall.

"You fucking bitch! You shot me!" He took two steps toward her before crumpling to his knees and rolling on his side, wailing in pain. "Call me a doctor, you bitch. Do what I say!"

For the first time in her life, Emma did not do what her husband ordered. She looked toward her son and saw Cal's bruised and bleeding face. He was unconscious but breathing. Then, she took three steps toward her husband and looked down.

Ace opened his eyes and saw her standing there. "I said call the doctor." He spoke between clenched teeth, fighting the pain and trying to remain conscious, staring up at her from the floor.

Emma lifted the pistol with both hands and fired twice more. Each shot nearly bucked the big gun from her hands, but she held on. The bullets smashed through Ace's chest, and his breathing ceased. He still stared, but his eyes were empty, devoid of all awareness and emotion. No anger, no hatred, no rage, or taunting. The man whose very presence terrified her was ... nothing ... just an empty thing on the floor. The blood seeping from the wounds had more life than the body from which it seeped. Ace Buxton would never torture them again.

Satisfied, she lowered her arms and stood for a moment in the middle of the room, uncertain what to do next. Cal remained curled up and battered in the corner but alive. She thought for a moment, then shuffled unsteadily to the kitchen, where she took a notepad and pencil from a drawer. It was the pad she used to make her grocery lists for the rare times Ace allowed her to go into Dykes to the store.

Placing the gun on the table, she fell back into a chair and wrote on the pad. The alcohol made it difficult, and the pencil was hard to control, her handwriting a wavy, whirling scrawl. When she finished, she lifted the pad and squinted at it for several minutes, making sure she had written everything down. Once, she lifted the pencil and added a few words, then looked at the pad again and nodded.

She stood from the table and, taking the gun with her, returned to her chair and the bottle of bourbon. She took a few sips before making a call on the phone she kept by the side table.

When she finished, she surveyed the scene. Cal—still huddled in the corner. Ace—dead and, for once, harmless on the floor. The note—on the kitchen table.

The pistol was too heavy for her thin arm and hand to hold to the side of her head, so she leaned back, rested it on her breast with the barrel under her chin, and with her thumb, pulled the trigger.

Emma's pain ended.

31. A New Hell

Ace missed the morning strut around the courthouse square with his brother, Ox. It was a ritual they had practiced for years and included taunting, smirking, intimidating, bullying, and generally being a pain in the ass to anyone who crossed their paths.

Locals who watched them from a safe distance and out of hearing sometimes made comments under their breath.

"Look at them. Two roosters strutting around the barnyard, letting everyone know who the cocks of the roost are."

"More like pricks," someone would add.

"Wrapped up in assholes," another might chime in.

Then the onlookers would chuckle softly among themselves, careful not to let the Buxton brothers overhear.

Ace had occasionally missed the ritual, usually when he was sleeping off a drunk from the night before. When he didn't show up later that day for the afternoon pint of bourbon they routinely sipped sitting in the shade of an old oak, Ox became concerned. He tried calling Ace's cell phone, then the house, and when there was no answer, he decided to investigate.

He arrived to find the yard filled with vehicles. Sheriff Sutter and two deputies, a hearse from the funeral parlor in Dykes, and an ambulance from the fire district in the next county had parked their vehicles in an arc facing the front door. He rushed into the house, saw Ace and Emma's bodies, and spotted Cal, still huddled and barely conscious, in the corner.

"You little son of a bitch, you did it!" Ox Buxton roared. "You fucking killed my brother!"

"Calm down," Sheriff Sutter said. "Cal didn't do it. We got a call from Emma ... said she had done it ... that Ace was dead and we should come pick up Cal and take him to foster care."

He held up the notepad they'd found on the kitchen table. "She left this. Says what she did, goes on about her being a failure as a mother, but she had to protect Cal."

"Protect Cal!" Ox whirled to stare at Cal again. "Ace was his father. You don't protect a boy from his father! If Ace whipped his ass, the little pissant deserved it."

"Anyway." Sutter shrugged. "Pretty clear that she did it. Even without the note, we found the pistol in her lap." He nodded at Emma's body still in the chair, head thrown back grotesquely, her face deformed by the impact of the .44 slug. "Murder suicide, for sure."

Two deputies photographed the bodies. Ox stepped toward Emma, fist balled as if he might strike her corpse.

"Ox," Sutter said and moved between him and the body. "You should go outside. This is a crime scene. Everything needs to be left just like we found it. The state GBI boys are coming over to do an official investigation. They'll let you know what they figure out, but I'm pretty sure it's going to be what I said. Murder suicide."

Ox stood fuming for a few seconds, then turned toward Cal. "He's coming with me."

He walked to the corner, grabbed Cal by the arm, and jerked him to his feet. Cal wailed in pain.

"Emma was pretty clear in the note that she wanted him to go to foster care," Sutter said but made no effort to intervene.

"He's my brother's boy, and I'm his next of kin," Ox said, looking hard into Sutter's face. "He's coming with me, and no one's going to stop me."

And no one did.

As Sheriff Sutter predicted, the GBI investigators concluded that the deaths resulted from a murder suicide. Their report concluded that Emma Buxton killed her husband and then herself in a fit of rage. No mention was made of her confession or the guilt she felt for failing to protect her son. Cal's injuries were never mentioned.

***

Ox Buxton retained custody of his nephew, despite Emma's plea in her note that Cal be placed in foster care. The Georgia Department of Child Protective Services sent a caseworker from Dahlonega. She visited Ox and Mimsy Buxton at home and found no reason for Cal not to remain with his uncle. Mimsy was sympathetic and gentle and assured the caseworker she wanted to care for Cal. Ox was gruff, but there was no sign that he abused his son, Harley, who was in good physical and mental health and showed no signs of abuse.

Despite the wishes outlined by Emma in her suicide note, Cal did not go to a foster home. The caseworker decided that the note was written by a woman who was clearly unbalanced, had just murdered her husband, and was about to take her own life. There was no reason to use it as a guide to her child's placement in foster care or to believe that Ox and Mimsy would not provide a safe family environment for Cal.

Cal's injuries eventually raised questions, and the caseworker scheduled a thorough physical examination with the only available local physician, Dr. Rush. The day Ox brought Cal in for the exam, Rush was waiting with the caseworker, who wanted to meet with Cal privately for a few minutes before the exam began. Cal remained quiet and would only communicate nonverbally with nods or head shakes.

The caseworker began by asking, "Are you being treated well by your uncle?"

Nod—yes.

"And your aunt and cousin?"

Nod.

"Are you happy living with your uncle?"

A slight shrug, followed by a nod. The caseworker decided his hesitation was understandable. In her notes, she commented that being ripped from his family in such a tragic way would undoubtedly make him confused and unsure about what would happen next.

"Did your father or mother cause your injuries?" She smiled to reassure him. "It's alright to tell me the truth. You're safe here."

Cal nodded.

The caseworker frowned and asked, "Your father?"

Head shake—no.

That was a new wrinkle, and the caseworker scribbled it on her pad. "Your mother?"

Nod, then another nod.

Things were beginning to make sense. It was a reversal of the roles commonly played in these scenarios. Instead of the father, an abusive mother severely injured her son—unusual, she noted in the file. When the father returned home and tried to intervene, the mother shot him and then killed herself. Clearly, she was mentally and emotionally unstable. The guilt manifested in her suicide note for failing to protect her son stemmed from her own abuse of the boy.

The caseworker continued making notes for several minutes. This was one for the books, she thought. It might even be one to take to the symposium the department required caseworkers to attend as part of their ongoing education credits. She could picture herself leading the discussion as the other caseworkers listened to the unique story—an abusive mother and protective father who paid with his life to try and help his child.

Cal sat silently and stared at the floor while she wrote up her notes.

Ox and Dr. Rush waited in a separate exam room.

"You know how this goes down," Ox said. "No one speaks bad about my dead brother. We made sure the boy knows what to say ... what he better say. Do I have to go over things with you?"

"That won't be necessary." Rush shook his head. "What's done is done. I'll give him an exam and make sure there's nothing life-threatening about his injuries."

"And you got no opinion on how he got hurt," Ox said. It was a warning, not a question.

"I understand," Rush said.

A few minutes later, the caseworker escorted Cal into the exam room. "I'll leave him with you, Dr. Rush. He gets a thorough physical exam before we finalize his status."

"It'll be thorough," Rush said. "Now, if you'll leave us alone, I'll get busy. A teenage boy doesn't need an audience for something like this."

"Right." The caseworker turned to leave.

Over her head, Ox gave Rush a hard stare, a warning. Rush nodded. Message received.

The doctor took his time with the exam. It had to appear thorough. Now and again, he made a note on a clipboard chart, documenting Cal's injuries—numerous contusions, blood vessels broken in his eyes, a couple of hairline fractures in an arm and two ribs. He concluded by adding the notation that the injuries were consistent with those one would expect from a physical attack but not life-threatening.

Afterward, he waited for Cal to dress, then escorted him to the waiting room. The caseworker read Rush's notes slowly, then reviewed each documented injury, asking questions.

"One final question, Dr. Rush." Could a woman like the boy's mother have inflicted these injuries?"

"Yes, I'd say so," Rush said, avoiding Cal's eyes. "The injuries I documented there could definitely have been caused by a woman in authority, like a mother. A submissive personality like Cal's would be reluctant to defend himself. I imagine he huddled down and just took it, waiting for things to blow over." Rush shook his head sadly and cast a glance at Ox. "Too bad his father didn't get home in time to protect him."

"Fair enough." The caseworker closed her notepad and stood. "That should wrap things up." She put a hand on Cal's shoulder. "You can go along home with your uncle and settle in. Things will be better now, you'll see."

Cal left with his uncle to begin life in his new hell.

32. No One Had Done Right

Despite the promise made by the Child Protective Services caseworker, things did not get better for Cal. They became infinitely worse. Ox did his best to fill his dead brother's shoes and more than succeeded.

Given the slightest reason or no reason at all, he would lay into Cal with a vengeance. The mere sight of his nephew in the house reminded him that Ace was dead, and somewhere in his warped mind, he held Cal responsible for it.

As time passed, the abuse Ox heaped on Cal increased to the point that Cal would lie awake at night and wish he was back with his father. The beatings then might have been frequent, but at least there were breaks, times when he could stay out of sight and avoid being pummeled for a while, at least.

In Ox's house, there were no breaks. The violence directed against him was constant, and Ox soon had an assistant in tormenting the boy.

Ox's son Harley was thrilled to have Cal in the house to deflect his father's abuse. He soon discovered that by mimicking Ox, he could bully Cal without repercussions. In fact, his father took pride that his son was becoming more like him each day. Their joint abuse of Cal created a perverted bond between father and son.

Cal's life became a series of beatings, kicks, and slaps administered by Ox when he was present or by Harley when he was not. Ox and Harley ganged up on the boy like schoolyard bullies, looking for new ways to make his life miserable.

Cal's thoughts about his mother were confused and bitter. She had hidden herself in a bottle to dull the pain of watching her son's torment. Then, when she finally did something about it, she only made things worse by taking her life along with Ace's and leaving Cal at the mercy of his uncle.

In time, the years of abuse took their toll.

***

"Cal Buxton! Sit up straight and pay attention." Doris Mills stood beside Cal's desk in her history class and rapped the surface hard with her knuckles.

"What?" Cal grunted but barely stirred.

"I said, sit up straight and pay attention." Mills snapped.

"I ... I don't ..." Cal managed to open his eyes and gaze sideways up at the teacher. "What did you say?"

Mills turned to the rest of the class and said, "The rest of you open your books to chapter seventeen and read. Be ready for a pop quiz when I get back." She tapped Cal on the back. "Get up. You're coming with me to the office."

Cal tried to push himself out of the chair but could barely rise.

Mills turned around and spotted his cousin. "Harley Buxton. Come over here and help your cousin get down to my office."

"Yessum," Harley said, grabbing Cal under the arms to help him from the room and down the hall. "You done it now," he grinned and whispered to Cal. "Daddy's gonna lay into you good when you get home, and I'll be there to see it."

Mills led the way down the hall, opened the door, and turned to the two boys. "Set him in that chair and get back to class, Harley."

"Yessum." Harley let Cal drop into the chair and, with a final grin, left and headed down the hall.

Mills picked up the phone on her desk and dialed. When it was answered, she said, "Mimsy, this is Doris Mills at the school."

"What's wrong, Doris," Mimsy asked, and then with concern, "Did something happen to Harley?"

"No, Harley is fine. It's Cal. He can't keep his eyes open, and it's disrupting the class.

"Oh," Mimsy said.

"Is anything happening at home? Something that's keeping him awake at night?"

"Well, no," Mimsy said softly and began to worry about where this might lead.

As usual, it led nowhere. "I need you to come get him and take him home.

What was happening to Cal was no mystery to Doris Mills or anyone else who came into close contact with the boy. When questioned about the bruises and lumps that frequently appeared in random places on his body, he always said he tripped or crashed his bike, or if it was particularly noticeable, that he fell out of the oak tree beside the barn. Locals marveled at the variety of excuses he could concoct.

"That Cal has got to be the clumsiest boy I've ever laid eyes on."

"Clumsy hell," someone would respond. *"Those bruises on his face are Ox Buxton's work, and someone should do something about it."*

"Who? You?"

"Well, no, not me, but someone."

"Best to just take the boy's excuse that he fell and let it be."

"That's right. You don't go around poking a hornet's nest unless you want to get stung. You wanna get stung?"

"Well, no, I suppose not."

"Good. 'Cause if you start trouble with Ox, we're all gonna suffer sooner or later."

And the conversation would return to considering Cal's clumsy ways.

One person did at least make a small effort to see what he could do. One day, Doyle Sutter saw Cal walking by the courthouse and called out, "Come here, Cal. We need to talk."

"It's alright," Cal said, rubbing the arm that hung limply from his side. "I fell from the tree again."

"Again, hmm." Sutter tried to look into the boy's eyes, but Cal averted his gaze. "Why do you keep going up in the tree, Cal, if you keep falling out?"

Cal shrugged. "Dunno. Just like it up there, I guess."

"Why do you like it up there?"

"Dunno."

"Is there something you want to tell me ... something about what goes on at home?" Sutter asked.

"No, sir," Cal said quickly. "Nothing."

"Alright," Sutter said, nodding. "Well, if there ever is, you can come see me."

Cal nodded. "Yes, sir."

"Alright then." Sutter tried to give the boy a reassuring smile. "I'll be seeing you around, I guess."

"Yes, sir," Cal said and hurried away, his eyes darting around to make sure no one had seen him talking to the sheriff.

Sutter watched him leave, moving with an awkward, ambling shuffle. It was hard to watch but Sutter's conscience was at least partly relieved. He'd tried, he told himself, but somewhere in his gut, he was relieved that Cal had not wanted to tell him about what happened at home. After all, he couldn't force the boy to talk if he didn't want to. He promised himself he would keep an eye on the boy, but that was all he ever did. Doyle Sutter wanted no more to do with Ox Buxton than Harvey Pursall or the rest of the county had.

Cal's bouts of daytime sleepiness persisted. After a while, Dori Mills ignored them and let the boy sleep in class while his classmates laughed, but then some alarming symptoms began to develop.

Cal was finding it difficult at times to coordinate his body movements. Walking became a chore. At times, merely lifting a fork to his mouth required immense concentration and effort, and even then, he spilled as much food down his shirt as made it to his mouth.

One day, Cal spent the afternoon climbing up to the loft inside the old barn behind the house. It took him nearly an hour to move up the ladder rungs while clinging desperately to the side rails, but desperation was his life now.

That day, he was desperate to avoid Ox's homecoming and the abuse that was worsening with each passing day. Things might get better if he could just find a way to avoid Ox and stay out of sight.

He reached the loft and stayed hidden for a few hours. Then Harley came looking for him.

"You in here, boy!" Harley called out from the barn entrance. "I know it! You can't hide from me!"

Cal remained silent.

"I looked everywhere else, so you gotta be here!" Harley shouted and began searching the barn.

When he finished examining every corner of the lower level, he looked up and grinned. "You little son of a bitch. You must have found a way to drag your ass up to the loft."

Harley climbed the ladder to the loft and, in victory, let out a, "Hah! Got you, you little shit."

Cal huddled on a pile of rags in the far corner, staring wide-eyed in terror at his cousin. Harley walked over and stood over him. "Daddy's home. He's looking for you. Let's go."

Cal closed his eyes and didn't move.

"I said, let's go!" Harley grabbed Cal by the shirt, pulling him up and dragging him to the loft's edge. "Get down there. Daddy's looking for you."

Cal sat immobile, silent, and didn't move.

"That the way you want it," Harley said and shrugged. "You got it, boy."

Harley reached down, jerked Cal up by the arm, and pushed him over the edge. Cal tumbled and fell headfirst to the wooden plank floor.

Harley came down the ladder, hovering over Cal. "Get up!"

But Cal didn't get up. After a few minutes of trying, Harley went to bring Ox to the barn.

"You pushed him, didn't you?" Ox said.

"No, Daddy," Harley said and started to step away from his father. "I swear I didn't ..."

It was too late. Ox backhanded him in the mouth. "You dumb shit. I don't have time to deal with this shit."

Mimsy came running into the barn at the commotion. "My God," she said, kneeling beside Cal. "What happened?"

"He climbed up in the loft and fell," Ox said, glaring at Harley.

Mimsy examined Cal, and when she lifted his head, nearly let out a shriek. "Oh, Lord. Look at his skull. It's busted and swelling up. We have to get him to the doctor."

"For what?" Ox sneered. "Dumb shit fell out of the loft. He'll heal up in time."

"Look at him, Ox! He's hurt bad," Mimsy pleaded.

Ox shook his head, unmoved.

"He's liable to die," Mimsy said, looking up at her husband from Cal's side. "What then? He dies, and people will come snooping around. Sutter won't have any choice but to do some kind of investigation."

Ox frowned as he thought it through, then glared at Mimsy and said, "Alright. You take him to see Rush, but you remember, he fell from that loft on his own. You don't say nothing else."

"I won't. I promise." Mimsy looked at her husband and nodded. "Now help me get him to the truck, and I'll get him in to see Doc Rush."

The drive to Dykes took nearly an hour. By the time Mimsy pulled into Dykes, the doctor had already gone home for the day, so she drove to his house two blocks off the square and ran up to the house to bang on the door.

"Mimsy? Who's hurt?" Rush asked as he stepped outside, although he would have bet money on who the patient was.

"It's Cal," she said, then added softly, embarrassed because she knew Rush would see through the lie, "He climbed up in the barn and fell out of the loft."

"Fell from the loft, huh?" Rush frowned. "Where is he?"

"In the truck," Mimsy said and ran back down the sidewalk with Rush in tow.

When she threw open the truck door and Cal nearly fell out, Rush's eyes widened in horror. "My God, Mimsy. This boy needs to be in a hospital trauma center. I can't do anything for him here."

"Can't you just fix him up some, so I can take him home and nurse him for a while until he's better?"

"No!" Rush looked at her, and the shock on his face turned to disgust. "No, I can't fix him up! He'll die if we don't get him to a hospital. I'm calling the ambulance over to take him to the trauma center in Dalton."

Rush turned to hurry back to the house to get his phone. Mimsy grabbed his arm.

"Please. You know Ox isn't going to want to pay for any hospital treatment. He'll be furious."

"This time, I don't have any choice, Mimsy. The boy will die if I don't. There will be an investigation ... questions asked ... lots of questions, not just by Doyle Sutter. Besides, there is enough on my conscience as it is. I can't let the boy die if I can stop it." Rush looked at her, the sympathy on his face real. "I know how Ox will react, but it has to be this way. I'll try to smooth things over with Ox ... see if I can get Cal admitted as an indigent patient without financial support." Rush turned to hurry back to the house, muttering, "It has to be this way. They went too far this time."

Mimsy stood by the truck, sobbing and looking at Cal's battered face and misshapen skull. "I'm sorry, Cal. I tried to do right by you. I really tried, but ..."

Her words trailed off. There were no buts, and she knew it. No one had done right by this boy since the day he was born.

33. We Did

Predictably, when Ox found out about the hospital, he was furious. "Goddammit, I said you could take him to Rush!" he shouted. "Didn't say nothing about no hospital!"

"I didn't have any choice, Ox," Mimsy said, shrinking away from him as he balled his fists in her face. "Rush said he would have died. Then what? Don't you see? I had no choice."

"There's always a choice," Ox snarled. "Coulda left the little son of a bitch on the side of the road somewhere and say we didn't know nothing about it when they found him."

"He would have died, Ox!"

"Exactly. He'd have died, and we'd be rid of him and his bullshit for good."

Cal spent the next six months in the hospital, receiving care from various doctors assigned to work on charity cases where the prospects of being paid were slim. That meant that although they were all dedicated physicians, the faces changed frequently, and the continuity of the treatment Cal received was spotty.

They did repair his damaged skull, but the years of trauma culminating in being pushed from the loft by Harley had resulted in permanent brain damage. He would never walk again.

Ox refused to allow Mimsy to visit him in the hospital. "Far as we're concerned, we got nothing to do with the boy. Whatever it costs to put him in that hospital is up to the state. You go nosing around there visiting, and they'll start to think we're gonna pay the bill, and by God, we're not paying a damn cent!"

Even so, the bills started coming in. Dr. Rush had listed Cal as indigent, but the record of custody was on file with DCPS. Ox was even more furious to find that his insistence that his nephew remain in his custody now made him responsible for the bills.

He found an attorney in Dykes to plead a hardship case in court. The premise was that Ox Buxton provided a foster home as a good Samaritan but had never adopted or claimed Cal as his own. They were entitled to State assistance to cover medical expenses.

After some haggling, the judge agreed, and Cal's bills were covered by public assistance. Ox calmed down after that.

"Falling from that loft might be the best thing the little pissant ever did," Ox said when the State money came through for the hospital bills. "He's out of my hair once and for all."

***

Despite Ox's orders that no one was to visit Cal, Mimsy was able to sneak away and get updates on Cal's condition from Doc Rush.

"The brain damage is permanent, I'm afraid," Rush told her in his office one day. "Brought on by the injury to his central nervous system from repeated brain trauma."

"So, what's that mean?" Mimsy asked between sobs.

"Well, you already know he won't walk again," Rush said. "Truth is that all muscular and skeletal control is impaired, probably for life. Hand movements, eyes, speech."

"You mean he can't talk?" Mimsy sobbed.

"He can talk ... some. But it's difficult to understand him." He shrugged. "That might improve in time, but there's no way to tell."

"All of this because he fell from a loft." Mimsy shook her head and wiped her eyes with the backs of her hands.

"We both know it was from more than that, Mimsy. The fall was just the last straw in a series of injuries," Rush said. "Looking back, it seems that Cal's been showing signs of brain damage for years. Difficulty interacting with people. We all thought it was fear of his father or, later, his uncle, but it could also be from repeated brain injuries that affected his mental acuity. Then there's the chronic sleepiness during the day ... hypersomnia, they call it, and it's been linked to repeated brain trauma."

"How long does this last?" Mimsy looked up. "I mean when will he get better from the brain injury?"

"He won't," Rush said, shaking his head. "This type of injury ... repeated for years ... it's irreversible."

"Irre ..." Mimsy's brow furrowed.

"Irreversible," Rush said gently. "The injury to Cal's brain means he will be severely handicapped for the rest of his life."

"My Lord." Mimsy shook her head and buried her face in her hands. "How could God let this happen?"

"He didn't," Rush said softly, lifting a hand to wipe at the corner of his eye. "We did."

34. Justice

There were never any letters from home. Private William Hobson Buxton waited out the ordeal of mail call with his usual air of stoic indifference. For a while, members of his squad teased him about being the forgotten child, the one no one wrote to.

"Geez, Buxton. How come nobody ever sends you any mail, no birthday cards, not even an email?"

Hob would shrug it off and say, "No one I want to hear from anyway."

"Not even a girlfriend?"

Hob would look up from his bunk and stare until the questioner walked away, muttering,

"No offense meant, Buxton. Just asking."

The teasing and questions eventually ended. Most of his squad mates began to feel uncomfortable receiving emails, letters, and packages from family and friends while he sat alone on his bunk reading or cleaning his weapon. The few who didn't stop received a private visit from the squad leader, Staff Sergeant Arnold Payne.

The visits went something like this:

"Saw you giving Buxton a hard time," Payne would say.

The soldier usually grinned and said something like, "Just giving him shit, Sarge ... you know, having a little fun, that's all."

Payne's answer was to the point. "Knock it the fuck off, or I'll start having a little fun with you."

The grin vanished from the soldier's face, followed by a subdued, "Yes, Sergeant!"

"One more thing. You don't mention that we had this little talk, not to Buxton or anyone else. Is that understood?"

"Yes, Sergeant," the soldier would mutter.

"Speak up, Private!"

Then louder, "Yes, Sergeant!"

"Good. Now, get the fuck out of here."

"Yes, Sergeant," the soldier would say said and scamper away as fast as he could.

Hob never knew about Payne's visits with the soldiers, and in time, he became close to the other members of his squad, or at least as close as he could. Army life helped him focus on something besides the abuse he'd endured at Ace's hands and gradually put aside the years of physical and mental torture he'd endured.

Two deployments to Afghanistan, each with Sergeant Payne and most of the same squad members, helped weld his bond with the other soldiers. They may have regarded him as strange, a loner, and a recluse, but when the shit hit the fan, Buxton was always there in the mix, pulling his weight.

For some reason, Payne took a special interest in the quiet private in his squad. Hard-nosed and demanding of his troops, Payne never went easy on Hob. He expected as much, and sometimes more, of him than the others, but he also saw the young man's potential as a leader and took the time to mentor him subtly, giving him additional responsibilities and relying on him in critical situations.

Hob was nearing the end of his fourth year of enlistment and was seriously considering making a career in the Army. It wasn't a bad life for a young man with no expectations and nothing but misery waiting back home. In a few months, he would take his accumulated leave time and return to Bayne County for the first visit since his enlistment. The money he'd been stashing away in the bank in Dykes was still there. He had no doubt that his mother was afraid to touch any of it because Ace would surely take it from her or beat her for hiding it from him.

Hob planned to withdraw the money and make a real home somewhere far away from Bayne County. Once he established Cal and his mother in their new home, he would return to the Army and continue to support them. When he had leave, he would go home for a visit.

He never shared these thoughts with his mother or brother in letters, and sending an email was out of the question. Ace would intercept anything he sent them, and their lives would only worsen.

So, he made his plans and prepared himself for the confrontation with Ace when he returned home to take his brother and mother away. He was stronger now, more confident that he could face Ace and do what was necessary. Those plans became his life.

Then one day, the letter arrived. It came from his aunt, Mimsy, and it was blunt and to the point, as if she had rushed to get the words down and sealed in an envelope before someone stopped her. It read:

Dear Hob,

Your mother and father died two years ago. Emma killed Ace and then shot herself.

Cal is hurt real bad. Dr. Rush says he has brain damage that won't go away. Said he won't walk anymore and is in a wheelchair. The state has him in a hospital where they take care of people like that.

Sorry to have to write this. I should of done it sooner. You know I got to be careful around Ox. The manager at the bank helped me with where to send the letter, so I hope you get it.

I know its terrible news and I'm sorry about that but I figure you got a right to know and I know I should of told you sooner.

Be careful in the Army.

Your aunt,

Mimsy

Hob stared at the page for several minutes, rereading every line. *Emma killed Ace and then shot herself.* He blinked back tears and wondered why there were any tears at all, but he knew they were for his mother. If she became a drunk it was because Ace turned her into one. Life had been hard for Emma. He could not blame her for taking refuge there until she finally found the courage to stop her husband from hurting her children ever again.

Cal is hurt real bad ... won't walk anymore ... in a wheelchair. He wept harder at that and wiped at his eyes with his fists, grinding them into the sockets, trying to make the tears stop, but they wouldn't stop. He stood and shook his head, flinging them from his face. There was no time for tears.

Folding the letter into his pocket, he left his bunk and walked out of the hut he shared with his squad. The other soldiers watched, amazed that he had finally received a letter from somewhere, but no one dared comment or ask him about it.

Five minutes later, he sat with Sergeant Payne and handed the letter to him. Payne read it, stood, and placed a hand on Hob's shoulder. More tears came, and this time Hob just sat in the chair, upright and stiff as they ran down his cheek.

"I'm sorry, Buxton," Payne said. He could think of nothing else to say.

It took a month for Payne to help him arrange a hardship discharge, and then Hob was on an airplane to Atlanta. After touching down, the first order of business was to withdraw his money from the bank in Dykes.

"You've changed," the manager said, looking at the military ID Hob handed over.

Hob was no longer a boy. He'd put on muscle and his face had lost its boyish look to take on the hardened maturity of a man and a soldier who had seen combat and worse.

"Don't know that I'd have recognized you without this ID." The manager smiled. "You've bulked up some, grown a beard and all. I suppose it's the Army ... the things you've seen... it must change a man."

"I suppose," Hob said.

"How do you want your money?"

"A thousand in cash and a cashier's check for the rest," Hob said.

A few minutes later, he left the bank and stood on the sidewalk for a few seconds, looking at the town that had not changed at all since his departure. Doyle Sutter came out of the county offices across the courthouse square, got into his county car, and drove away, probably to his part-time job at the Kwik Pak.

Hob climbed into the rental car he'd picked up at the airport and drove back to Atlanta. The first order of business there was to open a new bank account and deposit the cashier's check. Then he found a cheap motel room on the outskirts of the city.

The next day, he went to the state rehabilitation hospital where his brother was housed. Cal was ecstatic to see him.

"Hob! You're here! I knew you'd come one day."

"I'm here, buddy," Hob said, sitting in the plastic chair beside Cal's bed. He looked around the ward at the seven other beds and their occupants, all with disabilities that made life alone on the outside impossible. "We're going to get you out of here."

It took another month, but Hob was able to arrange Cal's transfer to the Sagg Manor Nursing and Rehabilitation Center, using his savings to get him established. Additional costs would be paid from the salary he was now earning working in the city parks maintenance department.

Life changed dramatically for Cal. While the state facility didn't exactly neglect him, budget limitations meant it was chronically short-staffed and poorly maintained. Suddenly Cal had the attention of nurses and aides twenty-four-hours a day and a weekly visit from a doctor who thoroughly checked his physical condition.

Cal was happy and comfortable for the first time in years. His mental health improved with each visit from Hob.

As for Hob, he went to work at his new job with a vengeance, always willing to accept overtime to help pay for Cal's expenses. He also decided to rid himself of the family name that had been nothing but a curse to him and his brother.

The name change was a tedious process and required several more months. After filing a petition to change his name with the superior court, he was required to place a public notice in the newspaper, then attend a hearing before the judge. In the end, no one offered and objection and the judge saw no reason not to grant the name change.

He took the name of the one man in the world he respected, who had mentored him and made him feel part of a team, the one man who was more like a father to him than Ace had ever been. Hob Buxton became William Hobson Payne.

After that, he settled in and began planning. It was too easy to say life or fate or God had given him and Cal a bad beginning. Hob knew the truth. There were people responsible, and he knew who they were. If they had given him and Cal a bad beginning, their ending would be worse.

It wasn't revenge he planned. There had to be justice, and he would bring it to them.

Part Three –Sins

35. All It Takes

"You." Mimsy Buxton stood in the doorway staring at the young man on the porch, changed but the same. The same intent eyes and serious expression that had been too serious on a young boy, but now, on this man standing before her was somehow different, threatening.

"Me." Hob nodded.

Toby Jones and Brian Mecham had left the house less than half an hour earlier after giving her the news of Ox and Harley's deaths. They stayed with her a while she wept. Mecham was eager to be gone, but Jones felt compelled to stay awhile, knowing that no one else would sit with her and offer support, much less comfort. When the news of their deaths became public, the entire county was liable to throw a celebration.

Hob had watched from the woods, imagining what they were telling her, and the thought made him smile. When their taillights disappeared through the trees, he padded through the yard to the porch.

"It was you," she said. It was a statement, not a question. There was no doubt in Mimsy's mind about who had murdered her son and husband.

Hob's only answer was a nod and a smile. Then he cocked his head to the side and regarded her with interest, curious. "You're crying for them? Why?"

"Why do you think? Harley was my son ... Ox was my husband, and he took care of me." She wiped at the tears streaming down her face now. The reality that they were utterly gone, never to return, was sinking in. Hob's presence on the porch emphasized that.

"Took care of you? How many bruises and scars did they give you?" Hob laughed. "He treated you like shit. So did Harley. They won't be able to do that anymore."

"Still ..." She shook her head, sobbing harder. "What will I do now? I'm alone!"

"Cal was alone," Hob said quietly. "That didn't seem to bother you."

"It did bother me, but what could I do?"

"Something ... anything ... to protect him from them."

"I tried. I swear to God I did, but ..." She shook her head, this time sending tears streaming down her face. "Nothing would have changed."

"I suppose you're right," Hob said softly. "Nothing would have changed."

She looked into his face and took a deep breath to stop the sobs. "Am I next?"

"I've been thinking about that." Hob nodded. "It might be better than leaving you here alone ... for you and for me."

Mimsy looked down and nodded. "Can you just do it quick? I'm not strong."

"Turns out, neither were Ox and Harley." Hob grinned now. "They screamed and begged like little children ... the way Cal would scream and cry, or me sometimes ... when Ace lit into us."

"I know how he treated you."

"And how Ox and Harley treated Cal."

"Yes." Mimsy's sobbing returned, her shoulders shaking. "I knew. It was terrible ... what they did to you boys, your father, and Ox ... and yes, Harley, too, and it was a terrible thing to know. They all treated you real bad, and I didn't do anything about it."

"No, you didn't."

"Your mama tried ... in the end ... but it was too late." She looked up. "You know what happened to her."

"Yes, from your letter. She tried, and it was too late." Hob nodded, and now the thought of his mother threatened to send a tear from his eye. "She did the only thing she could think of to do, but what did you do to protect Cal?"

"What could I do? Ox was my husband, and Harley was my son."

"Cal and I were Emma's sons. She did something."

"I couldn't do that." Mimsy shook her head. "She was stronger than me."

"Yes, she was." Hob nodded and thought of his mother, heartbroken, desperate, making a plan that had to fail, hoping the state would somehow take Cal away and put him somewhere safe. Did she know in her heart it was hopeless, that Cal would end up here with Ox and Harley to take over where Ace left off, or did she really believe it would work?

Hob sighed. There were too many questions and no good answers, except maybe the one he had come up with. He looked into Mimsy's eyes and shook his head. "I don't suppose I could expect you to do what she did. That's why I'm not going to hurt you."

"Y-you're not?" Mimsy's forehead wrinkled, confused. "But I thought ... I mean, I knew you were back, took Cal out of the state place and put him somewhere else. Then when Ox and Harley went missing and tonight when they told me they were dead ... Well, I thought you'd want to finish things."

"Things aren't finished, but I won't hurt you. I figure you're about as much a victim as my mama or Cal." He stepped back from the door as if to leave, then turned back and almost as an afterthought said, "They'll be coming to talk to you, to ask you questions how things were, about me maybe. If you tell anyone I was here ... what we talked about ... I will come and finish things."

"I know," Mimsy whispered.

He turned, walked from the door, and down the porch steps. There was more, and she called after him. "Please, I have to know. How'd you do it? Those deputies wouldn't tell me how they found Ox and Harley ... just that they are dead, but I know it wasn't good.. Did they suffer?"

"How?" Hob gave an indifferent shrug as if he was about to describe how he put a bullet through a rabid dog's head. He shrugged. "Suffer? We all suffer, and the truth is, I didn't do anything."

"That can't be right. They're dead. Something killed them. You said you did it."

"I left them, that's all." Hob smiled. "Sometimes that's all it takes."

"You left them?" Mimsy shook her head, trying to understand. "That don't make sense. There had to be more than that."

"There wasn't."

She watched him disappear into the night, then closed the door and turned, leaning against it as she slid to the floor sobbing, alone as she always feared ... always knew ... she would be.

36. The Big Fish

"You take the lead." Bob Shaklee said as they pulled up to the courthouse square in Dykes.

"You sure?" George looked over. "Seymour will probably come around, and I'm not sure I've got the right temperament to deal with him. Besides, this is probably your last case. Thought you'd want to head things up."

"Exactly. It's my last case. Don't want to leave any loose ends when I go. This one could go on for a while, and besides ..." Bob shrugged. "Your temperament's just fine for dealing with that asshole."

"You think?" George shook his head, smiled, and climbed out of the driver's seat. "You might want to reconsider that assessment in a few minutes."

"I doubt it." Bob shrugged and laughed. "I'm up for the show if you are."

"Ready and willing," George said.

"Good. You take the lead."

"Alright, but it doesn't change a thing. You're the boss until you ride off into the sunset, and you know what that means." George grinned.

"Yep. Shit rolls downhill ... in your direction." Bob returned the grin.

"Nope." George shook his head. "It means you are the shit umbrella."

"Fair enough." Bob laughed. "You deal with Seymour and find the killer. I'll take care of the shit storm."

They walked through the front door of the hundred-year-old building and around a corner to a room by the back stairwell. "There," George said, pointing to the door where the number 107 was stenciled in black. "That's where Carol Digby set us up."

It was a conference room that had once been a jury deliberation room. When the juries were moved upstairs, it was transformed into a conference room. In time, it became an unofficial meeting place for the county commission to discuss matters away from public scrutiny, a questionable practice that violated the state's open meeting laws but part of politics as usual in Bayne County.

They went in and found Toby Jones and Web Seymour already waiting. Jones stood in a corner away from Seymour, clearly uncomfortable in the county commission's inner sanctum.

Seymour lounged at the conference table with a smug look, drinking coffee and eating donuts from a box. "Brought these for you," he said.

"I'll have a cup of coffee," Bob said.

"No donuts?" Seymour smirked. "I thought all cops like donuts."

"I'll pass," Bob said.

"Personally, I'm partial to eggs and bacon in the morning," George said, reaching for the coffee decanter. "But I will have a cup of coffee."

He filled one of the paper cups stacked on the table, sipped, and made a face. "Civilian coffee," he said. "A little weak for my taste." He put the cup on the table and plopped into a chair across from Seymour.

Bob sipped coffee and watched. Game on, he thought.

Seymour frowned. "So that's how you boys want to play this ... the tough cop act."

"First, we're not playing," George said. "This is a triple murder investigation, and we take it seriously." He leaned toward Seymour. "And for the record, there are no boys in this room. We're here because you called the governor for help, and he sent the best he had."

"Fine, have it your way." Seymour threw a scowl in Bob's direction. "How about telling your ace investigator there he needs to get to work finding the person who killed my sheriff and two of our citizens."

"Like he said. You called the governor, and that's why we're here," Bob said. "Agent Mackey is the lead investigator."

"Alright, fine." Seymour turned back to George. "So, here's what needs to happen. We start doing some real searching ... expanding things ... calling in more people. Get some more National Guard troops and State Patrol. We beat those mountains until we find the murdering piece of shit who did this."

"First, there is no we. This is a criminal investigation, and OSI will handle it." George shook his head and stood. "And second, no one goes up on that mountain unless we authorize it, and for the moment, we are not authorizing any more searches there."

"You say no to me?" Seymour looked up from the table, and the scowl deepened. "Take care, Mackey. Your boss may call you the lead investigator, but this is my county ... my turf, and I still have some clout with the governor. You're here because he sent you, and I want all the stops pulled out on this. We send everything we have to look for the killer. There are a hundred men in the county that'll step forward today to find Doyle Sutter's killer. We'll deputize every one of them."

"No," George repeated calmly. "That's our crime scene up on the mountain. I don't want a crowd of non-professionals up there tromping around, contaminating it."

"Fuck the crime scene!" Seymour shouted. "There's a killer up in those mountains, and I want him found!"

"Maybe," George said.

"Maybe? What the hell does that mean?"

"Maybe he's up there somewhere, but ..." George shook his head. "I don't think so. The murders, the manner of death, the hidden cave, chains pre-positioned. ... all of that took time and planning, and someone had a reason for planning it. The reason might not make sense to us yet, and it is definitely the product of a troubled mind, but the victims were targeted. We'll find the killer when we determine who would target them." He shook his head. "Stomping around in the mountains is only going to waste time and possibly destroy any evidence we might find when we know what to look for."

"How the fuck do you plan to find anything, sitting down here on your ass?" Seymour shouted, his voice taking on a shrill tone. The biggest fish in the Bayne County pond was unaccustomed to being denied. Even more aggravating was that George and Bob seemed completely unintimidated by his bluster.

"We won't be sitting," George said.

"Then what the hell will you be doing besides wasting time!" Seymour's face reddened, and a vein in his temple throbbed.

"We need to know what we're looking for ... who we're looking for ... who would want to kill them in the particular way the murders were committed. The killer planned everything in detail, including leaving them to die without actually killing them. Why?" George looked at Seymour and waited.

"How the hell should I know!" Seymour shouted.

"There you go. We can eliminate you as a witness and source of information. See how that works?" George smiled. "That's how we'll find the killer. We have to find out who would want to kill them and do it the unusual way the crime was committed because that's the key to the killer's identity. You don't know, but someone does, and when we find that person, we'll know where to look for the killer."

"Seems to me you're stalling because you don't have any idea how to find the killer. You sent people up on that mountain yesterday ... tromping around as you say ... a lot of them, and most were non-professionals ... as you call them. It didn't bother you then." Seymour pointed a finger at George. "Sounds like a load of horseshit to me."

"Think what you want." George gave an indifferent shrug. "Yes, we had people up there, and that was yesterday when this was a missing persons case. Today, it's a triple murder investigation, and we'll do things carefully ... without contaminating evidence and ruining any chance of convicting the killer once we find him and know what to look for."

"Mackey, you may be some sort of big deal, hotshot investigator down in Atlanta, but you don't know how things work up here!" Seymour fumed and stood. "I'm going to make a little call to the governor, and when I finish, we'll start investigating my way."

"All due respect, Commissioner," George said, but his tone made it clear that he had no respect for Seymour. "You couldn't investigate your way out of a paper sack. Now, we have work to do." He turned for the door, calling over his shoulder, "Deputy Jones, you coming with us? We've got a killer to track down."

Toby Jones looked doubtfully from Seymour to George and Bob, heading through the door. He could follow the OSI men and end up on Seymour's shit list, probably for life. Stay there in the corner and lose the chance to be part of the investigation.

Seymour solved the dilemma for him. "Get the hell out of here, Jones!" he shouted. "Go with them, but you better damn well let me know what they're up to!"

"Yes, sir." Jones scurried after the OSI investigators.

37. Yes, Sir

A gaggle of National Guard troops wandered around on the courthouse square. The café across the street was doing blockbuster business, supplying coffee and egg and sausage biscuits to those just arriving. So much so that Doris Blackmon, the owner, had to send her son to Dahlonega for supplies.

While the troops mingled, a lieutenant assigned to oversee them and assist the OSI team in securing the mountain crime scene leaned against an old Civil War cannon on the square, sipping coffee and waiting for someone to tell him what was going on. He'd arrived an hour earlier to relieve the sergeant who'd supervised the overnight shift of troops left on the mountain.

When the sergeant came down from the mountain, the briefing he offered about the point of their presence in this backwater town was minimal. "Damned if I know what's going on. I was told to keep snoopers away from a shack on the mountain. I've got ten people up there now. You'll need to send a relief up in a couple of hours. Truck driver over there will show you how to get up there. Me, I'm going home and get some sleep."

"So, what's the deal with the shack?"

"Dunno, exactly." The sergeant shrugged. "Some investigation they got going on, and they don't want anyone, including us, to mess things up."

"Who is—they?"

"State people ... law. They work for the governor, some kind of special investigations office."

"You mean the OSI ... the Hunters?"

"Yeah, that's it. Heard some locals call them that. A couple of big deal agents they sent to handle things for the governor.

"Well, I'll be damned. Just another day being all we can be," the lieutenant said, smiling. He was young, just out of college, and still thrilled with the adventure of wearing a uniform. Being involved in a case with the OSI was even more exciting.

The sergeant he was relieving had three tours in Afghanistan under his belt before leaving active duty and enlisting in the Guard for the extra cash. Unimpressed, he yawned and shrugged. "Whatever. Just put together rotating shifts to go up there and keep people away."

"Had many people coming around?"

"Nope. Not a person, but the OSI guys running things said they don't want to take any chances on someone messing up their crime scene." The sergeant gave the lieutenant a serious look. "Rumor is from one of the deputies that there was some kind of murder up there, but the OSI guys aren't talking."

"Murder?" That was the first the lieutenant had heard about why the governor had personally called them out. "Hasn't been anything in the news about it."

"Nope, and they said they want to keep it that way." The sergeant nodded at the troops mingling and grabassing on the square. "Information is on a need-to-know basis, and I was told we don't need to know." He shrugged. "So, there it is."

With that, he turned and walked across the square to a waiting truck that would transport him and the overnight crew to their vehicles parked in the Guard recruiting office lot in Calhoun. It had been a long night, and it would be a long ride before they could head home.

The lieutenant continued sipping coffee from a plastic foam cup, watching his troops and waiting for someone to give him instructions. A half-hour later, George and Bob, trailed by Deputy Jones, came through the courthouse door. They spotted the lieutenant still leaning on the cannon and headed his way.

"Morning," George said, looking at the nameplate on the lieutenant's uniform. "Lieutenant Davis. Have you been briefed?"

Lieutenant Davis stood up a little straighter. The OSI agent's face looked vaguely familiar. "Not much, sir. Just that we are supposed to keep snoopers away from some shack up on the mountain."

"Alright, then. I'm Agent Mackey. This is Agent Shaklee from the OSI." He took out his badge and held it out for Davis. "You know who we are?"

"Yes, sir." Davis's eyes widened a bit.

"That's right." George nodded. "And you don't have to call me sir."

"Sorry ... habit."

"No problem." George turned and surveyed the courthouse square. "I'm going to need you to get your people organized and everyone up on the mountain."

"Everyone?" Davis's brow furrowed. "I was told we go up in shifts, ten or so at a time."

"That's how it was, but everyone goes up today. Gonna be a lot of activity up there. I want all the security we have. No one is to get near the scene, not even close enough to use a camera with a telephoto lens. Keep everyone away."

"I might need more people then, so we can keep the shifts going."

"Not necessary," George said. "Everyone goes up this morning, and by this afternoon, we should wrap things up." He shrugged. "That's the plan, at least. If it changes, we'll let you know."

"Yes, sir ... I mean alright. Whatever you say."

"One more thing." George motioned to Lieutenant Giles, who had returned with his state troopers.

Before releasing him the night before, George had briefed him on the crime scene in the cave. The Body Recovery Unit would arrive by helicopter that morning. The forensics techs would lead them up and help them organize the helicopter for recovery. Giles and his troopers would assume responsibility for preserving the scene as the remaining law enforcement professionals on the mountain.

Giles walked over, and George said, "Lieutenant Giles, meet Lieutenant Davis. He'll be working with you today."

Giles gave the Guardsman an appropriately stern law enforcement nod, establishing who was running things.

"We have some business to take care of," George continued. "You take your instructions from Lieutenant Giles. The State Patrol will have control of the scene. If he asks you and your men to do something ... do it."

"Yes, sir," Davis snapped out reflexively, then embarrassed. "I mean, okay."

38. Secrets

"Let's start with you."

"With me?" Toby Jones was driving again. He turned his head to look at George in the passenger seat. "What do you mean? Start what?"

"You heard what we told Seymour. We need more information if we are going to find who would want to kill the Sutter and the Buxtons, and do it in the way it was done."

"I don't know," Jones said and threw a nervous glance at Bob Shaklee, watching from the rear crew cab seat.

"Not asking you to point fingers or give us a positive ID on the killer," George said to put him at ease. "We're just talking ... trying to get a feel for things up here ... you know. You can imagine it's a lot different from working a case in Atlanta."

"I suppose so."

"Trust me, it is." George changed directions. "I'm asking you what kind of men they were ... their character ... anything that might point us toward the person who would want to kill them."

Jones was silent for a few seconds, thinking, then nodded. "Alright. As far as Doyle Sutter is concerned, I can't think of anyone or any reason someone would want to hurt him, much less kill him. Doyle got along with everyone. People around Bayne County liked him. He always had a smile, a kind word, worked hard ... as sheriff and then at the Kwik Pak for extra cash. I can't think of one person who would do ..." Jones shook his head. "What we saw."

"So, he was a saint then ... no enemies." George spoke casually, looking out the window, trying to put Jones at ease without pressuring him. Two people just passing time on a drive through the mountains.

"No, not so much a saint," Jones said quietly. "More like he was just one of us ...the sheriff, yeah, but also just another guy working and trying to make ends meet without causing problems for others."

"Easygoing then," George said.

"Yeah, that's it." Jones nodded. "Doyle was easygoing. Not one to get ruffled over things. People figured that's what made him a good sheriff."

"How was he to work for? Did you get along?"

"Like I said, easygoing and ..." Jones scowled and turned toward George. "Wait! You asking because you think I might have something to do with this? That's what this is all about ... all the questions?"

"Relax. I'm not accusing you of anything. Just trying to understand how things work up here. Dig into the secrets because we'll find the killer hiding somewhere in the secrets."

"Well, there are no secrets about Doyle Sutter," Jones snapped at him. "And yeah, he was easy to work for. We never had a problem. Like I said, I can't think of anyone who would want to do what they did to him ... including me."

"Okay. No offense intended." George changed directions. "Were he and the Buxtons friends?"

"Friends?" Jones shook his head, and the scowl returned to his face. "I wouldn't call them friends."

"But they got along," George persisted.

"As good as he could ... like he did with everyone else." Jones was silent for a second, then added. "Matter of fact, he went out of his way to get along with the Buxtons since he was bound to run into them now and again, being sheriff and all."

"Okay. Good information." George nodded. "Do you know if he had ever been up to their shack on the mountain before?"

"I don't know." Jones shrugged. "Maybe. A lot of people know where it is, especially if they go up hunting in the mountains. They're liable to come across it by chance following a deer."

"How would the Buxtons take that if someone came to their shack ... like you said, by chance tracking a deer?"

"Take it?" The smile on Jones' face was back. "Hard to say because people I know wouldn't go around it if they thought the Buxtons were up there at the same time."

"Why not?"

"Let's just say the Buxton boys aren't the friendliest people around, and anyone who showed up at their shack would likely be run at the end of a rifle barrel."

"Alright, let's move on to them," George said. "So, you say they pretty much kept to themselves, or they didn't get along with people sometimes?"

"Sometimes!" Jones let out a laugh. "All the time."

"They must have had some friends."

"Nope." Jones shook his head. "Not to my knowledge, and I've lived here all my life ... like them."

"Enemies then." George turned to see Jones's reaction.

"Enemies ... that's a strong word, up here." Jones' brow furrowed. "Wasn't all that long ago that people were still fighting feuds in the mountains. People remember that, and these days most people just walk around trouble when they spot it.

"Trouble like the Buxtons?"

"Yeah." Jones nodded. "They were trouble. If they came around, people just went the other way."

"Okay, people avoided them ... they could be threatening ... they were trouble, and people tried to avoid them," George summarized. "The question is, who'd they have differences with ... differences so bad they might want to kill the Buxtons?"

"Who?" Jones' face twisted into a smirk. "Kill is another strong word, but I'll tell you this. No one I know of in the county would mind if something bad happened that took them away. Truth is, they'd probably throw a picnic."

"By something bad, you mean if Ox and Harley Buxton died?" George said.

"Yeah, that's what I mean."

Little by little, George's questions colored in the background of life in Bayne County. A country sheriff, well-liked by the locals, was not unusual. People in rural communities sometimes live in close-knit social groups and like to see one of their own do well as long as that person can get along with everyone.

Apparently, Doyle Sutter was that type of person, the local boy who got along and did well. If someone had a motive to kill him, it was for some hidden reason, something the locals did not know about. That reason was enough for the killer to risk being detected after killing the Buxtons, staying in the area long enough to do the same to Sutter.

Bullies like Ox and Harley Buxton were common, even in rural communities like Bayne County. Look hard enough anywhere, and there is always someone willing to push their weight around, take advantage, and intimidate those who won't stand up to them or just want to avoid confrontation.

George grew up in the rural south and knew something about the people there. People stayed because they liked things simple, uncluttered, and without confrontation. Serious disagreements—feuds even—might occur, but when they did, most people kept out of it. Let the ones at odds settle things between themselves as long as they didn't interfere with everyone else. If they killed each other, all the better. Problem solved ... almost. That might explain why the Buxtons were killed. Doyle Sutter was another matter.

He looked over his shoulder at Bob, who nodded. He'd recorded the interview. Toby Jones was not a suspect, but nobody else was either. It could be hard to get people talking in a closed community like Bayne County. Jones showed every sign of sincerely wanting to find the killer, if not for the Buxton's sake, for Doyle Sutter's, but with no way of knowing where the investigation would lead, his unofficial statement on record for later comparison might be important.

Jones drove on while George pondered the questions running through his mind. No one would care if the Buxtons disappeared. If Doyle Sutter was the man Jones claimed him to be, everyone would miss him. So, who would kill the man who got along with everyone?

There was a secret here, something just below the surface. Exposing the secret would lead them to the killer.

39. He Remembered

They knew him here. He walked down the hallway smiling at the attendants and nurses, exchanging greetings, and asking about families. Like clockwork, William Payne was a regular visitor every Wednesday and weekend, arriving at 8AM and departing twelve hours later when the assisted living residents were in bed. The staff joked you could set your watch and calendar by it.

"How you doing, Bill?" Cecil, one of the staff attendants, smiled as he pushed an older man in a wheelchair down the hall.

"Doing good." Payne smiled back and looked down at the old man. "And how is Mr. Stark today?"

"Not saying much," Cecil said in the soft-spoken, good-natured way that made him a favorite among residents and staff. He patted the old man on the shoulder. "But he's feeling pretty fine, I'd say. Gave me a big grin when I brought him a fresh orange today. He loves his oranges."

Payne knelt by the wheelchair so the old man could see his face. His neck permanently twisted to the side by a nervous system disorder, he managed to shift his eyes and see Payne's face.

Mr. Stark smiled, nodded, and whispered, "Cal will be glad to see you. He was already up in his chair waiting."

"Well, I guess I better get a move on, then." Payne stood. "You have a good day, Mr. Stark ... Cecil."

With a wave, Payne hurried down the hall, whistling softly, nodding, and saying good morning to everyone he passed.

"That's a fine young man," Cecil said. "Rain or shine, never misses a visit and takes care of that brother like he was his own child." Cecil pushed the wheelchair down the hall toward the cafeteria, smiling. "Gives a soul hope for the next generation, seeing such a fine young man like that in this crazy world."

Mr. Stark nodded and managed a smile, and whispered, "Yes, it does. A fine young man."

***

Sagg Manor Nursing and Rehabilitation Center sat on thirty acres that were once part of the old Sagg Plantation sixty miles east of Atlanta. As antebellum homes go, the ruins of the old house were unimpressive. Tucked away in a corner of the property far from the nursing care facility, the charred rubble and tumbled rock walls were an unpleasant reminder of an ignominious past. Sherman burned it to the ground on his way to the Atlantic.

After the Civil War, a few former slaves stayed and farmed the property, each receiving their forty acres and a mule, as the government promised. But most headed west as far as they could to escape the reminders of slavery and the harbored ill will of the defeated white population. The remainder of the tillable acreage went to sharecroppers who paid for the privilege of living there by toiling away as hard as the former slaves to pay their rents and survive.

At first, the thirty acres around the old house that old man Sagg had called 'The Estate' went to the Daughters of the Confederacy to preserve what they called their southern heritage, but it was a heritage very few in the area cared to preserve. People were too busy trying to rebuild their lives, and funding for the project never materialized. Eventually, the county took over the property for taxes and, soon after, washed its hands of it by giving it to the state.

Except for the hardcore rebels and race-baiters, most of the local population were happy to forget about it and the plantation legacy of human slavery that had existed in their midst for a century. After a few generations, most could not have told you where the old plantation was or that it had even existed.

It sat abandoned and forgotten for decades until a healthcare conglomerate specializing in disabled and senior care made an offer on the property. They had been searching for a rural setting for what was to be one of the premier facilities of its type in the state. Sagg Plantation was just what they were looking for. The land was cheap, construction costs were low, and the area had an abundance of trainable personnel looking for well-paying jobs that did not require them to commute to Atlanta.

***

On this Wednesday morning, William Payne bounced down the hallway to a room at the far end with a view of the manicured lawn and garden. The door was open, and he strode through to be greeted by a delighted shout, "Hob!"

"Morning, Cal," Payne said, smiling and pulling a stool over to the twisted form seated in a wheelchair in front of the window. He plopped down on the stool and asked, "How's it hangin', buddy?"

His brother shook his head in a stiff-necked, awkward way, which signaled he was laughing. "Howsh it hangin' ... thash a good one," Cal said in the slurred way he spoke, his tongue unable to form some sounds.

"You get lucky yet with that new nurse I saw by the reception desk?" Payne asked with a wink and a sly grin.

Cal let out a wheezing hiss that passed for laughter, his body shaking. "Whish one? They all wansth me. You should know thash."

"I'll bet they do." Payne laughed.

He tried to laugh a lot around his brother. Cal loved laughing because it was something he could still do. It didn't require his body to do anything. It might have been ravaged by amyotrophic lateral sclerosis, ALS, but his brain was intact. Considering what had happened to him, that in itself was a miracle.

Doctors told Payne that Cal's disease might be hereditary, even though no one else in the family had ever been afflicted by it. They also explained that some studies pointed to traumatic brain injury as a possible contributing factor, and Cal showed signs of repeated trauma. They emphasized that this was just a theory based on observational studies but could be a contributing factor. To Payne, it was not a theory. He knew full well who was responsible for his brother's declining condition.

"Hob, leth go for a walth," Cal said, nodding out the window.

Payne tried to control the pain that flashed across his face at his brother's slurred speech. "A walk sounds good." He stood, got behind the wheelchair, spun it around, and rocked it back so the front wheels were off the ground.

Cal let out a wheezing laugh. "Fast, Hob! Let's go fast!"

Cal called his brother by the name he had gone by as a child. To everyone else in the world, he was William Hobson Payne, but to Cal, he was still Hob.

"Fast it is!" Payne said, wheeling the chair around and out into the hallway.

Payne pushed the wheelchair out to the garden and began a brisk walk around the grounds, chatting nonstop with Cal. The doctors had warned that the CTE—chronic traumatic encephalopathy—would continue to deteriorate Cal's control of his vocal cords, tongue, and facial muscles until, like most CTE victims, he would one day lose all ability to speak. It was just a matter of time before the disease entirely destroyed his brain's control over his body.

On each visit, Payne—Hob—tried to get Cal to speak as much as possible. The thought of one day coming to visit and never hearing his brother's voice again as he watched the tortured body shrivel and die was almost unbearable. So, they talked and laughed, and Payne treasured each labored word that Cal uttered.

He stayed to have dinner with Cal in the cafeteria. Sagg Manor was a premier care facility, one of the best in the state, and they would have served Cal his meals in his room if he preferred, but Cal wanted to be where the people were.

Payne ensured that his brother had the best care available and paid Sagg Manor's pricey fee without ever thinking of himself. Cal worried about the finances, but Payne assured him he made a lot of money at his new job and could cover the expense while living a comfortable life.

In truth, he lived in a squalid apartment in one of Atlanta's low-rent districts. His meals generally consisted of peanut butter or bologna sandwiches and boiled eggs. Meals for guests were part of Sagg Manor's all-inclusive price, so Payne treated himself by eating with Cal during his visits.

As usual, Payne wheeled his brother to the cafeteria at noon and again in the evening. Cecil, the staff member who usually took charge of getting the residents where they needed to be, smiled and joked each time they passed. Cal always had a joke or funny reply ready.

Cal was a favorite of the staff and other residents. Despite his deteriorating condition, he always found a way to say something positive. He touched their lives in ways that he was too humble to see, but they saw it, and more than one wiped a tear from their eyes after he passed in the hall.

Payne saw his brother's effect on others. He knew his brother was a special soul, and as far as he was concerned, the greatest injustice in God's universe was what had happened to Cal. Payne would do whatever was required to make his brother's remaining days as comfortable and filled with as many smiles as possible, no matter the cost.

So, on his visits, they walked and had meals together, and when Cal's fragile body tired, they went back to Cal's room, where he rested and dozed in his wheelchair. Payne would watch his brother sleep, a tender look on his face, fighting back the tears that threatened to stream down his cheeks. Cal never wept for himself and asked his brother not to cry for him.

"No tears," Cal would say with a shrug, his twisted smile wide on his face, always philosophically accepting of his situation. "Things happen for a reason."

Payne nodded, smiled, and made sure Cal never saw his tears, but he was not so philosophical or accepting. Things happened for a reason, and Payne knew why Cal would spend the rest of his life in a wheelchair until his sweet but twisted smile was gone forever.

Cal might accept and forgive. Even in his tortured state, he worried about his brother. When he saw the anger well up in Hob's eyes, Cal would quote a verse from the Bible that he kept on the tray attached to his chair—*For I will forgive their iniquities and will remember their sins no more.*

Payne listened, nodded, and reassured him he harbored no ill will against God or anyone else. Cal looked into his face and knew it was a lie, but he gave his crooked smile and said, "I love you, brother. You need to forgive and forget, or the anger will eat you up."

For William Hobson Payne, there were no forgotten sins. There were others to find. Almighty God could forgive and forget sins if he wanted, but Hob would remember, and he would find them. They would be held accountable. That was his mission now.

Hob turned back to Cal, smiling. "I love you too, Cal," he said, and that was true. To reassure his brother, he added, "I do forgive." Then he looked away because he knew Cal could see the truth in them.

40. The Interviews

She was sitting on the porch in an old cane chair when they came. She'd been sitting there since Hob left the night before, knowing he was right, that they would come.

Toby Jones parked the county pickup in the yard and led the way to the porch, calling out. "Mornin' Mimsy."

She wiped her eyes and nodded without speaking. She felt like she'd been crying all her life long before Toby brought her word of Ox and Harley being found dead in a cave.

"Sorry to bother you," Jones said. "You remember Agents Mackey and Shaklee from the state. They want to ask you a few questions to help find who ..." He searched for the right words ... delicate words ... and could only come up with, "Who did what they did to Ox and Harley."

Mimsy nodded again but remained seated and did not invite them into the house.

"You look tired." George came up and leaned against the porch rail, one foot up on the steps, speaking softly. "I know this is a hard time for you, Mrs. Buxton. We won't take long, just a few questions."

They'd decided George would handle the interview. Jones had told them how she had taken the news and that Mimsy, always a timid sort and easily intimidated, was likely to be more so now. One person asking questions was better than three people firing them at her, and George had the knack for getting people to talk.

Bob took up position on the other side of the steps and turned his back, looking out into the woods across the yard as if unconcerned with the questions George would ask. He leaned against the porch, a man just passing time, not intruding, but standing where he could hear everything she said. Jones followed suit and took up position beside him, trying to mimic what the OSI agents did and look like a real investigator.

"I'm George. You go by Mimsy, right?" George smiled. "Mind if I call you Mimsy?"

She shrugged and nodded.

"Thanks, Mimsy." George said. "We're going to be working together pretty closely to figure this whole thing out, and I like to be on a first-name basis with people." He spoke in a folksy way, the way neighbors chat on a front porch.

She nodded again.

"Good. Just so you know, we wouldn't trouble you today if it wasn't important."

Mimsy spoke for the first time. "It's alright. I got nothing to do but set here."

Good. She was talking. Time to move on and see if he could coax a few more words from her.

"Still, I know it's a hard time for you," George continued.

She nodded and stared down at her lap. "It's alright."

"Okay then. I'll get to it." His smile was genuinely sympathetic. "Who do you think would be upset enough with your husband and son to hurt them?"

She gave the answer they expected. "I don't know," she said, shaking her head. "No one I know."

Mimsy Buxton was what Jones had described, a woman browbeaten into submission by her husband. She had never pointed a finger at him for his abuse, and she would not now point a finger at anyone else without Ox's permission.

"We think it might be someone with a personal grudge. Does anyone come to mind?"

"No." Mimsy shook her head.

"You know the people around Bayne County, right?"

"Some." She nodded.

"If you had to pick someone who might be upset with your husband ... for any reason at all, even something that might seem small to you ... who do you think it would be?" George asked mildly. "You know how people are. They can get upset over the silliest little things."

Unlike Deputy Jones, who had explained that virtually everyone in the county had issues with Ox Buxton and sometimes outright confrontations, Mimsy looked down at her lap and said, "No one I know."

George tried a different direction. "You told us he fixed things for people to make money. Maybe someone was upset about something he fixed for them ... or didn't fix?"

"No one I know," Mimsy said.

Time to change tactics. George looked around the yard at the surrounding woods. "A long way out here from town. What's it like, living way out here in the hills?"

"I guess it's alright."

"Must get lonely, though ... this far out of town. Get many visitors?"

"Not many."

"Maybe someone who showed up and argued with Ox or Harley?"

Mimsy shook her head.

Let's try it another way, George thought. "How would you describe your husband's relationships with other people?"

"Pretty good." She shrugged.

The rest of the interview was as unproductive as the beginning and didn't last long. According to Mimsy, Ox and Harley got along with everyone. No one she knew would want to harm them. Ox was a good husband, and Harley a good son.

The picture she gave was idyllic, and it was bullshit. Aside from it contradicting everything they'd heard about Ox and Harley Buxton since arriving in Bayne County, George knew even the best marriages had their problems, and the easiest going people had occasional run-ins, even arguments, with others. That she said nothing and nearly claimed sainthood for her husband spoke volumes. There was no point pressing her further.

"Alright then, Mimsy, that's about all we need for now." George smiled and reached into his pocket. "Here's my card. If anything comes to mind that might help us find who did this to your husband and son, please call me, even if you just want to leave a voice message."

Mimsy looked at the card from the chair but did not reach for it, folding her hands tightly in her lap. She looked like someone backing away from an animal that might bite. George placed the card on the porch step.

"Alright. We'll be going now."

The three men crossed the yard without speaking. When they were back in the pickup and a half mile down the drive to the county road, Jones said,

"Went about like I expected. Afraid to say anything, even with Ox dead. Sorry, that wasn't much help."

"It helped some," George said. "She may not have said much, but everything about her screams that there is a secret buried inside, and she is terrified it might get out. That secret is the key to why Ox and Harley and the sheriff were killed."

"Oh." Jones thought about that for a second and asked, "So, we have to figure out what the secret is.

"Right."

"How?"

"We do what investigators do." George looked at Jones. "Take it a step at a time ... dig into the background ... put the pieces of the puzzle together."

"So what's next? Where do we dig?"

"There's another grieving wife. Let's go see her."

***

The interview with Chloe Sutter was far more vocal but no more productive.

"Those damned Buxton men killed my husband!" Chloe sat teary-eyed in the living room, her face red with fury. "I'm telling you that son of a bitch, Ox, and his no-good son, killed my Doyle!" She glared from face to face and stopped at George. "What are you doing about it?"

"That's why we're here," George began.

"I asked what you're doing to do, not why you're here!"

"Yes, you did." George nodded. "And I'll tell you when you're ready to listen."

"Alright." Chloe took a breath and rubbed a fist over her wet eyes. "Tell me."

"We need to know who might be angry enough with your husband or the Buxtons to want to kill them."

"Angry with Doyle?" She glared at him. "No one! Doyle was the easiest-going man in the county." She lowered her head, and her voice softened. "I always worried he wasn't cut out to be the sheriff, no matter what old Harvey Pursall said. Doyle wasn't a hard man ... always tried to make people happy. And with the Buxtons ..." She looked up, glaring again. "There was no making them happy. They were just mean, that's all ... mean and nasty human beings. That's why I know they're behind him being killed."

"You understand they were killed also?" George said, reasoning with her. "How could they be responsible when they were victims too?"

She was quiet for a few seconds, considering the question, then shook her head. "Doesn't mean anything. Whatever happened, whatever the reason, whoever did it, Buxton and his boy are behind it. Doyle is dead because of them. I know it."

"Alright. If the reason is something Buxton did, what was it, and who did they do it to?" George watched her face. "Knowing that might lead us to the killer is."

"How should I know?" Chloe snapped, then was quiet, thinking again. After a minute, she looked up and said, "There's too many to count. People they wronged ... took advantage ... just treated poorly."

"Did they have any friends in the County? Anywhere?"

"Friends." Chloe's face twisted into a sneer. "There isn't a damned person in God's world that would have called them a friend!" She glared at Toby Jones. "You're to blame too, Toby Jones ... you and everyone who knew about the damned Buxton men."

Jones said nothing, looked away nervously, and stared hard at a bee bumping against the outside window glass.

Chloe pointed a finger at Jones's face. "This could have been stopped. Where were you? What were you doing, knowing Doyle was headed up to see Buxton? Why didn't you go with him ... help him ... or stop him?"

George watched and noticed but said nothing. It was natural for law enforcement officers to feel guilty over the loss of one of their own, even out in the country. Maybe, especially out in the country.

For the next half hour, Chloe vented her anger at Ox and Harley, at Jones and the other deputies, at God. There was no logic to her reasoning. Ox and Harley were killed just, along with her husband. That did not weaken her conviction that Ox and Harley were responsible for her husband's death and someone should have stepped in to protect him.

George stopped asking questions and let her vent until the boiling anger lowered to a simmering rage. When she quieted, and there was nothing more to learn, he stood. "Thank you, Mrs. Sutter. You've been helpful. I promise we are doing everything possible to find your husband's killer."

Chloe Sutter said nothing, staring at them as they left.

***

"That was interesting." George watched Jones, hands gripping the wheel, staring straight ahead through the windshield.

"It was? Seems like a waste of time to me," Jones said. "Chloe told you what I did. Ox and Harley didn't have a friend anywhere." He shook his head. "No one around here is going to grieve for Ox and Harley."

"What about for Sutter?" George asked, watching Jones.

"Well, sure ..." Jones hesitated, then said, "I mean, of course, everyone will miss Doyle Sutter. He was a good man."

"So, we have different types of men, but they were all murdered by the same killer." George smiled. "You see, the day was not a waste."

"I don't understand?" Jones shook his head.

Bob spoke up from the back seat. "Because with the character of the victims so different, there has to be a link."

"A link?" Jones shook his head. "I still don't get it. They didn't have anything in common."

"As different as Doyle Sutter was from the Buxton men, something linked them together ... some event ... something they all wanted or didn't want ... or some person ... some reason put them all in that cave to die. That's the link."

"Alright, so there's a link. How do we find out what it is?"

"We dig until we find it. That link will lead to Mimsy's secret, and I'm betting that secret will lead us to the killer."

41. The Man in Apartment 3-D

He sat on a folding chair, hunched over a TV tray, eating canned ravioli from a plastic bowl with one of the three spoons he owned. There were four in the set he bought at a discount store, but he bent one trying to pry open a bedroom window on a summer night because the air conditioning was not working, a frequent issue in the aging building.

The TV was on, but the volume was turned low because sound traveled through the apartment's paper-thin walls like a north wind through the branches of a dead oak. And it wasn't a matter of courtesy to his neighbors, who made plenty of noise of their own—loud music, shouted arguments, fights, broken furniture, drunken shouts, and curses.

For him, silence was a habit, a mission precaution, something he'd learned, patrolling the villages and hills of Afghanistan, searching for the Taliban. If anyone ever asked about the quiet young man living in the third-floor apartment where the traffic on I-85 roared by twenty-four hours a day, seventy-five feet from the jammed bedroom window, there would be little to tell them, including his television viewing habits.

Conversely, he could describe in detail the daily lives of his neighbors from the sounds vibrating through the walls. He knew their music, what they argued about, the beer they drank, the drugs they took, and which television shows they watched. He could hear their squabbles, knockdown drag-out fights, whispered secrets, sexual encounters, and feet thumping to the bathroom in the middle of the night.

He knew as much about his neighbors as one could without actually ever meeting them, but Hob Payne made certain that they learned nothing about him. He was an invisible man, a shadow, who came and went without a sound, never interacting with others and always alone.

If anyone ever inquired about the strange man living in apartment 3-D, they weren't going to hear much more than:

"3-D? Man, that's one weird dude."

"Couldn't tell you a damned thing about the fucker."

"Never said nothin'."

"Shit, I didn't even know there was anyone in 3-D."

He was alone, unknown. That's how he wanted it, and he diligently maintained his anonymity.

This night, he wolfed down his ravioli, leaning forward toward the television, reading the closed captioning scrolling across the screen because the volume was too low to hear what the reporter was saying. She stood in front of a small but neat house with green shutters and a large forsythia in the front yard.

The report was from the network's affiliate station in Macon, Georgia. Hob's brow furrowed in concentration as he read. It was a review and an update on a story he'd been following on the nightly news for several days.

Two children, a girl aged six and her nine-year-old brother, were kept locked in a closet, deprived of food, and sexually abused by their foster father. One of their teachers complained they had lost a significant amount of weight and that they showed signs of physical abuse. Nothing happened at first, but the teacher persisted. When she told Child Protective Services they had not been in school for two weeks, CPS investigated.

The two children were found huddled in a corner of a bedroom closet. Locked inside, they had been forced to use a corner of the tiny space to relieve themselves, turning the closet into a filthy cesspool. That problem ceased when their kidneys and bowels shut down from dehydration and lack of nourishment. When the CPS investigators finally opened the closet door, the children whimpered and curled in their filth in the closet's corner, terrified of the strangers and the fresh horrors they imagined would come into their lives.

The children were immediately removed from the foster home. The mother, Enis Walder, was home and was arrested on the spot. She had tried to leave while the investigators were going through the house, but a police officer, waiting outside to assist the CPS team, detained her.

When her husband returned from his job as an actuary at a life insurance company, another officer was waiting along with arrest and search warrants. While police detectives searched the house, Reggie Walder was arrested and charged with two counts of first-degree felony cruelty to a child, each punishable by five to twenty years in prison.

Enis Walder cut a plea deal and gave a sworn statement that her husband not only tortured the children but raped both repeatedly. In exchange for her testimony, the charges against her were reduced to third-degree child cruelty

and the promise of a reduced sentence. Pending her trial, she was fitted with an
electronic monitoring ankle bracelet and released on fifty-thousand-dollar bail,
using their house as collateral.

Based on his wife's testimony and the statements from the children, Reggie
Walder was additionally charged with several counts of child rape. He was
denied bail and remained in jail pending his trial.

The reporter on the screen looked sadly into the camera, concluding the
report, and sending things back to the anchors in the studio. Hob turned
off the television, tossed the bowl and spoon onto the floor, and took his
laptop from under the chair, where he kept it within easy reach for just such
an occasion.

There was no wireless or cable service in the building. The television
signal came over the air locally, so he used his phone's mobile hotspot to
connect the laptop to the internet. It was the one extravagance he allowed
himself.

It didn't take long to bring up the child cruelty story online. No addresses
were mentioned, but the reporter had given the name of the older, quiet
neighborhood where the Walders lived. Using a map app with street and
satellite views, Hob began searching for the house he'd noted and seen
pictured on the laptop's screen while the reporter gave her report.

It took time, but he had plenty of that. Using the street view, he moved
the image through the neighborhood, street by street. Sometime before
dawn, he stretched and smiled.

There was the house—the green shutters, forsythia, the tiny front stoop,
everything just as he'd seen on the screen behind the reporter. He noted the
address and went to shower for the day.

He waited a week to make sure the media attention had died down, then
at work one afternoon, he began complaining of a cold, letting out a few
coughs and a sneeze. His supervisor told him to go home and get some rest.
The next morning, he called in sick.

42. A Personal Observation

At George's request, Andy Barnes contacted the GBI's chief medical examiner after the bodies were discovered and requested his presence at the cave. The ME, a twenty-year civil servant and veteran of dozens of murder scenes, had no intention of climbing a mountain and going into a cave to examine bodies in advanced stages of decomposition.

"No need for me to be there. I'm sure your investigators and forensics team will process and document everything adequately for me to review back here."

"So do we," Andy said. "But this case has some wrinkles we haven't seen before, and our lead investigator believes a set of eyes from your office might be useful ... see something we don't."

"You're saying you don't have any leads to go on, and you want to spread the blame around when your investigation comes up empty."

"No, that's not what I'm saying." Andy shook his head in disgust. The ME might be a doctor, but he was also a government bureaucrat and had the typical bureaucrat's reflex to always cover your ass, and any request for help might be because someone else is covering their ass.

"I'm saying this case is high priority," Andy said curtly. "The governor personally instructed us to put all available resources on it. GBI, State Patrol, National Guard. You're an available resource, and he did not exclude your department."

"The governor?" The ME sighed. "Alright, I'll have one of my associate MEs come to the scene. Let me check the schedule."

A couple of minutes passed, and Andy assumed the ME was going down the list of associates to find one, either junior enough not to complain about the assignment or one that owed him a favor. "Looks like Doctor Singman is free in the morning."

"Good. Have him meet our pilot at Peachtree-DeKalb Airport. Eight o'clock."

"He'll be there."

The next morning, when Singman arrived at the airport, it was apparent that he had been selected for his subordinate status in the ME's office. He was as junior as they come and barely looked old enough to be out of high school, much less medical school.

Johnny Rincefield, the OSI pilot, watched the young, round-faced man start to trot across the tarmac toward the helicopter, then, out of breath, slow and continue moving his arms wide in a sort of animated shuffle. When the man arrived at the helicopter's door, Rince asked, "Doctor Singman?"

"That's me, Francis Singman, Associate ME," Singman said, his smooth face breaking into a smile, then turning red, cheeks puffing out as he breathed hard to catch his breath.

"Here, let me give you a hand up." Rince extended a hand from the door to Singman. "I'm Johnny Rincefield. Call me Rince."

"Thanks, Rince." Singman climbed in and noticed the doubtful look on Rince's face as he showed him how to strap in. "I know what you're thinking. I look a little young for the job ... associate medical examiner and all."

"Now that you mention it." Rince nodded.

"I get that a lot." Singman grinned and shrugged. "Guess it's my baby face, but I assure you I graduated from medical school ... Wake Forest. My specialty is pathology."

"Seen a lot of dead bodies?"

"To be honest ... no." Singam grinned again. "I chose pathology because I don't really like blood."

"You're a doctor, an ME, and you have an aversion to blood?" Rince frowned, considering whether he should let Andy know that the chief medical examiner was not only not taking the case seriously but was treating it like a joke, sending along an associate who was as junior as they come and squeamish at the sight of blood.

Singman read his face again. "I promise you, I'm good at what I do." He nodded and shrugged. "And, yes, I'm the low man on the totem pole, so I get the shit assignments. From what I hear, this is a shit assignment."

"Yep, it is, and your boss shoved the shit stick right in your face." Rince nodded. "You say you haven't seen a lot of dead bodies, so how do you do your job?"

"Mostly the lab stuff. That's where I excel." Singman sat up a little straighter in the seat. "I'm the best at it, actually. But the boss figured it was time for me to see things as they are in the field, at the crime scenes the way your people do, not all cleaned up in the lab." He shrugged. "I agreed. I need to get my feet wet sometime ... do some fieldwork. So here I am."

"Fair enough. You'll definitely get your feet wet on this one."

The helicopter lifted off and made the thirty-minute hop to Dykes. Deputy Mecham met them as they landed and transported Singman back to the clearing. Lieutenant Giles was standing by with his troopers, monitoring the National Guard troops securing the area. He eyed the ME up and down. "You're the medical examiner?"

"Yep," Singman said, grinning.

"Okay." Giles shook his head and shrugged. "Let's get you up to the scene."

He led the way along the deer trail and up the path to the ledge. The path had been widened by the passing of investigators and the forensics team but was still rugged and challenging for Singman to navigate.

The cave entrance was another challenge. The Body Recovery Team would widen it with jackhammers once the ME examined the scene, but until then, everything remained as the forensic techs found it, and the opening remained tight.

Singman squeezed through the narrow entrance, puffing and panting. He'd never been athletic, focusing on academics rather than sports, and this assignment was taxing the limits of his stamina. Grunting and squirming his way into the tight space, he felt claustrophobic. When he popped through into the cave, he had to stand with his back against the rock wall with his eyes closed for a moment.

When he opened them and saw the state of the three remains—decomposing, ripped apart by animals, falling apart at every touch of a hand, confined in the cave's tight space—he turned and put his head down, breathing hard to hold back the vomit. It took a minute for his stomach to settle. When it did, he donned a breathing mask to block the stench and began his examination.

He worked methodically, going over the scene before getting close to the bodies. The forensics team had processed, photographed, and documented everything the day before, but he made notes for his own use, recording his impressions without being influenced by the observations of others.

He checked the walls and floor, stopping periodically to take a photograph with his camera. At one point, he peered closely at the rock and took a photo.

"We already photographed the scene," one of the forensics techs standing to the side said.

"I know." Singman peered at the rock. "Did you get a sample here?"

"Where?" The tech came closer and bent over to see where Singman pointed. "I don't see anything there."

"Even so, would you get me a scraping from right there, please."

"Okay." The forensics tech shrugged and went about collecting a sample of the rock where Singman pointed.

Singman moved to the chains and handcuffs still around the wrists of the victims, peering closely at each without touching. Last, he examined the bodies.

Unaccustomed to this sort of death still in its natural, horrific, unsanitized state, he had to pause and steady himself as he moved to each corpse. He found that focusing on one small portion of a body as if examining it on a morgue table or a tissue sample under a lab microscope helped him handle the nausea that threatened to erupt like a volcano at any moment.

When he completed the examination, he turned to the forensics techs, anxious for him to finish so they could answer his questions and get the hell out of the cave. They confirmed that the crime scene was exactly as they had found it. They had discovered no signs that the victims had been tortured or beaten as they hung from their chains. There was also no sign of poison or toxic substances. Further review in the lab might reveal otherwise, but for now, there was no way to confirm the cause of death.

Singman thanked them and squeezed through the cave entrance to the ledge, where Giles steadied him so he didn't accidentally take a step toward the drop-off. He ripped off the face mask, sucking in fresh air, then coughed at the lingering stench hanging outside the cave entrance.

"Come on," Giles said. "Let's get you down to the clearing unless you need something more up here."

"Nothing I need." Singman shook his head, relieved. "Let's go."

While Giles led Singman and the forensics techs down to the clearing, the GBI's Body Recovery Team went to work, which took most of the rest of the day. They had considered lowering the bodies over the side of the ledge, but the rough terrain, cluttered with boulders and trees, made that unfeasible. The rock wall leading up to the mountaintop from the ledge was nearly vertical, so the decision was made to lift them up by winch for transport. Rince brought the helicopter from the airport, idling the engines on the mountaintop while the Body Recovery Team did their work.

Because of the need for rock climbers, half the team were volunteers with rock climbing experience but no prior exposure to bodies in this condition. Pulling someone from the bottom of a cliff, a wrecked vehicle, or the rubble of a fallen building was one thing. Having bodies fall apart in their hands was another thing altogether.

More than one volunteer turned white and gagged when they entered the cave and were only too happy to step aside while the professional forensics team wrapped and prepared the bodies for transport.

The rock climbers then loaded them into body baskets. Secured them with ropes and cables, each body was winched to the helicopter waiting at the mountaintop. A rescuer accompanied each as it ascended, scaling the wall on ropes beside it, ensuring the basket remained stable and the wrapped body secure.

Rince made three trips in the helicopter back to the airport with a body and a recovery team member in the back. From there, the bodies were loaded into hearses under contract with the state and transported separately to the GBI morgue in Decatur.

Below in the clearing, George, Bob, and Deputy Jones met Singman as Giles led him and the forensics team from the deer trail.

"Doctor Singman?" George said, eyeing the ME. Rince had warned him he was young, but Singman looked like he should be looking for a date to the prom instead of examining murder scenes.

"That's me." Singman panted, red-faced and perspiring heavily.

"Here, sit down." George took Singman by the shoulder and moved him toward one of the stools set up for the National Guard so they could get off their feet during their shifts in the clearing.

Singman nodded without speaking and sat. George reached into a cooler, pulled out a bottle of water from the melting ice, and handed it to him. Singman nodded again and drank half of it before coming up for air. "Thank you."

"Rough day?" George said.

"Different, for sure." Singman drank more water, then looked at George. "Are you one of the OSI people who called for me up here?"

"Guilty," George smiled. "I wanted to make sure we didn't miss something. Someone looking with fresh eyes ... a different perspective."

"Suppose I understand, but I gotta tell you. "That was one helluva mess up there."

"It was." George agreed. "Any opinion yet? And I know all this is very preliminary. Just wanted to get your first impressions."

"My first impression on the cause of death?" Singman shook his head. "Hard to say without closer examination of the remains. Lots of possibilities ... dehydration, starvation, poisoning, wounds, or trauma that will take more examination to find because of the deteriorated condition of the bodies."

"Alright, how long for a final report on causes of death?"

"It'll take a few days to do the exams, lab workups, analysis." Singman thought for a moment. "I'll make sure this gets on the fast track and give you something within a week."

"Sounds good." George nodded. "Thanks."

"One more thing," Singman said, gulping some more water

George turned. "Yes?"

"I'm only an associate ME, and it's not my place to offer an opinion on the perp's mental makeup, but from what I saw, I'd say the killer has to be one sick bastard." Singman shook his head and smiled. "A personal, not professional observation, of course."

43. Digging

"So, what do we have?" George leaned the chair back on two legs, resting his head against the wall, and looked across the conference table at Toby Jones. Bob sat to the side, listening but not part of the conversation.

Jones looked surprised and then confused, not expecting to be asked to render an opinion on any aspect of the investigation. He was a part-time cop, not a real professional. The OSI, George, and Bob were the pros. He was there to drive, watch, and listen.

"Deputy?" George said. "What do you think?"

"Me? Well, I'm not sure. I mean, I don't think I'm qualified to ..." He shrugged. "You know, say anything. I mean, I don't think I could ..."

"Bullshit. You're qualified," George interrupted, smiling. "You've got eyes and ears. You were with us all day ... saw the interviews ... heard what the medical examiner said up on the mountain ... helped find the bodies yesterday. You're not just our chauffeur. You're on the team, part of the investigation, a law enforcement officer. I'd like to hear what you think."

"Okay." Jones took a deep breath and spoke slowly. "Well, the medical examiner didn't really say anything, only that he had to do the examinations and would get back to you. So, until he gives you his report, there's not much there."

"Right." George nodded. "What else?"

"I don't know ... nothing really, I can put a finger on."

"What about the interviews and the stories Mimsy Buxton and Chloe Sutter told us?"

"Stories? I don't know what you mean about stories." Jones's eyes darted nervously around the room. "I don't know that I'd call them stories."

"Sorry. I didn't mean to imply they weren't being truthful. People remember things from their own perspective. That's normal ... the reason eye witness testimony is always so unreliable and easy for defense lawyers to pick apart."

"Right. That's it." Jones nodded. "They told things from their perspective."

"Exactly. And their perspectives were very different. What's your take on that?"

"My take?" He shrugged. "Not much, I guess. Just perspectives, like you said." He looked hopefully at George, hoping that might be enough.

It wasn't. "Let's look at it this way," George said, leaning back and reasoning things out. "Everyone in the county knew Ox Buxton. You said so yourself."

Jones nodded.

"Mimsy was married to Ox, so she probably knew him better than anyone."

Jones nodded again.

"But Chloe knew him too, not as a husband, but because, as you pointed out, everyone knew Ox and how he was toward other people ... they how he treated them. Is that right?"

"Chloe knew Ox. That's right."

"Good." George smiled as if they had just reached some major agreement. "So, they both knew him in different ways, but he was the same man. I would expect Mimsy to try and say nice things about her dead husband. But Chloe had nothing nice to say and even accused Ox of being responsible for what happened. What do you think that means?"

"Right, that." Jones swallowed nervously. "Well, I guess, Mimsy being married to Ox and all, she didn't want to say anything bad about him."

"But there were bad things to say? She just didn't want to say them?"

"Something like that, I guess. Wife protecting husband. Isn't that something that happens in these kinds of cases a lot?"

"It does." George nodded and abruptly changed directions. "Did Ox ever abuse Mimsy?"

"Abuse? You mean hit her?" Jones stared open-eyed, trying not to blink or look away to hide his nervousness.

"Hit her, yes. Beat her, rape her, assault her in any way?"

"No, sir." Jones shook his head. "Not that I know of, at least."

"Good." George smiled. "By the way, I appreciate you sitting here and going over all this with me. It helps me get my brain around a case to have someone to talk to and pick their brains. You know how that is."

"I guess so."

"It really does help," George said, leaning forward and tapping his fingers on the table. He appeared lost in thought for a minute, then continued, "So, let's see what we have. Chloe said what you'd said ... that Buxton didn't get along with anyone. Mimsy said she didn't know of any reason someone would want to hurt him and her son Harley or Doyle Sutter."

"That's right." Jones nodded, a look of relief on his face as if hoping George was finished with asking his opinion.

He wasn't. "Do you think Mimsy is keeping something from us?"

"I ..." Jones paused, thinking hard about what to say next. Once again, he looked around the room as if someone might be listening. "Look, I already said she probably didn't want to say anything bad about her husband. That's all. What else could it be?"

"That's right." George smiled at the question. "What else could it be?"

He tapped on the table for another minute, staring at the ceiling, as if unaware of Jones's presence or that his eyes kept moving around the room like a man looking for an escape.

"Tell me something, Deputy."

"Okay," Jones said, with no desire to say anything.

"Are you worried someone might hear what we're talking about?" George asked, sitting up straight in the chair. "You look nervous as a long-tailed cat in a room full of rocking chairs."

"Nervous?" Jones shook his head. "Well, no, not really."

"Not really, or not at all?" George leaned his elbows on the table and leaned forward just enough to let Jones know he would keep asking questions.

"Look, it's just I don't know what to say." Jones looked away from George's eyes. "Feels like maybe you think I did something ... like I'm some sort of suspect."

"Sorry about that." George shook his head. "Bad habit. Sometimes, I get focused on a case, and I forget how other people might see things and react." He smiled. "Like I said, you're part of the team here and definitely not a suspect."

"Okay, then." Jones nodded. "Are we done here? My wife will be wondering where I've been."

"Almost done." George smiled, sat back, and nodded. "Just a lot going on today ... a lot to process. Not the sort of thing you're used to."

"No, it's not." Jones looked up, gave a weak smile, and nodded. "Look, I really want to help. I just can't think of much to say that will."

"No problem." George smiled. "I guess we're about done for the day."

"Okay." Jones pushed the chair back from the table and started to stand.

Before he could, George said, "One more thing. Chloe Sutter blamed you."

"What?" Jones froze. "No, she didn't ..."

"Yes, she did." George shrugged. "She said something like ... it was your fault ... you and everyone who knew."

"She did? No." Jones shook his head rapidly. "I don't think she said ..."

"She did." George was leaning forward again. "I have a pretty good memory for these things. In fact, she pointed a finger and said you and everyone who knew were to blame. What do you suppose that meant? What was it everyone knew?"

"Well, I ..." Jones's eyes darted from side to side.

"We're alone, Toby." George's tone was quiet and understanding. "Web Seymour's not hiding in the corner."

"I can't really say."

"Can't say, or won't say?"

"Look." Jones looked up and took a deep breath. "I didn't have anything to do with Doyle being killed ... or the Buxtons, either. I wouldn't ever do anything like that."

"But Chloe said you knew something ... everyone knew it. What was it everyone knew?"

"I can't say ... I mean, I don't know. She's just upset and angry that someone killed Doyle." Jones's eyes narrowed. "I am, too, and that's the truth."

"I believe you," George said.

"Okay." Jones looked down at the table. "Can I go now? Like you said, it's been a long day, and I need to get home."

"Yep." George looked down and began jotting notes on the pad he carried as a prop, more than a tool, a way of distracting people. "By the way, be here at seven in the morning."

Jones stopped by the door and turned. "Tomorrow?"

"Yep. You'll be working with us on the investigation until we get it sorted out."

"But like I said, I'm just part-time. I have my carpenter work and ..."

"Don't worry. We'll clear it with Seymour, and if there's any lost pay to make up, the state will take care of it as part of the investigative expense." George looked up from his notepad. "We need someone who knows the people here ... the way things are. That's you, so, tomorrow morning, seven ... here."

Jones said nothing, nodded, and left.

When the door had closed behind him, Bob said, "Digging on him pretty hard, weren't you?"

"He knows whatever it is, everyone is hiding."

Bob nodded. "He knows the secret, as you call it. That was obvious, but keep in mind we need him working with us, not against us."

"Or maybe both." George shrugged. "He's a good man, trying to be at least, and we're going to give him a chance to prove it, or if it comes to it, go down with the others when we get to the bottom of things."

"Seems harsh." Bob shook his head. "Coming at him hard just because he, Mimsy, and Chloe ... are not very good liars."

"Decent people usually aren't," George said. "Doesn't mean they aren't lying, and we need to get to the truth."

"Alright." Bob pulled out his phone and grinned. "I guess I better let Andy know he's going to get a call when Seymour starts hollering at the governor, bitching about us ordering Toby to work with us for the duration. He won't be happy about it."

"Who? Seymour or the governor?"

"Both"

"Perfect." George nodded and smiled. He pulled out his phone and punched in a number.

"About time you touched base," she said. "Beginning to worry about you two lost souls up in deliverance land."

He laughed. "Nothing to worry about."

"Well, it's too early for sweet talk. What's up?"

"I need some information."

"Tell me," Sharon said and started taking notes. When he finished, she ended the call, all business now. "I'll get back to you."

George looked at Bob. "Ready for a beer?"

"Been ready." Bob stood. "Thank God this isn't a dry county."

44. Did They Scream?

The sun was setting when Enis Walder opened the door to see the smiling young man in a tan work shirt standing on the stoop, clipboard in hand. "Yes?"

"Evening." Hob glanced at the clipboard, nodded, and looked up, smiling. "Mrs. Walder?"

"Yes."

"Mrs. Walder, I'm Rick Sager. I contract work with the power company. They have me out checking breaker boxes, and I need to check yours. May I come in?""

"Well ... I don't know. Is there a problem with our electricity?"

"No, ma'am. Not exactly, but they want me checking all the meter boxes in the neighborhood."

"Well, it's late," Enis said, leaning forward to see his face in the afternoon twilight.

"I know. Sorry about that." Hob smiled. "Last call of the day, and I need to finish this one, or I don't get paid. Like I said, I'm a contractor, and they're pretty tough on us."

"And you need to check what exactly?"

"The breaker panel. There's been some unauthorized power consumption and surges in the neighborhood. They suspect someone is bootlegging power ... you know, stealing it and sending it to other people, so they don't have to pay up."

"People can do that?"

"You'd be surprised what people try to get away with." He smiled. "That's why I'm here."

Enis glanced at the name patch on his shirt and back at the smiling face. "I'm just not sure I should."

"Alright." Hob shrugged. "I'll just note that you didn't want to grant access. No offense, but since they suspect a theft of power from their system, they'll send someone around with a search warrant."

"A search warrant? That means the police ... here?" Enis Walder had no desire to see more cops standing in her house.

"Yes, ma'am. I'm afraid so." The pretext sounded absurd to Hob as he said it, but it was the best he had come up with, and he knew a sincere face and the right demeanor could convince people that the biggest lies were plausible.

"Alright, I suppose it's alright." She opened the door wider and stepped aside. "But can you hurry?"

"Yes, ma'am."

Hob walked in, went to the breaker box in the garage, and opened the panel, pretending to busy himself. He didn't have to pretend long. Enis watched for a minute, then went back inside and turned on the television.

He waited until full night had come on before he walked back inside the house. Enis was on the sofa in the living room, watching a sitcom.

"Thank you, Mrs. Walder. Everything seems in order. If you'd just sign here to acknowledge I was here and did the inspection, I'll get out of your hair."

Enis rose from the sofa and reached for the clipboard. "Where do I sign?"

"Right here." Hob pointed to a line on a piece of paper.

Enis took the clipboard and pen, stared at the takeout menu from a fast-food restaurant, and looked up, a question in her eyes. "But this ..."

Hob smiled, and the question in her eyes turned to fear. She dropped the clipboard and started to pull away, but not fast enough.

"What are you doing?" she screamed and tried to pull her wrists from his hands, but his grip was like steel, the house was empty, and her scream went unnoticed.

Hob spun her around and, with a knee in her back, forced her to the floor. Pulling two sets of handcuffs from one of the cargo pockets running down the legs of his work pants, he locked her wrists behind her and did the same to her ankles. Then he pulled out a knife and sliced through the ankle monitor band, so the bracelet fell off her leg.

"No." Enis shook her head. "I can't take that off, or they'll put me back in jail."

"You won't go to jail," he said, and although the irony was lost on her, the sarcastic smile and malicious tone in his voice were not. Enis began sobbing.

A roll of duct tape came from the other cargo pocket. He wrapped the tape three times around her head. She was now immobilized and silent.

Hob stood and surveyed his work, gave a satisfied nod, and went outside to back the service truck up to the garage. It was the same truck and similar pretense he'd used to get close to Doris Mills. He would have preferred to change his methods, but with Enis confined to her house, there were few options, and he hadn't had time to put together a better plan. Besides, it worked on Doris, and it was working now.

He backed to the garage's bay door and found Enis squirming along the floor like an injured caterpillar in the living room. The sight almost made him laugh. If he'd had time, he would have liked to sit and watch her frantic, helpless struggle, but there was no time.

There'd been no signs of snoopy neighbors ... yet ... probably because if anyone noticed, they assumed the service truck was there for some official purpose regarding her house arrest. Eventually, someone would question the truck parked in her driveway at night, and their curiosity might overcome their desire to avoid any contact with the Walders.

Lifting her legs, Hob dragged her through the house to the garage, her face down, bumping and rubbing over the carpet and tile. She tried to let out a frantic scream, but the duct tape muffled it. He threw her into the back compartment, closed the garage door, and drove away.

The drive to the mountains was shorter this time but still took a couple of hours. Navigating the dirt trail to the shack in the dark forced him to slow as he bumped over the ruts and holes.

When they arrived, the moon had risen, throwing enough light for him to see without a light. He opened the truck's service compartment and found Enis, wide-eyed and panting, hyperventilating as if she might pass out or worse.

He ripped the tape from her mouth and said, "Breathe. Slow deep breaths."

She screamed instead, and he smiled. "No one will hear you."

He dragged her from the truck into the house and dropped her on the floor.

"Oh my, God!" Enis wailed. "What is that?"

The shack's interior was pitch black, but the stench of the rotting bodies was overpowering. She vomited and then screamed again. "Help me! Dear God, someone, help me!"

"God?" Hob shook his head in disgust as he released the handcuffs.

Her eyes filled with hope for a moment.

The hope vanished, and fear returned when he jerked her upright, looping the cuffs over the chain between the posts and ratcheting them closed again. "You think God's listening to you?" he sneered.

Enis hung from the chain, inches from the decomposing bodies of Doris Mills and Henry Rush. Hob turned on a flashlight so she could see, and the screams came again.

"I wonder." He leaned close to her face. "Did they scream like that? The children?"

"No!" she cried, but he was gone.

45. Eyes and Ears

"Where the hell have you been?" Web Seymour said as Toby Jones walked around the back corner of the house.

He sat in a wicker chair under a trellised gazebo in the backyard of his home, three blocks off the court square in Dykes. The neighborhood of older homes was in what passed for the fashionable section of town, a place where the local elite lived. He sipped from the glass of bourbon at his side, took a long pull from a cigar, and stared down at Jones. "Well?"

"Been with the OSI people all day," Jones said. "Got here as soon as I could."

"And?"

"Well ..." Jones paused, looking up at Seymour under his gazebo, on his throne, holding court like the pompous ass he was. It wasn't a matter of how much to tell Seymour. He would tell him everything. He had to because doing otherwise would be foolhardy. The hesitation was so he could prepare for Seymour's inevitable response to the news that they, The OSI, wanted him to work with them.

He decided to wait before sharing that news and began by saying, "They have questions ... a lot of them."

"No shit." Seymour sneered. "Tell me."

"Mostly, they think people are keeping a secret from them that might lead to the killer."

"Who in the hell put that idea in their heads?" Seymour glared at him. "You?"

"No." Jones shook his head emphatically. "I didn't say anything. I swear."

"You had to say something when they started asking questions. What was it?"

"I don't know ... not much. What could I say?" Jones shook his head quickly. "I just told them Doyle was a good man, everyone liked him, no enemies ... that sort of thing."

"And the Buxtons?"

"Just said that they didn't get along with anyone, stayed to themselves." Jones shrugged. "Not much, really."

"Not much? Then why do they have questions about a secret?"

"Well, Chloe Sutter said pretty much what I said, so that was okay, but then she tried to blame the killing on them."

"On them? How?"

"Said that if it wasn't for Ox and Harley, Doyle would still be alive. That got George and Bob thinking."

"George and Bob?"

"That's their names ... the OSI investigators."

"I know their names, dammit!" Seymour's eyes narrowed. "You on a first-name basis with them now?"

"They told me to call them by their names," Jones said meekly. "I didn't think that was anything bad, so ..."

"Shut up!" Seymour growled. "What did it get them thinking?"

"Well ..." Jones took a breath, thinking how to say it all so it would make sense. "Ox and Harley were killed too, but if Chloe thinks they had something to do with it, it must be because they did something bad, and Doyle got caught up in it ... somehow."

"Anything else get them thinking about secrets?"

"Mimsy got them thinking, too." Jones hesitated again, then sighed and spit it out. "She told them Ox was a good husband and got along with everyone, said lots of nice things about him and Harley ... stuff no one else was saying. So, they figured she's hiding something, or her story wouldn't be so different."

"And what'd you say to all that?" Seymour was chewing the end of the cigar now.

"Not much, I guess." Jones shrugged. "Things like Ox was her husband, and maybe she didn't want to say anything bad about him, but I mean, they're the OSI, and they want answers."

"Of course, they want their damned answers!" Seymour's face reddened as his voice rose in volume. "Your job was to make sure they get the answers we want them to have."

"Right." Jones nodded. "Just that ... well, Doyle was killed, left to die in that cave, and it just seems we ought to do right by him, get the person who did it. The only way I see to do right for him is for that to happen."

"Too late for that," Seymour snapped back, then looked hard into Jones's eyes. "Doyle Sutter was part of this ... you too ... hell, everybody was. You want to do right by him, then we keep our mouths shut. If we don't, what do you think happens to the way people remember Doyle ... the sheriff who let it go on for all those years?"

Jones nodded at the ground, then said hopefully, "It was just those two boys. Everything else he did was on the up and up ... to help people and do the right thing. Won't people remember the good things, too?"

"Hell no, they won't. What they'll remember is the story that will hit the news reports in Atlanta ... sheriff in a backwater county let two boys be abused to the point that one ran off and disappeared and the other beaten so bad he can't feed himself or wipe his own ass. They'll dig and find out the mother killed herself and her husband too, and you know what they're gonna want to know?"

Seymour didn't wait for a response. He threw the lit cigar into the yard, red sparks flying from the tip, barely missing Jones. "They'll ask questions and want to know why, if the sheriff wouldn't step in, why didn't you, or me, or every other son of a bitch in the county step in to stop it. They'll want to know what kind of people wouldn't do that? They'll dig until they find out who knew what was going on, didn't do a damned thing about it except look the other way?"

"Maybe we can make up for it by telling the truth now ... apologize, sort of ... say we wish we'd done better."

Seymour cut him off. "Shut the fuck up! There isn't any making up for it, you dumb shit. Sutter and the Buxtons are dead, and we know why and never did anything to stop it from happening. That's all the damned reports are going to say. We'll be ruined!"

"I suppose." Jones nodded, then offered meekly. "It would be an embarrassment, but it seems people would forget after a while. Things would go back to normal."

"Did you not hear what I just said?" Seymour shouted. "We'll be ruined ... I'll be ruined! My reputation ... yours ... everyone's ... the county that stood by and let two little boys be beat to hell and back ... beat so bad their mama killed their daddy, then shot herself out of guilt. That shit will be all over the news."

Jones stood in the yard before the gazebo, waiting for Seymour's rage to ebb before giving him the next bit of news that was sure to send another tidal wave of fury in his direction. He allowed a minute to pass before he looked up and said, "There's something else."

"What?" Seymour snarled, glaring down at him.

"They want me to work with them on this."

"Work with them? What's that mean?"

"I don't know exactly." Jones shrugged. "But I'm supposed to be back at seven in the morning. They say they need someone local for background information and such."

"You're just a part-time deputy. You've got a job. Did you tell them that?"

"I did." Jones nodded. "Said they'd clear it with the governor ... make up any difference in pay, so it wouldn't be a burden on the county."

"Son of a bitch!"

The tidal wave rushed over him. Jones stood there and took it while Seymour raged on about his stupidity and incompetence. Finally, the tide subsided, and Seymour took a deep breath.

"Alright, you meet them ... you work with them ... but you are my eyes and ears." He pointed a finger at Jones. "Don't you forget it, and whatever you do, you don't say anything, do anything, even think anything that might let them know what's behind those men being left to die in that cave."

Jones nodded without speaking.

"Now get the hell out of here!"

46. The Right Questions

Bayne County wasn't dry. You could buy beer and wine if you knew where to look for it, and even hard liquor out at the package store on the county line, but finding a restaurant that served beer with food required a trip out to the state highway.

It wasn't that people didn't drink. They did but drank in private, where they weren't likely to run into their pastor, or deacon, or president of the Ladies Church Auxiliary.

Jean's Restaurant huddled in a gravel lot a mile from the Kwik Pak where Doyle Sutter had been employed. They walked into a room full of people eating and speaking in animated fashion. As the door closed behind them, heads turned, and conversations ceased, like a scene from an old western when the stranger enters the saloon. It was the OSI men everyone had heard about, but few had seen close up.

There wasn't much to see, just two men who looked like they might be traveling through to go fishing. Their curiosity piqued, but far from satisfied, the diners did the polite thing and returned to their meals, voices lowered, and conversations now whispered.

A rotund and smiling woman, her gray hair pulled back in a bun, came up, beaming with red-faced pleasure. "I was wondering if I was gonna see you in here." She leaned toward them and lowered her voice. "I thought I might since those high-minded places in Dykes won't serve a beer in public, and you ..." She stood up straight, looking them up and down. "You look like drinkin' men."

"That we are." George grinned.

"Good." She patted the back of her hair and added, "I'm Jean, by the way."

"I'm George, and this is Bob."

"Happy to meet you. Got a preference on where to sit?"

"How about that corner table back there?" George pointed to a table with good views of the front door and back kitchen area.

"You got it." Jean led the way, handed them menus, waited for them to sit, and said, "Beers?"

"Beers." Both men nodded.

"Any particular beer?"

"A cold one," George said, grinning.

"Yep, that would be the best kind." Jean laughed and bustled off.

George looked around the room. "Mostly locals, I'd guess."

"They do appear to be from around here," Bob agreed, noticing George examining the faces. "You think they know? Whatever it is everyone is so closed-mouth about?"

"Maybe." George shrugged. "I wouldn't be surprised."

Jean showed up with the beers and set them on the table. "Get you boys anything to eat?"

"Sure. What's good?" George reached for a menu tucked between the salt and pepper shaker and hot sauce.

"Save your time," Jean said. "I suppose I should say everything's good, but Ralph, my regular cook, is off deep-sea fishing in Florida. That leaves me in the kitchen, and I'm not nearly as good at slinging hash as he is, but ..." She leaned toward them, whispering conspiratorially. "I make a damned fine meatloaf, complete with mashed potatoes, gravy, fresh green beans out of my garden, and a salad if you want it."

"Meatloaf it is." George grinned and put the menu back in its place. "Blue cheese on the salad."

"Me too." Bob nodded.

Jean bustled off, and they sat for a minute sipping beer, scanning the faces of the diners. Now and again, one would look their way and then turn away quickly. Despite their exaggerated indifference, the topic of their hushed conversations seemed obvious.

"What do you suppose they're talking about?" Bob said wryly.

"Us." George shrugged. "Anything out of the ordinary is big news in a place like this."

"More out of the ordinary than three murders?" Bob looked at a man at an adjacent table, who lifted a forkful of mashed potatoes and turned away.

"Good point," George said and smiled. "See any guilty faces in the crowd?"

"Yeah." Bob nodded. "All of them ... guilty of hiding something, knowing something we don't."

George nodded. "You're right."

Jean returned with the platters of food and two more beers. "I figured you for at least two beers, so I brought another."

"You figured right." George smiled, downed the last of the first, and lifted the second. "Thank you."

"No problem. Let me know if you need anything else." Jean bustled away, stopping briefly at a few tables, no doubt to answer questions about the newcomers.

They finished the meatloaf, and as Jean promised, it was damned fine. She cleared the plates, and they ordered another round of beers. George's phone chimed just after Jean put them on the table. Once again, heads turned in his direction, curiosity, and something else. Apprehension, nervousness, guilt?

He waited for Jean to move away, then lifted the phone, holding it tight against his ear. It was Sharon. "Hey, babe. Still at supper. I'll call you when I get back to the motel."

"Got the info you wanted," Sharon said, without preliminaries. "Thought you'd want to hear it as soon as possible."

"You're still at work?"

"Nothing waiting for me at home but a microwaved frozen dinner, so I figured I'd see what I could find."

"And?"

"Found quite a bit."

George had asked her earlier to check for information about any other Buxton family members. He would have never called it a hunch. Hunches were for suckers. He preferred to think of it as investigative intuition based on the reactions they'd gotten from everyone regarding Ox and Harley Buxton.

He pulled out his pad and pen. "Let's have it."

Sharon recounted the family history she had discovered, going back to the first Buxton to move into the mountain forests that would eventually become Bayne County. From there, she brought things forward until she got to Ox and said, "Turns out, Ox was not an only child. He had an older brother."

"I'll be damned."

"I take it no one mentioned that little fact to you yet."

"Not a word. Fill me in."

"Clarence Buxton, Junior. Took the name of Ace ... unofficially ... and even used it as a middle name on legal documents. Ace had a wife, Emma, and they had two children ... sons, William Hobson and Calvin James."

George scribbled in the notepad, "Son of a bitch."

Each new detail solidified the theory that there was a secret in the eyes of the people sneaking peeks at them in the restaurant. Bayne County was too small for people not to know.

"Any address on Ace and his family? Are they still in the area?"

"Well, they might be. I would assume they are ... buried in the local cemetery."

"What?" George lifted his head and looked at Bob, waiting patiently to be briefed on the call, but reading in George's face that Sharon had just revealed an important piece of information.

"They're dead. Turns out, Emma killed Ace ... shot him, and then turned the gun on herself. Left a note to have her boys sent to foster care. When the state CPS investigator checked, the older boy had already been gone a couple of years earlier, but no one knew where."

"And the younger, Calvin?"

"Went to live with his uncle Ox," Sharon said.

"They thought they could get by without telling us any of this," George said in disbelief.

"Probably never thought it would get to this point."

"How could they think that?"

"My theory is they never expected the bodies to be found," Sharon said and added, chuckling. "They didn't count on George Mackey ... the human bloodhound ... and his instinct for sniffing out dead bodies."

"Funny." George looked at his notes. "So, if the older boy ran off and disappeared, where's the younger, Calvin? We never saw him when we visited Ox's widow, and she never mentioned him."

"In a rehabilitation center, Sagg Manor, about an hour's drive from Atlanta. He suffered some type of brain injury. And who do you think pays for that?"

"Enlighten me."

"All paid for by William Hobson Payne."

George put the pen down and shook his head. "He changed his name."

"Yep, and that got me digging some more. William Hobson Buxton enlisted in the Army. He changed his name to Payne shortly after receiving a hardship discharge."

"What was the hardship?" George asked but suspected he knew the answer.

"Haven't been able to track that down yet. Army red tape."

"So, mother kills father and then herself, but before that, one son runs off and joins the Army, and then the other ends up in a hospital with brain injuries." George shook his head. "And no one said a word about it."

"That's about the size of it."

"You never fail to amaze," George said, and meant it.

"Well, wrap this up and get your ass home," Sharon said in her teasing way. "And I'll show you something really *amazing*."

"Soon, babe. Soon," George said and disconnected.

"Let's get back to the motel so you can brief me." Bob had picked up bits and pieces, listening to George's end of the conversation. "Sounds like Sharon answered some questions for us."

"Better." George nodded, scanning his notes. "Now we know the right questions to ask."

47. No Deal

Toby Jones scurried away around the side of the house and out of sight. As night came on, Web Seymour continued to sit under his gazebo, a king with matters of state weighing on his mind. He poured three more fingers of bourbon into the glass on the table, took a long swallow, and fished in his shirt pocket for one of the cigars he kept there to hand out when glad-handing constituents.

Seymour had always been the biggest bullfrog in the county, like his daddy before him. He croaked the loudest, always had the upper hand, and controlled everything and everyone in his little mud puddle.

Even Ox and Ace Buxton, belligerent, loud-mouthed, and vindictive as they were, had a sort of mutual coexistence agreement with Seymour. They avoided trouble with him, and he allowed them a measure of tolerance he afforded to no one else, as long as they kept their bullying away from his inner circle. The three men understood that doing otherwise would have resulted in the same type of mutually assured destruction that had kept the superpowers from blowing the world apart during the Cold War. It would have been a struggle that no one would win.

Instead, they developed a system of détente, and it worked well enough until Emma Buxton killed Ace and took her own life. Damn that woman, Seymour thought, grinding his teeth. She started the whole damned thing ... could have run off with her boys ... shot Ace quietly in the head while he slept, and just left. People would have pretended to look for her, but everyone would have understood, and no one except Ox would have really cared.

The truth was, they would have privately appreciated the killing as an act of community service. They couldn't exactly give her a medal for murdering her husband, but no jury of her peers was about to find her guilty for killing the biggest asshole in the county.

But no, the bitch had to go and kill herself, make the boys orphans, get the state involved, and get Cal sent to live with Ox. If she had done anything else, they wouldn't be in this mess now.

No one was talking for now, but everyone knew that Hob Buxton was behind what had happened in the cave. Shame, guilt, fear of being tied to what happened all contributed to their silence on the matter, but it was only a matter of time before the damned OSI people put things together.

Fuck! He slammed a fist into the arm of the chair.

This was supposed to be a simple search for the missing men. Mimsy Buxton and Chloe Sutter had demanded that he do something, or they would let the world know what kind of people lived in Bayne County. Cowards who looked the other way while men beat and tortured their wives and children.

He wasn't sure Mimsy would follow through with the threat, but he knew Chloe would. She was no shrinking flower and could be a trouble maker, and not one to give in until someone did something to find her missing husband.

Fine. He would make a show of trying to find their husbands and promised to call the governor and have the OSI organize a search. Then, when they came up empty, he could go back to the women and tell them they did their best, but their husbands were gone without a trace.

He'd planned it all. He'd even pay off the mortgages on their homes out of his own pocket to show his good faith. The rest of the county would nod and smile and comment to each other what a good man Web Seymour was. Everyone would have felt better about everything ... about themselves ... about never speaking up or standing up to Ace and Ox for what they were doing.

Except the OSI didn't come up empty. They found the cave.

He slammed his fist into the chair again. Fuck Hob Buxton too! He should have picked a better place to do it.

No one could prove he was responsible, but everyone in the county knew he was. It was as if he planned it all so that the people in Bayne County would share the blame for what happened to him and his brother. What right did he have to do that?

The little son of a bitch! Why should they share the blame? The people of Bayne County never intentionally did anything to harm the boys. No one liked Ace and Ox, but what they did in their own homes was nobody's business. Now, if the news comes out about the reason for the murders ... Shit!

He shook his head. Not if it comes out. When it comes out. Seymour downed the bourbon and poured another.

He should have found another way to satisfy Mimsy and Chloe. Instead, he'd wanted to show he could flex his muscles with the governor and had gotten the OSI involved. Now, the media in Atlanta were sure to pick up the story. Reporters would start nosing around, prying into the secrets. Worst of all, his plan to expand his fortune would evaporate.

It was a simple enough business proposition. A Japanese manufacturer of electronic auto components was looking for a quiet, remote location with cheap land, low taxes, and proximity to the interstates and railroads to ship their product. Besides placing the site away from the turmoil of big cities, they emphasized they preferred privacy, a place with no controversy or scandal, where they could work closely with the local government to achieve their mutually beneficial interests without outside interference. Seymour assured them he *was the local government*. His door would always be open to them, and their interests protected.

He courted them for a year, regularly visiting Atlanta to meet with them in a luxury hotel suite in Buckhead. During those visits, he learned a bit about their business culture.

He picked up the habit of bowing, a quick nod of greeting and respect, and of waiting respectfully for the senior member of their delegation to address him. It seemed a good practice and one he wouldn't have minded importing to Bayne County, and though it would never happen, the thought of the backslapping, good ole boys coming around, bowing, and waiting for him to address them was appealing.

He also found that they were concerned that any business arrangement appears not only legal but moral, which meant it must seem beneficial to all. The lowest nōdo—serf—should be grateful for the opportunity to toil for their overlords.

He also learned they didn't mind using influence, but it could never appear to be bribery. There was bribery, of course, but it was always disguised as goodwill, a gift to show appreciation for his help.

Most importantly, he noted their cultural aversion to impropriety. In their politely indirect but clear manner, they made sure he understood that any business deal tainted with even the hint of corruption or scandal was intolerable.

Seymour assured them he understood their requirements and ushered them through the process of evaluating and acquiring the land they would need for the plant. Once they settled on the location, he purchased the land they planned to use, paying half what he would charge the Japanese company to buy it.

When the county commission approved the new plant—and he would make sure they did—he would sell them the land at a new, inflated price. The Japanese company was satisfied with this arrangement. Their CEO smiled and nodded, telling him his prosperity was theirs as well. His approval was a polite way of saying it is acceptable for you to take advantage of the arrangement, but remember this—you are our man and work for us.

When the deal closed, they would thank him and give a polite bow, knowing they were paying more than they could have, but happy to see their new partner flourish as long as they got what they wanted. Seymour would pocket a fortune from the sale and see they got what they wanted. Now, all of his planning, the ingratiating meetings with the CEO and his underlings, everything would go up in smoke.

The evening newscasts out of Atlanta would show reporters standing in front of the courthouse, talking about the county that didn't care about the little abused boys and their mother. When the news came out about the murders and the people of Bayne County who turned a blind eye to the abuse of children, the Japanese would walk away.

Loathe to be drawn into a local controversy, they would meet with him a final time in the hotel suite. He could see them sitting in the same room where he'd come to the business arrangement with them.

They would look at him solemnly and listen politely to his explanation. Then, the leader of the delegation, the company's CEO, would say sadly, "It is regrettable that this has happened. We had plans for much success together, but ..." He would shake his head. "No deal."

Seymour threw the glass across the yard, shattering it against the backyard shed. The shards of glass sparkled like mini-stars in the moonlight, tinkling and falling, then blinking out as they hit the ground.

48. Frightened

They were chance encounters, random events that sometimes alter lives ... or end them. If Carl Galman had accepted any of the other twenty or so assignments from the contract service that employed him, he would probably still be alive. But by chance, he selected the one that would cost him his life. It happened this way.

Mitzy Dorner had lived in Atlanta all of her life. She married there, raised two children, a son, and a daughter, and grew old as everyone does if they live long enough.

In the 1950s, she and her husband Sid opened a small retail clothing store downtown. Their business thrived, and they became known as a sort of high-end clothing boutique, employing three tailors to custom fit their customers' selections. It was a time when people still went into the city to shop and not to the sprawling suburban malls.

Along the way, Mitzy and Sid bought a house in the Piedmont Park district of the city. Unlike many of the original owners, they stayed, weathered the area's decline, and then saw it flourish once again as young, upwardly mobile professionals moved in and began renovating. Yuppies, Sid called them, but they were happy to have the neighborhood improve again.

In 2004, Sid passed away after fifty-two years of marriage, suffering a heart attack as Mitzy slept beside him in the same bed they'd shared most of those years. He was seventy-five. Their children encouraged Mitzy to enter a retirement home, where she would have comfort, security, and companionship with people her age, but she would have none of it.

"I've lived in this house for more than fifty years, and I have no intention of moving," she told her children. "This is my home, and I plan to stay here until I die."

No amount of reasoning could change her mind. Things were fine for several years. Both children had moved away to raise their families and make their lives, her son to the Boston area and her daughter to San Diego. Visits were regular but infrequent, mostly on holidays when they could schedule time away from their lives. Mitzy understood and always assured them she was fine living in the old house, surrounded by the life she and Sid had made and her memories of the man who was the love of her life.

In time, the years caught up with Mitzy. Now in her nineties, she was confined to a wheelchair by a neurologic disorder that left her slumped, her head perpetually on her chest and twisted to the side, and her legs unable to walk.

Her son and daughter insisted she enter a nursing facility, but again, she refused. Despite her physical disabilities, her mind remained keen and able to suggest an alternative. She would hire someone to care for her in her home, where she would stay until the time came for her to meet Sid.

The senior care service her children found would provide their mother twenty-four-hour assistance for the rest of her life. The out-of-pocket cost was modest, just a reasonable monthly fee, but as part of the contract, the service required a hefty percentage of her assets once she expired. Mitzy agreed to the terms, and her children, who were doing well for themselves, did not object to losing most of their inheritance as payment for their mother's care if it made her happy and comfortable in her waning years.

That's when the first chance encounter occurred. Carl Galman came into Mitzy's life. The senior care service he worked for as a contract nurse/attendant gave him a selection of possible assignments. Working the day shift for an old woman in Piedmont Park seemed like easy money, so Carl took the job.

It wasn't long before the night nurse, an experienced caregiver named Maureen, became concerned that Carl was neglecting Mitzy during the day. Maureen often had to clean her, finding that she had released her bowels or bladder, sitting in her wheelchair.

When she confronted Carl, he said that it must have just happened, and he couldn't help it if the old woman's bowel movements were timed to his departure schedule. He shrugged and grinned. Just the luck of the draw, he told her.

Maureen complained to the care provider service they contracted with but was told there had been no complaints from Mitzy or her family. It was best that she just learn to get along with Carl, do her job, and not make waves.

Nothing changed for several months. Then Carl's second chance encounter occurred.

His habit was to take Mitzy to the nearby park, assuring the daughter and son that he made sure Mitzy had plenty of fresh air every day. Placing her chair under a tree in a secluded section of the park, he would meet with one of the women he claimed were his girlfriends but who had to be paid for their company. Sometimes, he played cards and gambled with a group that gathered there daily.

He did all this while being paid a nice salary to care for Mitzy, leaving her for hours in the wheelchair. Head drooping, her chin on her chest, drooling because her facial muscles had atrophied, without food or water or restroom access, semi-conscious, Mitzy was unable to call for help.

Sometimes, one of the dealers lurking perpetually in the park's dark corners dropped by to sell him drugs, and Carl always walked away with an ounce or so of weed in his pocket. The senior care service drug tested their contractors periodically but not very often, and the tests were unsupervised. Carl could go into a bathroom alone, where he would pour in the small vial of clean urine he kept handy for just such occasions.

On this day, a parks department maintenance worker was repairing the plumbing in a secluded restroom in the same quiet section of the park. The assignment had fallen to Hob Payne, and after completing the repair, he came from the restroom with his tool bag and walked to his truck. Across a wide expanse of high grass, up against a tree line, he saw an old woman sitting alone in a wheelchair. He had noticed her earlier, hadn't thought much about it, and went to work.

Seeing the woman in the same position, slumped down and not moving, he hurried over to investigate. He found Mitzy Dorner unconscious, her face flushed bright red, and the air around her pungent with the smell of excrement and urine from emptying her bowels and bladder in the wheelchair.

"Ma'am?" He touched her arm and found it hot and dry. She was dehydrated.

He looked around, but there was no one in sight. He got behind the wheelchair and began pushing it toward his truck, planning to take her to the maintenance shop where there was water, and he could call for an ambulance.

"What the fuck you doing?" Carl Galman shouted as he emerged from the trees, pulling his belt tight around his waist. A thin, scantily dressed woman followed him.

"Getting this woman some help," Hob said, turning to see Carl advancing rapidly, fists balled.

"Get the fuck out of here!" Carl came up within inches of Hob's face, shouting and holding a fist in his face. "I'm responsible for her."

"If that's true, you're not doing a very good job." Hob stood his ground, eyes narrowed, glaring into Carl's. "You left this woman here without food or water, no restroom, alone where anything might have happened to her."

"That's none of your business. Get the fuck away, like I said."

Hob looked at the prostitute, who had stopped several feet away, watching the confrontation. "Get out of here."

"Sure you want me to? You seem awful uptight." She smiled and scratched under her left tit. "I bet I could put a smile on that face."

"Get out of here," Hob said, his voice quiet and hard. "Now."

"Okay, fine. I been paid." The prostitute scowled and looked at Carl. "Make sure your friend doesn't come around next time, big boy."

The prostitute scurried away, disappearing back into the trees.

"You son of a bitch! You cost me a good lay." Carl leaned closer. "I'm telling you to get the fuck away from here."

Hob ignored him and reached for the wheelchair to push it toward his truck.

"Goddammit!" Carl threw a roundhouse sucker punch, catching Hob behind the right ear.

It was just a chance encounter. If Hob hadn't been working on the restroom repair that day, if Carl had chosen a different assignment from the senior care service provider, if he had met the prostitute in another part of the park, if it had been anyone but Hob who saw Mitzy in the wheelchair, if any of a million other possibilities had had happened, what followed would have been avoided.

But they did happen, all of them. Carl's fist struck Hob on the side of the head, and Carl's fate was sealed.

The blow was hard and stopped Hob in his tracks. It came as a surprise but was far from disabling. He'd been hit harder by his own father.

Hob spun around, pulling the fourteen-inch pipe wrench from a loop in his tool belt. It was pure reflex, not how he would have planned things, but the wrench caught Carl in the forehead, sending him to the ground like a two-hundred-thirty-pound sack of wet cement. Hob looked around, scanning the area for anyone who might have seen.

Had anyone been watching, he would have called for help and explained that he was defending himself from assault while trying to help the old woman, but no one saw. This section of the park was almost always deserted, too far from the usual parking and picnic areas for someone taking a casual stroll. The only people who came this far were the serious runners who always moved in groups as a precaution against the muggers, druggies, and whores, known to hang out here.

Seeing they were alone, Hob turned to Carl, moaning in the grass, blood pooling around his head. He lifted the wrench high over his head and brought it down, crushing Carl's skull with one blow. The moaning ceased, but Hob hit him again and then once more for good measure. Then he turned to the old woman and pushed her rapidly away toward his truck.

After lifting her bodily into the front passenger seat, he stowed the wheelchair in the truck bed, then raced to the park's maintenance shed, calling for an ambulance from his phone. At the shed, he left the truck running and the air conditioner blowing, ran inside, and retrieved a bottle of cold water from the case the department kept in the refrigerator.

"What the hell happened to you?" His supervisor looked up from his desk, face wrinkled in disgust. "You smell like shit."

Hob grabbed the water and ran back to the truck. When the paramedics arrived, he was trying to get the old woman to take a sip.

Mitzy Dorner was immediately given an IV and whisked off to the hospital. She was near death, but William Hobson Payne, a parks department maintenance worker, was credited for saving her life.

In his report to the paramedics, Hob said he'd found her abandoned in a section of the park far from where he encountered Carl Galman by the trees. Seeing that she was in distress, he immediately put her in the air-conditioned truck, called 911, and brought her to the maintenance shop to get some water.

Mitzy recovered eventually, and her children dismissed the senior care service company. There would be no more arguing with her. She would go into an assisted living facility where she would receive proper supervised care. Her only memory of what happened was a young man trying to give her some water. She called him her angel.

The company Carl worked for issued a dismissal letter but had to hold on to it. No one knew where Carl was. It wasn't until five days later when the landscape crew came around to cut the grass, that his body was discovered.

Identifying him as Mitzy Dorner's missing caregiver didn't take long. Police developed a working theory that he'd left Mitzy alone in the area where Hob had reported finding her. Then he went to the park's secluded section to buy drugs, meet a prostitute, or both. There were some signs that he had recently had sex, but the condition of the body made that difficult to prove. The elevated level of THC in his system was conclusive evidence that he'd consumed cannabis in some form shortly before his death.

As far as police were concerned, the death of Carl Galman was just another drug deal gone bad. William Hobson Payne received a nice letter of thanks from Mitzy's son and daughter, and the parks department gave him a commendation and recognized him as the employee of the month.

For days after, Hob lay awake at night, thinking about the events. It was not the way he would have ever planned it.

His mind was in a turmoil. Whatever he was, he did not consider himself a killer, not like that, not with the brutality and rage he'd felt as the pipe wrench crashed into Carl Galman's skull.

Yes, he had caused the deaths of others, planned them all in minute detail. There was purpose in the planning, a meaning to it all. It wasn't about justice. That seemed too presumptuous, a high and mighty concept best left to judges and juries, and he knew from experience that too often justice was not just.

He held no grand illusions about what he was doing. He was not some righteous avenger. It was a balancing he sought. Those who caused pain must suffer like pain. Nothing more, and nothing less. They could not be allowed to live their lives inflicting pain without consequence. The terrible things that had happened to him and Cal had to be balanced somehow or the universe—his universe—would spin off kilter until it destroyed itself, until it destroyed him.

He could have simply helped the old woman in the park, seen that she was cared for and protected her. Instead, he had acted out of rage.

He thought about what happened, the words exchanged, Carl Galman's red face, being hit in the head. Most of all, he remembered how it felt when the pipe wrench crashed into Galman's skull, the visceral thrill and release from within.

He remembered all this, and wondered what he was becoming, and that frightened him. He had a mission to complete, and Carl Galman had been a distraction.

He had to talk to someone, and there was only one person he could go to for that.

49. To Him, It Is Sin

"Think he'll be there?" Bob asked.

It was six-forty-five, and after talking over the information Sharon had provided the night before and coming up with a strategy for the day, they were headed to the courthouse. George nodded without looking away from the road. "He'll be there."

"You know, he left us yesterday and went straight to report to Seymour."

"Seems likely," George agreed. "Doesn't change anything. Seymour wants to know what we know, so he'll make sure Jones shows up."

George was right. Toby Jones was waiting for them in the conference room that had become their headquarters. He looked up and put on the best smile he could. "Morning. What's on the agenda today?"

"Let's start with you?" George said bluntly, dropping into a chair across the table.

"Me?"

"You." George nodded solemnly.

"I already told you everything I ..."

"You lied."

"No." Jones shook his head emphatically. "No, I wouldn't do that."

"Yes, you would, and you did," Bob said from the end of the table, forcing Jones to turn his head to throw him off balance. It was a technique sometimes used when interrogating a suspect. Toby Jones wasn't a suspect, but they now knew he had been less than cooperative as a witness.

"No. I swear. I wouldn't do that."

"Sure, you would," George said, smiling sadly. "Don't worry, though. We know you're not the only one. Everyone has been lying to us."

"Maybe others, but not me." Jones's face reddened at the unexpected tone the OSI men had taken with him. "I told you the truth, and I ..."

"Stop." George raised a hand, cutting him off. "You told us part of the truth, not all of it, and that's the same as a lie. You're supposed to be a law enforcement officer working to help solve three murders, but you kept important information from us."

"What information?" Jones asked, but the look in his eyes told them he knew exactly what they were driving at.

"Time to cut the bullshit, Toby. You're cop enough to know that we would want to know about all the family ... anyone associated with the Buxtons." George shook his head, staring hard into Jones's eyes. "But you never said a word about Ox's brother, Ace. Never told us that his wife Emma killed him and then herself. Nothing about their sons, one who ran off and joined the Army and the other who went to live with Ox until he ended up in a rehab center after he suffered a brain injury and was confined to a wheelchair."

Jones sat openmouthed for a moment, then looked down and nodded. "What do you want me to say?"

"How about telling us why." Bob spoke softly now, changing the tone, and once again, the change between the two investigators, one harsh and demanding, the other taking a softer approach, was intended to throw Jones off balance. It worked.

The floodgates opened, and it all spilled out. Ox and his brother Ace weren't just assholes that people preferred to avoid. They intimidated everyone. People feared them and what they would do if they crossed them. Hell, Jones was afraid of them. So were Doyle Sutter and Harvey Pursall before him.

Afraid of the bullies, everyone looked the other way and ignored the abuse the men heaped on their wives and children, especially on Hob and Cal Buxton. Interfering meant having to spend the rest of your life sleeping with one eye open, worried that a mysterious fire might start in the middle of the night, or livestock would turn up dead, equipment damaged, dogs shot ... whatever retribution the Buxtons could take on the offender. And it would be never-ending because the Buxtons never forgot or forgave. No one wanted to live like that.

George and Bob listened without interrupting. When Jones ran out of steam, George shook his head. "Hard to understand how a whole county of supposedly decent people turn their heads." He looked hard at Jones and the badge on his chest. "Even when a boy was beaten so badly, he suffered brain damage, no one spoke up. No one did a damned thing."

"You're right. I don't know what to say." Jones shook his head, staring at his lap. "Hard to explain what it's like ... trying to deal with someone who doesn't care about the law, or what's right ... when all they want is revenge. We're just not the kind of people to know what to do about that. Then after a while ... when it goes on all the time for so long ..." Jones shrugged. "Then it's just the way things are. You accept it because you know that no one else will stand up to change things. So, you do what everyone else does, and when everyone does nothing, it seems normal ... just how things are."

"How things are?" George could not hide the tone of disgust in his voice and didn't try. "You did nothing. An entire county did nothing."

"You're right, and we were shamed by it. That's why no one ever says anything about it," Jones said, still staring at his lap, his voice low and embarrassed. "It's a terrible thing to live ashamed. You kind of put a shell around what causes the shame and push it out of sight, so you don't think about it. Everyone stayed away from the Buxtons because they were afraid of them and, at the same time, ashamed of being afraid." He looked up and, for the first time, looked George in the eye and nodded. "But staying away doesn't mean you aren't ashamed ... you are. So, you don't talk about it ... to anyone."

"Therefore, to him that knoweth to do good, and doeth *it* not, to him it is sin," Bob said softly.

George and Toby Jones turned toward him. "What?" George said.

"The Bible, James 4:17." Bob smiled and nodded.

"Didn't know you were a Bible scholar," George said, mildly surprised but not overly so. Bob had always been a bit of an enigma for a hard-core investigator, thoughtful while the rest of the team worked frantically to break open an investigation.

"Mom and Dad taught Sunday school growing up," Bob said, shrugging. "Something stuck, I guess. Seems to fit in this case."

"It does." Jones nodded. "We sinned ... all of us."

"Well, if you think that, then let's do some repenting," George said, standing. "You're going to help us finish this."

"Tell me what to," Jones said.

"We're going to see Mimsy, and you can tell her what you told us."

***

Toby Jones did just that, and when George told her, "We know about Ace and Emma, William and Calvin Buxton," Mimsy became terrified, shaking, her eyes darting around the front room of her house.

"There wasn't nothing I could do," she sobbed, shaking her head, and wiping her eyes. She looked at Jones. "Who was I gonna call about it all? You?"

Jones looked away, the shame back on his face.

"Doyle Sutter?" Mimsy said. "Or Harvey Pursall before him? They was all afraid. No one wanted to come up against Ox and Ace." Her brow furrowed, and she looked up, angry now. "It was left to me and Emma to deal with them. We did what we could ... more than anyone else did."

"You could have gone somewhere ... anywhere," George said.

"Gone where? With what money." She shook her head, sobbing again. "You don't know how it was ... how it still is remembering it all, afraid I'll lose the house or be run out of the county 'cause no one was going to have anything to do with me for fear of what Ox would do to them."

The interview didn't take long, and they left soon after that with enough to seriously consider William Hobson Buxton-Payne a suspect. The abuse by his father and uncle established a motive for the murders. It would not have been the first time an abusive relationship ended in murder.

Mimsy stood on the porch watching them leave, sobbing and scanning the trees and hills, wondering if Hob was watching again, fearful that he might think she had betrayed him. She didn't want to be left alone in a cave to die. "I didn't tell them," she whispered. "You said not to tell them, and I didn't."

***

The follow-up interview with Chloe Sutter provided more icing on the cake. Unlike Mimsy, she was defiant and angry.

"Of course, I knew what was happening to those boys." She glared at Jones. "Everyone did, didn't they, Toby? You knew too, didn't you, Toby?"

Jones said nothing, her words just adding to the shame he already felt.

"Including your husband, Doyle. Is that right?" George threw in to let her know no one was without blame for what happened leading up to the murders.

"What was he supposed to do? Alone against those Buxton men? Not a damned soul in the county would stand up with him. He did the best he could ... what Harvey Pursall before him did."

"You mean he did nothing," George said, standing. "I think we have what we need. Thank you, Mrs. Sutter."

"Just like that?" Chloe Sutter followed him to the door as he led the others out to the porch. "You have what you need? What the hell's that supposed to mean?" She was shouting now. "It's their fault ... those Buxton! They're the cause of all this! Brought it all down on their own heads." She leaned against the doorpost as they walked across the grass to Jones's pickup, and, for the first time, she sobbed as she called after them. "And on my Doyle's head too, and all he was doing was to get along as best he could and keep the peace like they pay him to."

They climbed in the pickup, and Jones drove out to the county road.

"Peace at any price," Bob said.

"What?" George raised his eyes, amused.

"Doyle Sutter was trying to keep the peace, she said. That was Neville Chamberlain's philosophy back when Hitler was planning to take over the world."

"Oh." George smiled. "First Bible quotes and now history. You trying to educate us?"

"Nope. Just a thought. Peace at any price was Chamberlain's philosophy." He shrugged. "We ended up with World War II."

"Hmph." George folded his arms and stared out the window. "I like the Bible quote better."

50. Goodbye

"Hob!" Cal lifted his head from its usual hanging posture as his brother walked in and gave his lopsided grin.

"Hey, Cal. How's it hanging?" Hob walked to the wheelchair and put a hand on his brother's shoulder.

"How's it hanging! Good one." Cal wheezed and laughed.

"How about a walk?"

"Yes! Been waiting for a walk! Let's do it."

Hob pushed the chair down the halls of Sagg Manor, past the nurses and attendants, each calling out their usual greetings. He smiled and nodded, said a word here and there, but not with his usual good-natured exuberance.

Outside, he wheeled Cal's chair around the grounds to a far corner, set the brake, and dropped onto a bench placed there for visitors. He sat resting his elbows on his knees, looking past his brother to the trees at the edge of the property, staring as if focusing on something beyond them, something invisible that only he saw.

Cal allowed him his reverie for a minute before speaking, then said, "We need to talk."

Hob looked at him, surprised. "Is it that obvious?"

"Yes." Cal nodded. "Something is bothering you. Something big. I can see it in you."

"Really?" Hob looked into his eyes, wondering what it was Cal thought he saw. Wondering if he saw the truth.

"I know what it is." Cal forced his eyes up in his drooping head to look into Hob's face. "You've done some bad things."

"I have." Hob nodded and looked away. "How did you know?"

"I'm not on a desert island here. Maybe I don't talk so good, but I see the television reports ... the bodies in a cave in Bayne County ... Ox and Harley and Doyle Sutter. I knew it was you."

Hob nodded. Cal might be physically limited and confined to a wheelchair, but his mind was as alert and active as ever.

"Was it our cave?" Cal asked.

"It was." There was no point lying.

"I wish you had done it somewhere else."

Hob looked at Cal, studying his face, and saw the sadness there. It surprised him for a second, and then he realized he shouldn't be surprised.

"That was our place ... where we were safe," Cal said, shaking his head. "Now, it can't be that anymore. Now it's a place where bad things happened."

"They were bad people," Hob said, then nodded. "But, you're right. I'm sorry, I should have thought of that, found a different place."

"No." Cal shook his head. "You should have found a *different way* to make things right. Killing them was ..."

"I didn't kill them," Hob interrupted, shaking his head. "I left them. That's all."

"No." Cal shook his head, his eyes sad and wet. "I love you, Hob. That's why I can say this. I saw it on the news. You killed them. I wish you had done something different, anything different, so you could forgive and be at peace."

"I did forgive," Hob said and shrugged. "I had to even things out. Everything was all lopsided ... them doing what they did, going on like they always have ... and you here. I couldn't leave it like that."

"I told you I'm fine. But you ..." Cal shook his head, and tears rolled down his cheeks. "I worry about you ... for what you've done. How can you find peace now?"

Hob sat silent, staring into the trees. He'd come to see Cal to clear his mind and share it all with the only person in the world he could confide in, the only one he trusted. He had to tell him the rest. "There's more," he said.

"I thought there might be." Cal nodded, his shoulder sagging even more than usual in the wheelchair. "Tell me."

Hob talked for an hour, explaining everything he'd done ... how he'd done it ... where and when. Ox, Harley, and Doyle Sutter in the cave. Doris Mills and Henry Rush in the shack. Then, branching out when he saw the report of the children raped and tortured by their parents, unable to control himself, raging until he left Enis Walder at the shack. Then Carl Galman in the park, the feeling as he swung the pipe wrench and felt the man's skull cave under the blow.

Hob shook his head at that and added, "They were mistakes. Just to filled up with anger, I lost focus."

Stunned, Cal listened, sagging lower in the chair as Hob spoke, his chin on his chest, staring at the ground, saying nothing. He was the father confessor to his brother, hearing the terrible things Hob had done, he also heard the pain pent up for so long and now rushing out in a torrent as Hob told him everything.

Cal began to feel that he was the more fortunate of the two. Despite his disabilities and all that had happened, he'd found peace and learned to accept and look at the world through forgiving eyes. But Hob was in anguish, a tormented soul.

Cal wept silently as his brother spoke, the tears rolling down his cheeks and dampening his shirt. When everything was out, and there were no more secrets to share, and the confession ended, he looked at his brother and offered the only absolution he could. "It's all in the past. We're here now. That's what matters. Move on, Hob."

Hob looked up and touched Cal's tear-dampened cheek with a finger. "I will," he promised. "If anyone comes looking for me when this is all over, you know where I'll be."

He pushed the wheelchair back to Cal's room, leaned over, and kissed his brother's forehead. "Goodbye, Cal."

There was no promise to see you again soon. They both knew that would have been a lie, and Hob would never lie to Cal. He would never be back to visit. How could he after all that had happened and all that he'd done?

He'd done what he came to do ... confess his sins to the one person who might understand. Find peace, Cal had told him.

Hob wasn't sure how to do that. There had never been peace for him. Maybe there was a way to find it, but he knew it would not come from watching his brother slowly die in a wheelchair.

51. Mutiny

"So, how do we find him?" Toby Jones was behind the wheel of his pickup, headed back into Dykes. Now that he'd purged himself of the secrets he'd kept about the Buxton family, he was energized, a man with a load off his conscience and ready to make amends. "When do we arrest him?" he asked.

"Arrest?" Bob shook his head in the back seat. "Still work to do. We might have a suspect, but we don't have any hard evidence to hang it on."

"No evidence?" Jones turned his head. "What about everything everyone said ... what I told you? That's got to mean something."

"It does," George said. "Gives us a working theory, a good one. It shows William Payne, or Buxton, has a good reason to be angry, and yes, anger can be a motive, but it doesn't prove murder."

"Hob," Jones said.

"What?"

"We all called him Hob ... for his middle name, Hobson. His brother Cal started it, and everyone followed suit."

"Alright then ... Hob." George looked at Jones. "People didn't speak up about the type of men Ox and Ace were. That's not evidence of anything but their character and doesn't prove Hob did anything."

Jones flinched at that but remained silent.

George noticed and said, "Sorry, no offense intended, just reality."

"It's alright. I deserved it." Jones nodded. "We were weak. I was weak."

"For now, we don't have any concrete evidence. Only a theory, and a shaky one at that." George shook his head. "No judge I know is going to give us a search warrant, much less an arrest warrant, based on what we have."

"But you think Seymour will give you something that can be used as evidence?" Jones said doubtfully.

"I don't know. Maybe," George shrugged. "He's the next logical witness to confront."

Jones took a deep breath at the word confront. This would not be some simple get-together to take Seymour's statement. Confronting Web Seymour about anything would not have been in the realm of his possibilities a few days earlier.

"You understand this could be harsh," Bob said from the back seat. "Seymour will not be happy having you there."

"Just doing what he told me to do ... being his eyes and ears." Jones put on the best smile he could. Despite the attempt at bravado, the nervousness showed, and he drove hunched over the wheel as if it might turn on its own accord to avoid the coming confrontation.

When they reached Dykes, he parked by the courthouse's side entrance and stayed behind the wheel. George looked at him and shook his head. "Come with us."

"You sure?" Jones's bravado of a few minutes earlier dissipated.

"I'm sure. He needs to look you in the eye ... know that we know what's been going on."

"Okay." Jones sighed, stepped out of the pickup, and trailed them inside. The closer they came to Seymour's throne room, the more he drifted behind, a reluctant patient trying to avoid taking his medicine.

They found the commission chairman in room 107. His cell phone lay on the conference table, the speaker on, and the voice on the other end of the call immediately recognizable.

Seymour looked up, a smug expression on his face. "Here they are now,"

"Shaklee, what the hell are you doing!" Governor Fullman boomed at them over the speaker.

"Solving a murder," Bob said calmly.

"That's not what I sent you there to do. You were supposed to find the missing sheriff. You did that. If there's some sort of crime, turn it over to the locals or GBI, and get your ass back to Atlanta."

"There is *some sort* of crime ... a triple murder ... and the resources here are minimal. There's no need to send in the GBI. We're already on the scene. We can handle it."

"Did you hear what I said?" Fullman's voice raised a couple of decibels.

"I heard, and I think we'll just stay here and work the murder case." Bob remained adamant and unflustered.

George smiled. Toby Jones looked on, wide-eyed, as if the governor's anger might bring the roof down on them. Even Web Seymour stared in astonishment.

"Are you defying me?" Fullman sputtered. "I won't have it! You and Mackey head back to Atlanta now and report to me today!"

"No, sir."

"I'll have your job!"

"You already have my resignation, Governor. I'm retiring. Remember? Doesn't matter much if I move the date up some." Bob smiled. "Celia will be happy, but if you push things, I'll make sure the word gets out that the law-and-order governor did not want his investigative team to pursue a murder ... for political reasons."

"You wouldn't dare."

"You know me better than that," Bob said. "And you know I would."

"Dammit!" Fullman thundered. "Mackey, are you there? Can you hear me?"

"I hear you, Governor."

"You get your ass back to Atlanta now!"

"The last conversation we had, you wanted me gone." George looked at Bob and shrugged. If Bob was going down, he might as well follow suit. "In your words, you wanted me gone for a long time ... out of your sight. I'm just following your original order."

"I'm changing the order!"

"No," Bob said. "The order stands. I'm still the Director of the OSI, and I am ordering Investigator Mackey to stay here and lead the investigation. If you would like to dispute that publicly at your next press conference, I'll be happy to explain that this is a sound investigative decision and should be separated from politics as usual."

Fullman said nothing for several seconds. George smiled.

Bob Shaklee was a master at navigating the political currents behind the scenes, currents that would have swamped George. He imagined Governor Fullman sitting red-faced behind his desk, trying to figure a way to deal with their mutiny without turning it into a public relations disaster with the press.

Bob helped him along with his decision. "By the way, Governor, when we solve this murder, and we are very close to doing so, you will be a hero ... the governor who sought justice even for the remote voters in rural Bayne County."

It was masterful ... political checkmate tied to a life preserver. At once, Bob Shaklee defied the governor and made him a partner with something valuable to gain from the partnership.

Fullman could concede losing nothing. A successful investigation would bolster his relations and image with the Atlanta media. A failure would land on the OSI team's back, not the governor's desk.

"Get it done," Fullman said suddenly. "Keep me advised."

"Will do," Bob said.

Web Seymour stared at the faces in the room, fuming, trying to understand what had just happened. This was his county, dammit!

52. Loose Ends

He sat on a bench under an old hickory tree, eating a hamburger from a paper sack and drinking a Coke from a can. The food and drink came from Fran's Café across the street. Fran was there, sold him the food with a smile, and told him to have a good day. The woman he'd known as a child and youth, who had eased her conscience by sneaking candy to Hob and Cal when their father wasn't looking, never recognized him.

He finished the hamburger and leaned back on the bench, watching people pass, some moving briskly on errands, others just strolling. Toby Jones drove around the square in his pickup and parked by the side entrance. Two men got out with him and went inside. They were the men from the state, Hob knew, the ones who were sent to find him and bring him to justice.

He smiled. But not yet.

He watched the square. A few old men sat together on the other benches, talking, and laughing, telling old jokes, discussing the weather, or the deer season. None recognized Hob. He remembered all of them.

Many he knew by name; others were faces from the past, but all were part of the life he'd lived in Bayne County. He watched them all, living their lives and oblivious as they had always been to the things happening under their noses.

Here he was, the man who'd eliminated Ox Buxton and his bullying son Harley from their midst. If they knew, would they thank him? Throw a parade for him? Arrest him?

In a way, he was their savior, but it didn't matter. As Cal tried to convince him, God might forgive and save them, but as far as Hob was concerned, they didn't deserve to be saved.

So many were guilty. Hell, they were all guilty, had all looked the other way, safe as long as they dared not interfere with the Buxtons.

He couldn't make them all pay for what they'd done, or hadn't done, but some deserved it more than others. Ox and Harley, Doyle Sutter, Doc Rush, and Doris Mills.

And there, across the street. What about Pastor Sams coming out of the hardware store? He'd found Hob and Cal hiding out in the church after they snuck out and spent the night walking into Dykes to get away from Ace. They'd planned their escape from hell for weeks, waited until the weather was right, and the night was dark enough so that when Ace came looking for them, he'd never see them.

When they got to Dykes, they were exhausted. The sun would be up soon, and they needed a place to rest. The door to the church was unlocked, as was the habit in those days. They crept in and went into the sanctuary to hide. That's where Pastor Sams found them, asleep on a pew.

"Morning, boys."

Hob and Cal sat up, startled.

"Don't worry," Sams said, smiling. "Looks like you boys had a long night. You hungry?"

Both nodded. Hob said, "Yes."

"Come with me, then."

Sams led them into the little room at the back of the building that served as his study and prayer room. It wasn't much more than a closet with a shelf for a Bible and a few other church books, a small writing table where Sams prepared his sermons, and some chairs for visitors who came for his counseling.

"Wait here." Sams smiled and closed the door softly behind him.

A little while later, he returned with two plates of scrambled eggs, grits, and biscuits his wife had prepared. "My wife fixed you some breakfast. You eat now, and I'll check back on you in a while."

They dug into the food. They were sopping up the last of the grits with the biscuits when the door opened. Pastor Sams stood there but not smiling anymore. He stepped aside.

Ace Buxton pushed past him, thunder on his face. "You little sonsabitches, thought you'd sneak away on me? Couple of little chickenshits running in the night."

Ace was on a rampage, had roared into town at sunup, threatening everyone, swearing that anyone hiding his boys would pay for it. Everyone knew what that meant, including Pastor Sams.

Hob tried to stand between his father and Cal and caught a backhand across the mouth. Cal stood and was knocked to the floor by a fist to the side of the head.

"Brother Buxton! This is not the place for that!" Pastor Sams exclaimed, as if some other place would be just fine.

"Don't brother me. I ain't your damned brother!"

Ace grabbed each boy by the neck, a beefy fist locked around their throats, and dragged them outside. He tossed them bodily into the cab, pushing them down behind the seat, and roared out of town.

As he was dragged to the truck, Hob noticed others on the street walking by, standing on porches, driving slowly by. They looked at what was happening for an instant, then turned away, drove by, went back indoors, pretending they didn't see. But they saw. They all saw.

The beatings went on for weeks. Hob went to school bruised and lumpy, telling Doris Mills that he'd gotten into a scrape with some out-of-town boys who stopped at the café. Cal was out for two weeks, hurt so badly Emma wouldn't let him show his face, not that Ace would have cared what anyone thought. She told the school Cal caught a bad case of the influenza going around.

No one believed the excuses. Everyone knew what had happened.

Pastor Sams was an old man now. Hob watched him and the others, trying to decide what to do. There was more work to do right here in Bayne County. Enis Walder and Carl Galman were mistakes. He'd been distracted. Caught up in the euphoria of his successes, he lost his focus. Dealing with the Buxtons, Doyle Sutter, Doris Mills, and Doc Rush had filled him with a hunger for more, but the work to be done was right here, not in Atlanta.

Cal begged him to forgive, to move on, to be happy. Cal's saintly ability to forgive was his way of dealing with the life of abuse that had put him in a wheelchair. Hob found another way ... the way for him.

Cal would be disappointed in him. Maybe God would send him to hell for it, but Hob intended to send the others there first, the ones who deserved it.

He watched the people on the square and knew he had to finish the work here. Afterward, they could all stand before God and ask for forgiveness. If He granted it, so be it. Hob wouldn't complain because he'd helped send them there and would accept whatever judgment came down on their heads and his.

Across the street, Pastor Sams hobbled along the sidewalk past the café. Fran came out to greet him. They chatted, the old man smiling in his godly, benevolent way. After a minute, he gave her a pat on the hand and shuffled along the sidewalk.

"Fucking hypocrite," Hob muttered.

He had promised his brother he would move on, but it was a lie, and Cal knew it was a lie. The weary sadness in Cal's eyes told him he knew he lied, but there was nothing more he could say.

Hob watched Pastor Sams. There were too many loose ends for him to move on.

53. No Respecter of Butts

"But, Governor!" A stunned Web Seymour jumped from his chair after Governor Fullman abruptly disconnected the call. The smug smile had been wiped from his face and the fire in Seymour's eyes dimmed to a sputtering candle. He slumped back into his seat. "What now?"

"We'll keep it short," George said. "Do you know who killed Doyle Sutter and the others?"

"Hell, we all know." Seymour sighed, staring at the table. "That son of a bitch ... Ace Buxton's boy, Hob."

"Any proof of that?"

"What kind of proof?" Seymour looked up. "Anybody who got treated like Ace treated those boys would be primed to murder someone. Shit, most of us would have done it a long time ago."

"I'd have to call bullshit on that," George said sharply.

"What the hell is that supposed to mean?" Seymour sputtered.

"It means no one ... not a damned person ... did anything," George fired back. "You say you knew Hob would be primed to kill the people who hurt his brother. Did you try to stop it?"

"What the hell could I do?" Seymour scowled and shook his head. "You don't understand. You're not from here ... don't know how things are."

"Bullshit!" George leaned over the table.

Seymour backed away in his chair, startled. "You best keep in mind that I'm ..."

George cut him off. "I don't give a shit what you are. Right now, you're on the verge of obstructing a murder investigation. That's a felony in Georgia."

"You wouldn't dare."

"The hell I wouldn't. You heard the governor. We're about to make him a hero of the people when we arrest William Hobson Buxton for murder. You need to decide if you want to be a hero too, or go down as the small-time politician who tried to get in the way and cover up what was really going on in Bayne County."

Seymour slumped in the chair, deflated, and shook his head. "I swear I don't know any more than anyone else." When he looked up, the arrogance was gone from his eyes. "Lots of people might have a reason to kill Ox and Harley Buxton, but not Doyle Sutter. All he did was what the rest of us did."

"Nothing." George shook his head. "Just like everyone, he did nothing, except he was supposed to do something ... just like you."

"Like me?" Concern flickered across Seymour's face. "I'm not the sheriff."

"Maybe not, but the one thing we have learned since we got here is you run this county. That's the one secret no one tried to keep from us," George said. "And if Hob's out to even scores, it seems like you'd be on the list."

"Shit." Seymour looked up. "But I didn't do anything?"

"Exactly." George smiled. "Tell me what happened to Hob's brother, Cal."

"I never saw it," Seymour said. "No one did, but Doyle found out when Mimsy took Cal to see Doc Rush."

"Doc Rush?"

"Yeah." Seymour nodded. "Henry Rush ... local doctor. Had a practice here for nearly forty years, then retired somewhere ... down south ... Valdosta, maybe."

"He knew about what happened to Cal Buxton?"

Seymour nodded. "He's the one who got him admitted to a state hospital where they could take care of him."

"Anyone else know about the injuries to Cal or Hob?" George asked Seymour.

"Like I said, everyone knew they were mistreated, but firsthand ..." Seymour's brow furrowed for a few seconds before he said, "Doris Mills over at the school had the most contact with them and would know better than most. I know she and Doyle talked about it."

"Got an address for her?"

"No." Seymour shook his head. "Last I heard, she retired and moved over somewhere by Lake Lanier ... Cumming, I think."

Bob pulled out his phone. "I'll see if Sharon can get us an address for both of them."

Seymour had nothing to add beyond what everyone else had told them. No one wanted to make enemies of the Buxtons. They were mean, spiteful, and getting on their bad side was bound to have a heavy cost.

"Alright." George ended the interview and turned for the door.

"Is that it?" Seymour asked. "You've got what you need to arrest him now, so he doesn't hurt anyone else ... right?"

George flashed a look of disgust and left without answering.

They were halfway to Atlanta when Bob's cell phone chimed. He put it on speaker. "What do you have?"

"Checked missing persons reports around the state. Henry Rush disappeared from a retirement center in Valdosta, and Doris Mills went missing from her home in Cumming."

"Good work," Bob and George and exchanged nods. Good news and bad.

The pieces were coming together. That was good.

Mills and Rush were missing. That was probably very bad for them if Hob Buxton-Payne was behind their disappearance.

"One more thing," Sharon said. "The report came in from the medical examiner."

"That was fast," Bob said. "We weren't expecting it for a few days."

"It's a partial, but that young ME, Singman, figured this might be important. Some of the toxicology is still pending, but he wanted you to know that the sheriff, Doyle Sutter, died of natural causes."

"Natural?" Bob and George exchanged looks over the seat. "Chained up in a cave?"

"The report says he suffered a heart attack, no doubt brought on by the stress of his confinement," Sharon explained. "If not for the heart attack, you might have got to him before he died."

"And we'd have our witness," Bob shook his head. "Nothing we can do about that now, but do us another favor. See if you can get an address for William Hobson Payne."

"Way ahead of you. He lives in an apartment down on the south side of the city." She rustled through her notes and gave them the address. "Tracked him down through his job at the parks department."

"Alright, one more favor, then."

"I should charge for all these favors," Sharon joked. "But name it."

"We'll be tied up with another witness for a while. See if you can get a judge to sign a search warrant. We should have enough for that at least ...

motive for three murders and two others missing, all with some association with the Buxtons."

"I'll get the warrant," Sharon said. "I have a way with judges."

"I'll bet you do," George said, loud enough to be heard over the speaker. "You're there, after all. I was wondering if you would pipe up and say something."

"You and Bob were doing just fine without me. Didn't seem to be any reason to butt in."

"Speaking of butts, how about getting yours back to Atlanta?" Sharon said.

"Miss me that much?"

"Nope, just bored."

"Hate to break up the love banter," Bob said, "But when you get the warrant, organize some people to execute it, maybe Atlanta PD or the GBI."

"Told you not to worry. I'll get the warrant, and Andy and I have been looking for an excuse to get out of the damned office and away from the governor. We'll handle it."

"Alright. Be careful, check back, and let us know how it goes."

"Will do." Sharon ended the call.

Toby Jones listened to the call and found himself smiling for the first time in a while.

"What are you grinning at?" George asked.

"Not much." Jones shrugged. "Just that to us country boys, you OSI fellas are like supercops, and she told you to get your butt back to Atlanta. Kind of puts things in perspective again."

"Well, Sharon Price was never a respecter of butts," George said. "Mine included."

"Especially yours," Bob added.

54. No Promises

Sharon was true to her word. She had a way with judges and secured a search warrant for William Payne's apartment within an hour. Andy made a couple of calls and had two Atlanta PD uniforms, and a pair of homicide detectives meet them at the location.

They entered with a key provided by the landlord and found the apartment empty. That was no surprise. Payne's supervisor at the parks department told Sharon he hadn't been at work for a few days and hadn't answered his phone when they called to check on him.

The apartment was bare, the sort of place a bachelor on a limited income would call home. A couple of cheap chairs in the kitchen. A cheaper sofa in the living room and a television from a discount box store. Beyond that, there was nothing out of the ordinary.

The bedroom was the same. A flimsy spring mattress on a steel frame and cardboard boxes used as dresser drawers. No notes, no books, no maps, nothing to show what he might be planning next, if anything. Then they opened the tiny closet.

Sharon pulled out her phone and punched in George's number. "He's not done," she said as he answered.

"Tell me."

"Handcuffs, chains, duct tape in the closet ... laid out in neat little separate piles like each was reserved for someone."

"How many?" George asked.

Sharon looked at the items in their little piles on the closet floor. "Looks like five more. At least that's what he has ready here."

"Alright. Have Rince bring the chopper out to Sagg Manor. There should be enough space somewhere on the grounds to set it down. If we get any useful information here, we'll be moving fast."

"Will do," Sharon said.

George disconnected as they walked into Cal's room. A young man, his body twisted and shriveled, struggled to look up at the newcomers. The attendant standing beside him smiled and asked, "Can I help you?"

It was Cecil, Cal's favorite member of the staff. He took up a protective position between Cal and the men with the gold badges on their belts.

"We need to talk with Cal," George said. He craned his head around to see behind Cecil and smiled. "Hello, Cal."

Cal ignored him, lifting his head as far as he could at a sideward angle, staring at the man standing to one side. "I know you."

Toby Jones nodded without speaking and looked down at the floor.

"How are you, Toby?" Cal asked as if they were friends reuniting after an absence.

"Okay." Jones nodded and raised his eyes. "How about you, Cal?"

"Just lettin' it hang," Cal said with a lopsided grin, repeating the expression his brother always used. The grin faded as he shifted his eyes to George and Bob. "Hob did some bad things."

"He did," George said honestly. "That's why we could use your help."

"He told me. I was hoping he would stop." Cal shook his head. His chin pointed perpetually down at his chest, making it an awkward movement. A tear ran down the side of his face. "He was here, you know."

Cecil stepped out of the way, and George sat in a chair facing Cal. He leaned forward, his elbows resting on his knees. "When was he here?"

"Last time, a few days ago." Cal shook his head. "He won't be back. I know that."

"It would help if you would tell us everything he said."

"I should have told someone." Cal shook his head, his eyes pleading for understanding. "But I couldn't. He's my brother. If I told, it wouldn't change what happened to the others. I just hoped he would find some peace and put it behind him ... move on."

"I know, Cal." George gave a sincerely sympathetic nod. This was no hardened criminal. The young man in the wheelchair had spent much of his life suffering at the hands of those who should have protected him. Still, sympathy could not excuse what had been done, and George said, "Tell us what you know ... for Hob's sake."

Cal began speaking in his slow, forced way, pausing at times as if struggling with his conscience. He told them of their conversation, his admonition to forgive and move on, and Hob's promise that he would move on.

Cal raised his sad eyes and looked into George's. "He said he would forgive, but I knew it was a lie. I could see it in his eyes."

George wanted to say something to ease the young man's conscience, but there wasn't time. "Who else? Who are the others that he might hurt?"

Cal thought for a moment and began naming names. All were people who knew what was happening and could have stepped in and stopped the torture the boys had endured. Web Seymour was on the list, and others.

George noted the names and asked, "Do you know who might be next?"

"Any of them," Cal said, shrugging. "All of them."

"We know he's not at his apartment. Where would he go? Someplace he might feel safe?"

"Two places," Cal said immediately, then nodded and lowered his head. "The house where we lived with my mother and father."

George noted he did not call it home. "He would feel safe there?"

"No, not safe. But I think he would go there to remember." Cal shook his head. "All the reasons for everything he did are there ... all the memories, the bad ones."

George looked at Toby Jones. "Do you know where the house is?"

"I know." Jones nodded. "In the hills a couple of miles from Ox and Mimsy's place."

"Alright." George turned to Cal. "And the other place. Where is that?"

"He would feel safe there." Cal smiled. Finally, a memory that brought some peace to him. "He took me there for the first time when I was five. We would sneak off when we could get away from Ace."

"Where is it?"

"Not too far. Just a place in the hills we knew about." Cal's smile widened, lost in what must have been a rare moment of pleasant reverie for him.

"Can you tell us where?" George said, pulling him from the memory.

The smile faded. "Yes." Cal nodded. "Just a clearing back in the hills. There's a tree ... a big oak. We called it the Giant Tree. Hob said it would protect us. It was up there, right on top of the hill. We used to sit under the Giant Tree, and it was like our own private world. No one knew where we were. The Giant Tree wouldn't let them know."

He described it and the trail they would follow through the woods and over the hills.

George looked at Toby Jones. "Can you find it?"

"I can." Jones nodded. "Cherokee Hill ... highest point on the Buxton property. No one ever went around there because it belonged to the Buxtons, but you can see it from the valley below."

"That's the place." Cal nodded. "Where the Giant Tree is." He looked off into the distance, remembering. "Ace wanted to know where we were once when we ran off, and Hob wouldn't tell him. Got a beating for not telling, but Hob just took it, and then the next day, we went back to sit under the Giant Tree, where no one knew where we were." He shrugged and added, "We didn't want them there, anyway. Not any of them."

A roaring clatter overhead signaled the arrival of Rince and the helicopter. George stood. "We have to go now." He laid a hand on Cal's arm. "Thank you, Cal."

As they turned to go, Cal let out a desperate cry. "Please don't hurt my brother."

There was no way to know how Hob would respond if they found him and tried to take him into custody, and George knew he could make no promises. The best he could offer was, "We'll do our best."

55. Yes

"Evening, Bob ... Miss Sally." As was his custom, Pastor Grady Sams shuffled along the sidewalk, making his rounds. That's what he called the daily strolls he took around the courthouse square—his rounds—glad-handing people, smiling beatifically. The good shepherd looking after his flock.

"Evening, Pastor." Bob Thornton and his wife Sally stopped and smiled. Sams had been the leader of their church's congregation since they were children. Even now, after retiring two years earlier, they had a special affection for the old man who always had a kind word and a smile on his face.

Each day, morning and evening, Sams made his rounds around the square, stopping to greet his former parishioners. Some, like the Thorntons, went out of their way to be there, doting on him as if he were an aged and beloved grandfather. They laughed at his little jokes, smiled, patted him on the back, and invited him to supper. Their acts of goodwill were undoubtedly sincere, but in their hearts, they also took comfort in the belief that their kindness toward this man of God would surely stand them in good stead when their time came to face the judgment.

Now, Sally Thornton raised up on her tiptoes to give him a peck on the cheek. "God bless, and you take care now, Pastor Sams. We'll see you tomorrow."

"Yep. If the good Lord lets me hang around another day to see to my flock," Sams replied, grinning.

"Well, we pray he will," Bob Thornton said as the old man moved down the sidewalk.

"I just love that old man," Sally whispered to her husband, watching Pastor Sams stop in front of the hardware store to greet a man coming out carrying a new chainsaw.

"Got you a new saw, Charlie," Sams said. "Looks like a good one."

"Yep. Firewood to cut, and the old one gave out. Gotta get ready for winter, you know."

"That's the truth," Sams said, smiling. "Seems like winters get colder every year at my age."

"I've got some good seasoned oak that'll burn hot and long. I'll bring you a load for your fireplace," Charlie said.

"Oh, don't bother yourself, Charlie."

"No bother, Pastor. Happy to do it. I'll bring it around on Saturday."

"Well, I thank you for your kindness, Charlie." And Sams continued his shuffling round around the square.

Watching from a bench in front of the courthouse, Hob's face twisted into a disgusted sneer. The hypocrisy of it all was more than he could stomach. How wonderful it must have been for Sams to be so venerated by others for a life of service, doing the Lord's work. How wonderful for them to feel so sure of their salvation.

Hob wondered if he thought he was doing the Lord's work when he called Ace Buxton to come pick up the brothers, desperate to escape their father's brutality. Was it the Lord's work when he offered them food as a ploy to keep them there until Ace came to the church and dragged them home? Was the good pastor praying for them an hour later when Ace nearly beat them to death?

"You'll be doing some praying soon enough," Hob muttered, leaning forward on the bench to spit on the ground between his feet.

Sams completed his circuit around the square and, oblivious of the young man watching from a bench in front of the courthouse, turned down a side street. He walked the three blocks to the small frame house he'd lived in for forty years. The house sat next door to the church he had pastored. When he retired, the congregation took up a collection to pay off the small mortgage he still owed.

Sams lived comfortably enough now. He missed his wife, Jeanie, who had passed three years earlier, but he went to bed every night, praying that they would be reunited when he passed on.

He was just frying an egg for his supper when the knock came at the door. Turning the burner flame off, he went to the door, pulled it open, and a moment later found himself thrown back, tumbling to the floor from a two-handed thump on his scrawny chest. Startled and terrified, he looked up at the bearded young man standing over him.

"What ... who?" There was something familiar about the young man's eyes.

"Remember me?" Hob said.

Sams shook his head. "No son, I don't."

"I'm not your son," Hob sneered.

"I only meant ..." Sams's brow wrinkled as he studied the young man's face. "Who then?"

"Think back. There was a family you never visited ... never said a kind word to my mother or offered her the help she needed. Think hard. You have to remember the night two scared boys hid in your church thinking they would be safe? You found them the next morning ... fed them some eggs." Hob let out a snort of disgust. "As if that would make up for what you did."

"But I didn't do anything."

"No?" Hob glared at him, anger and disgust twisting his face. "You made a call."

"Ace ... you're Ace Buxton's boy." The pastor's face paled, and his eyes widened. "Which one?"

"Does it matter?" Hob said, glaring down at him. "You could have fed us and sent us away ... said nothing, but you made the call instead."

"I had to call," Sams whimpered. "You don't understand. There wasn't anything else I could do. If Ace had found out ..."

"*If Ace found out*! That's what they all said. There'll be hell to pay if Ace finds out." Hob sneered and reached down, jerking the old man bodily from the floor. "Well, hell is here, and it's time to pay up, old man."

Hefting him over his shoulders, he carried Sams to his pickup outside. Night had come on. A dim yellow glow from the single streetlight at the end of the block hardly penetrated the dark beyond the circle of light it cast below the pole. The neighborhood was old and quiet, made up of small frame homes. The residents, mostly retired like Sams, were inside their snug homes watching television and eating their suppers. No one noticed the young man moving through the dark, throwing a bundle into the back of his pickup.

"What are you doing?" Sams asked, close to tears as Hob pushed him into the truck

"Taking you for a ride."

"A ride? Where?"

"You've never been there. Never came to visit. Never checked on my mother ... my brother ... me. Never even came out to the place where Ace took me and my brother the day you called him."

"No." Sams shook his head feebly, his eyes pleading. "No, please."

"Yes," Hob said.

56. Nothing Left to Do

"How you doing back there?" Rince asked over the headset.

"Doing fine," Bob said, watching the Appalachian foothills pass below. He stretched out in the seat that would have been the co-pilot's if there were one.

The helicopter rattled and lurched in an updraft as it passed over a mountain ridge. "How about you, George?" Rince called out, grinning.

"Just get us there, Rince," George said tensely through clenched teeth.

To say he was not a good flier would have been an understatement. He hated flying, clinging to the sides of his seat in a white-knuckled grip, and pulling up as if physically lifting the chopper into the air. As far as George Mackey was concerned, soaring around thousands of feet in a tin can was unnatural and foolhardy. Sure, risks were part of the job. He accepted that, but they were risks he could control. Trapped in the confined space of the chopper, he had no control and could only hold on for life as the aerodynamically absurd machine—in his opinion—bumped and jolted through the air.

He hated it whenever he was required to go up with Rince and only did so out of necessity. It was necessary today, so he held onto the seat, subconsciously willing the helicopter to remain airborne and not plunge into one of the mountaintops passing by a few hundred feet below.

"Fifteen more minutes," Rince said calmly, accustomed to, and always amused by, George's discomfort in the air.

Seated beside George, Toby Jones was fascinated. He'd never been in a helicopter before, and this was an adventure he might never have again, something to tell the two other deputies over a beer.

The sun was setting as Rince circled once over the Bayne County Airport and set the chopper down near a hangar. Once the engines were cut and the rotor slowed, George was the first to hop out, taking a deep breath before turning back toward Rince. "We may need you. Can you find it in the dark?"

Toby had pinpointed Ace Buxton's abandoned house on a map for them, the place that Cal said held all the memories and where he thought his brother might go. The area was secluded and difficult to see from the air at night.

"I'll get close, but I'll need a signal from the ground. You have your lights?"

George nodded and pulled a powerful LED light from one of the kit bags Rince kept stocked in the chopper.

"Good," Rince said. "I'll fuel up and get in the air. Let me know where and when you want me."

"Will do." George turned to Toby. "Ready?"

"Ready." Toby nodded toward the hangar where Brian Mecham and Dave Pascal waited with their pickups.

"Let's go then."

A half-hour later, they bounced up the dirt road toward the house.

***

Handcuffed and chained to an eyebolt anchored to a wall stud, Pastor Grady Sams let out a low mewling whimper that lasted nearly a minute until he'd expelled all the air from his lungs. Then, sucking in another breath, he began again.

Hob watched from his mother's chair in the living room, wondering how long it would take before Sams gasped in his last breath, let out his final moan, and died. He hadn't been present for any of the others. They'd been left to die alone, but things were changing.

Now, there were the investigators from the state looking into the disappearances. It was only a matter of time until they put things together and came for him.

Before that happened, he wanted to know what the others—Ox and Harley, Doyle Sutter, Doris Mills, Doc Rush—felt as their lives sputtered out. He'd left them to die but had not been there to witness those last moments, to see the scales balance.

When he began this mission, that hadn't seemed important. Now it did, and he wondered why.

Sams squirmed in the corner, the chain dragging on the floor. His struggles became feebler with every minute that passed. Is that how it was for Ox and Harley, trapped in the cave?

Hob watched, curious and surprised that he wasn't taking more pleasure from the experience. This was what he had wanted. It was only fair that Sams should suffer the way he and Cal had, but this ... this was not suffering. Not really. The old man was simply fading away. Is that how it was for the others? They just faded away until there was nothing left?

The equation didn't balance. They should suffer ... truly suffer the way he and Cal had for so many years.

He began to doubt—not the mission but his methods. They were flawed. He'd left them to die, thinking that abandoning them, as he and his brother were abandoned and forgotten, would be sufficient. It was not. Cal had suffered for years—not days or hours—until he ended up mangled, broken, bound for the few remaining years of his life to a wheelchair. A true balancing of the scales demanded that those responsible should suffer equally.

Watching Pastor Sams fade away in the room's corner, he considered the dilemma. How could he increase the suffering to even things out and at least approximate the torment he and Cal had endured for years? There were ways. Methods he could employ, techniques he'd seen the Taliban use in Afghanistan, but they were distasteful to him, brutal and violent. Most importantly, they would require more time, and he sensed he was running out of time.

The old house shook with a sudden thumping roar overhead. It was a sound he knew well from his time in the military. A helicopter approached. He went to the window. A flashlight beam blinked upward for a second, signaling the chopper. They had put the puzzle pieces together and were coming for him.

Hob stood and walked to the corner, his hand on the pistol butt tucked in his belt. Pastor Sams looked up, shaking his head. "No ... please no."

Hob smiled, vindicated. They were all the same—pathetic creatures, content in their little worlds, willing to let others suffer as long as the suffering stayed away from their doors. No one wanted to die, not even the man who'd preached salvation to his flock and promised them a better life in another world. Hob wondered if Sams still believed in that better world.

"You'll know soon enough," he said, looking down at the old man.

"What will I know?" Sams whispered, eyes fixed on the pistol, shaking his head. "Please don't. I never hurt anyone ... never meant to."

The helicopter descended toward the house. They were coming for him, and there was nothing left to do.

57. For All the Others

Killing their headlights, the ground team left the pickups along the dirt road while Rince circled the chopper overhead. They made the final approach to the old house on foot, staying concealed as much as possible in the trees lining the dirt road along the last quarter-mile. When they reached the clearing, they fanned out into the woods, George motioning Toby and the other deputies to the rear of the house.

Approaching cautiously in the dark without lights, they surveyed the scene. The house had been abandoned since Emma killed her husband and then herself. Overhead, Rince circled in the dark. Lighting up the structure with the chopper's floodlights would expose the team on the ground and make them easy targets for anyone watching from inside.

When everyone was in position, George flashed his light once. They rushed the house front and rear, Toby leading the other deputies through the back door and George and Bob through the front.

The dank interior was musty with age and abandonment, and there was no sign that anyone had been inside for years. Electrical power had been turned off when the house was abandoned, and Ox Buxton decided there was no reason to pay the bill for his dead brother.

They moved slowly, turning the flashlights on to check the rooms, then off again to avoid becoming a target for anyone waiting inside. They were moving toward the back of the house when George clicked on his light and swung the beam to a far corner. Two wide and terrified eyes shone back at him.

Pistols in front, George and Bob approached to find a frail old man handcuffed, trembling, and staring up at them. He shook his head. "Please … no. I never meant for anyone to be hurt. You have to believe me … please."

"You're safe now." George knelt by him while Bob watched the room for any concealed threats. He took out a handcuff key, freed the old man's wrists, and helped him sit up and lean against the wall. "Are you alone here?"

"I don't know." The old man leaned toward George. "Don't let him hurt me."

"We won't," George said. "What's your name?"

The old man took a sobbing breath, nodded, and said, "Grady Sams."

Toby Jones led the deputies into the front room from the rear of the house and walked to the corner where George knelt. "Pastor Sams?"

"You know him?" George looked up from the old man.

"Everybody knows Pastor Sams," Toby said.

"I'll be damned," Brian Mecham muttered from behind

"Where the fuck did he come from?" Dave Pascal said.

"Where do you think?" Toby snapped at him, annoyed. "And watch your language in front of the Pastor."

"You figure he's going to hold a little coarse language against me with the Lord after we just saved his life?" Pascal smirked.

Toby glared without speaking, and Pascal shrugged and looked down. "Okay, fine."

"Can you tell us what happened? Who brought you here?" George asked.

"He was just a boy then," Sams mumbled, trembling, almost incoherent, shaking his head. "Back when I knew him ... just a boy." Tears welled up in his eyes. "And I let it happen ... all of us did. I wasn't any different." He looked up at George, the fear in his old, damp eyes replaced by guilt. "Not a boy anymore. He remembers it all ... everything." Sams shook his head again. "But he doesn't understand. I couldn't do anything ... none of us could."

George looked over his shoulder. "Did you clear the back of the house?"

"Couldn't find anything," Toby said.

"Alright." George stood and motioned Mecham and Pascal over, nodding at Sams. "Get an ambulance enroute and stay with him until it gets here."

"Right," Mecham said and pulled out his portable radio.

"Let's go." George led the way through the house to the back door. He nodded at Toby. "You sure you know where to go?"

Toby nodded. "If it's where Cal said it is, we should be able to find it."

"Let's go." George led the way through the house to the back door.

***

It was still there, its outline barely distinguishable in the dark. He could sense it more than see it. The wind humming deeply through its branches was the breath of the protecting giant.

Hob crossed the hilltop clearing until he stood beneath the Giant Tree. He reached out to touch the trunk and found the bark dry and crumbling.

He slid his hand along the bark and walked around the tree's massive circumference. Once, he stopped at a deep vertical gash, extending from the ground up as high as he could reach and beyond to the very top branches.

He raised his fingertips to his nose and touched them with his tongue. Ash and charred wood, the scars of a lightning strike ... a bad one.

He looked up and through the thick but now bare branches. A few stars blinked down. There should have been no stars visible through the tree's branches and foliage, but the leaves were gone, many of the heavier limbs already fallen and littering the ground like dead bodies after a battle. That's what the tree's life had been on the hilltop, a battle to fend off the elements. From the time it was a sapling, it had waged war against the elements—wind and rain, frost and freeze, snow and ice, spring thaws and summer droughts—and if it hadn't won the war, at least, it had survived.

The Giant Tree was dying now. To Hob, that seemed fitting.

He turned, leaned back, and slid down the tree, sitting on the ground with his back resting against its ancient hulk. Staring off across the clearing to where the hill sloped away, he could make out a few stars.

What now, he wondered? Then he smiled and shook his head. That was a stupid question, and he knew the answer. There only could be one answer. He had always known it.

He closed his eyes and remembered sitting there on the bare earth with Cal, the Giant Tree's branches hanging so low to the ground that they concealed the boys from anyone who might pass by, but no one ever did. It was their place, safe and secure, protected by the tree.

Cal would lean his head against Hob's shoulder and close his eyes while Hob told him about the tree's magic powers to protect them. If anything bad ever happened and Hob was not around, Cal should go to the tree and wait. Hob promised to come find him there.

It was a child's promise, but still, he felt guilty that he hadn't kept the promise. Instead, he'd run off and joined the Army, abandoning his brother when he should have stayed to protect him. He hung his head and whispered. "I'm sorry, Cal."

A sudden roaring overhead jarred Hob from his thoughts. The tree shook as if the giant was awakening from a deep sleep. Bright spotlights lit the hilltop surreally, the white glare casting ghostly shadows at unnatural angles through the branches.

The rotor wash from the helicopter hovering low overhead descended like a mini-tornado. Dead twigs, branches, and dried leaves showered down on Hob. He lifted the pistol and waited. The time had come.

At the edge of the clearing, Toby knelt in the trees. "There it is, just like Cal said."

"There it is." George nodded, taking a knee beside him.

"Lot of open ground between here and there." Bob scanned the area, assessing the situation.

"Yep." George looked around the clearing for a more concealed approach to the tree and the young man they could just make out, leaning against the trunk, watching, and waiting. "Doesn't seem to be any other way to get there."

"We could hold up. Wait for a reaction team," Bob said, then shrugged and shook his head. "But that won't work, will it?"

"No, it won't. Any show of force, and they'll take him out." George looked at Bob. "I'd like to take him in alive. We owe that much to him and his brother."

"We try to talk him out, then," Bob said, the decision made.

"Make sure Rince keeps the lights on so he sees I'm not a threat, and have him climb a couple hundred feet so we can hear over the engines."

"Right," Bob said, relaying the message to Rince over the portable radio.

Still hovering, the helicopter rose, and the engine noise diminished to a dull roar.

George stood, ready to take a step out into the clearing

"I'll do it." Toby Jones stood beside George.

"You?" George looked at him doubtfully. "I'm not so sure that's a good …"

"It should be me," Toby said. "Someone he knows."

George thought for a moment. "Do you have any experience with this sort of thing? "The old pastor said he has a gun. He might use it if he feels threatened."

"I don't have any experience, but he knows me and hasn't shot anyone yet. If he sees strangers, that might change."

There was some logic in what Toby said, but looking into his eyes, George saw something else. Guilt. The need to atone, to do something right after all the wrongs that had been done.

George remembered Cal's plea as they left—*Please don't hurt my brother.*

He nodded. "Alright. You try to talk to him. That's the key ... get him talking. We'll be watching, but if he looks like he's about to use the gun, you hit the ground. We'll do the rest."

Toby nodded and said, "Okay."

Then he took a deep breath, stepped from behind the tree into the clearing, and shouted. "Hob, it's Toby Jones! I just want to talk."

"You should stay back," Hob called out in a voice stronger and deeper than Toby remembered.

"I just want to talk ... so we can figure things out. Look, I'll show you." Toby loosened the gun belt, laid it on the ground, and stepped forward, hands in the air. "Just talk, Hob. That's all."

"I know those men from the state are with you, somewhere in the trees." Hob shook his head. "I got nothing to say to them."

"Then talk to me." Toby advanced toward the tree. He saw Hob sitting with his back against the tree, a pistol in his lap.

"You?" Hob laughed. "I've got nothing to talk about with you or anyone else in this damned county."

Toby took a few more steps. Under the chopper's lights, they could see each other's faces and eyes now. And didn't have to shout as loudly to be heard. "What can I say, Hob? I'm sorry. If I could go back and change things, I would."

"I know you," Hob said, raising the pistol, not pointing it at him but making sure he saw it.

Toby tensed, ready to fall to the ground as George had instructed.

"You're weak, like everyone else," Hob said, shaking his head. "Not bad ... just weak and afraid ... like everyone else ... staying out of the way, minding your own business."

Toby could say nothing. Hob was right.

"But what about us? What about Cal?" Hob asked more softly. "He couldn't stay out of their way. Did you ever think about that?"

"You're right. I should have ... we all should have thought about it," Toby said. "That's why I know we can work this out if you'll put the gun down and just talk."

"There's nothing left to talk about, Toby."

The drama playing out under the Giant Tree ended in the next instant. Hob lifted the pistol without another word, pushed the muzzle under his chin, and pulled the trigger.

"No!" Toby shouted, then sank to his knees. "We could have talked,"

George and Bob rushed from the trees, running past him, but they'd watched it all and knew there was nothing more they could do.

Toby stood in the clearing and watched, his shoulders sagging under the guilt he carried for all the others who weren't there ... but should have been.

58. Wages of Sin

Despite all that had happened, Pastor Grady Sams volunteered to conduct the funeral service for William Hobson Payne, formerly Buxton. He told his congregation of his plans at a Sunday morning meeting, using his pulpit to preach a sermon on forgiveness. They all knew of his ordeal, had seen the news, had heard it described in his own words many times as he greeted them on his rounds around the courthouse square.

"Forgiveness is the highest form of godliness," Sams told them, casting his eyes upward toward heaven. "I stand before you today to say that I forgive that troubled young man for the terrible things he did to others." He lowered his eyes to the congregation, a pious smile on his face. "And yes, to me."

Women and men in the congregation nodded solemnly and brushed a tear from their eyes. That he could forgive the horrors he had endured proved that Grady Sams, their beloved pastor, truly was a godly man.

Sams concluded his sermon with an admonishment to his flock. "Brothers and Sisters, God expects ... demands even ... that you forgive the sins of others. It is our duty,"

He did not mention the need to overcome their sins or the weakness that brought them on. Everyone left the meeting feeling it was one of the best sermons Sams had ever preached.

Cal declined the pastor's offer to officiate at the funeral. As Hob's only living blood relative, he decided his brother would be buried near him, as far away as possible from the ghosts and nightmares and hypocrisies of Bayne County.

Sagg Manor maintained a small cemetery. It was an extension of the old plantation's graveyard where family members had been laid to rest for generations. Slaves had been buried in a separate plot not far away, but now the two were joined together to create a single resting place for Sagg Manor patients who died there without surviving family to make funeral arrangements.

Using some of Hob's savings, Cal arranged for a small burial plot for his brother and one for himself beside it when the time came. Hob's remains were released to him once the investigation was completed, the reports written, and the case officially closed. A funeral home transported the body from the GBI's State Crime Lab Morgue in Atlanta, and the coffin was lowered into the hole the Sagg Manor grounds crew had prepared with a backhoe.

Cal sat for a long while beside the grave. His friend, Cecil, the attendant, stood patiently beside the wheelchair while Cal read from his Bible.

Only one other person showed up for Hob's burial. Cal looked up and smiled when Toby Jones crossed the lawn to the grave.

"I'm glad you came," Cal said. "I think Hob would be glad too."

Toby nodded, then stood beside Cal while he read Bible verses, ending with, "For the wages of sin is death; but the gift of God is eternal life through Jesus Christ our Lord."

"Do you believe that, Toby?" Cal looked up. "That we ... you, me, everyone, even Hob ... can still go to heaven after everything that's happened?"

"I want to believe it," Toby said, then shook his head, took a deep breath, and added honestly, "But I don't know."

Cal was silent for a moment. When he spoke, his voice was stronger than it had been for years. "I believe it."

59. Forgotten

The phone chimed at George's desk. He saw the number, frowned, and picked it up.

"Mackey, get your ass over to my office now!" It was the governor.

"I'll be right over." George hung up and walked from the OSI offices across the street to the capitol, ready to settle things with the governor once and for all.

Toni Garber met him in the anteroom. "This way," she said, her face blank as she opened the door for him to go in.

"George Mackey!" Fullman beamed with a grin. "Had you worried, didn't I?"

Bob and Andy were seated with the governor in the overstuffed chairs around his coffee table. They smiled, not flashing teeth like Fullman, but with looks that said they were pleased.

"Have a seat, George." Fullman indicated a chair to his right. "We've got some planning to do."

"What kind of plans, Governor?" George asked.

"You're gonna get your ass back to Savannah. We're taking over the cartel investigation from those stupid sons of bitches," Fullman said, using the expression that had George exiled in the first place. He leaned back, grinning again. "And you're going to lead it."

The media was calling Ben Fullman a hero. The law enforcement governor was credited with sending the OSI team in and finding the serial killer. At the same time, he cleaned up what the press described as a hornet's nest of dirty politics in Bayne County that led to the efforts to conceal the killer's identity.

Fullman's aide, Toni Garber, and her PR team made the most of the press coverage. That Bayne County voters had supported Fullman in his electoral runs actually played in his favor.

The middle-of-the-road, fence-sitting voters who might have never supported him in the past now looked at him as a man who put principle above politics. Law Enforcement Ben, as they called him, even went after his supporters when they broke the law. The couple of hundred voters he lost in ruining the county's reputation were more than offset by the additional support he garnered around the state.

It was a masterful exercise in spinning the narrative and massaging the facts. Fullman, the consummate politician he was, was not about to waste an opportunity to garner more favorable coverage. He intended to expand and take full advantage of his hero status.

Andy and Bob helped by stoking the furnace in Fullman's ego. They made the case that breaking up a cartel drug ring would be a monumental coup and the next logical step for the law enforcement governor. His hero status would be enhanced.

Toni Garber agreed and pointed out that a successful investigation would offset any fallout from the Savannah mayor's office. Fullman's reputation and poll numbers would skyrocket again.

To do all of this, they needed someone with a proven record of conducting successful investigations. They convinced Fullman that George Mackey was just the man to ensure the plan succeeded.

**

A few weeks later, a survey crew in the north Georgia woods frantically called a local sheriff. They'd been sent out to survey a piece of mountain property for purchase by a development company when they discovered a small shack that was unmarked on their maps. Inside were three decomposing bodies.

The remains of Doris Mills and Henry Rush were quickly identified and tied to the Bayne County killer. It took longer to identify Enis Walder, who'd gone missing not long after her husband was imprisoned for child abuse and molestation.

The murder of Carl Galman was never tied to the Bayne County case, but Sharon Price and the OSI team put the other pieces together for the governor. Once again, Toni Garber tied it all up in a nice package that portrayed the governor as ever-vigilant in protecting the people of Georgia and a man who left no stone unturned in his pursuit of justice. Fullman's poll numbers climbed up another couple of notches.

**

As his widow, Mimsy took possession of the title to Ox's house. The remaining Buxton property, including the hill where the dead Giant Tree still stood, was sold off, and the proceeds were put aside to pay for Cal's care at Sagg Manor.

Mimsy went to visit him there ... once. Seeing his deteriorating body, she fought back tears and sobbed, "I'm so sorry, Cal."

"Not your fault, Aunt Mimsy," Cal said through his lopsided smile and tried to absolve her of her sins. "There was nothing you could do."

After the visit, she sold the house and moved to Savannah to live with an aging aunt. She had always been invisible around Bayne County, living in Ox's shadow, staying out of the way as much as possible. Now, her sudden absence was barely noticed by the county's residents. Besides, they had other concerns.

***

An in-depth report by one of the Atlanta television networks, titled *The County That Closed Its Eyes,* became a regional embarrassment. Spotlighting the indifference and outright neglect of everyone, including politicians, local officials, and neighbors, the report detailed the abuses suffered by the Buxton boys. It went into great detail about Cal's injuries and confinement to a wheelchair and the lack of response from anyone until his brother was driven to murder and suicide.

The report aired as part of the evening news for five nights, painting an almost sympathetic picture of the killer, William Hobson Buxton, who had changed his name to Payne in a sad effort to erase ties to his family, but, as the reporter solemnly said, "There was no escape from his past."

In fairness, it also reviewed what happened to Hob's victims and the details of their unpleasant deaths, but by the time the reporter finished, there wasn't much sympathy for the victims. Viewers were left with the conclusion that Hob only did what he did after being driven to it by a lifetime of abuse. That did not excuse the deaths he had caused, but it tied things up neatly with an understandable motive.

***

For his part in hindering the investigation into the murders, Web Seymour was removed as the commission chairman. A special recall election was held, overseen by the county clerk, Carol Digby. The vote wasn't even close. Seymour lost by a landslide and never held public office again. His dreams of expanding his fortunes by bringing in the Japanese manufacturing plant evaporated.

He was not the only one to suffer setbacks. The scandal gave a black eye to everyone in the county. Being from Bayne County became information people concealed from others. Even locals with only scant knowledge of the abuse—mainly because they avoided contact with Ace and Ox Buxton—found their reputations tainted.

What remained of the sheriff's department also suffered. The county commission cut funding, and it was eventually disbanded. The Georgia State Patrol and GBI took over law enforcement duties, such as they were.

Once a quaint community in the Appalachian foothills, Bayne County became a seedy rural backwater and the butt of jokes around the state.

***

Before the sheriff's department was disbanded, Toby Jones moved his family away from Bayne County. He took a job with his brother in Charleston, where he applied for a North Carolina contractor's license to continue his trade as a carpenter.

Brian Mecham and Sam Pascal stayed in the state but also moved away, Mecham to Atlanta and Pascal to Macon. They never mentioned their service as deputies in Bayne County.

None of them ever attempted to find another job in law enforcement.

***

Cal lived another five years. The traumatic brain damage finally took its toll, shutting down his organs one by one until nothing was left to keep him alive. He passed away one night in his sleep.

Cecil and the other attendants at Sagg Manor, along with a few of the residents, attended the service at the grave. Sagg Manor's chaplain, a local preacher, read a few of Cal's favorite Bible verses. Then they sang a hymn.

If anyone in attendance remembered the terrible ordeal that brought Cal to Sagg Manor, they didn't speak of it. Instead, they tried to think of his goodness and the sweetness of the smile he always flashed as he struggled to lift his head from his chest and greet them.

When the final hymn was sung and the prayer offered, the backhoe scooped the dirt back into the grave, covering Cal and the sins of those who put him there. In time, they would be forgotten by all but a few.

End

Thanks for reading *Forgotten Sins.* If you would like to know when my next

book is available, you can follow me on Book Bub[1]   [2]
https://www.bookbub.com/authors/glenn-trust and receive an alert whenever there is a new release, preorder, or discount!

---

1. https://www.bookbub.com/authors/glenn-trust

2. https://www.bookbub.com/authors/glenn-trust

Your Next Suspense Thriller is Here!

Looking for another thriller? Check out **_Sole Survivor_**[1], Book 1 in the Sole Justice Series is another edge of your seat thriller by Glenn Trust. You can find it at this link >>>

https://www.bookbub.com/books/sole-survivor-a-sole-justice-thriller-book-1-by-glenn-trust

1. *https://www.bookbub.com/books/sole-survivor-a-sole-justice-thriller-book-1-by-glenn-trust*

2. https://www.bookbub.com/books/sole-survivor-a-sole-justice-thriller-book-1-by-glenn-trust

Don't Forget to Sign Up for Your Free Book – Here!

Thanks for reading and, *to show my appreciation, here's* a FREE Book.

Join us at Glenn Trust Books and receive a free download of his modern-day western crime thriller **Mojave Sun.** You can download your Free copy today at <u>this link</u> >>> **https://bf.glenntrustbooks.com/h31utr5ms2**

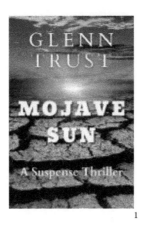

1

No Spam – We never share your address... Ever.

A Review is Always Appreciated

I know reviews aren't for everyone, but as an independent author, reviews help get the word out about my books. Whether you choose to leave a review or not, I greatly appreciate the time spent reading one of my books and hope that you enjoyed it.

Best - Glenn

Contact Glenn Trust

I love hearing from readers, so feel free to email me at gtplots@gmail.com I respond to all emails personally, so be patient. I promise to get to yours.

You can also follow me at BookBub[1] >> https://www.bookbub.com/authors/glenn-trust

---

1.   https://www.bookbub.com/authors/glenn-trust

About the Author

Glenn Trust is the author of the bestselling *Hunters, Sole Justice, and Journey Series* of mystery/thriller/suspense novels. He has also written standalone works, including *Dying Embers, Mojave Sun, and short stories.*

There are no superheroes or knights in shining armor in his stories. According to Trust, knights are for fairy tales. His books are gritty and based in the real world, with characters who face their frailties while dealing with their roles in the story. The heroes are average people doing the best they can.

The villains, as real villains often do, look like us. Trust's monsters hide behind the smiling faces that pass us on the street. They look like us, and this makes them more frightening.

He is a Georgia native but has lived in most regions of the country at one time or another. Varied experiences, from construction worker to police officer, corporate executive to city manager, color and provide insight into the characters he creates. His stories are known for detailed plots, solid research, and realism.

Today, he writes full-time and lives quietly with his wife and two dogs, Gunner and Charlie. You can find all of his work on his **Book Bub author page**[1] or check out his **Facebook Page - Glenn Trust Author,**[2] where you can sign up for his email group to receive updates on new releases and upcoming book promotions.

---

1. https://www.bookbub.com/authors/glenn-trust
2. https://www.facebook.com/GlennTrustAuthor/

More Books by Glenn Trust

Short Stories Collections
Lightning in the Clouds—Features the novella The Note

Milton Keynes UK
Ingram Content Group UK Ltd.
UKHW010808081123
432193UK00001B/118